SANCTUARY

BOOK TWO OF THE SUBVERSIVE TRILOGY

RAENA ROOD

ONE FOUNDATION PUBLISHING, LLC

SANCTUARY

BOOK TWO OF THE SUBVERSIVE TRILOGY

By: Raena Rood

"Everyone who does evil hates the light, and will not come into the light for fear that their deeds will be exposed. But whoever lives by the truth comes into the light, so that it may be seen plainly that what they have done has been done in the sight of God.
--John 3: 20-21 (NIV)

This book is dedicated to the memories of
Jared and Philip.
You fought the good fight, you finished the race,
and you kept the faith.

CHAPTER ONE

Holding the bow steady, Gemma locked eyes with the buck.

The animal stared back at her, coal-black eyes unblinking, unshed strands of thick velvet dangling from its antlers. The buck was massive compared to the does she often saw wandering the woods in small groups, its powerful, nine-point rack a testament to its ability to detect and avoid danger.

But the buck hadn't avoided danger today. Today, it had moseyed right into Gemma's hunting grounds and come to a sudden stop only thirty feet from her tree stand. Despite the slight breeze, she didn't think the animal could smell her. Her tree stand was upwind of the game trail. But the buck continued to stare her down, its ears twitching, the human-like intensity of its gaze unnerving her.

Gemma stayed perfectly quiet and still, which wasn't easy to do since her stomach was rumbling and she had to go to the bathroom. After hunting all afternoon, she'd been about to head back to camp for supper when she'd heard snapping branches and observed the buck approaching from the east. Of course the stupid animal would show up at the last minute, when dark was fast approaching and she just wanted to go home.

The buck flicked its white tail in a last-ditch effort to get a reaction out of her. When she still didn't move, he took a few meandering steps and bent over a patch of clover, presenting her with the perfect broadside view of its body.

Automatically, her mind superimposed a bullseye over the deer's left lung.

Moving quickly and quietly, Gemma drew an arrow from her quiver, nocked it in the bow, and pulled the string taut. She loved how the string resisted her pull at first before finally relenting and stretching to its full expanse. The green feathers at the top of the arrow brushed against her cheek as she worked to control her breathing.

"Aim behind the shoulder, but not too close," she whispered, repeating Abram's hunting advice. "Halfway up the body. A lung shot kills quickly."

Her eyes found the sweet spot about five inches behind the deer's shoulder. She loosened her fingers and held her breath, waiting for the string to snap forward and send the arrow hurtling toward the animal, waiting for the spurt of blood she'd seen many times before, but only when Abram's hands held the bow, waiting for the buck to run—as many of them did—but not very far, before finally slowing to a walk and then slumping onto the ground.

But nothing happened.

She glanced at the bow.

The arrow was still there.

Gemma pulled in another breath of air. Exhaled slowly. Tried again.

Nothing.

She closed her eyes and imagined herself chewing a tender piece of venison that some culinary genius on the kitchen crew had marinated in Italian dressing for twenty-four hours prior to grilling. Her empty stomach responded with another rumble, loud enough to make its thoughts on the matter known, but not loud enough to reach the deer's still-twitching ears.

Gemma opened her eyes, her arm shaking with the effort of holding the bowstring tight.

She couldn't do it.

She couldn't let the arrow fly.

"Shoot!"

The buck's head jerked up, its beady eyes zeroing in on her location for a split second before it bounded into the brush, flicking its tail the entire way, as if to mock her.

Frustrated, she tossed the bow sling over her shoulder, unclipped from the safety strap, and climbed down the ladder, muttering to herself. She walked a dozen yards away from her tree stand, squatted behind a sturdy oak to relieve the pressure on her bladder, and then set off in a steady jog toward the Sanctuary. She wasn't in any rush to get back, not after another long day of hunting with nothing to show for it.

And she had no one to blame but herself.

After nearly a week of daily bow-hunting expeditions, she'd seen one massive buck and fourteen grey squirrels, and she hadn't been able to bring herself to kill any of them. Coop and Oliver always brought something back from their hunts, whether it was a two-hundred-pound deer or a handful of skinned rabbits. Brie and Max regularly brought home buckets of bluegills after a day of fishing at the shallow brown pool of water known as Mire Lake.

They weren't hurting for food, not like at the Station, but the extra food was still nice. Plus, Oliver wanted them to hone their hunting and fishing skills—or, in Gemma's case, *acquire* said skills—in case things ever got bad again.

A banshee-like screech from above gave Gemma's heart a jolt, and she answered its scream with one of her own. Covering her pounding heart with her hand, she searched the trees for whatever otherworldly beast had made that terrible sound. Finally, her eyes landed on a low-hanging tree branch where a barn owl watched her from its perch.

When their eyes met, it screeched once more for good measure.

"Mouse-breathed little jerk," Gemma snapped. The rapid pounding beneath her palm seemed to slow down. She walked forward, and the owl's white head rotated to follow her progress. "You're lucky I don't put an arrow through your belly and eat you for dinner."

Clearly offended by the suggestion that it belonged on her dinner plate, the owl spun its head away from her, stretched out its wings, and flew off.

Gemma hated owls. They ranked only a few rungs above spiders and millipedes on her list of God's worst creations. Barn owls were the absolute worst with their pale-white faces, unnaturally long beaks, and jet-black eyes.

Little winged demons.

The wind picked up during her hike back to the Sanctuary, liberating hundreds of leaves from their branches. They drifted down from the sky and settled on the forest floor like giant, colorful snowflakes. Autumn had always been her favorite time of year, when the nights grew cooler and the lush green foliage of summer slowly surrendered to autumn's muted yellows, oranges, and browns.

When she reached the outskirts of the camp, a flutter of movement drew her attention to the box-shaped deer blind that sat atop a set of rusted stairs. Resembling a small treehouse, the deer blind blended seamlessly into the surrounding forest, providing more concealment than Gemma's tree stand. But it was decades old and in rough shape. No one hunted from it anymore. Not even Abram. Cut into each side of the structure were two small rectangular windows, and as she stared up at the blind, she saw a flash of red in one of them.

Red.

The color of blood…and poison…and Task Force patches.

It was Mullen.

Somehow, the soldier had found her. He was in that deer blind, watching her. *Hunting her*. Just as she'd been hunting the buck.

Gemma ducked behind the nearest tree. She wanted something sturdy between herself and the blind. Something that could stop a bullet. The Sanctuary was so close, the nearest cabin only a few dozen yards away. She could make a run for it, but that would leave her exposed for too long. She might as well paint a bullseye on her back. Plus, if it was Mullen, she didn't want to draw him any closer to the Sanctuary.

She pressed herself against the tree, the rough bark digging into her shoulder blades. With shaking hands, she drew an arrow from her quiver and placed it on the string. The bow felt natural in her grip, an extension of her own body. With the loaded bow came an overwhelming sense of power. She'd split two arrows at forty yards since first learning to shoot. What she had told no one, including Taylor, was that she'd insisted that Abram teach her archery for one reason, and one reason only.

And it *wasn't* so she could take down a deer.

Her brief but terrible encounter with Private Mullen on Dragon's Back Mountain six months earlier had left quite an impression. After Addie told her she'd seen a soldier matching Mullen's description lurking outside of Oliver's barn just before it went up in flames, things got even worse.

That was when the nightmares began.

Gemma never had nightmares about Colonel Carver, nor did she have nightmares about Private

Nowak, with his lecherous grin and abundant sexual innuendos. No, it was Mullen who invaded her sleep, night after night. Mullen, who she imagined endlessly searching the mountains for the prey that had somehow escaped his trap.

Leaning out as far as she dared, she aimed the bow's sight at the window, closed one eye, and waited for Mullen to make the critical mistake of revealing himself again, for another flash of red hair to morph into the pimple-covered face of the Task Force soldier. She aimed low, intending to put the arrow through his throat.

And then—yes! Another flash of red at the base of the window. He was crouching down, trying to hide from her. Slowly, the soldier rose, revealing himself one painful centimeter at a time.

Tracking the movement with her eyes, Gemma exhaled and loosened her grip on the arrow. Was she really going to do this? She'd felt no hesitation about killing the buck, yet she still hadn't been able to let go of the arrow. Uncertainty washed over her like the cloudy water of Mire Lake, making it impossible to see what was right in front of her. Her right arm trembled from the effort of holding the string.

This wasn't murder. This was survival, pure and simple. Mullen intended to kill Gemma and her friends. He'd proven that once already, back at the farmhouse.

She would *not* afford him another opportunity.

The soldier's eyes appeared in the window, wide and frightened. And the shock of those eyes staring back at her nearly caused Gemma to let the arrow fly. Then, her terrified brain went into overdrive and rearranged the face in the deer blind into another face. One entirely different—and even more horrifying—than Mullen's.

"Sophia?"

The redheaded girl peered at Gemma through the window and then ducked her head back down again, trying and failing to be unseen.

Gemma lowered the bow and released the string, the realization of what she'd nearly done causing her insides to roll. For a few seconds, she thought she might be sick. A horrific image appeared in her mind.

Sophia with an arrow through her throat.

Moving at a glacial pace, she slid the arrow back inside the quiver and slung the bow over her shoulder. She stared at the ground and worked to compose her anger. She *had* to calm herself down before she did or said anything rash. The fear and horror of the situation gradually gave way to anger, and then to relief, and then to the parental frustration that Gemma only experienced with Sophia.

Finally, she stepped out from behind the tree. "Sophia Grace Dillon," Gemma said, groaning internally at her use of the girl's full name. At only twenty-two, Gemma was already sounding like her mother. "Come down from there right now."

A whispered response came from behind the blind. "I'm so sorry!"

"I said *get down*."

Gemma made her way to the blind, her eyes searching the nearby shadows for the soldier, unable to shake the feeling that Mullen was near. She paused at the base of the ladder, arms crossed, and waited as Sophia descended the rungs. The moment the girl's boots hit the ground, Gemma grabbed her by the hand and dragged her toward the Sanctuary. "How many times, Sophia? How many times have I told you not to leave the camp by yourself?"

"But there's nothing to do there," Sophia whined, tossing her red curls over her shoulders. "It's so boring. And that treehouse is so cool."

"It's not a treehouse! It's a deer blind for hunting animals," she snapped. "I thought you were a soldier, Soph!"

The girl dropped her gaze to the ground. "Sorry, Gemma. I didn't mean to scare you."

But Gemma wasn't done being angry yet. Not by a long shot. "If you leave the Sanctuary, you're in danger. Don't you understand that? If you want to come hunting with me, that's fine. All you have to do is ask, and I'll bring you along."

"But *you* get to leave the camp by yourself…"

"Because I'm an adult!" Gemma snapped. She'd never spoken so harshly to Sophia before, but she couldn't stop thinking about that arrow. She'd almost let it go. "You're only eleven, Soph. Why do you need to leave the camp when you've got your fort at Neverland, friends your own age to play with, and an entire camp to explore? Why can't you just stay where it's safe?"

Sophia burst into tears. "Because I hate it here!" she cried, wrenching her hand out of Gemma's grasp. "I don't belong in this stupid camp! I miss my mom! And I hate you!"

The girl sprinted toward the camp, leaving Gemma behind.

The surrounding shadows grew larger and took shape, but Gemma remained rooted in place, unable to bring herself to go back. Her eyes burned, and she rubbed at them with her cold fingertips, but she did not cry. A puff of cold air caressed the back of her neck, and she rotated in a circle, searching the gloomy forest one last time for the soldier who'd taken up residence in her nightmares.

Nothing.

The forest was empty.

With Sophia's words ringing in her ears, Gemma resumed walking toward the faint lights of the Sanctuary.

CHAPTER TWO

Ten minutes later, Gemma stepped out of the woods and onto a footpath that wound through the entire camp. On the north end of camp, the path snaked past an in-ground pool (empty, of course), the Neverland ropes course, and a shale quarry. From there, the path curved into the heart of the camp and encircled the dining hall, which was Gemma's intended destination.

Before it was a hideout for subversives, the Sanctuary used to be an old Boy Scout campground. Back then, people knew it as Camp Mahantango. According to Abram Cleary, the Sanctuary's first occupant and resident historian, Mahantango was a Lenape word meaning "good hunting grounds."

Something about that name gave Gemma the creeps.

Pausing at the entrance of the old ropes course, she ran her fingers over the faded green sign.

Welcome to Neverland.

She stared at the hulking structure in the center of the field. It looked like some kind of medieval torture contraption. Over time, the untreated lumber that composed the rappel tower had faded to a dull gray, as had the thick stilts that supported its base. Colored handholds dotted the climbing wall and made the tower look as if it were suffering from a severe case of acne. A series of wooden poles sprang from the ground like errant weeds, ancient ropes strung from one to the next, linking them to the tower like blood vessels.

A murder of crows had gathered on top of the tower, squawking loudly.

Gemma hated that sound.

Two days after her group had arrived at the Sanctuary, Sophia had scaled the tower by herself, using the climbing wall. No one had been with her, and she hadn't worn a harness or used any ropes. She'd discovered the tower while exploring the camp and free-climbed all the way to the top before anyone realized she was missing.

Knowing they wouldn't be able to keep Sophia

away from the tower now that she'd conquered it, Abram and Taylor had made the climbing wall as safe as they could. They'd attached a harness system and made Sophia promise to use it anytime she climbed to the top. At Gemma's urging, they had also constructed a little fort at the top of the platform, complete with three walls and a roof, making it less likely that Sophia would fall. The girl spent a lot of time in her fort, drawing and reading, and she'd plastered the walls with her artwork. It was her own little corner of the world—the only place that belonged to her and no one else.

But it creeped Gemma out, the idea of the girl playing near all those crows.

Across the grassy field from Mire Lake, tucked up against the base of the mountain, were two ranges—one for rifles and one for archery. The rifles were gone, but for some inexplicable reason, the scout leaders had left the bows behind, locked away in a dusty storage closet at the archery range. That was where Abram had taught her to shoot a compound bow. To her surprise, as well as Abram's, she'd discovered a natural talent and affinity for archery. The bow felt so natural in her arms, almost like an extension of her own body, that when she went back to her cabin after a day of practicing, she felt as if she was missing a critical part of herself. When her arrows hit the bullseye every time, Abram moved the targets farther away, and then farther still, until even he couldn't compete with her accuracy.

After she split her first arrow at forty yards, Abram decided she was ready to hunt.

Even if they'd had the rifles, they wouldn't have used them to hunt. Despite the Sanctuary's isolated location, they weren't taking any chances.

An arrow was much quieter than a bullet.

Farther down the pathway, she passed a clearing where a group of coffee-colored cabins formed a half-circle around a covered picnic pavilion. While eight of the cabins remained empty, awaiting more Christians fleeing persecution, refugees from the Station filled the other four—well, all except for Gavin, who'd chosen to live with complete strangers in one of the larger cabins on the opposite end of the campground. While those cabins could comfortably house up to twenty people, the cabins used by Gemma's group held only six. Their metal roofs extended a few feet out from each structure, giving each cabin the benefit of a covered front porch. The cabins had no windows, and it sounded like the world was ending whenever it rained, thanks to the metal roofs. But the cabins were homey and warm.

Gemma took in her bare ring finger. She'd returned Gavin's pearl promise ring soon after arriving at the Sanctuary. She'd placed the ring inside his palm, hardly able to see anything because she was crying so hard. But Gavin had simply said, "Well, that's that," and walked away.

They hadn't spoken since.

She approached the stone facade of the L-shaped dining hall, her eyes lingering on the three empty flag poles that stood in front of the building. The sight of those empty flag poles always made her a little sad. She climbed the steps to the entrance, passing a faded sign that read: "Do a Good Turn Daily. Ask a Boy Scout. He Knows."

Inside the dining hall, Christians filled each of the long tables, as they always did during designated meal times. Others stood with their plates in their hands, their cups precariously balanced on the decorative shelf that encircled the room. Over one-hundred people called the Sanctuary home now. At last count, Abram said the number was somewhere north of one-hundred-and-twenty.

Gemma's nerves were still raw from her encounter with Sophia, and she couldn't handle the clanging of silverware and plates. She wanted to get her food, consume it as quickly as possible, and get back to the peace of her cabin.

She headed for the food line, which stretched clear to the back of the room, but someone shoved a full plate of food into her hands.

Gemma knew it was Mia before she looked up. The white-gold band on her ring finger had given it away. Mia and Oliver had gotten married back in July.

"Eat it while it's hot, honey." Mia put a hand on Gemma's back. "I know how much you love my spaghetti, so I set a plate aside for you."

The plate was almost too hot to hold. Gemma's eyes traveled from the twin slices of homemade garlic bread to the massive pile of spaghetti in the center of the plate, and she inhaled the scent of Mia's famous sauce. Only a culinary mastermind like Mia could combine tomato sauce, tomato juice, ketchup, and a variety of spices and make it taste amazing. "Mia, you don't know how hungry I am," Gemma said, rolling her fork in the spaghetti. "I spent the entire day in the woods, thinking about your spaghetti."

"You probably smelled it. Want to know my secret?" Mia lowered her voice, as if the dozens of nearby people currently shoveling pasta into their faces cared one iota about her secret recipes. "Pay attention, because you need to learn to cook like me if you want to eat this good after I'm gone. I'm not going to live forever, you know."

Gemma—who'd heard some variation of this declaration on dozens of occasions—responded with an internal eye roll. "Are you going somewhere, Mia? Can I come?"

"Don't get cute. Now, listen. The trick is to simmer the spaghetti in the sauce for at least two hours—longer, if possible. This isn't a meal you can whip up in thirty minutes. If you cheat the clock, you're cheating yourself."

Leaning against the wall, Gemma brought a huge forkful of spaghetti to her lips. She gave it a halfhearted blow before scarfing down the entire thing. "Cheat the clock," she said through a mouthful of spaghetti. "Cheat yourself. Got it."

Mia wrinkled her nose in disgust, but a tiny smile played on her lips. "Enjoy your dinner, honey."

"Thanks."

Mia returned to the kitchen, leaving Gemma alone with her plate of spaghetti. She scanned the room, hoping to glimpse Taylor among the tables, but he wasn't there. He usually ate his meals alone or in Cabin 4—the cabin he shared with Gemma, Sophia, Kyle, and Addie.

And, of course, Weston—Kyle and Addie's newborn son.

After Gemma finished eating, she carried her empty plate to the kitchen and then hiked back to

Cabin 4. Despite the mound of spaghetti currently digesting in her bloated stomach, she practically vaulted into the cabin, hoping to find Taylor sprawled out on his bunk, waiting for her. She hadn't seen him all day, and she missed him.

But he wasn't there.

In a wooden chair by the fireplace, Addie rocked a sleeping Weston in her arms. Despite enduring the physical and emotional trauma of the barn fire, Addie carried Weston to term and had given birth in late July. The baby had been born totally healthy and perfect, with his mommy's button nose and his daddy's messy blond hair. He'd only weighed six pounds at birth, but between his third and fourth month, he'd gotten positively chubby. He had no knees or knuckles to speak of, and the folds of his thighs held more fuzz than a dryer lint trap. When he sat up straight, his lolling head appeared to sit directly atop his shoulders. Gemma wasn't sure he even *had* a neck.

Taylor called him Tank, which annoyed Addie to no end.

Addie gave her a tired smile. "Did you get some supper?"

"I got *a lot* of supper," Gemma replied. "Way more than I needed."

"Good. How was the hunt?"

Gemma propped her bow and quiver against the wall and slumped onto the bottom bunk of the bed she shared with Sophia. The ancient springs creaked under her weight. "I saw a buck today. Nine points. He was huge, Addie, and he was so close. I could've shot him, but I didn't do it."

"Why not?" There was no judgment in Addie's tone, just curiosity.

"I don't know. I couldn't seem to let the arrow go."

"Probably because you're not a hunter, Gem," Addie said. "Besides, we don't *need* the meat. No one's starving to death around here—at least not with Mia slinging around in the kitchen."

"I know." Gemma used her feet to push off her boots and then fell back on her bunk. "I just..." She wasn't sure how to put into words what she was feeling. "I didn't shoot the arrow because I didn't *want* to kill it. Does that make sense? That's just not who I am. I didn't ask for any of this."

"None of us asked for this." Addie nodded at Weston, who gurgled his agreement. "This little stinker certainly didn't. You know, sometimes I feel guilty for having him, and then I feel guilty for feeling guilty." She looked at Gemma. "Was it selfish of me to want a family with my husband?"

"Of course not." Although, Gemma couldn't

imagine bringing a baby into this world. She often imagined marrying Taylor, but she never allowed herself to imagine having a child with him. On the few occasions when she had allowed such thoughts to enter her mind, she'd always pictured the soldiers ripping her crying baby from her arms and carrying it away. And she would be powerless to stop them.

No. She would never introduce a child into this world. Not now. Not ever.

Addie's voice pulled her back from her dark thoughts. "Earlier today, I was sitting here feeding Weston and thinking about how the Sanctuary has been such a blessing for us. But we might never have found it if you hadn't been detained. Finding Letty's flyer at the church like that…I mean, what are the odds of you putting *that* piece of paper in your pocket?"

Addie was, of course, referring to the advertisement that had been hanging on the bulletin board in the old church in Ash Grove. The one featuring a dark-skinned old woman with a kind smile, standing in front of a bookstore.

Letty's Book Cellar—New and Used Books in Winter's Dam.

Looking for a good book? We've got a towering selection!

Mention this ad to save 10 percent off your purchase.

Or visit our website and use our discount code: PV1810.

"It got knocked down when Taylor and Colonel Carver were fighting," Gemma spoke in a quiet voice. "When I picked it up, I didn't know why I was doing it. I just felt like it meant something."

Gemma hadn't realized it, but the piece of paper she'd plucked off the floor and stuffed into her pocket on a whim had contained a hidden message for subversives. She also hadn't realized that there were hundreds of flyers just like it, hanging in various locations throughout central Pennsylvania. It was Mia—with her keen eye and affinity for puzzles—who'd noticed the secret code embedded within the advertisement. The phrase "good book" had drawn her attention, and after studying the flyer for a few minutes, she'd grabbed Gemma's Bible and followed the coupon code to the Book of Proverbs, chapter eighteen, verse ten.

"The name of the Lord is a fortified tower; the righteous run to it and are safe."

"God used what happened in Ash Grove," Addie said, "to bring us to safety. To a place where we can finally breathe. Which means He must want us here, right?"

"Right."

"But I think He doesn't want us here."

"Huh?" Gemma massaged her temples, only half-listening to Addie. She could feel the beginnings of a headache coming on. "Is this one of those postpartum delirium things?"

"I'm serious, Gem. I have this nagging feeling that God doesn't want us here."

Rolling onto her side, Gemma propped her chin in her hand. "I'll bite. Why wouldn't God want us here? We're safe, and we're free to worship Him."

"I don't know." Addie dropped her gaze to Weston's cherubic face. "I've just got this feeling that we aren't doing what we're supposed to be doing. The world needs the Church, but the Church is gone. The ministers are gone. Most Christians have either renounced or are in detention centers, and the rest of us are in hiding."

"What are you saying?"

But Gemma already knew. She just didn't want to hear it.

"The world needs the Truth, Gemma. Their ears are *itching* for the Truth, and we're the only ones who know it and still have voices. And what are we doing? We're hiding away like a bunch of fat old gophers in a comfy hole."

Weston sputtered out a wet, hacking cough and squirmed in Addie's arms, as if he, too, was uncomfortable with the topic. Addie brought him to her chest and rubbed his back until he quieted down.

"How's he doing?" Gemma asked, eager to change the subject, although she didn't like the new topic much better. Weston's cough worried her. It seemed to get worse at night. The previous night, Gemma had crept over to Addie's bunk and offered to take him for a little while, but Addie never wanted to put Weston down. Even Kyle had to coax his wife into letting him hold their baby.

"Oliver thinks it's just a stubborn cold." Addie brought a trembling hand to her lips, probably searching for a nail to chew on, an old nervous habit she'd broken after meeting Kyle at the Station, that had recently reemerged. "I had Claudia examine him this morning, and she said his lungs sounded clear, so that made me feel a little better." Claudia was a retired emergency room nurse. Before Oliver, she'd been the only medical professional at the Sanctuary. She'd been overjoyed to find out that Oliver was a doctor, especially after she'd noticed Addie's bulging tummy. "Not that I don't trust Oliver," Addie continued. "But...you know..."

"Foot doctor," they said in unison and laughed.

"Is he still running a fever?" Gemma asked.

"Not since yesterday morning. So, that's good. I've been letting him breastfeed whenever he wants and giving him Tylenol when he fusses." Addie kissed Weston on the forehead. "He's Mommy's little stinker."

The door swung wide and Sophia burst into the cabin, red-faced and out of breath, as if she'd been running nonstop since she left Gemma alone in the woods. A green glow stick hung on a cord from her shoulders. After spending hours trapped in the root cellar underneath the charred remnants of Oliver's barn, Sophia had developed an intense fear of the dark. With Letty's help, Taylor had procured an entire box of glow sticks for Sophia so she would never be trapped in the dark again.

The crimson flush of the girl's cheeks deepened when she saw Gemma lying on the bottom bunk. But she recovered quickly, racing over to Addie and wrapping her arms around the woman's neck.

"How is he?" she asked, deliberately ignoring Gemma.

"Better. Not as fussy as this morning."

"Good." Sophia touched Weston's nose with the tip of her index finger. "I missed him."

Addie lightly swatted Sophia's hand away. "Don't touch him until you've washed those filthy little piglet hands of yours. What have you been doing, anyway? Juggling road apples for fun?"

Giggling at Addie's slang term for horse manure, Sophia held out her hands to examine them. "They're not that dirty."

Addie snorted. "I can *smell* them, you little hellion. And why weren't you at dinner?"

"Because I don't like Mia's gross spaghetti." She scrunched up her nose as if she smelled something bad. "She puts ketchup in it."

"Sophia Grace! You daresn't let Mia hear you say that you don't like her spaghetti." Addie covered her mouth with her hand, stifling a laugh. "Alright, go wash up, brush your teeth, and get ready for bed."

"But can't I help you with Weston?"

"Not until you're clean. Weston doesn't want your smelly little germs crawling all over him. When you get back, you need to redd up the cabin a bit."

Sophia laughed at another one of Addie's famous Pennsylvania Dutch-isms. "You want me to redd it up? You mean paint it red? Where do I get the paint?"

"When you get back from the bathroom, you will *clean up,*" Addie said, emphasizing the words, "your part of the cabin. This place is looking and smelling like a hog pen at feeding time. Then—and only then—can you help me with Weston."

Groaning, Sophia grabbed her pajamas, toothbrush, and toothpaste and dashed out of the cabin. The door slammed shut behind her.

The noise woke Weston, and he began to cry.

"It's okay, little man." As soon as Addie fed him, he quieted right down. "That's a good boy."

Gemma stretched out on her bunk and closed her eyes. On the other side of the room, Addie sang a quiet lullaby to Weston. Addie made up most of her lullabies, as if the old standards weren't sufficient for someone as plucky and adorable as Weston.

Gemma couldn't be certain, but it sounded like tonight's lullaby was about scrapple.

With Addie singing a song about her favorite mystery meat in the background, Gemma stretched out on her bunk and closed her eyes. She only intended to doze for a few minutes, but the moment her head hit the pillow, she felt as if she were falling backward into a deep abyss. The sound of Addie's lullaby faded away as sleep seized Gemma in its long-fingered grip and pulled her—headfirst—into oblivion.

✝

She woke to the sound of the cabin door creaking open.

People crept in and out of the cabin all night long to use the bathroom, but Gemma still hadn't gotten used to the sound. It always woke her up. She took a quick survey of the beds. The dark lump sleeping in the bunk above Addie and Weston was Kyle. Although she couldn't see Sophia, she knew the girl had made it back from the bathroom by the small hand dangling from the bunk above her own.

It could only be one person.

She tilted her head toward the door and watched as Taylor slipped inside the cabin and eased the door shut behind him. All of her worries —the stress with Sophia, Addie's thoughts about the Sanctuary—instantly evaporated at the sight of him. If Taylor was around, everything was going to be okay.

His bunk bed was perpendicular to hers, pressed up against the opposing wall. The bunk directly above his was currently unoccupied, although, one day, it would belong to Weston.

She watched as Taylor slipped off his boots and hung his coat over his bunk's top railing, but he didn't climb into his bed. Instead, he expertly side-stepped the creaky floorboards as he made his way to Gemma's bed. She shifted closer to the wall to make room for him.

Everyone in their cabin—and probably a few people *outside* of their cabin—knew that Taylor's bed was just for show. He and Gemma slept together every night. But things never got *too* romantic in Cabin 4. Gemma was the virgin in the relationship, but waiting for marriage hadn't been her idea. They'd discussed it only once, in a stilted conversation soon after their arrival at the Sanctuary, when Taylor began sneaking into her bed at night. Taylor had admitted that he'd made mistakes in the past and that he didn't want to make any more of them, especially where Gemma was concerned. Although she hadn't expected a twenty-five-year-old man—especially one as attractive as Taylor—to have saved himself for marriage, the realization that he'd shared that level of intimacy with anyone else broke her heart. And the guilt and regret she'd heard in his voice made her heart ache even more.

Their vow to wait had sounded honorable at the time. Old-fashioned in a sweet way.

And Gemma regretted it with every fiber of her being.

Taylor slid into the bed and stretched one arm across her pillow. She slid against him, burying her face in his neck and inhaling the scent of him.

Smoke. Cinnamon. Pine. Those were the scents that made up Taylor. He hadn't cut his hair since going AWOL from the Task Force six months earlier, and it was getting long now. Now, his dark hair was always a little disheveled, as if after having a military buzz cut for so many years, he'd forgotten how to use a comb. But what she loved most was the rough feeling of his slight beard against her cheek when he kissed her.

Little by little, he was shedding pieces of the soldier he'd once been.

Sometimes, she allowed herself to daydream about a future where they could get dressed up and go out to dinner. She couldn't imagine Taylor in a suit, although she knew he'd look incredible. What kind of cologne would he wear? Probably something subtle and inexpensive. A drug-store cologne. He was too practical to buy an expensive brand.

But the most expensive cologne in the world could never compete with the familiar smell that invaded her nostrils as he wrapped his arms around her.

If she could, she'd bottle that scent and call it *Safety, by Gemma Alcott.*

"Where were you?" she whispered.

"Hiking the perimeter."

Of course he was. Taylor hiked all or a portion

of the four-hundred acres of the Sanctuary almost every day, searching for any sign of trespassers, looking for tracks that might show someone had been sneaking around in the woods, maybe even attempting to get eyes on the camp.

She ran a finger along his rough jaw. "Did you find any bad guys?"

"No bad guys. Did you shoot a deer?"

"No. But I gave a barn owl something to think about."

He smiled at her. There was nothing better in the world than an understated Taylor smile. "I've got a supply run with Letty in the morning. You want to come with?"

"With *me*," Gemma corrected. "Stop taking grammar lessons from Addie."

"Do you want to come with or not?"

"Sure." She tried to sound nonchalant, but it thrilled her to be invited along. Rarely did she get to accompany Taylor on pick-ups or supply runs, as he thought they were too dangerous. She'd only gone a few times before, and she'd had to throw a fit to get him to agree to it. She did not know why he would invite her out of the blue, but she wasn't about to question it. "Anything to get me out of that tree stand for a few hours."

By the dim light of the lamp, she could see the

mischievous glint in Taylor's eye. "You're going to regret it."

"Why?"

"Because we're leaving at four," he said. "I want to get everything loaded at the bookstore and get out of town before the sun comes up."

Ugh. Four a.m. Gemma had forgotten how early he left for supply runs. She looked at her watch. It was almost eleven. If they were going to wake up that early, then she needed to get some sleep.

But first, she needed to kiss Taylor. A lot.

Going up on one elbow, she brushed Taylor's hair away from his forehead and brought her lips to his. She knew every inch of those lips well enough to draw a roadmap of them. From the subtle slope of his lower lip to the barely there dip in the middle of his upper lip, no part remained a secret to her.

Taylor still bore scars from the crippling beatings he'd suffered at the hands of Colonel Carver and the townspeople of Ash Grove. Some of those scars were visible, and some weren't. But the more time that passed, the more Taylor resembled the boy from the carnival. The one who'd rescued her from the carnie and then returned hours later to dig her precious necklace out of the garbage can. He'd kept her necklace safe for eight years and had only given it back after the Task Force had detained her parents.

The same night he'd proposed. And she'd refused.

Her necklace dangled over his chest as their kiss grew deeper, more urgent. She felt her resolve slipping, as it always did with Taylor. They were playing with fire, and they both knew it. But they couldn't help themselves.

She pulled away and rested her head on his chest, breathing heavily. They were both sweating now—partly because of the hot cabin, but mostly because they'd spent the last few minutes making out. Gemma's hair stuck to her forehead until Taylor brushed it away. "We're getting up early," she said. "We should go to sleep."

"Yeah." Taylor blew out a long breath. "We definitely should." He kissed her again, on the forehead this time. "I love you, Gem."

"I love you, too," she whispered into his t-shirt.

Her head rose and fell with each of Taylor's breaths, the steady sound of his heartbeat reassuring her as he slipped his fingers through her damp hair. Eventually, his fingers stopped moving and his breathing slowed into the steady rhythm of sleep.

When she slept, she dreamt of a redheaded soldier with a predator's eyes moving stealthily through the woods, closing in on her cabin. She lay paralyzed on her bed, watching as he opened the door and stepped inside. His head turned slowly, scanning the room before finally landing on her.

Desperate, she searched the cabin for Taylor, but he was gone. Where had he gone? Why wasn't he there anymore? Then, she realized the cabin was empty. There was no one left.

No one but Gemma...and Mullen.

I've come back, he said. *To finish what I started.*

And then he climbed on top of her, his breath hot against her face, his hands closing around her neck. Tightening. Squeezing. His dark eyes dancing with glee.

This is how I'm going to die, she thought.

Unable to scream. Unable to breathe. Unable to gasp for air.

Sputtering. Coughing.

Coughing.

Her eyes snapped open.

She was in the cabin.

Taylor was beside her, one arm cast over his head, snoring softly.

Mullen was gone.

On the other side of the room, Weston was coughing again, the sound weaving its way into Gemma's nightmare.

Pulling in a deep breath, she reached up and

touched her neck. Where Mullen's hands had been, there was only her cross necklace. Beneath it, her skin felt warm and tingly, and she wondered about the strange connection between her sleeping brain and her nervous system. How did her body—right down to the nerves buried beneath her skin—know what she'd been dreaming?

Or was there more to it? Was Mullen out there somewhere, still hunting her and growing closer by the minute? And on some primitive level, did her body already know it?

She closed her eyes again.

Four o'clock couldn't come soon enough.

CHAPTER THREE

Gemma jerked awake as Taylor turned the Charger into the parking lot of Letty's Book Cellar. The dashboard clock read *4:31.* She'd dozed most of the way to the bookstore, which really was a shame since it was the first time she'd left the Sanctuary in weeks. But between Weston's constant coughing and her own terrible dreams, she wasn't sleeping much.

Rubbing her eyes, she peered through the windshield at Letty's store. With its gambrel roof and fresh white paint, the bookstore appeared homey and welcoming, even in the early morning darkness. It was a quaint, mom-and-pop establishment that people discovered by accident on their way to somewhere else. A canary-yellow newspaper vending machine sat to the right of the front door, and on the opposite end of the porch, a wooden swing hung suspended from the roof. A green-shingled roof jutted over the porch like the bill of a ball cap, and three baskets of mums dangled from the overhang, dripping water onto the porch railing. It didn't surprise Gemma that the flowers had already been watered. Letty was an unapologetic early-riser.

Aside from the windows at the front of the store, there were no other windows on the first floor of the building, but twin dormer windows jutted out from each side of the second floor like suspicious eyes keeping watch over the parking lot. Letty lived up there, directly above the store, in a two-bedroom apartment. According to Taylor, she spent most of her evenings perched on that swing, a cup of coffee in one hand and a romance novel in the other.

A sign with green lettering hung above the porch's roof: *Letty's Book Cellar.*

Taylor backed the Charger into a spot near the porch steps.

Except for Letty's Subaru, the Charger was the only vehicle in the parking lot. Through the front windows of the all-night convenience store next door, Gemma could see a young man with a piece-meal goatee sitting behind the counter. But Gemma wasn't concerned about being spotted by the teenager. Like most people in his age bracket, he was busy tapping away on his phone, oblivious to the world around him.

She stepped out of the Charger and followed Taylor up the creaky wooden steps to the front porch. Although the sign on the door said the store was closed, they let themselves in through the unlocked front door.

Unlike its cheerful exterior, the inside of the bookstore was perpetually gloomy. Letty despised overhead lighting, claiming that it faded her books and highlighted the dust on her shelves. During the day, the only light came from the windows at the front of the store. Occasionally, she would switch on a few standing lamps only when it was too cloudy outside for her customers to see what books they were holding, but she did so begrudgingly.

The lamps were on now, casting the room in shadows.

"Who's there?"

Letty emerged from one row, a stack of paperback books clutched in her arthritic hands. Unlike her dark and cluttered bookstore, Letty always looked bright and put-together. Today, she wore a purple cardigan, floral blouse, and dark slacks that perfectly complemented her slightly plump frame. She barely wore any makeup because she didn't need it. Her youthful chocolate skin and megawatt smile made her look significantly younger than her sixty-eight years. On the outside, she didn't seem at all like a woman who was managing a business by herself while also running an underground railroad for subversives.

When she saw Taylor, Letty's face lit up brighter than the overhead lighting she despised. She dropped her books on a table and rushed to accost him, casting her arms around his shoulders and planting what sounded like an extremely wet kiss on his cheek. Since Letty was only five-three, Taylor had to bend over to accommodate her kiss. "How is camp life treating you, baby? They feeding you enough over there?" She wrapped a hand around one of his biceps and squeezed. "You holding up okay?"

Gemma covered her mouth to hide her laughter.

Letty was like a grandmother to Taylor.

A feisty, lascivious grandmother.

An embarrassed smile formed on Taylor's lips. It was too dark to be certain, but Gemma thought he was blushing. Gently, he extricated himself from Letty's grip. "Ma'am, as we've discussed before *in great detail*, sexual harassment is not okay. Even when a sweet old lady is doing it."

Letty snorted. "Who are you calling an old

lady?" She gave him a firm smack on the butt before directing her attention to Gemma. "And you brought Stormy with you! What a pleasant surprise!" She pulled Gemma into a sincere—but decidedly less enthusiastic—embrace. No butt slaps or wet kisses for her. "Have you been keeping my boyfriend in line, Stormy?"

Letty never used Gemma's actual name. On the day their group had first arrived at the bookstore, a powerful April thunderstorm had been raging outside, and Gemma had burst into the store before any of the others, hair dripping, clothes sopping wet, a loud clap of thunder announcing her arrival.

She'd been Stormy ever since.

Letty released Gemma from her grip and then slipped behind the counter and reappeared with a reusable grocery bag filled with paperback books. "Will you see that Sophia gets these? I know she loves drawing, so I threw in some art books, as well as a few Nancy Drew mysteries I thought she might like."

Gemma accepted the bag and peeked at its contents. "Oh, that's wonderful, Letty. She'll love this. Thank you."

The woman grabbed a small bottle of lotion from the counter and squirted a little on her wrinkled hands, filling the air with the smell of coconut. "By the way, the town druggie—Melinda

Tuttle—gave me a bottle of amoxicillin for that baby of yours."

Gemma shot Taylor a look. "You got amoxicillin from...a drug addict?"

Letty laughed as if she had heard nothing so funny in ages. "Oh no, Mindy's the pharmacist. I just call her the town druggie to irritate her. Mindy's husband, Gerry, was a few years behind me in school. He's got this long neck. We used to call him Tuttle the Turtle." She winked at Gemma. "Some of us still do, just not to his face. Anyway, you let me know if that baby doesn't get better quickly, okay?"

"I will."

"What else do you have for us today?" Taylor asked.

Letty tossed him a set of keys that unlocked the storage room in the rear hallway. "There are a few boxes of nonperishables. Canned vegetables. Cereal. Enormous bags of rice. Boxed meals. The Fishmans sent another thirty pounds of ground beef. That's in the freezer. You should be able to make that last a few weeks."

The Fishmans owned the butcher shop in town and regularly provided fresh meat for the Sanctuary. In the beginning, Letty had paid them for their meat, but now they insisted on donating it. Like most of the sympathizers in Winter's Dam, they had renounced their faith early on, and Gemma suspected this was their way of trying to make amends with God. Although Letty only sought help from people she trusted, none of the other sympathizers—not even the Fishmans—knew the location of the Sanctuary.

Taylor unlocked the storage room and went inside.

When Gemma followed him, a fleshy arm fell over her shoulder, pulling her close. The smell of coconut grew stronger. "Let your man handle the hard work, Stormy," Letty said. "You'd just get in the way."

"I really should help him."

Taylor emerged from the storage room, a cardboard box cradled in his arms. He winked at Gemma. "Nah. You'd just get in the way."

She followed Letty to a round table near the checkout counter. Letty gestured to one of the wooden chairs, and Gemma happily collapsed into it, thankful to be spared the job of carrying dozens of heavy boxes to the car. She wasn't much of a feminist—especially at four-thirty in the morning.

"Give me a minute," Letty said. "I'll fix us some coffee."

While Letty made the coffee and Taylor carried boxes to the car, Gemma glimpsed the cramped hallway that led back to Letty's office. Six months earlier, Gemma and her group had followed Letty down that same hallway into the overcrowded office where boxes of books cluttered the floor of the windowless room. A faded oriental rug covered part of the unfinished wood floor, and at Letty's direction, Taylor and Kyle had each taken an end of the rug and rolled it toward the desk, exposing a hidden door leading into the cellar. When they lifted the door, its unoiled hinges squeaked in protest.

Gemma shuddered. She would never forget the sound of the door slamming shut, sealing them inside the dark cellar. Or of huddling in the darkness with the rest of her group, her eyes on the thin bands of light peeking through the sagging floorboards, her icy fingers grasping Taylor's forearm. For her, the experience had been a miserable one. But for some others—the ones who'd spent hours trapped in the root cellar beneath the barn as it smoldered and collapsed on top of them—being locked underground again had almost been unbearable.

Letty reappeared and set a mug of coffee in front of Gemma, along with a saucer of cream and a few packets of raw sugar. While Gemma stirred a little cream and sugar into her coffee, Letty went behind the counter and came back with a mug that read: *It's Not Hoarding if it's Books*. She also brought with her an unopened package of Lotus Biscoff cookies and two napkins. "What's on your mind, Stormy? Whenever I see you, you always look worried."

At that moment, the only thing on Gemma's mind was that little red package of cookies. She hadn't eaten breakfast yet, and her mouth watered. "Do I?"

Letty pushed the package toward her. "Dig in, honey. They go great with coffee."

Gemma didn't need to be told twice. She opened the package and pulled out two cookies. To make them last longer, she dipped them in her coffee and nibbled on them. She'd never had this brand of cookie before, but they were heavenly. Warm and fresh and cinnamon-sweet.

"Letty…I can't even…There are no words…" She trailed off, unsure of how to express how strongly she felt about the cookies. She wanted to marry them, write songs about them, name her children Lotus and Biscoff. But when she reached for her second cookie, her fingers came away with only crumbs. She glanced at the napkin in front of her and realized that she'd already eaten both cookies.

Groaning, Letty grabbed the bag of cookies and shoved them at Gemma. "For heaven's sake, child, would you *eat*? I don't even like these nasty things. That's why I save them for company."

Gemma didn't know if that was true or not, nor did she care. She pulled out five more cookies and then wrapped a protective arm around the rest of the pack.

Maybe it was the early hour. Or the caffeine. Or the immense amount of sugar she'd just consumed. Likely, the combination of all three had lowered her inhibitions, because the next moment, she blurted out the question that had been on her mind ever since she'd arrived at the Sanctuary. She stuffed another cookie in her mouth. "So, how did you end up buying Camp Mahantango?"

The old woman took a long sip of coffee from her mug, no doubt killing time while she considered how much information she wanted to divulge. Finally, she set the coffee down and interlaced her hands on the table. "Stormy, have I ever told you that my daddy was an atheist?"

"Definitely not." She would've remembered that.

"Well, he was. It was my momma who got us into the faith. She took my sister and me to church every Sunday, but my daddy never went. Carlton Webb hated God more than taxes. He hated God so much that he married my mother at the local district justice office just to avoid setting foot inside a church. Don't ask me why he hated God, because he never divulged that information to me. It was just the way he was. The first time I remember seeing him in church was at my baby sister's funeral. She died in a car accident when she was nineteen."

"Oh, Letty." Gemma put a hand on top of Letty's. "I'm so sorry."

The woman responded with a shrug, but there was pain in her eyes. "It was a long time ago, Stormy. She's in heaven with our momma and Jesus," she said. "Just so you know, I don't judge my daddy for his failures. Lord knows, I've had a few of my own."

Letty didn't come right out and say it, but Gemma knew what she was talking about. Like so many others, Letty had renounced her Christian faith to avoid being sent to a detention center.

"There were so many wonderful parts of my daddy. Like, he was funny as all get-out. And he knew a good thing when he saw it—that was how he got my momma, after all. And that was how he built a company worth over five million dollars."

Gemma felt her eyes grow wide. She couldn't fathom having that kind of money. "Wow. What company?"

Letty brought the mug to her lips but didn't drink. Instead, she stared into the coffee, as if the answer to Gemma's question might float in the black liquid like tea leaves. "Real estate, mostly. He owned dozens of rental properties in Philadelphia and West Chester. Nice places, too. He employed the best property managers and kept after them. But he always dreamt of doing something else. Something bigger. When he heard that an old Boy Scout camp was going up for auction, I think he saw it as his biggest opportunity yet. He purchased all four-hundred acres in a cash sale one week prior to the scheduled auction. He said he wanted to create an upscale campground for city folk. People who wanted the camping experience without all the bugs and dirt. I guess they call that glamping now." She raised her eyes to meet Gemma's. "Believe it or not, he was going to call it The Sanctuary."

Goosebumps erupted on Gemma's arms, and she took another sip of her coffee to chase them away. "That's crazy."

"The man had crazy ideas," Letty continued. "He wanted his guests to stay in air-conditioned cabins with their own outdoor Jacuzzis. He wanted a kitchen that served five-star cuisine. Bless his heart…he even wanted a midnight buffet, just like they do on the cruise ships!" She pinched her lips together. "Stormy, I asked him, 'What about all the black bears? Is it a good idea to have a bunch of drunk city-dwellers stumbling back to their cabins in the middle of the night with full plates of food?'"

Gemma laughed. "What did he say to that?"

"He said, 'Don't worry, baby. I'm going to make them sign a release.'" The woman grabbed her belly and laughed until tears sprang from her eyes. Then, her laughter faded and only the tears remained. "He never got around to fixing the place up, though. He bought it about four months before he passed."

Gemma scooted her chair close to Letty's and wrapped an arm around the old woman. Somehow, Letty felt both sturdy and frail at the same time. An ancient tree in danger of collapsing. "The way you describe him…he sounds a lot like you."

Letty sniffed and dabbed her cheeks with a napkin. "We were a lot alike. It made him so happy when I renounced Jesus. I felt like the biggest coward, but he said it was the bravest thing I'd ever done. I'd love to tell you he came to know the Lord before it was too late, but he never did. My daddy denied God right until the day he collapsed and died while filling his plate at a Fourth of July barbecue. The man died a millionaire, but all he took into the afterlife was a glass of lemonade and a half-eaten bowl of potato salad. Everything else—all of his millions and his real estate holdings—went to me. Including the Sanctuary."

Gemma squeezed Letty tighter, her own eyes leaking tears now. She didn't know what to say.

She'd thought she understood how it felt to lose her parents, but she didn't. Her parents were still out there somewhere, and she might see them again one day. Letty didn't have that hope anymore.

"It's ironic, isn't it?" Letty continued. "My daddy had lots of money, and lots of investments, but in the end, none of those things could save him." She reached for Gemma's hand on her shoulder and squeezed it. "But I'm going to use it all to save others."

Gemma kissed her on the cheek. "And we love you for it, Letty."

"Hey." Taylor emerged from the storage room, wiping his dusty hands on his jeans. "The only one who gets to kiss Letty is me."

Beaming, Letty quickly switched back into lascivious-grandmother mode. "Oh, honey. Don't tease an old lady."

Taylor approached the table but didn't sit down. Gemma knew right away that something wasn't right. The coloring of his face was a little off, and he stood there awkwardly, not speaking, with both hands stuffed in his front pockets. Maybe he wasn't feeling well. Or maybe it was just nerves. He didn't like to stay in Winter's Dam for very long.

"Did you find everything, honey?" Letty asked. "Is everything good?"

"It's better than good," Taylor replied. Then, he surprised Gemma by leaning down and pulling Letty into a tight hug. "Thank you."

Letty squealed with delight and immediately dropped both of her hands to his butt. "Oh my! You just gave me something to dream about tonight!"

Taylor pried Letty's hands from his rear and sprinted for the exit.

Still laughing—honestly, how long had it been since she'd laughed this much?—Gemma stood and followed Letty to the front of the store. When they got to the door, Gemma hesitated. "Letty? What would he think about all of this?"

"Who?"

"Your father. What would he think if he knew you were hiding subversives at his campground?"

"Oh, Stormy..." A mischievous sparkle lit up the woman's damp eyes. She pushed the half-eaten package of cookies into Gemma's hands. "That man would absolutely *hate* it."

✝

The young cashier with the bad goatee was still thumbing away at his phone when Gemma and Taylor pulled out of the parking lot.

Gemma popped another cookie into her mouth.

Her stomach felt uncomfortably full, but she couldn't help herself. She tilted her head against the seat and closed her eyes.

"Gem, I want to show you something before we go back," Taylor said. "There's a place nearby, only about ten minutes from here. We drove past it on the way in, but you were asleep. It's called Halfway Lake. I think we have enough time to—"

"Halfway Lake?" she repeated without opening her eyes. "Halfway to what?"

"I don't know. Maybe the next town? Who cares?"

She swallowed. Another cookie down.

Might as well finish the package.

When she reached for another one, she heard Taylor pull in a sharp breath.

"Gemma."

"Yes, yes...I was going to offer you one." Reluctantly, she pulled the pack from between her legs and held it out to Taylor. "But there aren't many left. And Letty gave these to me, so—"

"Gemma. Look."

"What?"

She opened her eyes and saw Taylor pointing at the road ahead.

Gemma glanced out the windshield, expecting to see a deer crossing the highway. Or a fox. Maybe even a bear. But when she saw what Taylor was pointing at, the fight-or-flight response dilated her pupils, brightening her vision so much that the camouflaged vehicle blocking the road ahead appeared to be glowing.

"Taylor?" she whispered.

He tightened his grip on the wheel, his next words confirming what she already knew.

"It's the Task Force."

CHAPTER FOUR

Gemma's field of vision narrowed to a small circle that included the camou-flaged Humvee blocking the highway leading out of Winter's Dam and the two Task Force soldiers leaning against it. At the sight of their olive-drab uniforms and black tactical vests, memories flashed through her mind in rapid succession: soldiers dragging her up the basement stairs, Private Mullen's fist hurtling toward her face, Nowak howling as she plunged a letter opener into the meat of his thigh.

One soldier walked into the center of the road and held up both hands, indicating that Taylor should stop the vehicle. The other soldier—an older man with a gray mustache—remained next to the Humvee, his thumbs hooked into the straps of his vest.

The Charger came to a stop, and Taylor pressed a button to roll down his window. "Don't talk. Just let me handle it."

As the younger of the two soldiers strolled up to the driver's window, Gemma propped her elbow on the passenger door and tried to look nonchalant. Maybe even a little bored.

But she felt like tossing her cookies. Literally.

"How's it going, Private?" Taylor gestured to the Humvee and the orange-and-white A-frame barricades blocking the road. "What's all this?"

Gemma hadn't heard Taylor use that voice in months. It was his authoritative soldier voice. The same one he'd used on her when they'd first stumbled across each other on Dragon's Back Mountain before he realized who she was.

The soldier—whose nametape read Haywood—leaned into the window and locked eyes with Gemma's. She gave him a coquettish smile, and he responded with a nod that was all business. "We're setting up a barricade. We believe some folks in this town are helping a group of subversives. Possibly even hiding 'em." The deep-south twang of the soldier's voice brought to mind barbeque joints and boiled peanuts. "We're shutting everything down until we can get this straightened out. Do you folks live in town?"

"No, we're just passing through." Taylor glanced back toward the town, his expression a mixture of curiosity and annoyance. "You mind letting us out before you shut everything down? We have somewhere to be."

Even before Taylor finished speaking, the soldier was shaking his head. "I'm afraid that's not possible, sir. As of twenty minutes ago, we shut this town down. We blocked the other end of town off, too. We're still waiting for the rest of our unit to arrive, but we're under orders to enforce the barricades immediately. Sorry for the inconvenience, but no one's allowed to leave."

"But I *said* we don't live in town." There wasn't a hint of fear in Taylor's voice. No sign at all that he was speaking anything but the truth. "You mean you're going to detain us for driving through a town?"

"Can I see some identification, sir?"

Taylor leaned forward to dig his wallet out of his back pocket. His shirt pulled up a little, giving Gemma a glimpse of the pistol on his right hip. For a split second, she thought about grabbing the gun. She didn't want to hurt anyone, but what if the gun was their only chance to get away?

As if reading her thoughts, Taylor brought his

elbow down to cover the weapon. He pulled his Task Force ID out of his wallet, along with his government ID card, and handed them both to the soldier.

Gemma silently thanked God that neither had expired yet.

The soldier examined both cards and appeared to take special interest in the Task Force ID. He turned it over in his hands, his thumb covering the dark swirls of Taylor's fingerprint. Without raising his eyes from the card, he said, "Sorry for the trouble, Sergeant. What unit are you attached to?"

Was it possible that Haywood hadn't heard about Taylor? About what had happened in Ash Grove with Colonel Carver? The Task Force kept the whole thing out of the newspapers, as Carver's rogue operation would've been a giant black eye for them, but surely a soldier within the Task Force's own ranks would've heard about Taylor and known he was AWOL.

"I'm attached to 2nd Battalion under Lieutenant Colonel Drum. A scout, obviously." Taylor gestured to his out-of-regulation hair and then nodded at Gemma. "I'm on leave this week, so I'm spending some time with my girlfriend. We're supposed to meet her parents for brunch this morning. The app on my phone said this road was a shortcut to the highway, but apparently it doesn't take government barricades into account."

The soldier furrowed his eyebrows. "How did y'all get through the barricade on the other end of town?"

"It wasn't there when we came through," Taylor said. "But that was at least a half-hour ago. We'd already been driving for a few hours, so we stopped at the convenience store in town."

Haywood appeared to be satisfied with Taylor's answer. "Alright, Sarge. Now that I know you're Task Force, I'll have y'all out of here in a minute."

"Thanks, man. I appreciate it."

Haywood pointed at Gemma. "I'll just need to see your identification, ma'am. Then you folks can be on your way."

Gemma's heart dropped. Except, it didn't just drop—it smashed through the floor of the car and splattered onto the highway. She glanced at her lap where her purse would've been if she had anything close to a normal life. But there was nothing in her lap except for a few brown crumbs and a near-empty package of cookies. She didn't even own a purse anymore. And she certainly didn't possess a government ID card.

She swallowed her fear and put on her most sincere smile. "This is terrible, I know, but I left my purse at home this morning. We had to rush to get an early start, and my purse, my ID card...every-thing is back at the house. I only realized it when we stopped at the gas station, but since Taylor was driving, I didn't think it would be an issue."

Haywood's voice took on a hard edge. "You're required to carry your ID with you when you leave the house, ma'am. That's not a new rule."

"I know. And I usually do. Can't you give us a break today, please?"

"I'm afraid that's not possible." Haywood would not budge. He was a Task Force soldier, and the Task Force trained their soldiers well. They en-forced the compliance laws without question. *No matter what.* "Ma'am, I need you to step outside the car."

"She's not going anywhere, Private."

Haywood's eyes shot back to Taylor. "Sergeant Nolan... like I said earlier, I'm sorry for the trou-ble, but there are rules we need to—"

"You know what?" Taylor pulled out his cell phone, opened his list of contacts, and tilted the phone so Haywood could see the names. "Since you seem to be intent on wasting my time, why don't we clear this up by calling General Jameson? He's a close family friend of mine, and he can vouch for both of us."

The soldier winced as if someone had slapped him, his Adam's apple jumping up and down like a bobber on a fishing line. *"Brigadier General Jameson?"*

"That's the one. I'm sure the general won't mind me bothering him at five o'clock in the morning. I'll just explain that Private Haywood of... What company are you with again?"

"I'm with, uh...Captain Haggerty's unit," Haywood stammered. "Charlie Company. Second Battalion."

"Great," Taylor said. "I'll explain that Private Haywood of Charlie Company, Second Battalion wasn't comfortable letting a Task Force NCO pass through a barricade that wasn't there ten minutes earlier."

"Sarge, it's not about—"

Taylor held up a finger to silence him. Then, he pressed send and brought the phone to his ear. "Don't worry, Private," he muttered over the faint sound of the phone ringing. "You're just doing your job."

Haywood's cheeks turned as red as the Task Force patch on his uniform. He spoke through gritted teeth. "Go on through, Sarge." He stepped away from the car and pulled the orange-and-white barricade to the side, allowing enough room for the Charger, then circled his hand in the air, signaling for Taylor to drive. The older soldier unslung his rifle and jogged toward the barricade, but Haywood shouted something and waved him away.

Taylor put the phone on his lap and drove through the barricade, offering Haywood a wave as he passed by. The soldier did not return the wave.

Gemma twisted in her seat and watched through the rear window until the soldiers and the barricade faded from view. Only then did she let out the breath she'd been holding.

They'd made it out. Thank God.

She twisted in her seat to face Taylor. "I can't believe that just happened. Who were you calling back there?"

His eyes darted between the road ahead and the rearview mirror. "My old cellphone. I'd programmed the number into my phone under General Jameson's name. In the event I ever got stopped during a supply run, this was my Hail Mary." Taylor handed his burner phone to Gemma and passed a hand through his damp hair. She hadn't noticed it before now, but he was sweating. "Give Letty a call. Tell her what's happening. Tell her to get out of town if she can but to avoid the highway. There must be other roads they haven't blocked yet."

Gemma nodded and dialed the number for Letty's phone.

The call went to voicemail, but Gemma didn't leave a message.

It was probably already too late.

They didn't speak during the drive back to the Sanctuary. Not even when a Task Force convoy appeared on the opposite side of the highway, an endless parade of camouflaged vehicles rolling toward Winter's Dam. Gemma counted six Humvees followed by four large trucks with canvas stretched over their cargo beds. Two flatbed trucks carried what appeared to be water tanks and port-o-johns, and the largest tow truck she'd ever seen brought up the rear of the convoy.

"That's the recovery vehicle," Taylor said, as if reading her mind. "It's always the last vehicle in a convoy in case another vehicle breaks down."

"What about all those enormous trucks?" Gemma asked. "The ones with the canvas?"

"Those were deuce-and-a-halves. They're military transport vehicles." He paused before adding, "They're usually filled with troops."

This isn't just a roadblock, Gemma realized. *They're setting up an encampment.*

CHAPTER FIVE

At a table inside the old Camp Mahantango trading post, Gemma sat with her hands clasped tightly in her lap to keep them from shaking. Using her tongue, she pushed a rubbery piece of cinnamon gum around in her mouth. The gum no longer possessed even the faintest hint of cinnamon, but she couldn't bring herself to spit it out.

That piece of gum was the only thing keeping her from screaming.

Set apart from the rest of the campground, the old trading post doubled as a makeshift base of operations and a security office for the Sanctuary. The security office was comprised of a small room with a metal desk and a single laptop. The laptop displayed live feeds from each of the twelve closed-circuit surveillance cameras that were posted around the perimeter of the camp. Guard volunteers, who pulled twelve-hour shifts, constantly monitored the surveillance cameras at the trading post.

They also played a lot of Solitaire.

Although there were cameras in other vulnerable sectors, their group's primary concern was the access road leading into the Sanctuary. Just south of the camp's entrance, the access road crossed over a creek, the bridge creating a natural barrier between the camp and the rest of the world. Very few vehicles traveled the country road that passed by the bridge. But to discourage any nosy passersby, Letty had installed a locked gate on the other side of the bridge. She'd also hung many strongly worded signs to discourage trespassing. One camera remained focused on the gate at all times.

Gemma never worked security at the trading post, so she had spent little time inside the building, but the interior looked just as she had imagined. No merchandise remained, leaving only raw wood floors and empty shelves. Several time-yellowed Jamboree flyers clung to the walls, as if unwilling to relinquish their claim to the camp. Inside the door, a long counter with a glass display case extended halfway across the room. Once, young scouts had probably paid for their merchandise at the counter, although the cash register was long gone.

There was also a flat-top display freezer, the kind with the sliding glass doors on the top. Those types of freezers always held novelty ice cream treats like ice cream sandwiches and Drumsticks and Good Humor bars. Despite her anxiety and frayed nerves, Gemma had checked the freezer immediately upon entering the trading post, hoping against hope for a freezer-burnt strawberry Good Humor bar, even though she knew the freezer hadn't been operational for years.

But it was still empty.

Gemma and Taylor had arrived back at camp just before six a.m. An hour later, eight people had gathered in the trading post. Five were members of the Sanctuary's leadership council: Abram Cleary, Susan Richardson, Marcus Derrick, Oliver Barnes, and Mia Weber. Gemma and Taylor were present to discuss what happened in Winter's Dam.

The eighth person in the room was Gavin.

Gemma didn't know why he was there, but her best guess was that Oliver had invited him. Oliver was always trying to pull Gavin back into the fold, trying to make a leader out of him when Gavin obviously didn't want to lead anyone or anything. He'd come to the meeting—likely more out of curiosity than any genuine desire to help—and promptly slumped low in his seat, his eyes on the floor. He looked as if he hadn't slept in a week, his caramel hair somehow looking both dry and greasy at the same time.

Taylor dialed Letty's number again, and Gemma held her breath until he frowned and ended the call.

Voicemail again.

"For now, let's agree to keep this between us." Abram Cleary leaned against the glass display case, standing while everyone else sat. In his old life, he was a police officer, and he still had an air of authority about him. "There's no reason to panic the entire camp before we know what's happening."

The others nodded their agreement.

Abram was a man of few words, and he preferred his own company to the company of others. He spent most of his time at the trading post, monitoring the cameras, even when it wasn't his shift. He always ate alone, usually standing near the exit of the dining hall. No one knew much about Abram, where he came from, or who he'd been before the Sanctuary, except that he used to be a cop. Even Mia, with all of her prying, hadn't been able to get any additional information out of him.

But when Abram spoke, people listened. He filled whatever room he was in—both literally and figuratively—towering over the rest of them at six-foot-six. With his penetrating blue eyes and thick mustache, he reminded Gemma of Wyatt Earp.

"The first thing we have to do is establish communication with Letty." Abram spoke around the toothpick jutting out from his lips. One other bit of information Mia had gleaned was that Abram was a lifelong smoker. He'd reluctantly given up cigarettes when he went into hiding, and he'd done so by gnawing on toothpicks.

His new addiction was toothpicks.

Mia shook her head. "How could this happen?"

Susan Richardson, one of the first occupants of the Sanctuary after Abram, sat with her thin arms crossed over her chest, her strawberry-blonde hair twisted into a French braid. A middle-aged, widowed mother, Susan had arrived at the Sanctuary penniless and struggling with depression, her three teenage girls in tow. "Maybe someone figured out the flyers," she offered. "Or else someone in Winter's Dam has been talking to the Task Force."

Marcus Derrick's dark fingers worked overtime as he straightened a paperclip with painstaking precision. "At least no one else knows about the Sanctuary," he said. "Letty's contacts in town know there's a Sanctuary, but they don't know that it's *here,* because she purchased the camp under the name of her father's corporation. No one knows but Letty, and she won't give us up. Doesn't matter what they do to her."

Oliver stroked his beard. "Let's pray it doesn't come to that."

Mia rested her chin in her palm. "So, the Task Force might interrogate some people, but if they don't get any information, they'll eventually have to leave town, right? I mean, you can't get blood from a stone."

Taylor tore his eyes away from his phone and glared at Mia. "Why don't you ask Max Yelchin about their interrogation techniques? They got quite a lot of blood out of him."

Gemma cringed at the memory of Max's emaciated form sprawled in the backseat of the Task Force SUV, his face and body sliced to pieces after a week in the hands of the two interrogators. Both Brie and Gavin had wanted to shoot them—and if she was being completely honest, so had Gemma—but Taylor wouldn't allow it. Instead, they'd left the men hog-tied inside the house and driven back to their camp at the Mount Pisgah Altar.

Oliver stood and began pacing the room. "This isn't the same situation. Those soldiers knew Max was a subversive. The people in Winter's Dam are just regular citizens. The Task Force doesn't go around torturing regular citizens."

Abram massaged his bald skull with the tips

of his fingers. "I wouldn't be so sure about that. Do we even know how many contacts Letty really has in town? Because it only takes one person to break. If someone squeals to the Task Force that Letty is the one behind everything, they're going to come after her with everything they've got."

"She won't give us up," Marcus insisted. "I'm telling you, she won't. No matter what."

The toothpick in Abram's mouth wagged from side to side as if displaying its disagreement. "Letty's a tough woman, but even she's not *that* tough. Interrogations aren't about whether a person breaks, but at what point they break."

Taylor dialed Letty's number again. Then he bolted upright in his chair and practically shouted into the phone, "Letty? Yes! Why didn't you— Yes, we made it out of town. What's going on there?"

"Put her on speaker," Susan whispered.

Taylor pressed a button, and Letty's voice filled the room.

"...setting up some kind of camp on the other side of town. They've got these powerful lights that stretch clear up into the sky. I can see them from my attic window. A few people tried to leave earlier, but the soldiers told them to go back to their houses and wait for more information. So, that's what we're doing."

Gemma fought the urge to grab the burner phone out of Taylor's hands. "Are you okay, Letty?"

"I'm okay so far, Stormy," Letty's voice cracked a little, and Gemma knew the old woman was struggling to maintain her composure. "But I don't got a good feeling about this."

"Have you talked to anyone else in town?" Taylor asked.

"I talked to Lizzie Fishman. She called here a few minutes ago. She said two soldiers came to the butcher shop and hauled Clyde away. Claimed they wanted to talk to him because he's the mayor. Now, most people in this town couldn't tell you who the mayor is, so how in the heck do these soldiers know?"

"Where is he now?" Abram interjected. "Do you know where they took him?"

"I...uh...I assume wherever they're setting up shop," Letty replied, sounding distracted. "Lizzie said...uh...something about a town meeting tomorrow around noon. I guess we're all supposed to sit tight until then."

"Letty, can you get into your cellar?" Taylor asked. "Maybe hide down there?"

"Oh, no. I'm not going down there, honey," she said. "I'll be fine. Listen, I can see a few people outside my window. They're gathering in the gas station parking lot. I better walk over and see what's going on. I'll call you later when I know more."

A feeling of dread gripped Gemma's heart, a terrible certainty that she might never hear Letty's voice again. This time, she didn't stop herself from grabbing the phone away from Taylor. "Letty, what can we do? Is there anything we can do?"

"Oh, Stormy. Just pray for us."

There was a soft click as Letty ended the call.

✝

Afterward, the small group bowed their heads as Oliver led them in prayer.

Only Taylor refused to pray. He *always* refused to pray.

When the prayer ended, Gemma raised her head and saw Taylor staring at the table, one hand absently spinning the burner phone like a dreidel. She opened her mouth to ask him what he was thinking, but Abram beat her to it.

"Something on your mind, Nolan?"

Abram could read Taylor so well. He'd spent a few years in the Army prior to becoming a police officer. Although it wasn't the Task Force, both men were soldiers at heart, cut from the same cloth. Abram always knew what Taylor was thinking—probably because he was thinking the same thing.

Taylor picked up the phone, folded it into his fist, and shook it at Abram. "I'm wondering what we're going to do about this. How much time are we going to waste sitting on our—" Gemma elbowed him in the side, cutting off the profanity before it left his lips. "On our...hands," he continued. "Look, it comes down to this: those people helped us, and now they're in trouble. So, what are we going to do about it?"

On the other side of the table, Oliver cocked his head. "What *can* we do? They've closed off the town. They're establishing a base of some sort. Do we really have any options?"

"There are always options."

Mia leaned forward, eyebrows raised. "Like what?"

Taylor gestured at the front window of the trading post. "Those soldiers don't know where the Sanctuary is. Neither does anyone else in the town, except for Letty. There are thirty miles between us and them, our security is awesome, and we've got enough nonperishable food in storage to last us for months. For the time being, we've got nothing to worry about. Our focus needs to be on the town."

"Meaning...?"

Taylor put the phone down and rubbed his

hands together. "I say we get a group together—just a few people—to leave the Sanctuary. I volunteer to lead the group. Since we can't risk being followed, we won't return until everything is over. We'll set up a base somewhere close to town so we can monitor what's happening. Hopefully, the Task Force doesn't get the information they're looking for and withdraws quickly. If that happens, our group comes straight home, and we all live happily ever after."

Mia tucked a strand of hair behind her ear. Even with all the comforts of the Sanctuary, she'd aged a lot in the last six months. Her short, choppy hair was gray with barely a hint of brown remaining. "But they won't leave quickly, right? You don't really believe they will."

Taylor shook his head. "They brought a lot of equipment with them. They are obviously preparing for an extended operation, which means they must have good intel to suggest that Winter's Dam is involved with something big. But if they knew Letty was behind it all, they would've already detained her. That's why we need to sneak into the town ASAP and extract Letty."

Gemma's eyes flicked to Oliver, wanting to see how their unofficial leader would react to Taylor's idea. But Oliver rarely reacted to anything without considering it for an obscene amount of time, and today was no exception. Oliver said nothing, only continued to caress his beard the way he always did when he was thinking. Finally, he said, "But won't that endanger the town? If we sneak Letty out, aren't we leaving the rest of them to bear the burden themselves?"

"That's just a chance we're going to have to take," Taylor said, his voice as hard as marble. He leaned back in his chair and crossed his arms. "For the safety of this camp, Letty is the only one who matters. I'm sorry if that's not what you want to hear, but it's the truth. We can't save everyone."

No one said anything. Gemma kept her eyes down and watched the seconds tick by on her watch. She knew this side of Taylor—the unemotional soldier side—existed, although he kept it hidden most of the time. But it was still hard to hear him sound so cold, so callous, about the people who'd risked their lives to keep the Sanctuary running.

Abram spat his toothpick into the garbage can and extracted another from his pill bottle. "Well? Anybody have any thoughts on Nolan's plan? Speak now or forever hold your peace."

At first, no one said anything. And then Gavin burst into laughter. Not the warm laughter that Gemma remembered from their time at the Station, but a bitter chuckle that made the tempera-ture in the room drop by ten degrees.

Taylor fixed his eyes on Gavin. "You got some-thing to contribute, Bonnar?" he demanded. "I mean, you've been so helpful until this point. Why stop now?"

Gemma put a hand on his arm. "Taylor."

"What? I'm just wondering what's so funny? Does he think it's funny that the Task Force might interrogate Clyde Fishman? Or does he think it's funny that Letty is in real danger right now?"

Gavin smirked at him. "I wasn't laughing at the situation. I was laughing at *you*, Nolan. Once a sol-dier, always a soldier, isn't that right? After all this time, you're still making those cold and calculated decisions about who gets to be free...and who doesn't. I can't say I'm surprised. You're the same guy who used to drag people out of their homes and throw them into detention centers."

Taylor shot out of his seat, the metal legs of his chair scraping against the floor and leaving a long scratch in the wood. He started around the table toward Gavin, but Gemma jumped up, put her hands on his back, and pushed him toward the doorway. *"Let's go."* The tone of her voice left no room for argument. *"Now."*

Thankfully, he didn't resist, and they exited the trading post together.

Abram followed on their heels. Once they were outside, he pulled the door shut behind them. Then, he spun around and frowned at Taylor. "Cool down, kid."

Taylor pointed at the closed door. "Did you hear what he said?"

"Yeah, I heard him baiting you. And you fell for it." Abram tapped Taylor on the chest with a thick index finger. "This plan of yours...it really sucks, man. And I wish you were wrong, but you aren't. I'll convince the others to go along with it. You just figure out who's going with you."

With that, he slipped back inside the building.

Underneath the trading post's covered awning, four picnic tables stood side by side, their surfaces marred with deep grooves and faded initials. When they'd first arrived at the Sanctuary, Taylor had added their initials to one table in a cheesy display of romanticism. Now, Gemma grabbed Taylor's arm and dragged him to their table. They sat across from each other, and she took his hands in hers. "I'm going with you."

"No, you're not."

Gemma brought his hand up and held it against her cheek. It felt like Taylor—strong and warm and a little rough. "Whether or not you like it, we're a team. We've always *been* a team. Now, you can waste time arguing with me about this, and you can get mad at me, but you won't change my mind."

They locked eyes across the table, and a variety of different emotions played across Taylor's face—anger, frustration, acceptance—each one vying for dominance. For a moment, it appeared anger was going to win out—as she'd expected it would. But then he surprised her by leaning across the table, cupping her cheek in his hand, and bringing his mouth to hers in a gentle kiss. It was cold outside, but his breath felt warm against her lips.

When they pulled apart, Gemma blinked at him in surprise, heat still flooding her cheeks. She could hardly think straight. Maybe that was part of his plan. "So...is that a yes?"

He lifted his shoulder in a half-shrug. "It's more of a, 'What choice do I have?' Or a, 'I'm too tired to argue with you.' Maybe even a little of a, 'We have no time, so let's just get going.'"

She gave him her brightest smile. "Now for the big question: Who's coming with us? It should only be people we know and trust. How about Abram?"

"No, Abram should stay here. If anything happens to us..." His voice trailed off. He didn't have to finish the sentence. "He should be here."

"Okay, what about Kyle? You trust him."

"Yeah, but I hate for him to leave Addie while Weston is sick."

That was true. Addie certainly had enough on her plate without having to worry about Kyle going off on some sabotage mission. So, she said the next name that came to mind. "Max Yelchin would be good. He's tough. Look at what he survived at the hands of Carver's goons."

Taylor's eyebrows scrunched together in concern. "You think he can handle it?"

Things had been rough at first after they'd rescued Max from Carver's interrogators. For almost a month after his rescue, he'd suffered from nightmares every night where he woke up in a cold sweat, thrashing against his sheets and fighting invisible assailants. "Brie says he's not having the nightmares very often anymore," Gemma said. "Plus, if you get Max, you get Brie as a bonus. They're a package deal."

"You mean the crazy punk-rock girl who shot me in the leg?" Taylor raised his eyebrows. "Why would we want her?"

"We want her *because* she's crazy, and she's not scared of the Task Force. Do we need anyone else?"

A strange look appeared on Taylor's face. She'd never seen this look before and couldn't quite decipher it. "Yeah, I have someone in mind. I'll try to get in touch with him."

Get in touch with him?

She was about to ask Taylor what he meant by

that when the door to the trading post swung open and Gavin walked out. He paused on the front stoop long enough to suck in a mouthful of mountain air. Then, he turned toward the picnic tables, and his eyes landed on Taylor.

"I'm going with you," he said. "The others already agreed to it."

Before Taylor or Gemma could protest, he walked away.

CHAPTER SIX

Seated on the dropped tailgate of his pickup truck, Corporal Mullen popped a handful of sunflower seeds into his mouth and crunched them between his teeth. *Mmm.* Jalapeño Hot Salsa. His favorite flavor. Hot enough to burn his tongue. Mullen worked them around in his mouth, using his tongue to separate the seeds from their shells. Then, he spat the husks into the gravel beneath his dangling feet.

"You failed your mission, son."

Mullen raised his head but did not turn around. The voice had come from behind him. It *always* came from behind him.

"It's not over yet, sir," he replied, licking jalapeño dust from his fingers.

"Yeah. You keep saying that."

Mullen smiled. Colonel Carver was back.

If he *had* to be criticized by a dead man, he was just glad it wasn't his father.

Douglas Mullen Sr. had succumbed to liver disease when Mullen was sixteen, and Mullen hadn't shed a single tear at his father's funeral. But even death hadn't stopped the old man from berating him regularly. For a few years after his death, his father had frequently made his thoughts about his only son known, never failing to remind him he would never amount to anything. Douglas Mullen's whiskey-coated prognostications used to bounce around Mullen's brain like a pinball in a machine until Mullen was ready to jam needles into his ears to make it stop.

After he joined the Task Force, the old man didn't talk as much, although he still popped up from time to time. Recently, however, a different corpse had taken up residence inside Mullen's skull, easily drowning the old man out.

"That's why I come back to this place often, Colonel," Mullen said. He could sense that Carver was still listening, even though the colonel wasn't speaking. "To remind myself that my mission isn't complete yet."

Mullen lowered his gaze from the bulldozed

plot of land in front of him to the corporal rank sewn onto the sleeves of his uniform. Initially, the promotion had taken the sting out of the dumpster fire that was Ash Grove. For those first few months, all it had taken to make him feel better was to look down and see those two black chevrons pointing up at him as if to say, *You earned this. While others failed and defected, you served your country well.* Now, those same chevrons seemed to point at him judgmentally, as if he were the one at fault for everything that had gone wrong, and Mullen felt nothing but shame at the sight of them.

A bottle of Mountain Dew sat next to him on the tailgate, and he picked it up and took a swig. The rush of sugar lifted his spirits a little, and he smiled as he remembered the black duffel bag in the backseat of his truck.

Some secrets he kept, even from Carver.

To his right, the decaying farmhouse loomed over him, looking far worse than it had six months ago. The good men and women of Ash Grove had taken their frustrations out on Papa Roach's humble abode. They smashed every window and spray-painted curse words and X-rated images all over most of the first-floor siding. Someone had even sprayed a giant pentagram between the two windows on the second floor. Probably some drunk teenager with a ladder in the bed of his truck.

Mullen hawked a mouthful of shells into the dirt, and they landed in such a way that they resembled tiny black gravestones jutting out of the ground. The last funeral he'd been to was Colonel Carver's. There hadn't been many civilians present, only Task Force. No surprise there. Carver bled olive-green. Mullen had shared a few beers afterwards with Private Nowak, who had served under Carver in Ash Grove.

The primary topic of conversation had been Sergeant Nolan.

According to Nowak, Sergeant Nolan and the female roach were *together*—whatever that meant. Apparently, Nolan had tried to break the girl out of the church and had gotten himself captured. Then, in an insane twist that Mullen still couldn't wrap his brain around, two *other* subversives had broken into the church, overpowered Nowak and another guard, murdered Carver, and escaped with the roaches.

When Mullen had asked the obvious question, which was how a couple of untrained subversives had overpowered him, Nowak had heaped all the blame on his chain-smoking compatriot, Brady, who'd received a dishonorable discharge from the Task Force because of the Ash Grove incident.

Mullen's upper lip twitched at the thought of Brady. His lip had been twitching lately whenever he got good and angry. He took out his aggression on a difficult seed, crunching down so hard that he ended up biting his lower lip. He swore loudly, the sound echoing through the trees, and then he dug the shell out of his mouth with a dirty finger and flicked it to the ground. When he swallowed the seed, the taste of blood lingered on his tongue.

It was the female soldier, Private Dietrich, who'd discovered Carver's body in the basement, a hunting knife plunged into his guts. Her official statement was that she'd reported for duty as usual that morning and hadn't seen a thing. By the time she got there, everything was already over. When Dietrich located Nowak and Brady, she'd freed them and called the higher-ups at their base, the Gap. They had immediately sent a squad of soldiers into the town to mop up the mess.

To Mullen, that all sounded awfully convenient.

Mullen hopped off the back of his truck and strolled forward, carrying the bottle of Mountain Dew with him. He continued to chew and spit as he walked, leaving a trail of shells behind him like Hansel's breadcrumbs.

He stopped just short of the spot where the old barn had once stood.

There was nothing to see anymore. The barn

was gone, bulldozed to the ground, the charred wreckage hauled away. But when Mullen closed his eyes, he could see it clearly in his mind. He could hear the screams and the coughing. He could smell the smoke. It was all still there, just in a different dimension that only he could access.

The higher-ups had never connected Mullen to the barn fire. All they'd found was a destroyed barn, its metal doors still chained shut, and the charred cadaver of the fat slob, Carl Lovell, lying a few feet away. The chains and the dead body hadn't told the total story, but it hadn't taken the authorities long to piece it all together. Everyone in Ash Grove knew how much Carl Lovell hated subversives, so it surprised no one when he'd tried to torch a barn full of them. The *real* surprise was Carl offing himself at the scene, presumably out of guilt. Carl Lovell wasn't a guy who felt guilty about anything.

But no one cared enough to investigate it further.

It was only Carl Lovell, after all.

The barn was gone, but the trapdoor to the root cellar remained, half-buried under a thin layer of dirt. He took another step forward and stopped in the exact spot where Lovell's body had tumbled after Mullen had blown out his brains.

Mullen poured a little Mountain Dew onto the

ground, and it carved yellow trails through the dirt that reminded him of urine. He always paid a brief homage to the fat slob when he visited the farmhouse. Lovell was a far cry from a soldier, but he'd given his life for the cause, and Mullen would always be grateful for his sacrifice.

Mullen stared at the trapdoor, the taste of jalapeños and blood intermingling in his mouth. The black hole inside of him was expanding again. He could feel it, pulling and stretching at his skin, expanding a bit each day, like an embryo of hate growing in his belly. That was why he came back to this spot, over and over. To keep his hate-fire burning.

The subversives had survived.

Not just a few of them.

All of them.

A fat raindrop splatted on Mullen's cheek, and he wiped it away, his eyes rising from the trapdoor to the sky. Thunder rumbled in the distance. The gunmetal sky appeared ready to open up and—to use an expression he'd learned from the roaches—*wash away the sins of the world.*

It would take one heck of a storm to wash away Mullen's sins.

He walked back to his truck, kicking rocks into the ankle-high grass as he went, and slammed the tailgate.

It wasn't Carver's death that was eating away at him, nor was it Sergeant Nolan's defection or Mullen's own failed attempt at exterminating the roaches in the barn. Those things bothered him, of course. Especially the barn. But he'd found plenty of other roaches in the months since April.

He'd more than made up for it.

No, what upset him most was the girl. The one he'd caught in the woods. The one who'd disrespected him. Kicked him in the junk. Ran away from him. She'd been Mullen's catch, and those incompetent idiots in Ash Grove had let her get away.

No, Mullen's mission wasn't over. It wouldn't be over until he found the girl and finished what he'd started on Dragon's Back Mountain, all those months ago.

He was ready. Now, all he had to do was wait for fate to bring her back to him.

"She's still out there, you know," Colonel Carver spoke up again from just over Mullen's left shoulder. "She's probably laughing about you right now, cuddled up in the arms of her traitor boyfriend."

"Yes, sir." Cold raindrops pelted Mullen's head as he jerked open the door to his truck. The old hinges squealed in protest, and he made a mental note to squirt some WD-40 on them when he got home. "But she won't be laughing for long, will she, sir?"

He took the colonel's silence as agreement.

Before Mullen stepped inside the vehicle, he tilted his head back and sniffed the air, inhaling the earthy scent of the coming rain.

There was a storm coming.

He wondered if the girl could smell it, too.

CHAPTER SEVEN

They left at dusk, just before the sky opened up.

Gemma rode next to Taylor in the passenger seat while Max, Brie, and Gavin crammed into the back seat of the Charger. At Taylor's request, they'd each packed an extra set of clothing and a few toiletries, and they carried everything in the backpacks on their laps. Taylor's backpack was on the floor between Gemma's boots. They filled the trunk with a few blankets, flashlights, and enough food and bottled water to last them a week.

Despite Taylor's last-minute objections, each of them carried a gun.

Gemma didn't know where they were going. She assumed Taylor had contacted Letty and arranged for some kind of shelter since they had brought no sleeping bags or tents with them. He'd gone missing for most of the afternoon, during which Gemma had packed and said her goodbyes to Addie, Kyle, and Sophia. She'd tried not to worry, but her mind always went there. What if she got detained? What if this was the last time she ever saw her friends? Or what if something terrible happened at the Sanctuary while she was gone? Weston had medicine now, thanks to Letty, but Gemma hated leaving while he was still sick.

Taylor stopped the car when they reached the bridge, and Gemma pulled the hood of her jacket over her head and jumped out. Icy raindrops pelted her bare hands as she unlocked the metal gate and walked it open. She kept her eyes on the lonely dirt road that passed by the bridge, watching for any headlights cutting through the rain, but there were none. She held the gate open while Taylor drove through and then pushed it shut and locked it behind them. Casting one last glance at the narrow lane that led back to the Sanctuary, she hurried back to the car and hopped inside, warming her chilly hands in front of the heating vents.

Rain hammered the windshield as Taylor followed his normal route to Winter's Dam—a roundabout course that added fifteen minutes to their travel time but avoided any major towns. He gripped the wheel with both hands and turned the wipers up as high as they would go, but it was still difficult to see anything. Even if they had wanted to talk—which none of them did—the deafening sound of the rain would've made it nearly impossible to hear one another.

So, they rode in silence.

By the time they turned east on Highway 192, the rain had passed, and the downpour had left behind scattered dark patches of standing water on the roadway that Taylor swerved to avoid. He drove neither too fast, nor too slow, but at a pace unlikely to draw the attention of any bored state troopers who might lurk in the overgrown driveways of the deserted hunting cabins that punctuated the highway. On either side of the vehicle, ancient pine trees stood guard over the road like battle-worn soldiers, their limbs sagging under the additional weight of the rain from the storm. They boxed the car in, giving the illusion of safety.

But Gemma knew it was only an illusion.

She stared out her window as a hunting cabin appeared as a flash of white through a gap in the trees, its driveway overgrown with waist-high weeds. Most of the cabins were empty now, but when hunting season kicked off in a few weeks, they would come to life again, their driveways weed-wacked into submission, their chimneys belching smoke into the sky.

Gemma reached for the dashboard and turned up the air, adjusting the defroster so the windshield wouldn't fog up. It was really stuffy inside the car, especially with the irritation wafting off Taylor like a cheap cologne. He couldn't stand being around Gavin, which was probably exactly the reason Gavin had volunteered for this mission.

He'd wanted to upset Taylor, and it was working.

Gemma slid her hand across the center console and wrapped her fingers around Taylor's. He met her eyes, and something passed between them—an understanding of sorts—and he offered her that adorable half-smile of his, the one that always made her heart do somersaults. He raised her hand to his lips and kissed her knuckles.

"That's it," he said, nodding at the driver's window. "That's Halfway Lake."

Halfway Lake. The place Taylor had wanted to take her this morning, before they had encountered the roadblock in Winter's Dam. They must have passed it on their way back to the Sanctuary, but Gemma had probably been so distracted by the Task Force convoy that she'd completely missed it. Now, she leaned forward in her seat to get a better look.

The glassy lake and accompanying quarter mile of sand was like a secret treasure hidden amongst a forest of towering pines. On this dismal October evening, the lake shimmered like polished onyx, and the barren strand of beach resembled the coast of an abandoned island, entirely devoid of life and ripe for exploration. As they drove by, the rain started up again, pelting the dark surface of the water so that the lake appeared to shudder at their passing.

"Wow," Gemma whispered. "I wish we could've gone there together." She wanted to know how it felt to walk, hand in hand, across the beach with Taylor, her bare feet sinking into the hot sand. Or to dive beneath the surface of the lake, the water so cold it made her teeth chatter.

Taylor gave her hand a light squeeze. "We will."

A few minutes later, he eased his foot off the accelerator. The Charger slowed almost to a complete stop before Taylor suddenly made a left-hand turn directly into a cluster of trees.

"What are you—?" Gemma grabbed the door handle and braced herself for a crash as Taylor drove straight into the forest. But the impact never came. Instead, the Charger slipped through a narrow gap between the trees and plunged down the steep slope of a hidden driveway.

Thick brush and branches scraped at the sides of the car, as if trying to catch the trespassers and fling them back onto the highway. Gemma stole a glance at Taylor and saw his jaw tighten at the awful scraping noise.

He loved his car.

Up ahead, a green metal arm jutted out from the trees, stretching the width of the driveway. Taylor slammed on the brakes, and the Charger came to a halt inches from the barrier gate. The sudden stop, coupled with the steep angle of the driveway, threw the three backseat passengers forward against the front seats.

"Learn how to drive," Brie muttered, rubbing the sleep from her eyes. Blinking, she peered through the windshield. "Okay…where *are* we?"

Ignoring her, Taylor reached underneath his seat and pulled out a bolt cutter. Then he got out of the car and slammed the door behind him. Gemma watched him through the windshield as he cut through a padlock and unchained the gate. He pushed the metal arm open and hopped back inside the car.

With nothing blocking their path, they continued down the driveway into a small clearing. A ramshackle hunting cabin stood to the right of the driveway, completely hidden from the highway by a thick cluster of trees. Green algae crawled up the faded yellow siding, and a concrete chimney jutted out from a slanted roof. The rain had slowed a little since Halfway Lake, and water spilled from the roof, creating a lovely waterfall effect over the front door. Given the neglected condition of the cabin, Gemma assumed at least ten years' worth of dead leaves clogged the gutters. A disconnected propane tank sat to the right of the screen door, the once-white tank so overrun with algae and mold that it was practically black.

"Taylor?" she whispered. "Where the heck are we?"

"We're home."

A covered carport extended out from the left side of the cabin, but Taylor didn't park beneath its roof. Instead, he drove through the carport and pulled around the back of the cabin. The roof extended over a wooden porch supported by four concrete pillars. There was another door on this side of the cabin, along with two boarded-up windows on the first floor and a dormer window on the second floor. A rickety-looking green park bench sat to the left of the door next to a pile of firewood that appeared as if it had been cut and stacked when Kennedy was in the White House.

Taylor parked next to a pine tree and threw open his car door. "Unload our stuff from the trunk." He leaned over to grab his backpack from between Gemma's feet. "I'll work on the door."

Slinging her backpack over her shoulder, Gemma followed the others to the trunk. The canopy of branches overhead did little to slow the deluge, and rain quickly found its way down the back of Gemma's neck. Max shoved a cardboard box filled with canned beans and soups into her hands, and she hurried up the steps and crowded onto the porch with the others. They huddled in a group near the door and waited as Taylor examined the lock. Another padlock. He left the porch and jogged back to the car.

Droplets of rain beaded on Max's leather jacket. He brushed his damp curls away from his eyes as Taylor returned with the bolt cutter. "Wait…it's locked?"

"Why wouldn't it be?" Taylor replied, cutting through the second padlock as easily as the first one. He tossed the broken lock behind the woodpile and pushed the door open.

Gavin stepped forward so his body was blocking the doorway. "Whose cabin is this?"

Taylor glared at him, the bolt cutter still clutched in one hand. "It's my Uncle Dave's cabin," he said, his voice dripping sarcasm. "He said we can use it; we just have to tidy up before we leave."

Gavin's hands clenched into fists at his sides, his eyes blazing embers of fire. He turned to Max and Brie, completely ignoring Gemma. "Nolan just broke into someone's cabin. We can't stay here. What if the owner stops by to check on his place?"

"Did you see the rust on that padlock?" Taylor gestured toward the gate. "No one's been here in years. Not for months. *Maybe years.* I scouted out a few of these cabins back in the summer, just in case we needed to leave the Sanctuary in a hurry. No one's opened the padlock on that gate since I first discovered this place."

"What about hunting?" Max's eyes darted back and forth between Taylor and Gavin. "What if the owner only comes here once a year to hunt? It's the fall, you know."

"They didn't use this cabin last year, either."

Gavin held his arms out to his sides. "How could you possibly *know* that?" he demanded. "The answer is…you can't. You don't know when the owner was last here. The guy could've parked somewhere else and hiked in. You act like you're in charge of this operation, but you're no leader, Nolan. I wouldn't stand behind you if we were in line at Hershey Park."

A laugh burst through Brie's lips, and Max elbowed her lightly in the side.

"Whatever, man." Pulling a flashlight from his jacket pocket, Taylor strong-armed his way into the cabin, his left shoulder slamming into Gavin's before he disappeared into the darkness.

Gavin's nostrils flared at this most recent offense, but he didn't go after Taylor. He remained in the doorway, blocking the others from entering.

Gemma shifted the box in her hands. It was getting heavy, and the wet cardboard was disintegrating beneath her fingertips. "Look, can we please just go inside? Something tells me if I stand here much longer, I'm going to crash right through this porch."

Gavin gaped at her. "It really doesn't bother you that we're breaking into someone's cabin?"

It was the most he'd said to her in months, which should've felt like some kind of victory, but it didn't, not when he continued to stare at her as if he didn't know who she was anymore. His expression broke her heart because she still loved him and wanted him in her life. But not in the way he wanted. Friendship with him wasn't a possibility.

Hurt coursed through Gavin's veins, and his veins ran deep.

She wouldn't continue to wait for a forgiveness that would never come.

"No," she replied. "It really doesn't bother me at all."

Pushing past him, Gemma stepped into the cabin and placed her crumbling cardboard box on the floor. "Taylor?"

"Try the light switch!" he called out from somewhere across the room.

Gemma's fingers trailed along the rough wood paneling to the left of the door, quickly finding the light switch.

Please, she silently prayed. *Please have electricity.*

She flicked the switch up.

Yellow light filled the room. Two pendant light fixtures dangled from the ceiling at opposite ends of the living room. A dining table occupied the right side of the room just in front of a staircase that led to the cabin's second level. The left side of the living room featured a massive stone fireplace, and some festive hunter had strung Christmas lights along the mantel.

But instead of normal Christmas lights, these lights were red and green shotgun shells.

Taylor appeared on the other side of the room, standing in the doorway to what looked to be the kitchen. He wore a triumphant smile on his face. "Found the breaker box. I'll be honest, I wasn't sure this place was going to have any power. That's why I brought so many flashlights."

Gemma couldn't imagine having to stumble around this cabin in the dark. The area in front of the fireplace was like an outdated furniture showroom with very little walking space between each piece of furniture. There was an old, gray couch and a tan recliner—both of which looked like they were home to a variety of creatures Gemma didn't care to meet. There was also a coffee table, two end tables, an upholstered rocking chair, and a huge box television. Gemma had never even *seen* a box television set before—at least not outside of the movies she used to watch with her parents.

Stumbling in beside Gemma, Brie gave a loud whistle. The yellow light made her look as if she were suffering from jaundice. She dropped her cardboard box, and a bunch of the cans tumbled out and rolled across the floor. "This place has a real murder-cabin vibe, doesn't it? Makes the basement of the Station look like Caesar's Palace."

"At least we have power."

"Great," Brie muttered. "But I think I would've preferred not being able to see."

For once, Brie wasn't exaggerating. The cabin was awful. There was no other way to describe it. Red carpeting covered the floor, unraveled and bunched up around the edges as if someone had tried to vacuum and accidentally sucked up a good portion of the carpet. A pale substance—likely mold, given the splotchy pattern—clung to the wood paneling and the exposed wood of the furniture. Aside from the mold, there wasn't much else on the walls, save for a poster featuring the many varieties of fish in Pennsylvania, the mounted head and antlers of an eight-point buck, and—inexplicably—a framed 5x7 photograph of a doe.

"What kind of person frames a picture of a deer?" Gemma asked. "It's a close-up, too. It almost looks like a family photo."

Brie wrapped her arms around herself and shivered. "If we find an old book hidden underneath the floorboards, we're not reading from it. I don't care how bored we are. We have enough problems. We don't need to be unleashing any ancient curses."

"I don't know about you," Gemma said, "but I don't plan on looking underneath any floorboards."

The others entered the cabin and placed their soggy boxes on the dining table. Gavin came in last and slumped onto the couch, sending a plume of dust soaring into the air. On the other side of the room, Max peeked inside the kitchen, his eyes widening as he surveyed whatever fresh horrors lurked in there. "I think you're right, Taylor. No one's been here for a long time. There's something on the kitchen floor. I think it might've been a rat...once."

"A rat?" Brie squealed, leaping onto one of the dining room chairs. "Are you serious?"

Brie wasn't afraid of much, but she *hated* rodents.

Max opened a storage cabinet just inside the doorway of the kitchen and peered inside. After a little searching, he pulled out a garbage bag. "This one won't hurt you, honey."

"What about his friends?"

"I think his friends ate him."

Gemma headed for the kitchen, intending to help Max, but as she approached the dining table, a section of floor sank beneath her weight. She hopped off the spot and made a mental note to never step there again. "Um…the floor over here feels a little…rotten."

Taylor bounced lightly on a section of floor beside the stairway, his boots sinking an inch into the floor with each bounce. "Same over here."

"This entire *cabin* is rotten," Gavin muttered. He still hadn't moved from the couch.

Gemma ignored him and walked into the kitchen where Max was finishing bagging up the rat. The kitchen appeared to be a late addition to the cabin, but it wasn't much better than the rest of the place. The cramped room more closely resembled a hallway than a kitchen. Jagged rows of exposed stone comprised the wall that adjoined the living room, jutting far enough into the limited space that, if someone wasn't careful, they could easily scrape the skin off their elbows. Clearly, that wall had once been the front of the cabin, and whoever did the kitchen addition had probably left the stone wall for aesthetic appeal. A square-shaped hole cut into the wall—once an exterior window—linked the living room and the kitchen together.

On the opposite side of the kitchen, four white cupboards hung above a white countertop. Two of the cupboard doors hung open, showcasing the unlimited number of mouse droppings inside.

Gemma had no desire to open the drawers to see what might lurk within them.

It wasn't all bad, though. There was a newer-looking microwave, as well as an electric oven and range. The refrigerator was empty but clean. Taylor crouched on the floor to plug it in, and its motor whirred to life.

Gemma almost cried when she found the tiny bathroom with a stand-up shower just off the kitchen. But her joy was short-lived. All the water had evaporated from the toilet, and when she turned on the faucet, nothing happened.

"Please tell me we don't have to use an outhouse," she said when Taylor walked up behind her. "If the cabin is this bad, what's the outhouse going to be like?"

"Do you really think I'd make you use an outhouse?" Taylor fiddled with the handle in the shower, but no water came out. "Don't worry. These cabins all have wells. We've already got electricity, and with any luck, we'll soon have heat.

Once I get the water turned on, you'll be in heaven."

She wrinkled her nose at the yellow stains around the base of the toilet. "Heaven's a bit of a stretch."

Taylor stepped out of the shower. But instead of leaving the bathroom, he closed the door, shutting them inside a room no bigger than Gemma's old bedroom closet. Then, he moved closer, backing her up against the empty wall between the sink and the toilet. He cupped her face in his hands and leaned down to kiss her. His lips lightly brushed against hers, but he did not kiss her, and her skin broke out in goosebumps in that way it always did whenever Taylor touched her. "You shouldn't have come along, Gemma."

"I know," she whispered against his lips. "But I bet you're secretly glad I'm here."

He wouldn't admit it, of course. Not with his words.

But his lips told her otherwise.

When they returned to the living room, Gemma's cheeks were still hot. If she'd had any water, she would've splashed it on them. Taylor pulled out a chair for her at the dining table, and she sat. Sitting was probably a good idea. Her legs felt a little weak.

The wooden stairs creaked as Brie and Max

came down from the second level. When they reached the bottom of the staircase, they both leaped over the soft spot in the floor. They joined Gemma and Taylor at the table.

Gemma clasped her hands together on the table. "Well, the kitchen isn't terrible, and the bathroom is nice." She glanced at Taylor and pinched her lips together to keep from smiling. "How's the upstairs? Are there beds, or are we going to be sleeping on the floor?"

Brie smirked. "Oh, there are beds, alright."

"Six beds, all with pillows and mattresses," Max explained, tugging off his leather jacket. "There's a dresser, a few bedside tables, and some lamps. There aren't any mints on the pillows, but it'll do for a few nights."

"So, what's the problem?" Taylor asked.

"Well..." Max's cheeks turned crimson, highlighting the pale scar running down the left side of his face. "It's not really set up for—"

"All the beds are in one room," Brie cut him off. She seemed pleased with herself, as if she'd been patiently waiting for the opportunity to drop this bomb. "But we're all friends here. It'll be just like summer camp. We can tell ghost stories after lights out."

"Wait..." Gavin turned around to face Brie. "There's only one bedroom?"

"Yeah, but it's huge!"

He gave a humorless laugh. "Yeah, not happening. I'd rather sleep down here with the rats."

Gemma couldn't take it anymore. "You're not sleeping down here, Gavin. Not when there's a perfectly good bed for you upstairs. Besides, do you have any idea what might live in that couch?"

"What do you care?" he snapped. "You haven't spoken to me in six months, Gemma. Don't pretend to care about me now."

"It's not my fault we don't talk." Even as the words left her lips, she knew they weren't entirely true. She avoided Gavin as much as he avoided her. "You cut me—and pretty much everyone else—out of your life when we got to the Sanctuary. It was your choice to do that, not mine."

His eyes burned into her. "None of this was my *choice*."

Gemma opened her mouth to respond, but then she heard something coming from outside—the unmistakable sound of a car engine. Not passing by on the highway. This was too loud. Too close.

Someone was pulling into the driveway.

Max and Brie ran for the windows, which they'd obviously forgotten were boarded up. Gemma made it to the rear door of the cabin a split second before Gavin. He stretched his arm across her back and snapped the interior lights off just as headlights splashed across the trees.

A dark SUV appeared in the clearing and pulled to a stop next to the Charger.

Gemma dropped her hand to the pistol on her belt and held her breath, waiting for whatever came next.

A man stepped out of the SUV. It was growing dark outside, but it wasn't raining hard anymore, and Gemma could easily see the details of his uniform...

And the blood-red patch on his left shoulder.

CHAPTER EIGHT

"It's a soldier," Gemma whispered to the others. "I think he's alone."

He didn't appear to have a care in the world as he jammed his hands into his pockets and practically skipped toward the back porch. He was whistling a song—Gemma was almost certain it was "He's Got the Whole World in His Hands."

That seemed an odd choice for a Task Force soldier.

Max grabbed Brie's hand and pulled her toward the kitchen, and Gemma knew what he was thinking. There was another door back there. The door that faced the highway. They might slip out the back and hide in the woods until the soldier left.

As the soldier climbed the steps to the porch, still whistling, Gemma and Gavin inched away from the door in perfect unison—partners in the slowest three-legged race in history. But Gemma's right boot caught on a patch of unraveled carpet, and she fell backward.

Taylor grabbed her from behind to steady her. "It's alright. Don't worry."

Then, he squeezed her shoulders, stepped around her, and opened the door.

For one crazy moment, Gemma wondered if Taylor had betrayed them. Was it possible that bringing them out to this isolated cabin was an elaborate ruse to deliver them into the hands of the Task Force? Certainly not her, but maybe the others. Gavin in particular. But that made little sense. This was Taylor—*her* Taylor. He didn't like Gavin very much, but he would never do something like that.

"Yost. It's been a long time, man."

"Too long, brother." The soldier pulled Taylor into a bear hug and thumped him on the back. "I almost didn't recognize you."

Yost? Gemma peered around Taylor's body. Who in the world was Yost? She couldn't see him very well, but he sounded friendly enough. Lighthearted. Far from dangerous.

"What's with the hair, Nolan? Isn't that mop top of yours a little out of regs?"

"Yeah, well, *I'm* a little out of regs." Taylor

stepped back and motioned for the soldier to come into the cabin. "Come in, man. I guess it's time you meet everyone."

Gemma backed away from the door until her legs hit the couch. Three minutes earlier, everything had been normal. Well, not normal, exactly, but as normal as things could be when Taylor and Gavin were in the same room, sharing the same oxygen.

Now, a uniformed Task Force soldier was standing inside the cabin.

Even after Taylor closed the door and flipped the overhead lights back on, no one spoke. Brie and Max stared at the soldier from the doorway of the kitchen, their faces identical masks of confusion. Gavin had retreated to the stairway. With one hand hovering over the hunting knife on his belt, he looked hungry for a fight.

With the lights on, Yost wasn't very intimidating. He was a few inches shorter than Taylor, a little stockier, and although his eyes were friendly, they weren't nearly as intelligent as Taylor's. There was a Band-Aid stuck to the bottom of his chin where he'd probably cut himself shaving. When Gemma realized the Band-Aid had tiny G.I. Joes on it, she nearly laughed out loud. With chocolate hair, squinty eyes, and full lips, Yost was handsome in a goofy way. There was something childish and sincere about him. He reminded Gemma of a young Tom Hardy.

He even had a small gap between his front teeth.

Yost glanced around the living room, eyebrows raised. "Nice pile of sticks you got here, man. How many people have died on that couch?" He winked at Gemma and gave her a gap-toothed smile that—despite herself—she found quite charming.

"None," Taylor said. "Yet."

Brie moved into the living room, head tilted to one side, and studied Yost with a quiet intensity that only she could pull off. "We didn't know that Nolan had any friends." She extended her hand to Yost. "And who might you be?"

He took her hand, kissed it, and gave her a little bow. "I'm the man of your dreams."

This time, Gemma *did* laugh out loud. She couldn't help it.

"Who *is* this dude?" Max demanded, his voice equal parts annoyed and amused. "And why is he kissing my girlfriend's hand?"

Yost dropped Brie's hand like it was on fire. "Whoa. Sorry, dude. My bad."

Taylor put a hand on the soldier's back. "Every-one, this is Mike Yost. Former Task Force scout and current full-time lothario. We met at Basic Training, and then we served in the same unit for a few years. He's the only person I kept in touch with after I went AWOL."

Gemma blinked at Taylor. "I didn't know you kept in touch with *anyone*."

"Sometimes I use the burner phone, but never at the Sanctuary," Taylor explained. "I needed to know if the Task Force was looking for me. Yost kept me informed and never once tried to get information out of me. Plus, he's not Task Force anymore. He had the chance to re-up last summer, but he didn't take it."

Max appeared to relax a little. "So, if you're not Task Force anymore, what's with the uniform?"

"Nolan told me to wear it. Said it might come in handy."

"I said to *bring* it," Taylor threw in. "Not wear it."

Yost shrugged. "Half of one, six dozen of the other."

Gemma laughed again, and Yost raised an eyebrow at her. He didn't even seem to realize he'd misspoken. "So, why did you get out of the Task Force?"

He flashed her another flirtatious smile. "I didn't like detaining gorgeous women."

Taylor rolled his eyes. "Bro, seriously?"

"Sorry, sorry." Yost raised his hands in surrender. "I take it you're Gemma." He shook Gemma's hand, but—thankfully—did not kiss it. "I wasn't sure which one of you was Nolan's girlfriend, but I thought flirting would be a fun way to figure it out. I didn't think it would be the scary one."

He tilted his head in Brie's direction.

Brie feigned offense. "Gee. Thanks a lot." But she had a smile on her face.

Gemma couldn't believe it. Even *Brie* liked Yost.

Yost's expression turned serious, a look that seemed wholly unnatural on his face. "All kidding aside, I got out of the Task Force because I couldn't deal with it anymore. What we were doing…it had been eating at me for a while. And then everything changed after Nolan went AWOL." He spoke without looking at them, toeing at a loose pile of carpet with his boot. "I started breaking the rules. Whenever I found little groups of subversives hiding somewhere, I'd let them go and wouldn't report them. I could've gotten court-martialed for that alone, but I didn't care. When the time came for me to decide whether to stay in the Task Force, there was no question. I had to get out."

A heavy, uncomfortable silence followed his confession, the quiet broken only by the songs of the crickets and the rushing water of the swollen creek.

Gavin finally broke the silence. "So, that's it? You expect us to believe that you had some Paul-on-the-road-to-Damascus moment, and we're all just supposed to trust you?"

Yost's forehead wrinkled in confusion. "Paul on the road to where?"

Gavin looked at Gemma as if to plead his case to her. "I don't buy this guy."

"Dude, you don't buy me?" Yost looked genuinely offended, and he pointed a finger at Taylor. "Why do you trust him and not me?"

"That's where you're wrong. I don't trust him *at all*," Gavin retorted. "In fact, I trust you more than I trust him."

Yost's face brightened a little, and he gave Gavin a thumbs up. "Hey! It's a start, brother." He tilted his head to the side and cracked his neck. "Listen, I don't blame you guys for being suspicious. I doubt you've met many good Task Force soldiers." He smirked at Taylor. "So, I brought a peace offering to help ease tensions. Hold on a sec."

He exited the cabin and jogged back to his SUV, which Gemma now realized wasn't a Task Force vehicle but an aging Chevy Tahoe. He came back a minute later with two white boxes cradled in his arms.

Gemma stared at the bright orange-and-pink logo on the top of the boxes. Her eyes seemed to have trouble processing what she was seeing and sending those signals to her brain.

Standing in the doorway, Yost offered them all his gap-toothed grin, and then he held up the boxes like Rafiki presenting Simba at the beginning of *The Lion King.*

"I brought donuts."

✝

After Taylor and Yost got the cabin's water pump working, the group quickly washed up and then gathered around the table to devour both boxes of donuts. They didn't bother with plates or napkins, and the wooden surface of the table was soon coated with donut crumbs and white powder. Everyone consumed at least three donuts. Everyone except for Yost, who'd reluctantly taken a donut only after Gemma had insisted he eat one. And it was the only one left.

The dreaded jelly donut.

"So, whatever happened with Nurse Amelia?" Taylor asked, his lips coated with powdered sugar. He wiped his mouth on the back of his hand. "Did you ever get that date?"

"Nurse who?"

Taylor laughed. "I guess that answers my question."

"Oh, right!" Yost exclaimed. "The hot nurse who changed your bedpan."

Gemma slugged Taylor in the arm. "Um…what hot nurse?"

"She wasn't hot, Gem. And for the record, I never required a bedpan."

"First, she *was* hot," Yost countered. "And the bedpan thing is still a big question mark. But since you asked, no. Things didn't work out between Nurse Amelia and me." He took another bite of his donut. Jelly oozed out through the hole in the pastry and slid onto his fingers. "I took her to Applebee's."

Brie laughed. "Big spender."

Yost waved a hand at her. "You women are all the same. You all want Red Lobster or Olive Garden or something equally classy, but then you expect *us* to foot the bill. That little nurse should've been grateful I didn't take her to Burger King. I got her everything she asked for, including a butter pecan blondie!"

Gemma licked granulated sugar off her fingers. "She sounds very unappreciative."

"Yeah, well, she got even more annoying as the meal went on. She kept wanting to talk about herself and her job, but I guess I wasn't giving her enough attention or something. She actually walked out on me right before the bill—" Yost's cheeks flushed red, and he dropped his gaze to the table. "Oh."

"What?" Max leaned forward, clearly invested in the story. "What happened?"

Yost covered his face with his hands. When he spoke, it was through splayed, jelly-stained fingers. "Well…I *might* have gotten a text from another girl. And I *might* have responded to it. At the table."

"Not surprised." Taylor shook his head. "Not surprised at all."

They all laughed. And then something incredible happened. At first, Gemma thought it was a hallucination—the result of too much processed sugar after a long sugar drought. But then she locked eyes with Brie across the table, and Brie's subtle nod told her that—yes—she, too, was seeing the same thing. It wasn't a hallucination. It was actually happening.

For the first time in six months, Gavin was smiling.

✝

The upper level of the cabin consisted of a single, massive room with six beds, three on each side of the room. A double bed sat closest to the stairway while the rest of the beds were twins. There were no sheets or blankets, only stained mattresses set atop ancient box springs. Judging by the tiny mouse droppings scattered across every mattress, Gemma assumed the stains were mouse urine, but it was impossible to be sure.

Still, they were beds. Actual beds. And they were comfortable. More comfortable than anything Gemma had slept on in the past two years. Taylor had discovered some wool blankets and pillows in a metal storage cabinet in the living room, and they'd carried them upstairs, pleased to not have to sleep directly on top of the soiled mattresses.

Brie and Max took the double bed. No one questioned or debated which couple should have it. They just took it. Gemma watched in amusement as Max took the stairs two at a time to make it up before Brie so he could brush the mouse droppings off of the bed. He finished just as Brie rounded the top of the stairway.

"There better not be any mouse poop on my bed," she said.

"Of course there isn't, babe." Max winked at Gemma. "I disinfected and sanitized it myself."

"What a gentleman."

As much as Gemma wanted to curl up next to Taylor, she couldn't fathom the idea of sharing a bed with him in a room that was also occupied by Gavin. So, while Gavin collapsed onto the twin bed directly across from Max and Brie, Gemma lugged her blanket and pillow to the other end of the room. She claimed the bed next to the window that overlooked the driveway at the side of the cabin. As a bonus, her bed seemed to have the least amount of mouse droppings on it. Taylor took the bed nearest to hers, and Yost dropped his blanket on the bed across from Taylor's.

Unlike the first-floor windows, the windows on the second level weren't boarded up, so their group couldn't turn on any lights upstairs. The cabin wasn't visible from the highway during the day, but they couldn't risk anyone noticing the lights at night, so they navigated the room using flashlights aimed at the floor.

The lack of light was probably for the best.

The less Gemma saw of the room before closing her eyes, the better.

Once everyone claimed a bed, they took turns using the downstairs bathroom. When it was Gemma's turn, she brushed her teeth and splashed cold water on her face. She dried her face on a faded hand towel that was damp and stiff to the touch. Movement drew her attention to the floor, and she glanced down in time to see a large spider scurry into a crack between the wall and the baseboard heater. A soft cry left her lips but thankfully it wasn't loud enough to be heard by the other inhabitants of the cabin.

She wasn't afraid to face the Task Force again—

especially if it meant saving Letty—but she still *hated* spiders.

When she left the bathroom, she noticed the back door hanging open. Taylor waved at her from the porch, his cell phone pressed against his ear. Probably trying to call Letty again. He'd been trying for most of the evening—so far with no luck.

They were going into town tomorrow, whether or not they'd heard from Letty.

Gemma started for the second floor, carefully sidestepping the soft spot at the base of the stairs. The others were already in bed, although Yost was the only one snoring. He was also the only one lying underneath his blanket, instead of on top of it.

Gemma brushed the mouse droppings off her mattress and put down her wool blanket. Taylor hadn't gotten the propane heater working yet, and it was chilly inside the cabin. She wanted to cover up, but she didn't have an extra blanket, and she couldn't imagine sleeping directly on the filthy mattress. Brie and Max had each other for warmth, but Gemma had nothing.

She rolled onto her side, clutched her cross necklace in her fist, and shivered.

A little while later, she heard footsteps on the stairs followed by the creak of box springs as

Taylor settled onto the bed right next to hers. Although she was facing the window, she could see him clearly in her mind, unlacing his boots and placing them neatly beside his bed. Still a soldier. She heard him fumbling with the cord for his cell phone charger before placing the phone on the small table between them.

She ached for him. Every part of her yearned to be close to him. To lose herself in his gentle kiss and protective arms. To kiss him until she forgot all about what was going to happen in the morning.

A few seconds passed before Taylor's box springs sounded again, and she imagined him settling onto the bed, maybe putting his hands behind his head, elbows splayed, his eyelids growing heavy as he focused on the ceiling.

But then she felt warmth as he covered her with his blanket.

His *only* blanket.

She rolled over so she was facing him. "Taylor, no," she whispered. "It's cold. You need something."

His lips grazed her ear, and the warmth of his breath against her cheek did more to warm her than the blanket ever could. "I'm used to sleeping on the ground, remember? Just go to sleep."

Taylor returned to his bed and lay on his side so he was facing her. Only a few feet separated them, but the distance seemed insurmountable. The room was almost completely black, and she couldn't see his expression, only the outline of his body, but she extended her hand anyway, hoping he would sense it.

Her fingers dangled in midair. Her arm grew cold. He was probably already asleep. Taylor had an uncanny ability to fall asleep the moment his head hit the pillow. She pulled her hand back to tuck it under the blanket, but then she heard a single creak, barely audible.

In the near-total darkness, Taylor's fingers intertwined with hers.

CHAPTER NINE

Two Task Force soldiers stood on the footbridge behind the cabin.

Gemma stepped onto the back porch and froze in place, her eyes locked on the soldiers. She forgot all about the Styrofoam cup of long-expired instant coffee she was holding, and when her arms fell limply to her sides, the dark-brown liquid sloshed onto the porch.

"Whoa!" Brie came up behind her and grabbed the nearly empty Styrofoam cup out of her hand. "What's your problem? I know it tastes like garbage, but we don't waste caffeine."

Gemma didn't respond—she *couldn't* speak—but she reached for the pistol on her belt.

"Easy there, sharpshooter." Brie placed a hand on top of Gemma's and eased it away from the gun.

Then, she spoke loud enough for the soldiers on the bridge to hear. "Your boyfriend already has enough holes in that over-inflated head of his."

Both soldiers turned toward the cabin.

One was Mike Yost.

The other was Taylor.

Gemma's shoulders sagged with relief. She hadn't seen Taylor in his uniform since the day they'd rescued Max from Carver's interrogators. And it was like stepping through a time portal. His bed had been empty when she'd woken up at five-thirty, and now she could see why. He'd used the extra time to shave the scruff off his face, trim his hair, and put on his old uniform, magically transforming himself into the soldier he'd been only six months earlier.

She wasn't sure how to feel about it.

Brie gave Gemma's arm a supportive squeeze and called, "Shotgun!" over her shoulder as she leapt into the front passenger seat of Yost's Tahoe.

Taylor left Yost on the bridge and crossed the clearing, his cover flapping from his unbuttoned cargo pocket. A series of moss-covered rocks littered the ground between the creek and the cabin, and Taylor promptly tripped over one of them. He made a show of stumbling forward and briefly regaining his footing, only to trip over another rock. Finally, he caught himself on one of the porch's concrete support posts and stood there, panting.

"That was close," he muttered, his blue eyes traveling up to meet Gemma's.

"Idiot," Brie called from the Tahoe. "Fakest fall ever."

It was a struggle not to laugh, but Gemma managed.

When his act failed to get a smile out of her, Taylor nodded toward the spot where the driveway passed beneath the roof awning—a spot out of sight of the others. "Can I speak to you, Miss Alcott?"

She rolled her eyes at the formality but followed him around the cabin. The same sharp rocks that formed the wall in the kitchen jutted out from the side of the cabin, but the other half—the part that comprised the more recent kitchen addition—was plain old siding.

Avoiding the rocks, Taylor leaned against the siding and pulled her close to him. "Well?" he asked, gesturing to his uniform. "What do you think?"

Gemma immediately burst into tears. "You cut your hair," she cried, lightly pummeling his chest with her fists. "Why did you have to cut your hair?"

His eyes grew wide—he clearly wasn't expecting that to be her biggest complaint—and then he laughed. A genuine, adorable Taylor-laugh. He didn't laugh very often, but when he did, it always created a physical ache in Gemma's heart, as if she were listening to the song of a rare and beautiful bird.

The sound triggered something deep within her, and she grabbed him and kissed him hard, as if trying to reclaim what was hers. Finally, she released him and gave him a light shove. He staggered back a step and almost tripped over one of the moss-covered rocks for real this time.

"I seriously can't believe you cut it," she muttered.

Taylor wiped away the tears she'd deposited on his cheeks. "I knew you wouldn't be happy about the hair, Gem. But I had to cut it if I was going to put on the uniform."

She glared at him. "I hate the uniform, too."

"I know you do," he whispered.

"I never thought I'd have to see you like this again."

He moved closer to her and tugged at the front of his uniform jacket, just below the sergeant rank sewn onto his lapel. "This means nothing. It used to mean something to me, but it doesn't anymore. Now, it's a disguise. It's one of the few advantages we have. But I'm not going back to that life, Gemma. Not after us. I promise."

Wrapping her arms around his shoulders, Gemma ran her fingers through his too-short hair. Until he cut it, she hadn't realized how much she preferred his hair slightly long and disheveled. Her right hand slid from his shoulder to the blood-red patch on his arm—two intersecting swords in the shape of an upside-down cross. "It just feels like you'll never be free of this."

Tendrils of her auburn hair had broken free of her age-weakened hair elastic, and Taylor brushed them away from her face before kissing her lightly on the forehead. "I *am* free of it," he insisted. "This is a means to an end. That's all it is."

"I know." Gemma nodded. Of course, he was right. All that mattered was helping Letty and the other people in Winter's Dam. "But after this little mission of yours is over, you're forbidden from ever cutting your hair again."

Taylor tilted her face back to his and kissed her deeply, not holding anything back, as if he had something to prove to her.

Which, she supposed, he did.

✝

They approached Winter's Dam from the opposite side of the ridge that composed the town's northern boundary, hoping to avoid encountering any roadblocks. At Taylor's request, Yost parked at the town reservoir, located north of the town, halfway up the ridge. He pulled the Tahoe behind the reservoir building, where it wasn't visible from the road, and they exited the vehicle and silently slipped on their backpacks. Their plan was to descend the steep slope of the ridge as a group, using the woods for concealment, and then to split up into groups to reconnoiter the town.

A night of cold, unrelenting rain had washed away the unseasonably warm fall temperatures, leaving in their place a blustery and dreary fall day. Overhead, the wind tore at the colorful canopy of leaves, ripping them from their branches far too soon. Propelled by the wind, fast-moving clouds sailed across the pewter sky, creating the illusion that time was speeding up, pushing them toward a destination they did not wish to reach.

The wind beat against Gemma's face, lashing at her cheeks like a whip, making her eyes water. She had to wipe her eyes repeatedly on her sleeves just to see where she was going, but the rough material of her cargo jacket quickly made the skin around her eyes raw and sore. Finally, she tugged the hood of her cargo jacket over her head, which helped a little but limited her peripheral vision so much that it forced her to put the hood back down. She had to keep her head on a swivel. There was no reason to believe these woods were free of Task Force scouts, especially considering how close they were to Winter's Dam.

The woods abruptly ended, spitting them out into a cornfield. There was no one in sight, so they traversed the field at a light jog, careful to avoid tripping over broken corn stalks. On the other side of the field was a quiet back road that ran parallel to the highway that passed through Winter's Dam. To their right, several acres of cemetery covered the steep slope leading down to the road. According to Taylor, the road in front of them—fittingly titled Cemetery Road—linked up with the main road on both ends of town, so there were no roadblocks in sight, only houses in both directions. They stayed hidden in the corn as they surveyed the town.

The houses were all dark.

Every single one of them.

It was still early—just after seven—so it was possible that the town just hadn't woken up yet. Yes, seven was a little late for a weekday, but it wasn't like the residents of Winter's Dam could go to work. Their town was under Task Force occupation. They'd probably been told to shelter in place and await further instructions.

But as Gemma stared up at the dark windows of the house across the street, they felt like vacant eyes staring back at her. The unseeing eyes of a body devoid of a soul.

"What's going on here?" Brie asked. "Why is it so quiet?"

"Look over there."

Gavin rarely spoke anymore, and when he did, he used the gruff voice that she'd grown to despise over the past six months. So, when Gemma heard the familiar pitch of his old voice—his *real* voice— her ears perked up. She turned in his direction and saw him pointing at the cemetery.

Like most cemeteries, the oldest gravestones— the neglected, barely legible ones—were near the entrance at the bottom of the hill. Halfway up the hill, the older gravestones slowly gave way to new markers. The newer gravestones were flush with the ground and visible only by the sporadic bouquets of flowers and the American flags jutting out of the earth.

Gemma wasn't close enough to read the inscriptions on the gravestones, but she didn't have to be close to know that any crosses that had once been carved into the marble would've been covered up, haphazardly scratched off, or chiseled away until they resembled something else. Crosses had been among the first things to go back when things got bad, because the sight of them upset people. Removing them from headstones had brought an end to much of the cemetery vandalism that had been plaguing the country.

It had seemed a minor concession at the time.

But it wasn't missing crosses that had drawn Gavin's attention to the cemetery. Near the top of the hill, a black tarp covered a fresh grave. A square funeral tent stood beside the grave, the green canopy shielding two rows of black chairs from the elements—at least, that was the intention. But the tent had blown over, and an entire section of canopy had torn free of its support post. It whipped furiously in the wind, creating an eerie cracking sound, like the snapping of ancient bones.

Another gust of wind filled the canopy, giving it the look of a ship at full sail.

The sight of the empty grave sent a shiver down Gemma's spine. "Why would they do that? Why would someone just leave a tent to blow around like that?"

Taylor rubbed a hand over his freshly shaved chin. "They probably set it up yesterday to prepare for a funeral," he said. "Then the Task Force arrived and—"

"The poor stiff never got put in the ground," Yost plucked his cover off his head, held it over his heart, and bowed his head. "Man, that's a rotten break. No one deserves that."

Taylor ripped his gaze away from the billowing canopy and cleared his throat. "We need to start our recon, figure out where everybody is, because people obviously aren't in their homes. Let's break into groups of two and conduct a grid search. But no one draws their weapons today, understood?"

Except for Gavin, everyone nodded in agreement.

But Taylor continued anyway. "If we do this right, no one's even going to know we were here. Do exactly like we talked about last night. Stick to the alleys. Stay away from the main road. If you see or hear a vehicle coming, find somewhere to hide. Don't go inside any buildings. Just check things out and report what you find. Report back to this spot in sixty minutes."

Gemma nodded. "How are we pairing up?" Of course she wanted to be with Taylor, but she knew that would not happen even before he started listing the groups on his fingers.

"Yost and I are going to check out the high school on the east end of town. That's where Letty said the Task Force was setting up their base of operations. Brie and Gemma, you guys head for the bookstore. That's close to here. Once you get through the cemetery, you can use that next field for concealment most of the way. See if you can connect with Letty. I haven't been able to reach her since our phone call yesterday morning. If you find her, bring her with you."

"Okay," Brie and Gemma said in unison.

"Max and Gavin, you two search the main part of town, but stick to the alleys and side roads. But don't search any houses or businesses. Just try to see what's going on. If there are soldiers around, what are they doing? Are they using any of the buildings? What weapons do they have? Make note of everything you see. Soldiers, vehicles, weapons…everything. You guys understand?"

Gemma glanced at Gavin and saw the familiar flare of his nostrils. He couldn't bring himself to look at Taylor, much less take orders from him.

Max answered for both of them. "Got it."

"Good." Taylor pressed a series of buttons on his watch. "Sixty minutes from right now, meet back in this spot. If you're not here on time, you're walking home."

Brie gasped in mock alarm. "Yikes. We better get moving, Gem. Your kindhearted boyfriend just threatened to leave us behind if we're late." She grabbed Gemma's arm and pulled her toward the cemetery.

When Gemma glanced back, she saw Max and Gavin already jogging down the hill into Winter's Dam, sticking close to the buildings. She locked eyes with Taylor, and the fingers of her free hand found their way to her necklace, as they always did when she was frightened. The silver cross—once lost to a mountain of garbage—felt strong and sturdy beneath her stiff fingers.

Besides Taylor, it was the only strong and sturdy thing in her life.

He gave her one of his understated smiles, designed to reassure her, but there was worry in his eyes. He didn't want to let her go without him any more than she wanted to let him go without her. But she wasn't stupid. Taylor hadn't wanted her to come with him to the school for a reason. Probably because that was where he expected to find the most trouble.

She dropped the hand from her cross and gave him a small wave.

He raised his own hand in return, and his uniform sleeve slid down his wrist, revealing the numbers tattooed there. The telephone number he'd thought would eventually lead him back to her.

But in the end, God had brought them back together.

"Watch where you're going!" Brie barked at her, drawing Gemma's attention to the crumbling gravestones at her feet. They had made it to the cemetery. "If you trip and fall into a freshly dug grave because you were busy making googly eyes at your boyfriend, I'm not pulling you out."

Wrenching her arm out of Brie's grip, Gemma muttered, "Just keep moving."

The next time she looked back, Taylor was gone.

CHAPTER TEN

Rubbing his hands together for warmth, Gavin huddled next to Max in the alleyway between a bank and a twenty-four-hour diner—cleverly named That Dam Diner. But except for the blinking red OPEN sign in the front window, the interior of the diner appeared deserted. Gavin pressed his face against the glass and saw half-eaten breakfasts and dirty plates stacked on tables. A glass of orange juice rested on its side, and a dark stain had settled into the worn carpet beneath the table. Movement drew his attention to a pair of dippy eggs on a plate nearest to the window. The eggs had coagulated into a yellowish-white mass, and Gavin realized, with a stomach-churning wave of revulsion, that the movement he'd seen on the plate was maggots.

He doubled over, his hands on his knees, and gagged. Luckily, the five donuts he'd consumed the night before didn't decide to make an appearance.

"What is it?" Max looked worried. He'd been monitoring Main Street, watching for movement inside the houses, and thankfully, hadn't seen the maggots. He strained his neck to look in the window.

Gavin waved him away. The last thing he needed was for Max to see that squirming plate of maggots and lose his cool. "There's no one inside. Let's keep moving."

"Where to?"

"See that little store over there?" He gestured to a squat building at the end of the block. Fallon's Grocery. Like the diner, it had a red OPEN sign in the window. "The sign says they're open. Why don't we have a look inside?"

Max looked uncertain. "I don't know, man. We'd have to cross the main road, and Taylor told us not to go inside any buildings."

Gavin rolled his eyes in frustration. Max wanted to stick to the alleys because Nolan had told them to stick to the alleys, and he didn't want to go inside any buildings because Nolan had told them not to. For reasons Gavin would never understand, Max respected Nolan. But they didn't *have* to listen to the guy. Nolan definitely viewed himself as their leader, but he wasn't. Gavin had no loyalty to him. In fact, he had every reason to *not* be loyal to the guy. The only reason he'd volunteered to come along on this little mission was to annoy Gemma's soldier boyfriend.

Gavin held his arms out to his side. "Max, do you see anyone? Are there any soldiers rushing at us with their guns drawn?" He dropped his arms. "There's no one around, man. If something bad happened here, it's already over."

Max's eyes darted nervously between Gavin and the empty street. He ran his finger along the red slash on the left side of his face, as if to remind himself that he'd survived much worse. Finally, he nodded. "Okay. Let's see what we find."

But there wasn't much *to* find. Aside from the diner and the bank, there were only a handful of businesses in Winter's Dam. There was a health-care and rehabilitation center, a post office, and the little mom-and-pop grocer on the corner. There were a few cars parked on the street, but no people in sight.

The main drag was dark and quiet.

Except for the barking. Lots and lots of barking.

It had started just before they reached the diner. A little dog had appeared in a window of one house, jumping and barking like crazy. That set off a chain reaction where every dog on the block went crazy. Muffled barks drifted to them through the walls of the dark houses, but there were plenty of dogs outside, too, either tied up or running free inside their fenced-in yards. The farther Gavin and Max traveled down the street, the more the barking increased in both intensity and pitch. It sounded like every dog in Winter's Dam had noticed their presence. The noise level should've made it impossible for anyone to sleep, but no one came outside to shush their dog. No one opened their door to let their dog out to relieve themselves.

To Gavin, that could only mean one thing.

The houses were as empty as the diner.

When they reached the grocery store, Max slumped against the side of the building and ran a hand down his face. "They're gone, aren't they? They took the entire town."

"I don't know. Probably."

"But why would they do that? *How* would they do that?"

Gavin didn't think the Task Force would detain an entire town under suspicion of helping a group of subversives, but after what had happened at Oliver's barn, he believed anything was possible. He nodded at the door of the grocery store. "Come on. Let's get off the street for a few minutes. It might be a little warmer inside."

They tried the door. It was unlocked, and they quietly slipped inside. They didn't turn on any lights but stood in the darkness, giving their eyes time to adjust.

The store was tidy but small, the cramped aisles barely wide enough for two people to bypass each other without bumping elbows. The stocked shelves featured quick-fix staples Gavin remembered fondly from his childhood: cans of Chef Boyardee, Kraft Macaroni and Cheese, Hamburger Helper. He'd lived on that stuff for the first few years of his life, until his mother committed suicide when he was four. After she died, he went to live with his maternal grandmother, and she had insisted on cooking meals from scratch. But Gavin still remembered those early meals fondly, not because the food had been good, but because they'd been a source of comfort in an uncertain world. By the age of three, he knew how to open those little containers of Chef Boyardee and heat them in the microwave himself because his mother was usually too drunk or high to do it for him.

On the left wall of the store, two glass-door refrigerators housed quart jugs of milk and orange juice, as well as eggs, butter, and cheese. The refrigerators were lit up and running, and Gavin made a beeline for the nearest one. He grabbed a jug of orange juice off the shelf, twisted the cap, and chugged half of it before coming up for air.

Nothing had ever tasted so good.

They had a decent variety of food at the Sanctuary, but orange juice wasn't one of them.

Max came up behind him. "Dude, that's stealing."

But when Gavin held out the jug, Max grabbed it and took a long swig. "Oh, man. That's good," he said, wiping his lips on his sleeve. "I never used to like orange juice, but I do now."

While Max finished the juice, Gavin's eyes traveled to the second refrigerator. It held too many treasures to count. Raw cookie dough. Blocks of cheddar cheese. Hot dogs. Cinnamon rolls. Cream cheese. Bacon.

But then he saw another case, closer to the back of the store.

A freezer…filled with ice cream.

Gavin loved ice cream. His mother had provided it freely in order to keep him quiet whenever one of her boyfriends dropped by. A small pint of ice cream in front of the television would buy her at least an hour, maybe more, if he collapsed into a sugar-induced coma on the rug. He would eat until his stomach ached and he thought he might throw up, but he didn't care.

Ice cream took his sadness away. It made him feel better, just for a little while.

He shoved the memory aside—he'd been thinking about his mother too much lately—and flung open the freezer door. This wasn't a regular grocery store, so there were only a few flavor options. Chocolate and vanilla, of course. Peanut butter cup. He pushed aside a carton of cookie dough—the most overrated flavor of all time, in his opinion—and found his favorite flavor hiding in the back of the freezer. Mint chocolate chip. Turkey Hill brand, of course. In Pennsylvania, eating anything other than Turkey Hill ice cream was sacrilege. He tore off the lid and dug a finger into the carton, using it like a scoop to shovel the frozen goodness directly into his mouth.

The dessert was cold against his teeth and so incredibly sweet. He scooped more ice cream into his mouth and then held the carton out to Max. "Dude, try this."

Max backed away from Gavin as if he were holding a box of snakes instead of a carton of ice cream. "Gavin…"

"Just try it." Gavin pushed the carton into his hands and reached into the freezer to pull out another one. "It's not stealing if you're hungry. Besides, when are you going to get another chance to—"

"Stop right there."

Gavin pulled his head out of the freezer and turned in the voice's direction.

A young woman stood at the end of the row, near the rear of the store.

She was beautiful. And she was pointing a revolver at him.

If not for the ambient light from the freezer, he wouldn't have seen her at all. It was so dark back there. How long had she been watching him? How long had she been pointing that gun at his back?

Max raised his hands in the air, and the carton of mint chocolate chip splattered on the floor. "Don't shoot. Please. We're not stealing anything."

Gavin gave him a sidelong glance. *Really?*

"Well, what would you call it?" The girl spoke in an unnaturally husky voice, and Gavin realized it wasn't her normal voice. She was trying to sound intimidating. "So far, you've stolen a jug of orange juice and some ice cream. What's next?"

"We're leaving." Max edged backward toward the exit. "We're leaving right now."

But Gavin didn't follow him. Instead, he took a step closer to the girl. She looked to be in her early twenties. Tall and thin with pale skin that seemed almost translucent when set against her long, jet-black hair. She wore a flannel shirt and blue jeans with ripped knees.

Her hands were shaking.

"Don't come any closer," she warned, taking a step backward. "If you think I won't shoot, you're wrong."

"Gavin," Max called out from behind him. "Let's get out of here, man."

A familiar feeling twisted Gavin's insides. This girl—whoever she was—was alone and frightened. In that way, she reminded him of Gemma, the way she'd been back when he'd first met her at the Station. He'd allowed himself to fall in love with her, even as she held back from ever giving herself completely to him. And then she'd tossed him aside, as if their two years together had meant nothing to her. Gemma still did not know how much pain she'd caused him. And how much pain he still felt every time he saw her with Nolan.

Now, standing before him was another tragic girl in need of a savior.

The taste of mint lingered on Gavin's tongue. "What's your name?"

"Get out," she replied, cocking the revolver. "Now."

He swallowed his irritation. She was just scared. And judging by what he'd seen over at the diner, she had good reason to be. "Listen, if you want us to leave, we'll go. But we're not the enemy. Sending us away will not help your town, which is why we're here."

There was confusion in her eyes, but there was something else there, too.

Hope.

"You want to help us?" she asked. "Why? Who are you?"

Max spoke up first. "Some people in this town have been looking after us, and we wanted to return the favor."

The girl's eyes shot to Max and slowly widened. "You're from *there*, aren't you? The secret place?"

Gavin glanced at Max, who lifted his arms in a shrug. "You know about us?"

Slowly, the girl lowered the revolver. Gavin wasn't even sure if she realized she was doing it. The thing remained cocked. "Only what my dad told me, which wasn't much. I caught him putting food in boxes one day last summer, and I asked him about it. He tried to make up some story about donating to a local food bank, but he's a terrible liar. Eventually, he admitted there was a secret place nearby. A place for subversives. He said someone paid him for the food, but he always donated extra." Anger flashed in her eyes. "I told him he was making a mistake."

"No, he wasn't," Max muttered. "He was doing the right thing."

"Oh, yeah? Look where it got him."

"Where?" Gavin asked. "Where is everybody?"

She lowered the revolver a little more, pointing it at Gavin's waist instead of his chest. "They took everyone to the high school. After things died down last night, I snuck over there and saw two gigantic tents in the middle of the football field. There's a fence around the field, so there's only one way in and out, and soldiers are guarding the entrance."

"Why didn't they detain you?" Gavin asked.

Her eyebrows bunched together, and her eyes strayed to the floor. "My dad saw them coming. There were soldiers on the streets. There was no way to make a run for it. He made me hide inside the walk-in freezer, and he stacked a bunch of boxes in front of me." With her free hand, she scratched at her pale arm, which had goosebumps all over it. "I heard them take my dad." Her voice cracked a little, and she took a deep breath. "I kept expecting them to check the freezer, but they never did. I don't know how long I stayed in there, but it was a long time."

Max blew out a breath. "Wow. You got lucky."

"When you guys first broke in here, I thought they'd come back."

"We didn't break in," Gavin explained. "Your

door was unlocked. You should've locked it after the Task Force left with your dad."

She scowled at him. "And what if the soldiers came back looking for some food, and they discover that someone had locked the door? They would know I was in here."

Gavin couldn't say anything to that, because she was right. However scary it might've been for her, she'd done the smart thing in leaving the door unlocked. In the silence that followed, he stole another glance around the store. It was clear from the neatly stacked shelves and sparkling floors (well, sparkling except for the carton of rapidly melting ice cream) that this girl's father took pride in his business. A pride that his daughter had obviously inherited.

"What about your mom?" he asked.

Teresa shook her head. "She took off soon after I was born. It's always been just me and my dad."

"You can't stay here." The words were out of Gavin's mouth before he could stop them. But there was no way to unsay them, so he went all in. "Come with us."

She looked at him as if he'd just suggested she lick the ice cream off the floor. "No way. I don't know you people. And even if I did want to leave, I can't go anywhere. I have a responsibility to this store until my dad gets back. I can't stop the Task

Force from taking what they want, but I *can* stop people like you."

Behind Gavin, Max made an angry *harrumph* sound. "Let's just go, man."

But Gavin wouldn't stop trying. Once a savior, always a savior. "Just lock the place up and leave. The only thing you're doing by staying here is creating more trouble for your father. If the Task Force finds you, you're going to end up just like him. Or worse, they'll try to use you against him."

"What do you mean?"

But she sounded as if she already knew.

"If your father was helping us, that means he's got information the Task Force wants. Valuable information. I doubt he'll give up that information willingly, but if they capture you, they could use you to get to him. To make him talk."

He didn't go into any more detail, but it was clear from the expression on the girl's face that she got the picture. "Come with us," he repeated. "You have knowledge of the town. You can help us figure out a way to get your dad—and hopefully everyone else—out of there safely."

The girl glanced around the empty store, as if searching for another option—one that didn't involve leaving everything she knew and running off with two strange men. When her eyes met Gavin's again, she uncocked the revolver and tucked it inside her waistband.

"I'll go," she finally said. "But first, you're going to help me clean up this mess."

So he did.

While Max stood guard at the front window, watching the street for soldiers, Gavin and the dark-haired mystery girl mopped a carton of half-melted mint chocolate chip ice cream off the floor. It brought back memories of the time he'd mopped a floor with Gemma, back at the Station. The same night she'd run away with Taylor. That seemed so long ago now, like the memory belonged to someone else. And now here he was again, mopping a floor with another beautiful girl he suspected was eventually going to break his heart.

God certainly had a sense of humor.

After they finished cleaning, the girl snuck back to her house—which was located right next door—to grab a few things. She returned five minutes later with a pale-blue knapsack slung over her shoulders.

"If you have a cell phone, leave it behind," Gavin told her. "They can trace it."

The girl brushed a sweaty clump of hair away from her eyes. "I didn't bring it along."

"Good."

She followed Gavin to the front of the store, but

before they stepped outside, she turned to look at the dark aisles, her eyes lingering on every soup can, every microwavable meal, and every can of tuna as if seeing them all for the last time.

Gavin shouldn't have said anything. He should have remained quiet and let her have a few moments to say her goodbyes. Who knew what was going to happen? Who knew if she would ever see the store—or her father—again? But he couldn't stand the look of despair in her eyes. He needed to take that hopelessness away from her as much as he needed his next breath.

Old habits died hard.

He leaned close enough to smell the girl's lavender shampoo. "You'll see it again," he whispered. "When this is all over, I'll make sure you get back to your dad. Okay? I promise you that."

With what appeared to be great effort, she raised her eyes to meet his. Tears glistened within them, but she did not cry. Not a single tear rolled down her cheek. She was a lot tougher than she looked.

She held out her hand. It was so small his own hand swallowed it up.

"My name is Teresa," she said. "Teresa Fallon."

Gavin smiled. It was a beautiful name.

"Gavin Bonnar," he said, shaking her hand. He nodded toward the front window, where Max was looking increasingly irritated with the situation. "That's Max Yelchin."

But Teresa wasn't interested in Max. She kept right on staring at Gavin until it felt like she was trying to bore a hole straight into his soul. "Do you keep your promises, Gavin?"

He didn't hesitate, because it was true. "Always."

"You better. Or else."

Teresa dropped his hand. She pushed past Max and nudged the door open, checking both directions before leading them outside. The streets were as empty as they'd been thirty minutes earlier, when they'd first entered the store. The three of them jogged across the street, heading for the alley.

All around them, the dogs continued to bark.

Gavin felt lighter than he had in months. Maybe this was his second chance. Maybe he could claw his way out of the dark hole he'd been living in since April.

Maybe he could be happy again.

And then he heard the gunshots.

CHAPTER ELEVEN

The town was deserted.

Taylor and Yost didn't have time to search every house, but it quickly became clear that the Task Force had moved the residents of Winter's Dam *somewhere,* most likely into the high school. While most of the houses were dark, the football field on the east end of town was lit up like a carnival. The two ex-soldiers communicated without words, using the hand signals they'd learned in their scout training, and they hurried through the town.

As they passed a two-story tan house with pale-blue shutters, Taylor heard a whining sound coming from one window. Glancing up, he locked eyes with a small beagle in the window, its nose leaving wet streaks on the glass. This dog wasn't going crazy like most of the other dogs in the town, but it gave Taylor such a look of despair that he couldn't ignore it.

He jogged up the porch steps, pulling a small bag of beef jerky from his pack.

"Dude," Yost whispered. "What are you doing? You plan on feeding every dog in town?"

"Nope. Just this one."

Taylor tried the front door, and luckily, it was unlocked. The second he pushed the door open, the beagle rushed through the gap and threw itself onto its back, exposing its white underbelly. Its tongue lolled out of its mouth, and its tail repeatedly thwacked against Taylor's boot.

"You hungry, buddy?" He knelt and held out a piece of beef jerky. The little dog flipped over to inhale the piece of jerky while Taylor scratched behind its droopy ears. "Just don't do that howling thing you beagles do, okay? We're trying to keep a low profile here."

The dog gobbled up two more pieces of jerky before it trotted off into the backyard, and Taylor and Yost continued toward the school.

There were fewer houses on the west end of Winter's Dam, and the relentless barking that had followed them through the town faded away.

But they soon heard other noises.

Voices. Doors opening and closing. The hum of stadium lights.

A two-story red brick colonial sat in the lot next to the high school, its second-floor windows overlooking the school's rear parking area as well as the football field. Four white pillars supported an elaborate front porch that contained a swing and twin rocking chairs. Two carved pumpkins flanked the front door, and mums of various colors dangled from the porch overhang. The American flag and a POW/MIA flag flew from a pole in the yard.

Taylor and Yost gained entry to the house through an unlocked sliding glass door off the kitchen. The interior of the house appeared lived in and comfortable with family pictures on the walls and toys scattered in the hallway. Taylor didn't look closely at any of the pictures. In the kitchen, a loaf of white bread, a deli bag of American cheese, and a frying pan laid on the counter next to the stovetop. Whoever lived in this house had been preparing a grilled cheese sandwich when the Task Force came knocking on their door.

Yost stationed himself in the downstairs hallway where he could easily watch both the front door and the sliding glass door in case any of the soldiers at the school had noticed them entering the house.

Taylor climbed to the second floor and located a small bedroom that overlooked the football field. The heat was still on inside the house, and by the time he made it to the top of the stairs, he was sweating. He knelt in front of the window, unlocked it, and pushed it up a few inches, allowing cold air into the room. Both flags billowed in his peripheral vision, battered by the wind. The snapping of nylon and the clanging of the snap hooks against the pole—combined with his brief tour of the empty town—made him feel like he was the last man alive in some post-apocalyptic nightmare world, like Robert Neville in Richard Matheson's, *I Am Legend,* a book he'd read as a kid—mainly because his pastor father wouldn't have approved of it.

The bedroom he was in belonged to a child. Stuffed dinosaurs littered the bed, and Marvel posters decorated the walls. He tried not to think too much about the kid or where he might be now.

Taylor rested his phone on the windowsill. Paint chips adhered themselves to his uniform sleeves as he aimed the phone's camera at the two white detainee tents that occupied most of the football field.

He pressed record.

Long rectangular tents stood end to end, separated by a broken strip of white paint that had once been the fifty-yard line. The chain-link fence surrounding the field provided a natural barrier to keep the prisoners contained, and the armed soldiers stationed around the perimeter made any kind of escape attempt impossible. At least a dozen soldiers patrolled the foul line, their heads on a swivel.

All of them held M4 carbine rifles in their hands.

Taylor returned his attention to the tents themselves. There weren't many people in Winter's Dam, four-or five-hundred souls at the most. But they did not design those detainee tents to house over one hundred people, at least not comfortably, much less if each detainee got their own cot. It was possible the Task Force was keeping some detainees inside the school, but even if that were the case, he couldn't imagine how overcrowded and uncomfortable the tents must be.

As he watched, townspeople emerged from the tents, most of them bundled in coats and looking the worse for wear. They carried coffee-colored packages in their hands, which Taylor recognized as MREs—meals, ready-to-eat. The military's answer to TV dinners. Most of these civilians probably did not know what to do with their makeshift breakfasts. Hopefully, a veteran or two among the bunch could explain the complicated heating process to the uninitiated. Breakfast MREs were rare, so most of Winter's Dam would probably enjoy cold, coagulated meat in a variety of tasteless sauces for breakfast. A lucky few might get the highly coveted cheese tortellini, while the extraordinarily unlucky would inevitably stumble across the ambiguously named "Chicken Chunks."

Two water trailers—also known as "water buffalos"—sat on either end of the field. There would be no hot breakfasts or morning cups of coffee for the residents of Winter's Dam. Today, they would wash their congealed mystery meat down with paper cups of ice-cold, brackish water.

Instead of eating their MREs alone, most of the townspeople congregated in small groups on the field. A few plopped down on the metal bleachers, undoubtedly recalling better days when they'd wrapped blankets around themselves and cheered on the football team from those seats. Most looked resigned to their situation, as if they were just waiting for their detainment to end. Undoubtedly, the soldiers were reassuring them that as soon as they sorted everything out, the townspeople could return to their homes.

But Taylor knew that wasn't true. The Task Force wouldn't leave the town until they got what they wanted.

And they wanted the Sanctuary.

The unit commander was probably using the school as the tactical operations center. Taylor had yet to see anyone who ranked higher than a sergeant on the field, so those soldiers were probably inside the school. He couldn't see Letty among the people on the field. That didn't mean she wasn't there, but it was possible that some people were being housed inside the school. He didn't see too many old people milling around on the field. Maybe they were housing the elderly people inside.

The rear door of the high school swung open, and two soldiers emerged from inside. They walked purposefully toward the field, rifles slung over their shoulders. One was a bespectacled specialist who trudged, rather than walked, across the rear parking lot. The guy had the boorish look of a bully who wore glasses to make himself look smarter. The other was a fresh-faced second lieutenant, and he was struggling to keep pace with the specialist.

The lieutenant carried a clipboard in his left hand and a bullhorn in his right.

Taylor glanced back at the field where the crowd continued to expand. He couldn't believe how many people the Task Force had crammed into two detainee tents. He tilted his camera to capture the two soldiers as they approached the field. The soldiers guarding the entrance moved aside to allow the lieutenant and specialist to enter.

The crowd appeared to notice the approaching soldiers. Several people on the bleachers rose to their feet, including a bearded man wearing a leather vest and a hat that identified him as a veteran, although Taylor couldn't see what branch of the military or even what war. Gradually, the drone of conversation diminished until no sound remained. Nothing but the endless clanging of the brass snap clips against the flagpole.

The lieutenant raised the bullhorn to his lips. "Good morning, ladies and gentlemen!" He dragged the *good* out obnoxiously, reminding Taylor of Robin Williams in *Good Morning, Vietnam*, probably drunk on his newly gained power, as so many of the gold bars were. "I'm Lieutenant Keen, and I just need a moment of your time."

From the bleachers, the grizzled veteran shouted, "What choice do we have, Butter Bar?"

A few of his compatriots in the bleachers laughed nervously. An old woman—possibly his wife—slugged him in the arm.

The lieutenant did not show that he'd heard the old man, but when he spoke again, his playful tone had gone the way of the buffalo. "Our company commander, Captain Haggerty, apologizes for this inconvenience. Most of you do not deserve to be detained, and the Task Force does not want to keep you from your homes. But we appreciate your sacrifice for the good of your town as well as your country. Our goal is to get everything sorted out as quickly as possible, and then you can all get back to your lives."

"When?" the old man shouted. "When are you going to release us so we can get back to our lives?"

The lieutenant did not look at the man. "Soon, sir."

"*How* soon?" a woman yelled. "Some of us have animals to care for. Are you boys going to swing by on your way out of town and shampoo the dog crap out of my carpet?"

A chorus of voices shouted in agreement.

Another woman cried, "What about our jobs? What if we get fired for missing work? You're treating us like criminals, and we have done nothing wrong."

"That remains to be seen." The lieutenant shot a pointed look at the specialist. "But I promise to do everything in my power to get you back to your homes and responsibilities in short order. Until your release, please obey the orders of my soldiers and give them the respect they deserve." The officer looked at the clipboard for the first time. "Just one more item of business before I go. Captain

Haggerty would like to speak with Elizabeth Fishman."

Taylor knew that name.

Lizzie Fishman, co-owner of the butcher shop that supplied meat to the Sanctuary, and wife of Clyde Fishman, the mayor.

On the field, hundreds of heads swiveled as the crowd searched for Lizzie Fishman. The low drone grew louder, like a hive of irritated worker bees.

Taylor could feel something in the air—a tangible vibration that seemed to reverberate down his arms and into his hands. The same vibration he used to experience when raiding secret church gatherings. He'd chalked it up to an adrenaline dump. The raid rush, as he thought of it. But he was feeling the same thing now, and he wondered if the vibration wasn't something else entirely, some primordial part of his brain alerting him to danger.

To violence barely held at bay.

A middle-aged woman in jeans and a fleece jacket stepped out of the crowd. She raked her fingers through the unkempt mop of gray hair on her head, as if trying to ready herself for her meeting with the Task Force captain. But then the wind gusted again, sending her limp curls spiraling and undoing all of her hard work.

Lizzie Fishman.

With her free hand, the woman clutched the arm of a lanky, dark-haired boy in a Penn State sweatshirt. He couldn't have been over sixteen, and he was the spitting image of Lizzie.

Taylor closed his eyes and opened them again.

He didn't realize Lizzie and Clyde had a son.

The kid glared at the lieutenant, a dangerous glint in his eyes. It was the look of a boy trying to be a man. Taylor had seen that look on raids before, from other kids.

That look *always* got his attention.

Leaning close to his mother, the kid whispered something to her. She responded with a vigorous shake of her head.

"Ma'am, please accompany us inside," the lieutenant continued to speak through the bullhorn. He sounded almost bored. Clearly, he hadn't been in the field long enough to know when a situation was in danger of popping off. "This shouldn't take long at all."

Lizzie Fishman straightened her back and held her head high. "Where's my husband?" She wasn't shouting like the others, but the wind seemed to carry her voice to Taylor. "And what about the others? The ones you've taken into the school? Why haven't they come—"

"Enough!" The specialist lunged forward and grabbed the woman by the arm. "Let's go!"

But the boy—still clinging to his mother's other arm—pulled in the opposite direction, creating a crude game of tug-of-war with Lizzie Fishman as the prize. The match was even. While the bespectacled bully was short and stocky, the kid had the benefit of height on his side.

Taylor imagined two people tugging on a wishbone until the whole thing snapped in two.

Two older gentlemen suddenly materialized out of the crowd. One of them grabbed the kid by the arms and pried him away from his mother. Without another word, the lieutenant and the specialist each grabbed one of the woman's arms and rushed her toward the school.

The kid fought his restrainers with everything he had. Droplets of spit flew from his mouth as he screamed, *"Let go of me!"*

Briefly returning his eyes to the image on his phone, Taylor adjusted the camera so it was tracking the soldiers as they led Lizzie Fishman toward the gate. She wasn't resisting, but she kept twisting in their arms to look back at her son, imploring him with her eyes to calm down before things got any worse.

And then they did.

Lizzie Fishman was about ten feet away from the gate when her son broke away from his restrainers and barreled toward the soldiers.

Taylor's attention was still on Lizzie Fishman, so he only realized what was happening when the screams drew his attention back to the crowd. He snapped his head to the left and saw the boy sprinting after his mother, his head lowered like a bull, thin arms pumping at his sides. The two older gentlemen gave chase, but they had no hope of catching him.

"You're not taking her!"

Those were the kid's last words. Taylor would never forget them.

In a liquid-fast movement, the specialist performed an about-face and unslung his rifle. He didn't fire any warning shots, or order the kid to stop, or wait for one of the other soldiers to tackle the kid. Instead, he brought the rifle to bear on the teenager and fired a single round into the center of his chest.

"No!" Taylor shouted. The phone slipped out of his grip, but he grabbed it at the last second, saving it from a two-story plunge.

Had anyone heard him shout? He didn't think so. No one was looking in his direction. The crack of the gunshot and the screams on the field must've drowned out the sound.

With shaking hands, he aimed the phone at the dying teenager.

One word ran through his mind.

Evidence.

The kid stumbled to a halt halfway between the gate and the first tent. He went pale as the blood drained out of the hole in his chest. In the center of his Penn State sweatshirt, a tiny crimson smudge expanded and bloomed like a flower. The kid's gaze fell to his chest and widened as the cold recognition of what was happening to him set in.

That was when Taylor realized he'd been wrong about the kid's age.

He wasn't sixteen. He was fourteen at the most.

Over by the gate, Lizzie Fishman unleashed a high-pitched wail and fought to break free of the lieutenant who still held both of her arms behind her back. The lieutenant's expression was one of slack-jawed bewilderment. Taylor had seen *that* look many times. It was the look of a green officer who didn't understand how a situation could've gotten away from him so quickly.

Taylor wanted to throttle the guy. To straddle him and pound his head against the macadam parking lot until he realized what he'd just allowed to happen.

Yost burst into the bedroom and squinted at the window. His eyes were red, as if he'd been dozing. "What is it?"

Taylor couldn't answer him. He nodded at the window, at the boy dying alone on the football field. Yost crouched next to him and looked outside.

Something else was happening.

The grizzled veteran wasn't on the bleachers anymore. He was running, his thick legs carrying him across the field at an impossible rate. A soldier dove at him like a linebacker, trying to intercept him, but only snagged the edge of his vest. The veteran shrugged off the vest and kept running. He sprinted past the dying boy who'd collapsed onto his back in the grass. The veteran wasn't interested in the boy. His target was obvious.

He wanted the specialist.

But he had too much ground to cover. The specialist had plenty of time to see the veteran coming. He had plenty of time to take aim. And he had plenty of time to pull the trigger.

The round hit the veteran in the center of the forehead, just underneath the bill of his ball cap. The man's legs crumpled beneath him, and he went down hard and fast.

With Yost breathing hard next to him, Taylor kept the camera on the field as it erupted into chaos. Every soldier converged on the crowd gathered outside the tents, their weapons drawn, shouting orders, trying to herd them back toward the tents. But the crowd did not heed their orders. A group of people surged forward, and soldiers struck several of them—including a woman—in the heads with the butts of their rifles.

Better than a bullet.

Taylor wiped the sweat from his brow. With the window open, the bedroom was an icebox, but he was still sweating.

Since the lieutenant had mentally checked out of the situation, the murderous specialist doled out orders. *"Get that woman into the basement with the other HVTs!"* he barked at the lieutenant. But when the officer didn't respond, the specialist gave him a hard shove in the school's direction. *"Get going, LT!"*

The shove finally got him moving, and the lieutenant half-carried, half-dragged the wailing woman across the high school parking lot. She fought him the entire way and even got in a few good kicks. Just before they entered the school, Lizzie Fishman wrenched one of her hands loose and clocked him so hard on the side of the head that Taylor expected to see the lieutenant's head spin all the way around.

Back on the field, the soldiers had regained control through force, and the townspeople were filing into the tents. The dying kid wasn't moving anymore. If he was still alive, which Taylor doubted, he wouldn't be for long. He would not receive any medical attention. Not after what just happened.

The specialist crossed the field and halted next to the veteran from the bleachers. He nudged the man in the side with his boot, a cruel smile on his face.

Taylor looked at the camera in his hands.

The numbers at the top of the screen read: *00:12:57.*

Two civilians were dead, murdered by a Task Force soldier. One of them was a kid.

And he'd gotten it all on video. Every bloody second of it.

He stopped the recording, double-checked to make sure the video had saved to his phone, and then slipped the phone inside his pocket.

Yost looked at him. He was fully awake now. "What the heck are we going to do now?"

Taylor glanced around the room, his gaze falling on the unmade bed with the Looney Tunes bedsheets. The little boy who slept in that bed was in one of those tents.

"We're going to get out of here." Furious, Taylor pushed himself to his feet, no longer caring if someone on the field spotted him in the window. He was a Task Force scout, and he knew how to hide and evade capture. They would never find him. "We've got twelve minutes to get back to the rally point."

Yost grabbed his arm. "What are you going to do with that video?"

The kid's face—that steely look of determination—flashed in Taylor's mind again. He recognized that look, not from previous raids, but from the mirror. It was the same expression he'd worn when his mother was dying of cancer. He would not let her die. No, he would fix her. He would pray her right out of her sickbed.

The kid in the Penn State sweatshirt had only been trying to save his mother, just as Taylor had tried—and failed—to save his own mother.

In that moment, he knew exactly what he had to do with the video.

"I'm going to show it to the world."

CHAPTER TWELVE

Gemma couldn't stomach watching the video again.

When Taylor pushed the button to replay it, she excused herself from the living room, slipped into the cabin's tiny bathroom, and closed the door behind her. Standing in front of the mirror, with her hands braced on the sink, Gemma hardly recognized the person staring back at her. The person in the mirror looked much older than her twenty-one years. The overhead fluorescents highlighted all of her flaws, from her weary eyes, to her washed-out complexion, to her greasy hair. She wanted to break down in tears—it was the only thing that might make her feel better—but she was too tired to cry.

The audio on Taylor's phone wasn't great, and

it had captured little of what had been said on the field. They could easily hear anything the lieutenant said into the bullhorn, but between the distance and the wind, it was hard to hear the townspeople's responses.

But the audio didn't have to be perfect—the video spoke for itself.

Gemma splashed ice-cold water on her face, trying to rinse away the image of the dying kid. And the old man.

She and Brie hadn't located Letty at the bookstore. They hadn't expected to find the old woman holed up in her store, not after they saw the rest of the town. They could only assume that Letty was at the school with everyone else. Still, Gemma wished Taylor would've seen her on the football field. She hated not knowing if something terrible had happened to Letty. What if they had already hauled her off to a detention center and someone like Carver was interrogating her right now? The thought made both Gemma and her weary-eyed reflection shudder. Even if Letty was still at the high school with everyone else, several others in the town, including poor Lizzie Fishman, knew that Letty held the key to the Sanctuary.

They wouldn't break easily. Letty had trusted these people for a reason. But how long would they stay quiet? How much abuse could they withstand?

There was also the matter of the girl. The one Gavin and Max had found at the store in Winter's Dam. At first, Gemma had been happy to discover that someone had escaped the clutches of the Task Force. But when Gavin had introduced Teresa to the group, his eyes had lingered on Gemma, as if trying to gauge her reaction. As if he'd brought this girl back to their cabin for the sole purpose of making Gemma jealous. Of making her *hurt* the way she'd made him hurt.

When their group watched the kid get gunned down in Taylor's cell phone video, Teresa had clamped a hand over her mouth and sobbed. "That's Jason Fishman!" she'd cried. "That's Clyde and Lizzie's son. He's only fourteen. And the older man is Marty Glick. He comes into the store all the time."

Gavin had put an arm around Teresa and guided her outside. And Gemma had felt a strange pang of jealousy watching them together. Not because she still had feelings for Gavin but because he'd found someone who was the polar opposite of Gemma, in every way: tall and thin and stunningly beautiful, with striking black hair and a natural confidence that Gemma could only hope to emulate.

In the bathroom mirror, Gemma watched the water trickle down her cheeks and drip into the sink. She dabbed her face with the stiff towel, took a deep breath, and opened the door.

The video was still playing in the living room—she could hear the crowd screaming. She honestly felt like she might throw up if she had to watch it again, so she turned right and exited the cabin via the front door.

An eighteen-wheeler tore by on the highway, startling her. It sounded so close, as if it could easily veer off the road and come barreling into the cabin, killing them all. The cabin felt isolated, but it really wasn't. They were only a few dozen yards from a major highway, with nothing but a rusted metal bar to hold the world back.

She was too close to the road. If someone drove by and looked close enough, they might see her. She approached the rear of the cabin but stopped when her eyes landed on the metal bridge.

Gavin and Teresa were facing each other on the bridge. Their lips were moving, but Gemma couldn't make out what they were saying over the sound of rushing water. Teresa wiped at her eyes and nodded. Then Gavin pointed at something in the water and made a weird gesture with his hands, and Teresa laughed—*really* laughed—an endearing sort of snort-cackle that carried to Gemma over the sound of the water. When Teresa's laughter died down and the sadness returned to her face,

Gavin put an arm around her shoulders and pulled her close, their heads touching as they gazed into the water.

Gemma turned away from the scene playing out on the bridge. It was too much.

Everything was too much.

†

After returning from the bridge with Gavin, Teresa set up shop in the kitchen, quietly digging through the boxes of non-perishable food items and pulling out cans of beans and diced tomatoes. While Max and Brie dozed on the couch, Gemma sat in the upholstered rocking chair and watched through the open window between the living room and the kitchen as Teresa pulled a half-empty bottle of Dawn dish detergent from beneath the sink. She filled the sink with soapy water, retrieved a large pot, several bowls, and a handful of spoons from the cupboards, and dropped everything in the water.

Taylor was outside with Yost trying to hook up the cabin's propane heater. They couldn't light the fireplace because the smoke would give them away. Plus, Taylor had noticed a lot of debris sticking out of the vents. He hadn't called them mouse nests in Brie's presence, but Gemma wasn't dumb. They were mouse nests. If they started a fire, they would either end up smoking themselves out of the cabin or burning the place to the ground. But if he and Yost could get the propane heater going, they might avoid another night of everyone shivering in their beds.

With nothing better to do, Gemma made her way into the kitchen where Teresa stood over the sink, rinsing soap suds off a bowl.

"Hey." Gemma picked a can of beans off the counter and examined it. It had expired two years earlier. "What are you making?"

Teresa stacked the pot in the old dish rack without looking at Gemma. "Vegetarian chili. I need to take my mind off things. I have very little to work with, but I found some old spices in the cabinet over the stove. Hopefully, it'll taste okay."

"Can I help?" Gemma gestured to the beans. She pulled open the nearest drawer and dug around until she found a rusty handheld can opener. "Should I open these and rinse them off for you?"

Teresa gave her a quick glance before returning her attention to the dishes in the sink. "I don't need any help." When Gemma didn't move from the doorway, Teresa looked over at her. "I prefer to be alone when I cook, if that's alright with you. I need to concentrate."

You need to concentrate on dumping beans and

tomatoes into a pot? Gemma wanted to ask. Instead, she placed the can opener on the counter and retreated into the living room, her tail between her legs. She plopped onto the rocking chair, silently stewing about Teresa's hostile takeover of the kitchen.

And Gemma's life.

Brie smirked at her from the couch where she was curled up with Max. "I don't know about you guys, but I *love* the new girl. She really fits in."

Max nodded. "Maybe even better than Gemma."

Gemma rolled her eyes. "Both of you, shut up."

A few minutes later, Gavin descended the stairs and passed through the living room without saying a word to any of them. Gemma watched through the window as he entered the kitchen, grabbed the can opener, and started cranking the cans open, one at a time.

She wanted to scream.

"What's for dinner?" Gavin asked, hopping up on the counter.

"Vegetarian chili," Teresa replied, smiling at him. "Pass those cans to me after you open them, will you?"

Gemma fought the urge to jump out of her seat and turn the rocking chair so she wouldn't have such a clear view of the kitchen. "I don't get it," she grumbled to Brie and Max. "Why isn't she making *him* leave?"

Brie shrugged. "I assume she likes him better than you."

This prompted a hearty laugh from Max, and Brie leaned over and gently kissed the crooked scar on his cheek.

A sharp intake of air drew Gemma's attention back to the window.

Gavin's thumb was in his mouth. "Stupid thing bit me."

Gemma briefly lost herself in a daydream where Gavin developed a serious case of lockjaw from the rusty can opener.

He wiped his thumb on his pants and got back to work on the can. "I don't get it. The owners could afford this big cabin, but they couldn't spring for an electric can opener?"

Teresa accepted the can from Gavin and drained the juice into the sink. "What's the matter?" she chided as she ran the beans under the water. "Is this too much exertion for your skinny little arms?"

He grabbed a can of tomatoes and cranked even faster. "Hardly. If I wasn't such a gentleman, I'd rip them open with my teeth."

"Oh, give me a break," Gemma muttered loud enough for both Gavin and Teresa to hear.

Teresa glanced behind her at the window, a hint of a smile playing at the corners of her lips. But if Gavin heard Gemma's outburst, he gave no sign, only continued with his unabashed flirting. "I hate to question the chef, but it's technically not even lunchtime yet," he said, glancing at his watch. "Isn't it a little early to be starting dinner?"

"Haven't you ever made chili?" Teresa said. "It needs to simmer for hours to be any good."

Gemma didn't know if that was true or not. She'd never made a pot of chili in her life. But Mia swore by letting things simmer for hours. Gemma had a feeling that Mia was going to adore Teresa. They would easily bond over their shared love of long-simmering foods.

"Yeah, but I don't want to smell that all afternoon and not be able to eat it," Gavin said. "Can we plan for an early dinner? No later than five?"

"As long as you keep opening those cans."

They didn't make it to five. At four o'clock, they converged on the kitchen and filled their bowls with heaping portions of a vegetarian chili that even Gemma had to admit looked and smelled amazing. She hadn't intended to take much chili since she was still salty that her offer to help had been rejected, but the smell got the better of her, and she filled her bowl to the brim and then followed the group to the dining table.

They bowed their heads as Max offered the prayer, thanking God for His protection in getting them all back safely from Winter's Dam and asking Him for guidance in what to do next.

Gemma peeked during the prayer and saw Yost's head bobbing up and down, a paper towel tucked into the collar of his shirt as a makeshift bib. She half-expected to hear him shout, "Yes, Lord," halfway through the prayer or to see him throw his hands in the air and shout "Hallelujah!"at the end. Yost was growing on her. He was so goofy and sincere that he almost made her forget his past as a Task Force soldier.

Before she closed her eyes again, she glanced at Taylor, who sat directly across from her. She always wished to see his head bowed in prayer, but it never was. Even though he'd been living at the Sanctuary for six months, Taylor still refused to pray. He sat with his hands folded in front of him, his eyes on the table.

"Dig in, everyone," Max said after he concluded the prayer. "Thanks for making dinner, Teresa. It smells fantastic."

"You're welcome. Thanks for letting me spend the night."

"No problem," Gavin replied. "Stay with us as long as you need."

"Hopefully, none of us will be here much

longer," Brie muttered. "Things aren't exactly gravy at the Sanctuary, but they're a lot better than this."

Gemma stirred her chili, the rising steam warming her cheeks. It was still cold inside the cabin, but the temperature was rising now that Taylor and Yost had gotten the propane heater going. The heater was on the first floor. There was no heat source on the second floor, but they didn't need one up there. The second floor was already nice and toasty, thanks to the rising hot air. "Thanks for the heat, guys." She blew on her chili, eyeing Taylor and Yost. "I'm looking forward to a better night of sleep."

"Yeah, I'm not so sure about that." Yost shoveled another spoonful into his mouth. "You think these beans are a good idea, with the tight quarters and all? I don't know about the rest of you, but any time I eat beans, it's like someone set off an IED in my digestive tract."

Brie covered her mouth, probably to stop herself from spitting her chili onto the table. "I'm going to pretend I didn't hear that."

"What? It's the truth." Yost finished his first bowl and disappeared into the kitchen. He returned a minute later with another heaping portion. "Nolan can tell you. It happened once in his apartment." He paused, seeming to reconsider.

"Well, *most* of it happened there. A little also happened at the gas station down the street."

Taylor gawked at Yost, a spoonful of chili hovering halfway between his mouth and the bowl. "What are you *talking* about?"

"You know, man. Rutter's on the corner of Second and Market?" Yost dropped his spoon into his bowl. "How could you forget double-stuffed bean burrito night at Murray's Bar?"

Now, it was Gemma's turn to clamp a hand over her mouth. The sincerity in Yost's voice was her undoing. He sounded as if he couldn't believe that Taylor had forgotten this night, a night that obviously held some significance for him. The table erupted in laughter. Gemma laughed until tears rolled down her cheeks. Tears! She could cry again. As she dabbed her eyes with a paper towel, she glimpsed Gavin at the end of the table.

He was laughing, too. Great, body-shaking laughs.

Somehow, Taylor maintained a straight face—but just barely. "Don't believe anything this idiot says. I would never attend a double-stuffed burrito night with him. And even if I would, do you really think I'd be stupid enough to bring him back to my apartment so he could blow up my bathroom?"

"I couldn't make it to Rutter's!" Yost bellowed,

slamming a fist on the table, but he was laughing, too.

Everyone was…except for Teresa.

Gemma had almost forgotten about the girl who sat wedged between Gavin and Brie at the opposite end of the table. But now she could see that Teresa wasn't laughing *or* eating. Her bowl of chili was untouched. She'd been lighthearted earlier, flirting with Gavin in the kitchen, but something had changed in the last few minutes. Cooking and flirting had provided a much-needed distraction, but now she looked stricken, as if she was only moments away from bursting into tears.

The others noticed Teresa's expression, and the laughter died down.

When no one said anything, Gemma cleared her throat. "I'm sorry, Teresa. We weren't thinking. Are you doing okay?"

Teresa picked up her spoon and stirred her chili, but she didn't take a bite. When she spoke, her eyes never left the bowl. "You guys have a plan, right? Some way to get my dad and the others out of there?"

The question hung in the air. Everyone stopped eating and stared at one another, except for Yost, who continued to scoop food into his mouth as if nothing had changed.

Finally, Taylor pushed his half-eaten bowl of

chili away. "You remember how they talked about HVTs in the video? About putting Lizzie Fishman in the basement with the other HVTs?"

Gemma nodded. "Yes. But what are HVTs?"

"High-value targets. Military-speak for important people with information. The Task Force must know that Lizzie and Clyde Fishman have been helping a group of subversives. That's why they're being held separately from the rest of the town. I assume Letty's in the basement, too, since I didn't see her on the field."

Max brought his fingers up to touch his scar, something he did often, probably without realizing it. "Does that mean they're being interrogated right now?"

"Probably not yet," Taylor replied. "They're probably giving the prisoners a day or two. Trying to break them down in the hopes they might start talking."

Teresa's eyes widened. "Trying to break them down? What does that mean?"

"They might take away their clothes. Or deny them sleep or food."

Brie shoved her chair away from the table. "You talk so casually about this stuff, like it's just business as usual," she said, rising to her feet. "Taking people's clothes away. Starving them. How could you ever be a part of something like that?"

Gemma leapt to Taylor's defense. "Brie, he's not a part of it anymore, remember? He's on our side. He's helping us now."

"But he *was* a part of it. Those cretins in the government wouldn't have been able to create a Task Force if no one had signed their name on the dotted line."

Taylor nodded. "Good point. Thanks for sharing."

"And you're so freaking *smug* about it," Brie seethed. "That's what bothers me the most. You still see nothing wrong with the Task Force, do you? The only reason you're on our side is because of Gemma. If it weren't for your girlfriend, you'd still be putting us in cages."

"Actually, your *fiancé* would still be in a cage if it wasn't for me." The even pitch of Taylor's voice made Gemma think of the ocean, of the dangerous vortex lurking just below its calm surface. "A thank you would be nice."

"You want me to *thank you?*" Brie spat the words at him. "Go back to where you belong, Nolan. It's only a matter of time before you leave, anyway. With or without Gemma, you don't belong here. You're not one of us." She gave her chair a hard shove, and it slammed into the table. "And for the record, I don't regret shooting you. I regret missing my target." With that, she exited the cabin's rear door, slamming it shut behind her.

Max glanced at Taylor, an unspoken apology in his eyes, and then went after Brie.

In the silence that followed, Gemma replayed Brie's words in her mind. Much of what Brie had said was true. Taylor didn't belong at the Sanctuary. He proved that every time he refused to bow his head in prayer. Every time he skipped a church service. Every time he stuck up for the Task Force and defended the evils they perpetrated.

He was only there for Gemma.

Yost tilted his bowl to slurp down the last of his chili and then placed the empty bowl on the table. "I know she shot you," he said to Taylor, dabbing his lips with a napkin, "but I like her. She's got moxie."

Taylor shook his head, clearly not amused. "Shut up, man."

Determined to bring the conversation back on track, Gemma said, "Look, forget about Brie. Honestly, I don't care what she thinks about Taylor or our relationship. It's none of her business. We still need to figure out how we're going to get Letty and the others out of there." She turned to Taylor. "What options do we have?"

He shrugged. "Few. The school is heavily guarded. We believe the important prisoners—the high-value targets—are being held in the basement. But we have no way of knowing how many are down there or how many soldiers are guarding them. Even if we knew those exact numbers, we have no way of getting them out of the school without being spotted." He uttered a humorless laugh. "Short of tunneling underneath the school like Bugs Bunny, popping up inside the basement and sneaking the prisoners out through the tunnel, there's not much we can do."

Gemma tilted her head to the side. "But there has to be something, right? What if we create a diversion of some sort? Something to get the soldiers inside of the school to come outside?"

"Like what? And even if we could do something like that, it wouldn't work. You'd still have to sneak into the school *and* sneak a bunch of prisoners out. There's just no way to do that without being spotted—"

"I know a way."

All three of them turned to Teresa. The sadness had vanished from her face.

Now she looked excited.

Gavin spoke first. "What is it?"

"There's an old tunnel system," she replied. "I only thought of it when Taylor mentioned tunneling underneath the school. When I was growing up, the older kids talked about the tunnels beneath the school, but I always assumed it was just some urban legend—until one of my cousins showed me how to find them."

"Where exactly is this tunnel?" Taylor leaned forward, his eyes sparkling with interest. "How do we access it?"

"It's in the elementary school basement. Getting into the elementary school is easy since it's an older building. The door into the gymnasium doesn't lock correctly. Once you're inside, you just go to the basement, and there's a door near the boiler. That's the entrance to the tunnel. There are steam pipes on both sides of the tunnel, so you have to be careful, but you can follow it all the way to the basement of the high school. My friends and I used to sneak in there all the time."

Yost's eyebrows knitted together in confusion. "Why would anyone want to sneak into their own high school?"

Teresa fumbled with her spoon, turning it over in her fingers. "Have you seen our town? There's not a lot to do around here."

"Fair enough."

"But there's a problem," she said. "The tunnel is really narrow. That's why we don't use it very often. It freaks everyone out. And the steam pipes running along the sides of the tunnel are *boiling* hot. People have gotten burned."

Taylor turned to Yost. "If we access the basement through this tunnel and we sneak Letty and the other HVTs out, we'll have eliminated the Task Force's reason for being in Winter's Dam."

Yost nodded his agreement. "The HVTs won't be able to go back to their homes for a while. Weeks. Maybe even a month or two, until the Task Force stops looking for them. We'll have to hide them somewhere. You guys got any extra room in this little sanctuary of yours?"

"We'll make room," Gavin said.

Gemma didn't want to give voice to the idea running through her head, as if doing so might cause it to become a reality. But it was something they needed to consider. "What if Letty isn't in the basement?"

They all looked at her.

"I didn't see her on the field," Taylor said. "She's got to be in the basement."

"But what if she isn't? What if you just missed her?"

Taylor considered this for a minute. "If she's not in the basement, that just means the Task Force hasn't realized that she's the key yet. After we remove the HVTs from the equation, hopefully they'll release Letty along with the rest of the town."

The others appeared to be satisfied with this

answer. They all rose and cleared their dishes from the table, leaving Gemma alone with her half-eaten bowl of chili growing cold in front of her.

She wanted to be like the rest of them. She wanted to believe that Taylor was right, but she couldn't stop replaying the cell phone video in her mind. The boy chasing after his mother. The bullet ripping through his torso. Him falling to the ground and clutching his chest as blood leaked through his fingers.

Taylor knew how the Task Force operated, but he still didn't realize the evil of which some of these soldiers were capable.

What if their rescue operation was successful but the Task Force *didn't* withdraw from the town? Instead of withdrawing, what if they punished the people on the football field? The ones their group couldn't rescue. What if they used the friends and family of the HVTs as bait to get them to turn themselves in?

What if, in their efforts to save Letty, they ended up getting her killed?

CHAPTER THIRTEEN

The group huddled around the table until late into the evening, working together to complete the details of the rescue operation. Despite Gemma's earlier reservations about Teresa, the girl continued to prove her worth. She'd scribbled rough maps of both the elementary and high school on separate pieces of paper, including all the details she remembered of the tunnel system and the layout of both basements.

When Brie and Max finally returned to the cabin, Gemma had expected them to slink upstairs without talking to anyone, but they surprised her by returning to their spots at the table. Brie's eyes met hers in a silent apology, and Gemma gave her a tired smile.

Taylor filled them in on the plan.

When he finished speaking, Max asked, "When?"

"The sooner, the better," Taylor replied. "That Task Force unit will not hold the high-value targets for very long. We've got another day. Two at the most. I say we hit them tomorrow night, just after sunset."

"Is night better than daybreak?" Gemma asked.

"We should do a recon of the elementary school first. We don't want to go in there blind. Yost and I will do the recon first thing in the morning. Everyone else can stay here and rest up for to-morrow night."

No one argued. No one wanted to go back to that town any sooner than necessary.

Gemma fiddled with the cuffs of her sweater, her mind cycling through all the things that could go wrong. There were so many variables, so many things they couldn't be certain about, with Letty's location being the biggest one. They also had to worry about the number of soldiers in the base-ment and when those soldiers changed shifts. In an ideal world, they would've watched the school for a few days to gather information, but time wasn't on their side. The soldiers could transfer the prison-ers. Once the transfer happened, the Sanctuary was over.

They couldn't wait. They had to act now.

After they finished hammering out the details, Max requested they pray as a group for the next day's mission. Taylor quietly excused himself and slipped upstairs while the rest of them joined hands and prayed.

Afterward, it felt as if someone had flipped a switch. People yawned. Eyelids grew heavy. Heads drooped. The adrenaline they'd all been running on for hours was finally wearing off, and exhaustion—both physical and mental—was setting in. The group trickled away, one by one, first to the bathroom to wash up and then upstairs to sleep. Teresa filled the sink with water for the dishes, but Gemma put a hand on her arm to stop her.

"In my world, the cook *never* cleans up. Let me handle these."

Teresa gave her a grateful smile. "Thank you." She pulled a toothbrush and toothpaste from her bag and headed for the bathroom.

Taylor joined Gemma at the sink, and together, they washed and dried the dishes. At some point, Yost sprinted through the kitchen and slammed the bathroom door. Moments later, a choral arrangement of groans and other revolting noises came from the other side of the door. Exhausted to the point of mania, Gemma's and Taylor's maturity sank to the level of third-graders, meeting each of Yost's agonized moans with gut-splitting laughter.

"I'm glad you guys find this so funny!" Yost shouted from behind the closed door, making them laugh harder. Twenty minutes later, he emerged red-faced and with a dire warning. "Give the bathroom a good half-hour to recover," he said, fiddling with his belt. "After that, send in one person at a time, but attach a rope to them so you can pull 'em out if necessary."

Then, he jogged upstairs, leaving Gemma and Taylor alone in the kitchen.

Gemma stretched her arms over her head. "We should go to bed."

Taylor leaned against the counter, folding and refolding the damp dishrag in his hands. He looked strange, as if he was nervous about something—probably tomorrow's mission. Although, he hadn't sounded nervous when they'd been discussing it at the table. He'd sounded excited. "We can't," he said. "The bathroom is out of commission."

Gemma yawned. "It's fine. I'll hold my breath."

Taylor dropped the wet dishrag on the counter. "Hang on a second." He crept up the stairs, leaving Gemma alone in the kitchen's doorway.

When he came back downstairs, he looked even more nervous. Most of the color had left his face, and he avoided looking at her.

"What's wrong?" she asked, concerned.

"I told Yost we'll be back in a little while. Everyone else is already asleep."

She didn't want to go anywhere. She wanted to sleep, especially considering the day that laid ahead of them tomorrow. But there was an urgency in Taylor's voice that she couldn't ignore. "Okay," she sighed. "Where are we going?"

Taylor handed her a jacket.

"A ride," he said. "I want to show you something."

✝

Ten minutes later, Gemma stood on the beach of Halfway Lake, her bare feet sinking into the cold sand. Her toes were already going numb, but she barely noticed. In the moonlight, the sand looked almost white. The breeze lifted her hair from her shoulders and tossed it around. She zipped up her jacket to ward off the chill and continued toward the water's edge.

At night, the surface of the lake was as black and glassy as the coal at the Station. The full moon hung low on the horizon, and the water reflected the cloudless sky above, the infinite canopy of stars. Gemma's eyes flitted between the real sky and its doppelganger in the water, and she wondered what it would be like to step into that upside-down world.

Was life different in the upside-down world? Was it better?

She closed her eyes and imagined herself slipping beneath the black surface of the water and emerging on a beach identical to this one. In the upside-down world, she wouldn't have to hide because of her faith. There would be no Task Force. No closed and crumbling churches. No detention centers. No orphaned children. No dead teenagers.

Of course, she'd still be in love with Taylor Nolan.

Some things would never change, no matter what world she inhabited.

"Gemma."

She turned away from the water. Taylor stood a few feet behind her, his hands shoved into the pockets of his cargo jacket, the moonlight illuminating him like a spotlight. He'd hung back while Gemma strolled closer to the water, allowing her time to take everything in. Unlike Gemma, he hadn't stripped off his boots before walking onto the beach. One bootlace trailed behind him in the sand, untied.

He still looked nervous. Maybe he was regretting bringing her to the beach. They could see the highway from where they stood, which meant that any vehicles passing by might see them. What if a Task Force vehicle passed by and noticed them? What if the State Police patrolled this park?

"What's wrong?" Gemma felt her own pulse speed up. Her stomach muscles tightened with fear. "Was this a bad idea?"

He shook his head. "It's not that."

"Because we can leave—"

"Gemma." Taylor pulled a hand from his pocket and raked his fingers through his disheveled hair, giving Gemma another glimpse of the number tattooed on the inside of his wrist. "I brought you here for a reason—"

The sound of a car's engine drew both of their attention to the highway. Gemma shrank against Taylor, and he clutched her against his chest. Headlights speared the darkness, sweeping across the far end of the lake. The vehicle—a small pickup truck—drove slowly past the lake.

Gemma resisted the urge to run for the safety of the woods. Any movement might draw the driver's attention to the beach.

"Taylor?"

"It's okay. He's not slowing down. He didn't see us."

A few seconds later, the truck vanished around a bend in the road.

Gemma exhaled and tilted her head against

Taylor's chest. "We shouldn't be here," she whispered. "We should go."

But Taylor didn't move.

"Taylor?"

He released her and stepped back, putting a little distance between them. "Can you pretend things are normal?" he asked. "Just for one night. Pretend we don't have to be careful. Pretend we aren't going back to Winter's Dam tomorrow. Just pretend that we're two normal people, and this is a normal night. Can you do that?"

She cast another nervous glance at the highway, but the truck was long gone. "Sure," she said, giving him a tight smile. "Normal night, normal people. Got it."

Taylor took her hands and pulled her toward the water's edge. The sand beneath her feet went from dry and powdery to damp and clumpy. "I wanted this to be perfect for you, but then I realized I can't give you perfect. I can't give you the life you deserve, Gemma. I can't give you anything."

She released his hands and went up on her tiptoes to kiss him, her hands cupping his cheeks. They felt much warmer than hers. "You don't know how much you've given me, Taylor Nolan," she said. "I've been in love with you my entire life. You've made all of my dreams come true just by loving me back."

Gemma waited for him to wrap his arms around her, but he didn't. His body felt stiff against hers. Unyielding. She pulled away from him. "We should go," she said, trying not to sound as hurt as she felt. "The others might get worried."

Taylor nodded, and then he glanced down at his boots. "Hang on. I have to tie my shoelace." He crouched in front of her, tugged the dangling lace out of the sand, and brushed the sand off of it.

Gemma couldn't wait to get back to the cabin. Her feet were getting cold, and Taylor was acting really strange. They both probably just needed a good night's sleep. She returned her attention to the road. There were no headlights. The road was silent and dark, but it wouldn't stay that way for long. And Taylor was still kneeling in the sand, messing with his laces.

She reached for his shoulder. "Hurry. I want to—"

The sentence died on her lips.

Taylor held a ring in his right hand. A gold, twisted-cable band, topped with a pear-shaped emerald. The stone was small. It couldn't have been more than a carat, but it reflected the moonlight in a way the lake never could.

She looked from the ring to Taylor, trying to make sense of what she was seeing.

He wasn't tying his bootlaces.

"Are you proposing to me?" she whispered.

"It sure looks that way, doesn't it?"

Gemma wanted to draw this moment out forever. Gazing down at Taylor as he knelt before her on bended knee was her childhood fantasy come true. And it was so different from his hasty proposal in her parents' living room two years earlier. They were older now, and their love had matured into something much stronger, no longer fueled by the fiery emotions of adolescence, but by something much deeper. A bond that could never be severed.

"Oh, Taylor…" She brought a hand up to caress his cheek, her nose scrunching in faux disgust. "Please tell me my engagement ring hasn't been inside your dirty boot this whole night."

A smile dangled from the corner of his lips. "That's exactly where it's been. Are you going to wear it or not?"

Gemma shrugged. "That depends on how good your proposal is." She waved a hand in the air. "Go ahead. Get on with it."

He gave her a half-shrug. "That *was* my proposal."

"What?" She took a step away from him and put a hand on her chest. "Did I miss it? All I remember is you pulling a ring out of your boot and holding it out to me. Aren't you supposed to have a speech prepared? Not a single word left your mouth."

"I wish *fewer* words would leave your mouth." Despite her goading, Taylor still looked nervous, as if he believed she'd say no—which, of course, she wouldn't. "Gemma Alcott, if it's not too much trouble, will you put on this smelly engagment ring and marry me?"

When Gemma looked down at him, she saw the boy from the carnival. The one who'd always been pushing the dark hair out of his eyes. She remembered how he'd defended her against the carnie. How he'd abandoned his beautiful blonde demon girlfriend to walk her home.

She wished she could travel back in time to her front porch on the night Taylor had walked her home from the carnival. If she could, she would tell her starry-eyed, eleven-year-old self, "Don't worry. That boy is going to propose to you someday. Just wait for him to catch up to you. I promise, he's worth the wait."

Tears flowed down her cheeks. Dropping to her knees in the sand, she reached for his face and pulled him to her. Their foreheads touched, their lips inches away from each other.

"Of course I'll marry you," she whispered. "I should've married you the first time you asked."

Taylor's body sagged comically, his relief clear.

With their foreheads still touching, he took her hand and slid the ring onto her left ring finger. The ring fit perfectly, as if meant to be there. "I couldn't ask your father for permission." He glanced at her, his blue eyes searching her face. "So, I asked Oliver. He gave his blessing. I hope that's okay."

"That's okay," she assured him, although it hurt to realize that her father and mother wouldn't even know their only daughter was engaged. Would they ever know?

Not tonight, she scolded herself. *Don't think about that tonight.*

Pushing the thought from her mind, Gemma brought her lips to Taylor's. She wrapped her arms around his neck and kissed him deeply, both of them kneeling in the damp sand at the water's edge. The knees of her pants were wet, and her legs were freezing, but she didn't care. Taylor's body—and love—provided all the warmth she needed.

When they pulled apart, she gazed down at the ring. She had a feeling she'd be looking at the ring a lot over the next few days. It was beautiful. Nothing like the ring she'd always pictured for herself...but better. Because Taylor had picked it for her.

"Do you like it?" he asked.

"I love it," she whispered. "I love my smelly, beautiful ring."

Taylor touched the green stone. "I didn't think you'd care that it wasn't a diamond. Emeralds are rarer than diamonds. Plus, I thought the green would look nice with your hair. And I paid for it with my money," he added, as if it mattered. "I just wanted you to know that."

Before going to the Sanctuary, Taylor emptied the money from his checking and saving accounts, knowing that after the Task Force declared him AWOL, the government would freeze his bank accounts and all of his money would be lost. There had only been a few thousand dollars between the two accounts. Gemma had thought they'd burned through most of it buying gas and food, but apparently, Taylor had set some aside to buy her a ring.

"How?" she whispered. "I mean, where did you get it?"

"Letty got it for me after I described what I wanted. She found the perfect ring at a jewelry store in Harrisburg, and I picked it up yesterday on the supply run. I was going to propose to you after we left Letty's, but—"

"The Task Force shut down Winter's Dam," Gemma finished. She pushed his hair behind his ears. She didn't know what else to say, so she whispered, "Thank you so much."

"I wish the stone was bigger."

"Taylor, I love it. It's perfect."

They lay in the sand, alone in their mirror-world. He kissed her again, and his kiss was different this time. Deeper. More passionate. And she realized she was ready. She wanted to take it further. More than anything in the world.

Gemma pulled away from him long enough to shrug off her jacket and toss it onto the sand. She briefly met Taylor's eyes, eyebrows raised, and when he didn't offer any objections, she started to unbutton her flannel shirt.

"Gemma." Taylor grabbed her hands and shook his head. "Please don't do that."

"Why?"

His voice was firm. "You know why."

Gemma groaned. If she'd had a cupcake, she would've thrown it at him, just as she'd done that night at the Sweet Street Bakery. But Taylor was right. They had to stop before things went any further. She collapsed on top of him, rested her head on his chest, and distracted herself by staring at her engagement ring. Taylor kissed her forehead and pulled her into an embrace. She heard his heartbeat slowing down. Inside her own chest, her heart would be doing the same thing.

The moment was passing. Thank goodness.

"You know," she said, "we probably shouldn't have a long engagement."

"I agree," Taylor breathed into her hair. "A long

engagement isn't a good idea. Where engagements are concerned, my motto is, *'The shorter, the better.'*"

"So, how soon do you want to get hitched?"

"Real soon."

She smiled against his chest.

"Do you have plans for tomorrow?"

CHAPTER FOURTEEN

Colonel Carver led him straight to the roaches.

Mullen brought his rifle up and flicked on his night scope. The dark world blazed bright green. He squinted at the two-story cabin, searching for any signs of movement, but there weren't any. It was after midnight. The roaches were all tucked away in their beds.

They didn't know what was coming.

He never would've found them if not for the colonel. He hated sharing credit with anyone, but there was no way around that fact. Mullen relied on his instincts when tracking down roaches, and he was darn good at it. But the colonel had been helping him a lot lately, directing his path, telling him to go right instead of left. Whenever he received orders to search a new grid, he would ask Carver for guidance. He was practically *praying* to the guy.

Carver was Mullen's god.

Despite the chilly night air, there wasn't any smoke coming from the cabin's chimney. The roaches were either too smart to light a fire or too dumb to know how to start one. Mullen believed the latter. He'd been watching the cabin for hours, and he'd heard the clanging of pots and laughter as the roaches ate their dinner. They were acting as if they had nothing to worry about. As if the Big Bad Wolf couldn't possibly be lurking right outside their door, ready to huff and puff and blow their cabin down.

Digging into his rucksack, Mullen pulled out a can of Campbell's chicken noodle soup. He pulled the top off the can—it had one of those handy pop-and-pull lids—and brought it to his lips. He closed his eyes and slurped down the salty noodles.

He preferred his food cold.

When subversives went off the grid, they went many places. Some fled to the mountains. Others hid in their relatives' basements or attics. Mullen had even found groups of them squatting in vacant houses that were listed for sale. But most roaches didn't have the stomach to stay in hiding for long. They were too soft. Too accustomed to their cushy lives. Their televisions. Their phones. Their hot meals. The older ones needed medicine, and the younger ones needed diapers and milk. Even if they avoided capture, after a few months on the run, they usually gave up and renounced. The roaches' numbers were dwindling. Detentions were steadily declining while renunciations were skyrocketing.

Soon, there wouldn't be any roaches left to detain.

"Look at you," Carver spoke from somewhere behind Mullen, startling him. He didn't dare turn around to look, afraid he might see the colonel backlit by the moonlight, the hunting blade still protruding from his bloated belly. "Sitting outside like a dog, lapping up soup from a can, while the roaches are warm and toasty in their beds."

The colonel had been talking a lot the last few days. Way more than usual. It had to mean something, although Mullen didn't know what. He dropped the empty soup can and kicked leaves over it. "Sir, I was just going to—"

"What are you waiting for? The Second Coming? Are you hoping the Lord takes the roaches up to heaven so you can have the night off?"

If anyone else had spoken to him like that, Mullen would've throttled them. But this was Carver, and Carver had earned Mullen's respect.

"You know what I'm waiting for, sir. I can't go in there alone. That's violating protocol."

"Hogwash," Carver muttered, his ghost-voice thick with disgust.

Weird, Mullen thought. He'd never heard the colonel use that word in life. However, Mullen's own father had used it daily, usually as a retort to any opinions offered by Mullen or his mother. But Carver was in the afterlife now. Maybe death had changed him. Or maybe he'd been spending time with Mullen's old man, although Mullen couldn't imagine the two of them ending up in the same place.

Carver was a good man. Douglas Mullen was not.

"The others are coming, sir," Mullen said. "I called it in at twenty-three hundred. Shouldn't take them more than an hour to get here."

"Hogwash," Carver repeated. "You're screwing up again. Just like last time, when you tried to get fancy with that barn fire. Look what happened there. You don't want to be outsmarted by a bunch of roaches again, do you?"

"No, sir." Mullen hated thinking about the barn. Why did Carver always have to bring it up? "Give me an order, sir. What should I do?"

"We."

He lifted his head but did not turn around. "Sir?"

"What should *we* do? You aren't alone, son. Not as long as I'm still drawing breath."

"Roger that." Mullen didn't have the heart to remind the colonel that he hadn't drawn a breath since April. "What should *we* do, sir?"

"We burn it down, son," Carver said without hesitation. "We burn the whole thing down."

✝

Mullen hit them hard and fast, just like the colonel wanted.

He jimmied the cabin's door open easily enough, making far too much noise. But it didn't really matter. Even if the roaches were packing heat—which they usually weren't—his M-4 carbine was superior to any weapon they might have had.

Once inside, he did a quick sweep of the main level of the cabin. It was empty. Then, he inched his way up the staircase, keenly aware of Carver's presence behind him.

At the top of the stairs, he turned left at Carver's whispered direction and collided with someone in the darkness. Mullen triggered the flashlight attached to the stock of his M-4, illuminating a child's face. It was a girl, no older than five. She wore pink pajamas, a puffy coat, and fuzzy slippers.

Half-asleep, she blinked at the light, confusion clouding her eyes. "Bafroom?"

"Shut up," he hissed. "Little brat."

The girl's confusion morphed into fear, and she unleashed a scream that made Mullen's ears ring.

"Shut up!"

"Do something," Carver muttered. "She's compromising your mission."

Mullen knew what Carver meant. God help him, he knew what the colonel meant.

But it was too late.

Mullen shoved the girl to the floor and spun around in time to see a shirtless man tearing out of one bedroom. The flashlight blinded the guy who raised a hand to shield his eyes.

"Keely?" The man squinted at the light. "Who's there?"

A woman joined him in the doorway, her face wild with fear and confusion. "What's going on?"

Mullen lowered the flashlight from their faces and waited patiently, giving their eyes time to adjust. He could imagine how terrifying he must look in his dark uniform and his bulky vest. When the roaches realized what they were looking at, disbelief dawned in their eyes, and Mullen smiled. He couldn't help himself. Their lives, as they knew them, were over. The Task Force would send the parents to a detention center. Even if they wanted to, captured subversives could not renounce. Not until they completed the government's reintegration program, which took years. In the meantime, their daughter would be separated from them and sent to live with more suitable parents. Even if they were eventually released, regaining custody of her wouldn't be easy.

As their disbelief yielded to devastation, the woman wailed and fell to her knees. The man grabbed the doorframe for support. The brat said nothing, only wiped at her runny nose.

Mullen pointed the barrel of his rifle at the girl's head.

"What do you say we have ourselves a little campfire?"

†

Mullen forced them to watch their cabin burn. They knelt on the ground, their arms zip-tied behind their backs. He'd even zip-tied the little girl. They weren't crying anymore. They were all in shock.

He'd made a call to the fire department in case the blaze spread to the trees. It hadn't so far, but the fire whackers were on their way. They would probably beat the Task Force to the cabin. Detention teams were notoriously slow.

Mullen had considered leaving the family inside the cabin when he set it on fire. It would've made him feel a little better about screwing up at the barn. But there was no fat slob to pin this one on. He'd waited for Carver to voice an opinion on the topic, but when the colonel remained silent, Mullen had played it safe. No point in bringing any trouble down on himself.

His SRX 2200 squawked. He tugged the radio off his belt and raised it to his ear.

The voices on the radio weren't talking to him. He often listened in on other frequencies, mostly out of boredom. Being a scout was a lonely job—or it *used* to be, before Colonel Carver showed up to keep him company—and the voices on the radio provided a welcome distraction.

One higher-up was requesting a SITREP from Captain Haggerty's unit about the ongoing operation in Winter's Dam. The Task Force had raided the town to expose and eliminate a suspected network of sympathizers who were aiding a large group of subversives. The tip had supposedly come from the local minister who'd been among the first in town to renounce.

Mullen thought that was pretty funny.

What *wasn't* funny was that Haggerty was in charge of the whole operation. The incompetent broad had a knack for allowing simple sweep-and-clear operations to turn into multi-day sieges. He didn't know why the higher-ups hadn't demoted her yet. Probably worried about a lawsuit.

Tomorrow was Friday, the first day of Mullen's three-day weekend. He intended to spend most of the day asleep, but he was thinking about swinging through Winter's Dam on Saturday or Sunday, maybe talk to the guys he knew in Haggerty's unit, see what kind of trouble he could kick up. It wouldn't make him as happy as finding the girl from the mountain, but it would help.

A violent explosion rocked the night sky as the second-story windows of the cabin blew out, spraying the ground with shattered glass. The family barely reacted to the noise. The little girl had fallen asleep, her head in her mother's lap.

Flames stretched toward the sky like hell-bound arms reaching for heaven.

"Beautiful, isn't it, sir?" Mullen said to the colonel. "It went up so fast."

The woman glanced back at him, confused, before returning her attention to the dirt.

The colonel's voice filled his mind. "Don't pat yourself on the back yet, son. This was another failure. I would've left the roaches inside."

Mullen swallowed hard. He hated letting the colonel down. He could still shoot the family, execution-style, but that might get him in trouble with the higher-ups. Plus, he'd already reported the family to the detention team. They wouldn't be happy if they drove all the way out to the woods in the middle of the night for nothing.

"Sorry, sir."

No response.

Slowly, Mullen turned around, terrified of what he might see but curious enough to look. What horrible form would Carver take? The man had been intimidating enough in life. What would he look like in death? Would he still have the blade sticking out of his stomach as Mullen imagined? Or would he be bigger somehow? More powerful?

Had death made him indestructible?

But there was nothing behind him. Nothing but trees and shadows.

Mullen let out a shaky laugh.

Carver was gone.

CHAPTER FIFTEEN

Something wasn't right.

Gemma could sense it as soon as they pulled into the parking lot behind the reservoir. Her elation at Taylor's proposal the night before had faded, giving way to a gnawing sensation in the pit of her stomach, as if something small but mighty was trying to chew its way out of her. She'd been on edge for most of the day, but this was different. It was more than nerves. It felt like some kind of primitive warning system was going off in her mind, trying to alert her to imminent danger.

And she was ignoring it.

They'd driven both the Charger and the Tahoe to the reservoir since they would need the extra space to transport the HVTs back to the cabin. The plan was to spend another day or two at the cabin to ensure that the Task Force didn't follow them to the Sanctuary. That way, if the Task Force tried to retaliate by harming the remaining prisoners on the football field, their group would still be close enough to help.

But realistically, what would they be able to do against a company of heavily armed and well-trained Task Force soldiers?

Gemma had gotten engaged less than twenty-four hours earlier, but it felt as though a lifetime had passed. In the upside-down world, she would've already posted her engagement announcement on Instagram along with an artistic shot of her ring. The caption would've read something simple like, "I said yes!" with accompanying heart and champagne emojis. She would already be purchasing bridal magazines and calling friends to ask them to be her bridesmaids.

Instead, she was going to raid a Task Force stronghold to rescue a group of sympathizers.

With the sun descending behind them, they performed their last-minute equipment checks. Everyone was carrying either a Glock or an M9 pistol—except for Teresa, who had her father's revolver—and everyone had a role to play. Taylor, Yost, and Gavin were going to traverse the tunnel and break into the basement of the high school. Teresa and Gemma were going to stay in the elementary school basement to help any prisoners as they came out of the tunnel from the other side. Max and Brie were going to stand guard upstairs in the elementary school cafeteria where they could easily watch the high school and keep an eye out for any approaching soldiers.

Gemma crouched to tuck in her bootlaces. Her hands were shaking badly. When she stood, she saw Taylor and Yost talking at the trunk of the Charger. Both men were wearing their Task Force uniforms again. Taylor thought the basement guards wouldn't be as quick to shoot fellow soldiers who materialized out of thin air.

When Gemma stood, she noticed Max leaning against the door to the reservoir building, his face as pale as the sand at Halfway Lake. He did *not* look good. Not at all.

She walked up to him and put a hand on his arm. "Max?" She kept her voice low, not wanting to draw the attention of the others. "What is it? What's wrong?"

His eyes were wild. The eyes of a cornered animal.

Gemma had seen that look in Max's eyes before, after her group had rescued him from the two Task Force interrogators. They'd found Max curled up in the backseat of the SUV, half-naked, rail-thin, and bloody. Gemma hadn't been able to believe the damage done to his mind and body in only a week's time.

He grabbed her by the arms, his eyes drilling holes into hers. "We can't do this."

"Why not?" She tried to wiggle out of his vise-like grip. "Max. You're hurting me."

But he didn't loosen his grip.

Gemma's eyes flicked to Taylor, who was messing with his phone, oblivious to the situation. Gavin was still inside the Tahoe, and Yost had withdrawn to the woods, probably to go to the bathroom again.

Where was Brie?

Max noticed Gemma looking for help. He pulled her around to the other side of the building where they couldn't be seen and lowered his voice conspiratorially. "We can't do this, Gemma," he said. "I can't do this. I can't go down there."

"You don't have to do anything, Max. You're not even going into the school. Taylor and Yost are going into the tunnels."

"No!" He squeezed her arms harder and gritted his teeth. "The town. I can't go back down there. I got through it yesterday, so I thought I could do it today. But I can't."

Gemma tried to ignore the pain in her arms. She had to reason with Max. To bring him back from the brink. They needed him. "Max, you can do this. You're stronger than you think you are. And you're not alone this time. We're all in this to-gether, whatever happens."

Max shook his head, his dark curls snapping back and forth. "You don't even know what you're saying," he muttered, his eyes locked on Gemma's. "We're all in this together? What does that even mean? You don't know what it's like to be tortured, Gemma. You don't *know* what these people are ca-pable of."

"Max?" Brie appeared out of nowhere, her eyes wide with alarm. "What's wrong? Are you okay?"

Max whipped his head around to look at Brie, tendons straining in his neck. "You always ask me about my nightmares, and I never talk about them. Do you know why? Because, every night, I dream they capture you. Those same interrogators that hurt me… Every night, I watch them hurt you, re-peatedly. I watch them do horrible things to you. That's how they torture me." He shut his eyes tight, as if trying to unsee the terrible images that were burned into his mind. *"Why didn't you guys kill them when you had the chance?"*

"Hey!" Taylor came around the side of the reservoir with Gavin and Teresa following on his heels. When he saw Max holding Gemma against the building, Taylor lunged forward and grabbed Max's hands, trying to pry them from Gemma's arms. But Max refused to let go. "Get your hands off of her!"

Then, Gavin joined in, grabbing Max's other arm and wrenching his thumb backward—one of the self-defense tactics he'd shown Gemma back when they were a couple. Max howled in pain, and both of his hands fell away from Gemma's arms.

Gavin shoved him against the building. "What's your problem?"

"Stop!" Brie ran to Max and wrapped her arms around him. "What is it, baby? What's happening?"

Taylor examined Gemma's arms, lightly running his fingers over the angry red marks that would soon turn into bruises. "Are you okay?"

She wanted to cry her arms ached so badly, but she held back the tears. "I'm fine. He didn't hurt me."

A few feet away, Max dropped to the ground, his legs splayed out in front of him. Brie went down with him, her arms still wrapped around his shaking body. Tears streamed down his face. "I can't do this," he wept. "I'd rather die than go back there."

Gemma realized he wasn't talking about the town.

He was talking about his time in captivity.

"You're not going anywhere," Brie reassured

him. "We will not let that happen, okay? Never. Do you hear me?"

What had they been thinking, bringing Max along on a mission? He had all the symptoms of post-traumatic stress disorder: nightmares, paranoia, flashbacks. Yes, he'd been doing much better recently, but that was prior to sneaking into a town that was under siege by the Task Force.

Max wasn't fit to accompany them on this mission. He would have to stay behind. And since they couldn't very well leave him alone, that meant Brie would also have to stay behind.

Two down, Gemma thought. *Two down before we've even left the parking lot.*

"Well, this mission is off to a brilliant start," Gavin muttered.

Gemma stole a glimpse of her watch. It was already a quarter past six. They were losing daylight. She didn't want to be the one to say it, but she had no choice. "Max and Brie, you guys stay with the cars, okay? The rest of us are going into town."

Max raised his damp eyes to meet hers. "Huh?"

"It's better this way," Taylor interjected. "The fewer people we sneak into the town, the fewer people we have to sneak back out. Plus, if something goes wrong and we don't come back, you two can drive to the Sanctuary and tell the others to evacuate. If they capture us, it'll only be a matter of days—maybe not even that."

"What if we come back tomorrow?" Brie offered. "He'll be better tomorrow."

"He won't be any better tomorrow." Gemma knelt and took Max's warm hand in her cold one. "I'm sorry, Max, but we can't wait for you. Letty and the others are going to be transferred to the Task Force interrogators soon. Maybe as early as tomorrow morning. It has to be tonight. You *know* that, Max."

He stared at her, his unblinking eyes leaking tears. "I'm not a coward."

Gemma smiled at him. "A coward wouldn't have lasted a day in the hands of Task Force interrogators. Those monsters tortured you for a week, and you gave them nothing. You have nothing left to prove to us." She released Max's hand and pushed herself to her feet. "I'll take his place on the rescue team. You don't need three of us standing around, doing nothing. Teresa and Gavin can stay at the entrance, and I'll go with—"

"No, Gavin can do it," Taylor stated. "Gavin, you're part of the rescue team now. Teresa can be the lookout in the cafeteria, and Gemma will stay at the entrance to the tunnel."

"Got it," Teresa said.

Gavin nodded.

"But why can't I go with you?" Gemma demanded. "Give me one good reason."

Taylor walked back to the vehicles. "Because I want you at the entrance."

She could feel the others staring at her, waiting to see what she would do. They probably thought she was going to back down. The old Gemma certainly would have. But she wasn't that girl anymore. Ash Grove had changed her. Tilting her head back, she stared defiantly at the back of Taylor's head. "You can't stop me."

He stopped walking and turned to face her. She expected to see anger in his eyes, but there was no anger, only frustration. And maybe a little sadness. "You're right. I can't stop you." He unbuttoned his uniform jacket. "I just figured that since I gave up my career and personal convictions for you, maybe you would give me the respect of listening to me, just this once. If you want to go into that tunnel, Gemma, be my guest. But you're going without me." He tossed her his uniform jacket, which she tried to catch—and missed. Then, he crossed his arms over his chest and stared at her, waiting.

Her face burned with a combination of embarrassment and anger. The fingers of her right hand curled around her engagement ring. She twisted it, intending to rip it off and throw it at him.

He watched her, an angry glint in his eye, silently willing her to do it.

But she couldn't do it. With a sigh, she pushed the ring back into place.

Taylor was bluffing. All he cared about was protecting her. He would never let her go into the tunnel without him.

She was about to call him on his bluff when Gavin spoke her name for the first time in months.

"Gemma," he said, his voice soft. "I *really* don't want to say this, but…Taylor's right. We don't know what's going to be waiting for us when we get inside the high school. There could be a dozen soldiers on the other side of that door. I know you can handle yourself in a dangerous situation—I've seen it firsthand—but I think it's safer for everyone, including Letty, if I go."

She met Gavin's eyes and saw something like an apology there. After all this time, he didn't hate her. Not even with Taylor's ring on her finger. And she couldn't argue with his reasoning. Gavin had gone through months of police defensive tactics training while Gemma's self-defense moves left a lot to be desired. Gavin wasn't a soldier like Taylor and Yost, but he was a lot closer to one than she was.

Plus, she didn't want to put anyone in danger, especially Letty.

"Fine," she muttered, still angry but willing to

bend for the sake of safety. She retrieved Taylor's uniform jacket from the ground and tossed it back to him.

Of course he caught it.

Yost stumbled out of the woods a few minutes later. "Teresa, that nuclear chili of yours is still wreaking havoc on my digestive system. You've got a promising career ahead of you as a biological weapons specialist." Confusion clouded his features as he noticed Max and Brie slumped against the building, Taylor bare-armed and clutching his uniform jacket, and Gemma scowling at him. "Uh, did I miss something?"

They set out for Winter's Dam ten minutes later, leaving Brie and Max behind at the reservoir. The plan was to stick to the forest until they got close to the elementary school, which sat on the east side of the high school. An uncultivated field separated the school from the ridge. The tall weeds would provide excellent concealment as they snuck the prisoners into the woods.

Just before they reached the field, a twig snapped behind Gemma. She spun around, expecting to see a doe, or maybe a buck, like the one that had gotten away from her the other day.

But it was a soldier.

He stood high on the ridge, a roadmap of dark freckles beneath a shock of red hair. When her eyes met his, he threw his head back and unleashed a high-pitched, cackling laugh that only she could hear.

Swallowing back a scream, Gemma closed her eyes, counted to three, and opened them again.

Mullen was gone.

He wasn't hunting her. He'd probably forgotten about her months ago.

So, why did Gemma feel as if he was getting closer?

CHAPTER SIXTEEN

They entered the elementary school via the unlocked gymnasium door.

A windowless hallway linked the gym to the cafeteria, and Taylor led the group through the hallway in near-total darkness. They carried flashlights with them, but they had agreed not to use them on the main level of the elementary school in case the soldiers could see the light from the high school. They would only use them when they entered the tunnel.

Two double-doors at the end of the hallway opened into a cafeteria featuring a center aisle flanked by long tables with attached benches. Taylor held the door open while the others passed by. The whole school stank of reheated foods and disinfectant, but the stench was strongest in the cafeteria. There was nothing appetizing about it. He didn't remember his school ever smelling so badly, but maybe he'd just gotten used to it.

Beyond the cafeteria, a hallway on the right led to a grouping of classrooms. They continued forward, their destination a door up ahead on the right, just before the library. Taylor pushed the door open and motioned for Yost to lead the group down the dark stairway into the basement. Taylor brought up the rear of the procession, trying to catch Gemma's eye, but she still refused to look at him.

At least she hadn't thrown her engagement ring at him back at the reservoir. But she'd looked as if she wanted to.

She could be mad at him, if she wanted to. That was fine.

As long as she wasn't going into the tunnel with him.

They switched their flashlights on as they filed into the musty basement packed with boxes of moldy textbooks, outdated sports equipment, and bookshelves stacked with old yearbooks. Built into the wall on the opposite end of the room, the steel access door for the steam tunnel looked strangely out of place, like a portal to another dimension. Someone had painted the door white to match the surrounding wall, but the paint at the bottom-center of the door had chipped away, leaving behind an uneven pattern of dark rust that reminded Taylor of the Rorschach tests he'd taken during his application process for the Task Force. The access door had no lock of any kind, and Teresa said the high school side was also unlocked. At first, it had seemed strange that the school had employed no measures to keep curious students out of the tunnel, but after his morning recon, Taylor understood why the school hadn't bothered. He also understood why Teresa had only gone down there once.

The tunnel itself was enough of a deterrent.

Pulling the door open, he directed his flashlight into the darkness. Fluorescent lights hung in even intervals along the ceiling, but they couldn't risk turning them on. They had no way of knowing if those lights would be visible in the high school basement. A series of white steam pipes ran along both sides of the floor and the entire right wall, significantly narrowing the passageway. It was barely wide enough for someone to walk, single file, without their arms touching the pipes. According to Teresa, when the heat was on, those pipes were hot enough to sear your skin. She wasn't lying. During their morning recon, Taylor had sustained a minor burn on his right forearm.

He could feel the others behind him, their eyes

on his back, awaiting their orders. Somehow, in the course of a few days, he'd become their leader. Even Yost seemed to take his cues from Taylor now, even though they'd held the same rank in the Task Force. But Taylor had never wanted to be in charge of anything. He'd never wanted to lead anyone. He'd only ever wanted to be a soldier. A tiny cog in a gigantic machine.

He forced himself to make eye contact with Gavin. With Max out of commission, Gemma's ex-boyfriend had assumed a role on the rescue team. The only other option was Gemma, and Taylor would not let that happen.

But he would never fully trust the guy.

"The tunnel is cramped but passable," he said to Gavin, the only member of the rescue team who hadn't been on the morning recon. "But some of those pipes are hot. Moving the prisoners with no one suffering any first-degree burns is going to be tricky. The mission gets significantly more complicated if any prisoners are injured and unable to walk without help. But we'll cross that bridge if we come to it."

Gavin gave him a quick nod. "Got it."

He'd brought it up to prepare the others, but Taylor *really* didn't want to consider the possibility that any of the prisoners would need to be carried or that the Task Force might've already passed them off to an interrogation team, rendering the entire mission pointless. Both scenarios were equally likely. It was also likely that the Task Force would capture the rescue team. That was why Taylor had insisted on Gemma staying behind. It was also the reason he'd proposed to her last night. The practical side of him hadn't wanted to do it—not because he didn't want to marry her, but because it wasn't fair to her. What if something happened to him?

He couldn't go without first telling her how he felt.

Taylor cleared his throat. "Let's review this one more time. When we get to the other side, Yost and I are going to breach the door while Gavin stays behind in the tunnel. We will restrain the guards and remove their weapons and radios. After we neutralize any threats, I'll take up a security position at the base of the stairwell, and Yost will release the prisoners and lead them into the tunnel. Gavin, you're going to stay at the rear of the procession as straggler control. If anyone has trouble walking, you can assist them." He passed Gavin a length of rope he'd found at the cabin. "Leave this rope at the tunnel's entrance when you head back with the prisoners. After everyone is safely inside the tunnel, I'll use the rope to secure the door from the inside so no one can follow us."

Gavin tucked the rope into the back of his jeans. "Why are you giving it to me?"

"If anything goes wrong during the raid, you're going to seal the door so the Task Force can't follow you. Then, you're going to lead everyone back to the reservoir."

Taylor glanced at Gemma, noticed her stunned expression, and added, "Yost and I will find another way out. Give us thirty minutes. If we aren't back by then, head to the cabin. We'll catch up with you later."

Yost gripped Taylor's shoulder and squeezed. "My man sure loves his worst-case scenarios, doesn't he? Don't worry. We're going to hit these grunts so hard and fast their grandmas will feel the impact."

Taylor ignored Yost and turned to the girls. "Gemma, you're going to wait here by the tunnel. When the prisoners reach this end, get them moving toward the stairwell but don't leave the basement until we're all back."

Chewing on her lower lip, Gemma fixed him with an icy stare. "Fine."

He wanted to pull Gemma aside, to explain his reasoning to her, but he reminded himself to keep going. He couldn't worry about her right now.

"Teresa, you're going to stay in the cafeteria. The doors at the south end of the room should give you a decent view of the high school, but make sure no one sees you. If any soldiers come in this direction, yell down to notify Gemma, then you guys can sneak out through the gym. We'll meet up with you at the reservoir."

"Okay."

Teresa was a big concern for Taylor. He would've preferred to leave her behind at the reservoir with Max and Brie—or, better yet, at the cabin. Presumably, her father would be among the prisoners rescued. What if he couldn't walk and they had to leave him behind? Or what if the Task Force had already passed him off to one of the interrogation units? Would Teresa freak out and jeopardize their mission? He wished he could've removed her entirely from the equation, but her familiarity with the building and the prisoners might come in handy. So, he'd stationed her in the cafeteria, as far from the action as possible.

After the last-minute briefing, Teresa made her way upstairs while Gavin and Yost hovered outside the door to the tunnel, checking their weapons and flashlights one last time.

Gemma stood by herself, her arms wrapped around her waist, her cross necklace lying exposed on her chest. There was so much shared history there, with the two of them and that necklace. Taylor had a love-hate relationship with it. He hated that a piece of jewelry could put her in danger, but he loved pushing the chain aside to kiss the soft skin of her neck. She never wore the cross over her shirt, even at the Sanctuary—a force of habit, he assumed. But she pulled it out to clutch it whenever she was scared. He didn't even think she realized she was doing it.

Taylor approached her cautiously and took her left hand. "Can we talk for a minute?"

He pulled her away, out of sight of the others. She resisted at first, the emerald stone of her engagement ring jabbing into his fingers, but then her muscles relaxed, and she allowed herself to be led to the opposite end of the basement, near the stairwell.

He practiced his speech one more time in his head. He'd been working on this speech—a gentle but firm explanation of why she needed to stay behind—since they had left the reservoir. But when he turned to face Gemma, she surprised him by lunging forward and wrapping her arms around his shoulders.

"I'm scared," she whispered into his ear. "I have a terrible feeling about this."

He wrapped one arm around her waist and cupped the back of her head with his hand. "*You* have a terrible feeling about this? I'm the one who has to navigate a dark tunnel with your crazy ex-boyfriend."

"I'm not kidding, Taylor. You don't know what's waiting for you on the other side of that door. There could be four soldiers, or there could be forty. What happens if you're outnumbered? How are you going to get away? Aren't you worried?"

With no other choice, Taylor tried to channel his father. What would Joseph Nolan say? What meaningless words of encouragement would he offer? His father was a man who valued his relationship with the Lord more than he valued his own son. Taylor's mother had died of cancer on a Tuesday afternoon, and his father was so brainwashed by his faith that he'd been in the pulpit, preaching, the following Sunday. His beloved wife's death hadn't even warranted a week off to mourn. If watching the love of his life die a slow and agonizing death hadn't been enough to show Joseph Nolan that God didn't exist, Taylor thought nothing ever would.

Still, he knew what Gemma needed to hear. He knew what his father would say.

He took Gemma's face gently in his palms and spoke the same empty words his father would've used. "It all comes down to faith, Gemma. Your faith means everything to you, right? Otherwise, you wouldn't be here. But having faith is the simple part. Trust is a lot harder. That's where people stumble. That's why so many Christians renounced long before the Task Force ever showed up at their doors. They knew how to dress up in their Sunday best and parade their children around the church. But when God asked more of them, they had no trust, Gemma. But you do. I've seen it in action. You believe God is in control of what happens today, right?"

Tears sprang to Gemma's hazel eyes, and her head bobbed in his hands. "Yes."

He hated deceiving her with words that meant nothing to him, but he made himself continue. "We've got a good plan, Gemma. You guys prayed over this last night. You know I wouldn't be doing this if I didn't think it would work. But if you believe in God, you also have to trust in Him and believe that it's Him—not you or me—who's ultimately in control of what happens today. God already knows how this is going to end. The best thing you can do is to pray for us…hold the door open so we can see the light."

Nodding through her tears, she ran her fingers over the blood-red Task Force patch on his left shoulder. The intersecting swords with the soaring eagle. "I always hated this patch, Taylor," she said. "The way it looks like an upside-down cross. I understand why you have to wear it now, but I've always hated seeing an upside-down cross on your arm."

In that moment, Taylor knew what he had to do, what Gemma needed from him. He dropped her hand and tugged at the patch, digging his fingers into the tiny spaces between the stitches. One by one, the stitches gave way until, finally, the patch tore free from his sleeve. He felt a pang of guilt, but he pushed it aside and handed Gemma the patch. "I'm not one of them, Gemma. Not anymore."

She stared at the patch in disbelief, and then the corners of her lips slowly curved into a smile. She stuffed the patch into her pocket and whispered, "I love you so much, Taylor."

He lifted her hand and kissed her knuckles, and then he touched his lips to her engagement ring. Ripping that patch off his uniform had felt so final. He probably should've waited until after the mission to do it, but he also felt like it couldn't wait another second. "I love you, too."

Suddenly, he remembered his burner phone. He dug it out of his pocket and handed it to Gemma. "Here. Hang on to this for me. I put it on silent, but I don't want to risk it going off during the rescue."

"Okay." She tucked the phone inside her pocket without looking at it. "Taylor, I'm still so worried that—"

He pulled her close and kissed her to shut her up. A deep kiss. A kiss his pastor father never would have approved of. A kiss that lasted forever and left no room for argument. Eventually, when he couldn't justify kissing her any longer, not with Yost and Gavin on the other side of the room, waiting for him, he reluctantly pulled his lips away from hers. Her body drooped against his before she steadied herself, and he realized that his arms had been the only thing keeping her on her feet.

She whispered, "Please hurry back so you can marry me."

He smiled. "Roger that."

CHAPTER SEVENTEEN

The tunnel was hot. So hot Gavin couldn't breathe.

Wiping his damp forehead on his sleeve, he aimed his flashlight at the two dark figures ahead of him, cringing inwardly at the sight of those all-too-familiar black zip-ties poking out of their back pockets. Nolan led the way through the tunnel with Yost following close behind. Gavin brought up the rear of the procession like an afterthought. Sometimes, it was so quiet that he could only hear his own breathing echoing through the tunnel. But every so often, some distant piece of machinery kicked on, and steam rushed through the ducts overhead, rattling the tunnel and his nerves.

The cement beneath his boots sloped slightly

downward, which he knew from Nolan meant they were halfway through the tunnel. The other two were still within sight but steadily pulling away from him. Gavin increased his pace, mindful of the steam pipes stretched out along the concrete wall to his right. He didn't want to get burned, at least not any more than he already was.

Hold the rope. Shut the door if things go south.

It was insulting.

Gavin wasn't stupid. Nolan hadn't wanted him to come along on this mission. He'd wanted Max. It didn't matter that Max had post-traumatic stress disorder from being tortured by Nolan's Task Force buddies. The only reason Nolan had insisted on Gavin being on the rescue team was to keep Gemma out of the equation. On that point, at least, he and Nolan could agree.

The most important thing was keeping Gemma safe.

Yost glanced back at Gavin. "You okay back there?" His whispered voice echoed through the tunnel.

Gavin gave him the barest of nods, but even that seemed like too much.

Just like his role on this rescue team, back at the Sanctuary, Gavin was the third wheel. He was just *there*. Not important to anyone. Serving no real purpose aside from completing the menial tasks assigned to him. Expected to do his job and keep quiet. And, of course, stay out of Nolan's way.

Nolan got the glory—and the girl—and Gavin got nothing.

It hadn't always been that way. Gavin's life had been so different only six months earlier. Not perfect, by any means, but better in the ways that counted. Just like that song his grandmother used to sing to him after his mother committed suicide, "Count Your Blessings." At the Station, he'd been a leader, trusted to go on supply runs, growing in his faith each day, despite—or possibly because of— the adversity of his circumstances. He'd found a best friend in Kyle Hogue.

And he'd fallen in love with the girl of his dreams.

Now he had no blessings. At the Sanctuary, he was a follower, not a leader. No longer trusted with any important duties. Kyle had a wife and a baby to worry about now, and that left little time for Gavin. And the girl he loved was engaged to someone else.

And his faith... Well, he had very little of that anymore.

If his grandmother were still around, instead of rotting away in some detention center—or maybe she was already dead by now—she would lightly flick his ear and tell him to stop whining and to count his blessings. *It's not too late to find your purpose,* she'd say. *You just have to ask God to show you.*

But Gavin had done that before. After the Task Force detained his grandmother and Gavin went into hiding, he'd prayed and asked God to give him a purpose, a reason to keep going. And God had answered his prayer by giving him Gemma. His only job was to love her, make her happy, and keep her safe. And he'd tried to do it. He really had. Even after he'd realized something was holding her back from fully giving herself to him.

Not something.

Someone.

Before they entered the tunnel, Nolan had pulled Gemma aside. Gavin had heard them whispering, but he couldn't hear what they were saying. But then it got quiet, too quiet. When they finally walked back into view, they were holding hands and their faces were flushed.

The memory stabbed him like a knife in the chest.

He couldn't believe that his life had turned into *this.*

By the time they reached the metal door leading into the high school basement, they were all sweating and panting, not from exertion but from the smothering humidity of the tunnel. Taking slow, deliberate breaths didn't help. Gavin felt as if he was suffocating. It took every ounce of restraint he possessed not to push past Nolan and Yost and throw open the door.

Nolan turned to face them, sweat dripping from his brow onto his uniform. The guy looked like a soldier again. It wasn't just the uniform, either. It was the predatory look in his eyes. There was no fear there. No hesitation. Just a glimmer of excitement.

The excitement didn't surprise Gavin.

You can take the soldier out of the Task Force, but you can't take the Task Force out of the soldier.

Thankfully, Nolan gave no final rah-rah inspirational speech or words of encouragement. Raising his eyebrows, he looked at Yost first, and then at Gavin, silently asking them both, *Are you guys ready?* He stared at Gavin, waiting for some kind of acknowledgement, until Gavin gave him a hasty nod.

Nolan pulled his Glock from its holster and turned to the door.

Only then did Gavin realize that the Task Force patch on Nolan's left shoulder was missing.

A second later, the door swung open, and Nolan and Yost faded into the darkness.

CHAPTER EIGHTEEN

The two guards in the basement—a male and a female—huddled over a laptop, watching an old Jim Carrey movie. The one where the two idiots go on a cross-country road trip to Colorado to return a suitcase full of money to a redheaded lady.

Taylor liked that one.

The guards sat at neighboring chair-desks, facing away from the entrance to the tunnel. If they chose this moment to look behind them, they would see two unfamiliar soldiers standing in darkness twelve feet away, along with a civilian huddled in the entrance of a tunnel—a tunnel they probably hadn't realized was there. But they didn't turn around. Their attention was on the movie. The male snorted with laughter as Jim Carrey's character, Lloyd, proudly presented Jeff Daniels' character, Harry, with a motorized scooter for the last leg of their journey.

The presence of guards in the basement was a good sign. It meant the HVTs probably remained on site. But this was a poorly run operation, for sure. All entrances to the school should've been barricaded or guarded. There certainly should've been more guards in the basement. Captain Haggerty and her company were clearly nothing more than glorified babysitters.

Taylor slipped his pistol back into its holster and crept closer to Dumb and Dumber. He would not need the gun. Not with these two. Yost stayed behind him, mimicking his movements, like an extension of his own body.

Taylor focused on the male soldier, and Yost focused on the female.

They were seven paces away from the guards when Taylor caught movement out of the corner of his left eye. He rotated his head and saw four wire mesh lockers stretched along the left wall of the basement. The lockers were tall—at least seven feet high—but only about four feet wide. They didn't look new, which meant the school had probably been using them for storage prior to the Task Force's arrival.

Now, they were cages, each one secured with a

numbered padlock.

There were people in the cages.

As Harry and Lloyd made their way into Aspen to the tune of "Where I Find My Heaven" by the Gigolo Aunts, Taylor scanned the faces in the cages. He immediately recognized the distraught mother from the football field—Lizzie Fishman—in the first cage. Seated cross-legged on the floor, her head rested against the wall, the fleece jacket with her son's blood on it clutched against her chest.

In the next cage, an older woman was curled up on the floor, shivering but seemingly asleep. The pharmacist, maybe? What was her name? Tuttle? Taylor couldn't remember.

In the other cages, two men stood with their hands clutching the wire mesh, watching Taylor closely, probably trying to decide if he was a friend or foe. One man wore a red bandana over his head and bore a striking resemblance to Teresa. The last man—with the bald head and handlebar mustache —was easily recognizable from the *Re-Elect Mayor Fishman!* signs posted all over Winter's Dam.

Clyde Fishman.

Taylor scanned the cages again. There were only four prisoners. Not five.

Letty wasn't there.

He didn't have time to consider what Letty's absence might mean for their mission because, at that moment, the sleeping pharmacist bolted upright, as if awaking from a nightmare. Blinking rapidly, she scanned the basement as if searching for some invisible danger. Her eyes filled with dread when she saw Taylor and Yost, and a strangled cry escaped her lips. "Please! Please don't take us!"

One man shushed her, but it was too late.

The male private pivoted in his seat to look behind him, but he had turned the wrong way, trapping himself behind the metal bars of the chair-desk. Taylor put the kid in a chokehold and subdued him easily, releasing his grip on the kid's neck the second he stopped struggling. Lowering him back to his seat, Taylor dug two fingers into the guard's carotid artery, felt a strong pulse, and got to work. He cinched a set of zip-ties around the private's wrists then removed the guard's sidearm and slipped it onto his own belt. He also removed the guard's handheld radio and tossed it away. The guard regained consciousness as Taylor was placing a piece of duct tape over his mouth.

He looked at Taylor's uniform and rank, his eyes growing wide, but he did not fight.

With the male guard secure, Taylor glanced up and saw Yost holding the struggling female guard's arms against her sides. His free hand was over her mouth. However, Yost was nothing if not a gentleman, and he wasn't cutting off her air supply, only restraining her until he could get her into a cage.

"Stop fighting, please," Yost muttered as Taylor guided the disoriented male soldier toward the cages. "You two weren't paying attention, and now you've earned yourselves a time-out."

All the prisoners were on their feet now except for Lizzie Fishman. She remained on the floor, watching the scene unfolding in front of her with unfocused, lifeless eyes. But her husband, Clyde, was watching as Taylor dug the keys to the cages out of the male private's pocket. Like the locks, each key had a number, probably so the guards could easily remove the prisoners from their cages to escort them upstairs to the bathroom.

Clyde slipped his fingers through the wire mesh as Taylor unlocked his cage. "You're him, aren't you? The one Letty talks about?"

Taylor glared at the mayor and gave him a quick shake of the head.

No names.

"We're going to get you out of here." Taylor kept his voice low as he unlocked Clyde Fishman's cage. He wanted to ask the man about Letty. Was she still on the football field? Or had they already transferred her somewhere? But he couldn't say anything, not with the guards around. "Step out of there."

The mayor vacated his cage, and the soldier took his place.

When Taylor turned around, Yost was escorting the female toward the cage. A strip of duct tape covered her mouth, and her hands were zip-tied behind her back. She wasn't fighting him anymore, but she looked as if she wanted to stab him in the throat.

With both guards safely locked up in the mayor's cage, Taylor tossed Yost the keys. "I'm going to the stairwell. Signal me when everyone's inside."

"Copy that."

While Yost got to work unlocking the rest of the cages, Taylor pulled his Glock out of its holster and jogged over to the neon exit sign. The door was closed, so he peered through the vertical strip of tempered glass at the stairway beyond.

It was empty.

The stairs changed direction halfway up, and he couldn't see past the landing. If one of Haggerty's soldiers came around that turn, Taylor would only have a few seconds to get to the tunnel and seal the door behind him. An old mop rested against the wall near the exit. Since the door opened into the stairwell, Taylor picked up the mop and slid it through the handle, hoping the makeshift barricade would buy him an extra few seconds in the event of an unexpected guest.

Behind him, he could hear the prisoners filing into the tunnel. He heard Gavin warning them, "Watch the pipes. They're hot." One woman—probably Lizzie Fishman—was sobbing quietly, her pitiful cries working on Taylor's nerves. He wished her husband would quiet her down. There was a company of Task Force soldiers camped out just above their heads.

As Taylor watched the stairway, he couldn't stop thinking about Letty. It was probably a good thing that she wasn't among the prisoners in the basement. That meant the Task Force had yet to realize her importance. If everything went according to plan, the embarrassment of losing all of her high-value targets would be enough to send Haggerty back to the Gap, and the rest of the town—including Letty—would be released back to their homes.

The success or failure of this mission hinged on protecting a single person: Letty. She was the only one in Winter's Dam who knew the location of the Sanctuary. If they couldn't find her and the Task Force discovered that their highest value target was still among the prisoners, they would immediately transfer her to an interrogation unit. Captain Haggerty would probably deliver her there personally.

Letty would be gone forever, and so would the

Sanctuary.

A whistle came from the direction of the tunnel. Yost's signal. Everyone was inside, on their way back to the elementary school.

He backed away from the door...just as two sets of boots appeared on the landing.

Two Task Force soldiers.

And they were *moving*.

The shock of seeing the soldiers sent Taylor stumbling backward, away from the stairwell. A fraction of a second later, both soldiers hit the door. Hard. The mop bowed inward but didn't snap.

It wouldn't hold for long.

Taylor sprinted for the tunnel, his eyes passing over the two soldiers in the cage. One of them—the female—had something in her hand. A two-way radio! Why hadn't Yost taken her radio? The girl couldn't talk or even get it close to her mouth because her hands remained tied behind her back, but she was repeatedly pressing a button. Probably some kind of emergency alarm.

The exit door exploded inward. Shouting voices filled the room.

"What happened? Where are they?"

Taylor flung his body around the corner, out of sight of the cages, nearly losing his balance and wiping out on the turn.

He sprinted for the black mouth of the tunnel.

It was right there. He could see it. He was going to make it.

Gavin stood at the entrance. He'd stuffed his flashlight into the back of his jeans with the beam directed upward. The guy was practically glowing, like some kind of savior. He held the door open with one hand and the end of the rope in the other. The rest of the rope stretched taut over the pipe like an albino snake.

That was good. Gavin was ready. As soon as Taylor made it inside the tunnel, they could easily pull the door shut and tie it off before the soldiers reached—

Gavin's eyes darkened. His expression morphed from panicked to calm.

No. Not calm exactly, but relief.

The expression of a man who'd suddenly realized that the solution to all of his problems was *right in front of him*, staring him in the face.

The world slowed around him. The shouts of the soldiers faded away.

Taylor knew what was going to happen before it happened. He opened his mouth to yell for Yost, but it was already too late.

The door to the tunnel—his only hope of escape—slammed shut with a deafening clang.

CHAPTER NINETEEN

Gemma never allowed her eyes to stray from the tunnel.

It was eerie, staring into the darkness for so long. After a while, it felt like the darkness was staring back at her. Several times, she realized she was holding her breath, and she had to remind her lungs to breathe. The realization that her body's automatic functions weren't working properly frightened her, and she brought a hand to her chest and held it there briefly before dropping it with a sigh of relief.

At least her heart was still beating.

She talked to God the entire time, whispering prayers for the safety of the prisoners in the basement and for her friends in the tunnel. God didn't need to hear the same request a dozen times, of course. Once was good enough. But since prayer was all she could do for Taylor and the others, she would do it well.

Please, God. Bring them back. Bring them all back.

Overcome with nervous energy, Gemma bounced on the balls of her feet like a hyperactive child. It felt like the rescue team had been gone for hours, but it was probably only twenty minutes. She wished Teresa was in the basement with her so she would have someone to talk to. Someone to assure her that everything was going to be alright.

Finally, Gemma spotted a tiny pinprick of light in the darkness. Were her eyes playing tricks on her? But then, the tiny speck of light expanded into a glowing sphere, and relief washed over her like a wave. A flashlight! They were safe. They were coming back. The light bounced around the walls of the tunnel as its carrier jogged toward her.

Taylor.

Her heart sang his name as it always did. But it wouldn't be Taylor in the front. The plan was for Taylor to bring up the rear of the line. It would be Yost, then the prisoners, then Gavin, and then—finally—Taylor.

She couldn't wait to hug him—and Letty.

But when Yost jogged into view and Gemma got a good look at his face, her heart skipped a beat. Something was wrong. Never had she seen him so deflated. So utterly devoid of his usual good humor. He refused to look at her. Wouldn't even meet her eyes.

"What is it?" she demanded as he stepped out of the tunnel.

He ignored her and turned back to the tunnel. He directed his flashlight at the floor and called out in a half-whisper, half-shout, "Let's go! Almost there!"

Dark silhouettes shuffled toward the exit on uncertain legs. As they moved into the light, Gemma saw two women and two men, their clothes filthy, their hair drenched with sweat. Each of them spared Gemma the briefest of glances as they filed out of the tunnel. None of them seemed to be injured, thank God. She recognized Lizzie Fishman, the grieving mother on the cell phone video, but none of the others looked familiar.

Gemma grabbed Yost's wrist. "What about Letty? Wasn't she there?"

He twisted away from her. "I don't know who that is." Then, he strode to the other side of the room and—without warning—slammed his fist into the concrete wall.

Both female prisoners cried out, and Gemma slapped a hand over her mouth. She shuddered, imagining the pain he must be in. He'd probably just broken his hand.

"What?" Gemma cried. "What happened?"

A man in a red bandana stopped beside Gemma. His black hair and pale eyes reminded her of Teresa. "Letty wasn't with us," he said in a flat voice. "She was on the field—I saw her there myself—but they never brought her down into the basement with us, thank God."

The other man—Clyde Fishman—was holding his wife in his arms as she sobbed. He locked eyes with Gemma, the muscles in his face twitching in obvious anger. "Whoever ratted us out to the Task Force must not have known about Letty."

Gemma shook her head, unwilling to believe him. He must have been mistaken. Even if he was right, even if Letty hadn't been with the other prisoners, maybe they were holding her in another part of the basement. Maybe that was why Gavin and Taylor weren't back yet.

Gemma clung to this bit of hope with everything she had, unwilling to surrender it.

They could *not* leave Winter's Dam without Letty.

At the sound of running footsteps, Gemma peered inside the tunnel.

Finally.

Gavin was a few feet away, jogging toward the exit.

He was alone.

Gemma stepped into the tunnel, positioning her body in front of the exit. She went up on her tiptoes to see past Gavin, searching for another beam of light, far off. But there was nothing. No light. No sound except for the steady drone of the steam pipes.

Gavin tried to step around her, but she put an arm up to stop him. He glared at her, nostrils flared, his face a picture of angry defiance. But there was something else lurking in those familiar green eyes of his. An emotion he was working hard to hide from her. An emotion she recognized.

Guilt.

Guilt over not having rescued Letty? Or over something else?

"Where's Taylor?"

The muscles in Gavin's face contracted, his striking Roman features transforming into something hateful and ugly. "I had to seal the door."

"You...what?" His words made no sense to her. Seal the door? What did that even mean? An image of the white rope flashed through her mind, and she suddenly felt sick to her stomach. Gavin wasn't telling her he'd left Taylor behind, was he?

He couldn't be saying that. She'd heard him wrong.

But Gavin kept talking. He kept talking long after she wished he would stop.

"More soldiers broke into the basement. They were coming after us. They were coming toward the tunnel." He reached up to scratch the back of his neck, and Gemma saw an ugly-looking burn on the underside of his forearm. "I held the door open as long as I could. If I would've waited any longer, they would've gotten into the tunnel. I had no choice, Gemma. I had to seal the door."

She repeated the question, slower this time. "Gavin...where...is...Taylor?" Wanting a different answer. *Needing* a different answer.

"They got him. I heard them through the door. The Task Force got him—"

She grabbed Gavin's shirt and tried to slam him against one of the steam pipes, but he was too big for her. His body barely moved. No matter how hard she pushed, he felt as immovable as a tree. When she couldn't throw him into the pipes, she slapped him across the face, cursed at him, and slapped him again. *"What did you do?"* she shrieked. *"What did you do?"*

He didn't move. He allowed her to slap him.

Someone grabbed her arms and pulled her away from Gavin.

"Stop!" Yost shouted in her ear. "We can't help him! Not like this! The Task Force knows we're here, Gemma! If we don't get these people out of here now, we're all going down with him!"

She shoved him away. *"I don't care! I'm not leaving him behind!"*

The tunnel was right there, only a few feet in front of her.

She sprinted for the entrance.

Yost grabbed her jacket, tried to yank her backward, but she twisted her body, and the jacket slid off her shoulders.

She ran.

†

Running. Running. Endlessly running.

She couldn't see. Couldn't think. Couldn't breathe. It was a miracle she hadn't burned herself on any pipes yet. But she couldn't stop running. She could hear Yost behind her, shouting her name, gaining on her.

Her foot caught on something, and she fell onto her hands and knees. Her left hand landed in something squishy and wet.

Squishy, wet, and...furry.

Snatching her hand away, she bit her tongue to keep from screaming. She didn't know how close she was to the high school now. She couldn't scream. But what had she just put her hand in? She told herself to keep moving, don't worry about it, because she couldn't see anything without a flashlight. But it was all over her hand, the fuzzy wet-ness. All over her engagement ring. She needed to know what it was.

Wait…Taylor's phone! He'd given her the phone before he went into the tunnel. Using her clean hand, she pulled it out of her pocket, turned on the flashlight, and directed it at the dark lump on the left side of the tunnel.

A dead rat.

She recoiled, disgusted, and crawled away from the creature, but she'd forgotten about the steam pipes, and her shoulder pressed against one of them.

Her thin jacket offered little protection from the heat, and the pipe scorched the skin of her right shoulder. White-hot pain shot through every nerve ending in her body, its own unique and ter-rible agony. She'd burned herself a few times working at the Sweet Street Bakery, and the pain had been intense but nothing like this. Her entire body felt as if it were on fire. Her arms gave out, and she collapsed onto the concrete, her left pinky finger again sliding into the dead rat.

If Taylor really was gone—captured by the Task Force, as Gavin claimed—then Gemma wanted to stay in the tunnel. She wanted to ingest a bellyful of poison and find a dark, quiet place to lie down and wait to meet the same fate as the rat. Because without Taylor, there was no reason to keep going. No reason to keep fighting.

An AWOL soldier captured aiding the escape of known sympathizers would not fare well at the hands of the Task Force. If Taylor was lucky, they would imprison him for the rest of his life. But they could also execute him for treason.

Yost caught up with her, flashlight in hand, and she was still on the floor, arms wrapped around her knees.

"Gemma," his voice broke. "Please."

With that one word, Gemma realized how much pain Yost was in. He sounded close to tears himself. In different circumstances, she and Yost would've been enemies. For all she knew, he could've been the soldier who'd arrested her parents. But now they were strange comrades, mourning the same terrible loss, uncertain of how to move forward.

"We can't leave him," she whispered. "Taylor would never leave us. You know he wouldn't."

When Yost tried to speak again, he seemed unable to get the words out. He wiped at his eyes and cleared his throat. "He's already gone, Gemma. After Gavin told me what happened, I went back. I heard them through the door. The Task Force got him."

No. She wanted to wail. *No. No. No.*

"We can go back," he said. "The others left for the reservoir. It's just you and me now. We can do whatever we want."

She understood what Yost was saying. If she was going to sacrifice herself for Taylor, then he would do the same. If one of them was going down, the other would go down, too.

But Gemma knew that wasn't what Taylor would want. He wouldn't want them to risk their lives and their freedom when there was no hope of saving him. He would want Gemma to get to safety. To return to the Sanctuary. To take care of Sophia.

To continue forward...without him.

If she hadn't already been on the ground, the wave of grief she felt at that moment would've brought her to her knees.

Once again, her life had turned on a dime. Another person she loved, ripped away from her in an instant. No warning. No premonition. And she realized that every single moment of happiness—because of its fleeting nature—was a rare and precious gift from God, deserving of its own celebration. Last night, those few moments spent with Taylor on that isolated beach had been the happiest moments of her life. She'd thought it was the beginning of a new chapter, not the end of their story. How could she have known that her only chance at happiness would be snatched away less than twenty-four hours later?

Now, surrounded by darkness, with the remnants of some poor creature smeared all over her hand, she had to come to terms with the loss of the love of her life. Taylor was gone. He was *gone.* Probably forever.

She was nothing without him.

Just a frightened girl on the ground, covered in filth.

Finally, she allowed her eyes to rise to meet Yost's.

"Let's go home," she said.

Without a word, Yost extended a hand and pulled her to her feet. Then, he turned away and walked toward the elementary school.

Gemma tucked Taylor's phone inside her pocket and followed him.

CHAPTER TWENTY

Saturday morning dawned as cold and silent as a graveyard.

Sprawled on the cabin's musty couch, Gemma rolled over for what felt like the millionth time since she'd collapsed, sobbing, onto the couch at midnight. The only sign that it was morning came from the bit of light teasing its way through the kitchen window. Gemma silently cursed the sun for having the audacity to rise.

With four additional guests staying in the cabin, they'd adjusted the sleeping arrangements. Max and Brie had squeezed together in one of the twin beds, opening up the larger bed for Clyde and Lizzie Fishman. Yost's bed had gone to Teresa, and Gemma had willingly surrendered her bed to the pharmacist, Melinda Tuttle, despite the woman's insistence that she didn't mind sleeping on the floor. But Gemma couldn't imagine staying upstairs with the others. She couldn't imagine seeing another man sleeping in Taylor's bed, even if that man was Teresa's father.

Plus, she didn't want to be anywhere near Gavin.

Soon, the others would come downstairs, but she didn't want to face them. She didn't want to see them or talk to them. And she certainly didn't want to go back to the Sanctuary without Taylor.

She felt his absence like an amputated limb.

Lifting her head from the armrest, she checked on Yost. He'd held his post all night, good soldier that he was, sitting with his back against the cabin's door, his arms wrapped protectively around his body, his pistol on his lap. He was snoring softly, his head tilted backward.

What will they do to him? Gemma had whispered the question to Yost earlier, after the others had retreated upstairs to bed. She hadn't wanted to ask, but she'd needed to know.

He'd closed his eyes and thumped his head against the cabin's door. "It's treason. They can do anything they want."

The floor overhead creaked as someone left their bed.

Gemma pulled the wool blanket over her eyes.

If it were possible to remain on this couch and hibernate forever, she would do so in a heartbeat. She rubbed at her sore eyes. Her throat was scratchy, and she felt as if she was getting a cold. She didn't think she'd gotten any sleep at all last night, but parts of the night had gone by faster than others. From midnight until three a.m., every minute, every second had ticked by with a dreadful sort of patience, as if time itself had conspired to torture her. But she had no memory of the hours between four and six a.m., and she could only assume she must've drifted off during that time. The thought that she had slept made her queasy. How dare she? Taylor was out there somewhere. God only knew what was happening to him.

And she'd been *asleep*.

And then there was the matter of Letty. According to Todd Fallon, Teresa's father, he'd seen Letty on the football field with the others, and she'd been fine. Scared, but fine. To his knowledge, Haggerty's soldiers hadn't realized that Letty was also a sympathizer. All four prisoners believed there was a rat in the town, but no one knew who it was. At least the rat didn't seem to have knowledge of Letty. There was nothing left to do now but wait. Hopefully, the Task Force would pull out of Winter's Dam in the next day or two, and they would release the rest of the prisoners.

Someone was coming down the stairs.

Peeking out from beneath the blanket, Gemma saw the dark shape of someone passing behind the couch and hesitate in the kitchen doorway. Dim light drifted out of the kitchen, revealing Gavin's familiar features.

Of course it would be him.

He glanced back at the couch, as if sensing her thoughts, but Gemma receded under the blanket. She pulled her necklace out of her shirt and clutched it tightly, squeezing it until the metal cut into her palm. The pain felt good. It felt good to feel something other than devastation.

"Gemma?"

Go away. Go away. Go away.

She ignored his whispered voice. She couldn't stomach looking at Gavin right now, much less listening as he apologized for leaving Taylor behind. As a Christian, she had to forgive. If she couldn't forgive the sins of others, how could she expect God to forgive hers? She *knew* what she was supposed to do, but she couldn't bring herself to do it. Right now, she had nothing but hatred in her heart for Gavin. Over the last twelve sleepless hours, she'd come to terms with the fact that he wasn't the same guy she'd known back at the Station. That guy had been decent. Honorable. Kind.

That guy was gone.

She wasn't sure who Gavin was anymore.

Finally, his footsteps moved into the kitchen. The bathroom door closed quietly, and she breathed a sigh of relief. The others would be awake soon. Gavin wouldn't try to talk to her with other people around. She only had to avoid him until their group went back to the Sanctuary later today. Once they were all back there, she would retreat to her side of the camp, and he would retreat to his.

Only a few more hours.

A few more hours, and she would be home.

Without Taylor.

✝

"I'm driving Taylor's car."

Gemma spoke the words to no one in particular. Five people had gathered around the vehicles, preparing to head back to the Sanctuary: Gemma, Yost, the Fishmans, and Melinda Tuttle.

They all nodded their heads in agreement.

The others—Brie, Max, Gavin, Teresa, and Teresa's father—were still inside the cabin.

Gemma drummed her fingernails on the Charger's roof. "What's taking them so long?" she sniped. She had a headache, and it hurt to swallow.

She would ask Abram for a Tylenol when she got back. "If they don't hurry, we're leaving without them."

Yost shoved another box of leftover food into the trunk of his Tahoe and then came around to the front of the vehicle. He hadn't cracked a smile since the previous afternoon. "I agree. They've got five minutes, or they're walking."

When the others finally emerged from inside the cabin, they weren't carrying their backpacks. Max and Brie led the procession down the steps, their hands intertwined, and the sight sent a wave of grief crashing over Gemma's soul. It reminded her how, two nights earlier, Taylor's hand had enveloped hers across the space between their beds.

She should've crawled into bed with him, no matter what Gavin thought.

She should've let him hold her all night.

Gemma tore her eyes away from Brie and Max. "Where's your stuff? We need to get moving."

Brie glanced at Max. The normally unflappable punk-rock girl looked like she was going to throw up. "We're, uh...we're not going back." She sucked in a breath before continuing. "We're staying here."

"You're *what*?" Gemma's eyes searched Brie's and Max's faces for answers. "What are you talking about?"

Todd Fallon stepped forward. "I'm not leaving my store," he said in a gruff voice. "That's the bottom line. Besides my daughter, that business is the only thing I've got left in this world. Teresa and I are going back to our home. We'll lie low until the Task Force leaves."

Gemma couldn't believe what she was hearing. And she couldn't contain her anger, not after everything that had happened in the last twenty-four hours. "Are you kidding me? We risked our lives to rescue you!" she shouted. "Don't you realize that? We lost—" But she couldn't bring herself to speak his name. "They took one of our friends prisoner! Do you think he sacrificed himself so you two could have a vacation in the woods and then go right back to the town he helped you escape from?"

Todd Fallon's face turned as red as the bandana tied around his skull. "Like I said," he spoke through gritted teeth, "we'll keep a low profile until they leave. Teresa was there by herself for a few days, and the soldiers didn't find her."

"She was there by herself for *one day*. What happens if you go back to town and the Task Force is waiting for you at your home? They know you escaped! You don't think they'll be looking for you?"

"We will defend ourselves." His eyes narrowed into slits. "By any means necessary."

"You're an idiot." Gemma just blurted it out. She couldn't help herself. "So, your plan is to kill a bunch of government soldiers? And what happens when they keep coming? Are you just going to keep shooting them until you run out of ammo? And then what? What happens to your daughter when you're dead?"

Todd Fallon opened his mouth to respond, but Teresa grabbed her father's arm, and his mouth snapped shut. "This is something we have to do, Gemma." Teresa spoke in a gentle voice. "We don't expect you to understand."

"Good, because I don't understand." Something occurred to Gemma. "By the way, how are you planning on getting back to town?"

"We'll walk if we have to. It's not far. But we'd appreciate a ride."

A harsh bark of laughter escaped Gemma's lips. Todd Fallon was a lost cause and apparently so was his daughter. She turned her back on them both. "Can we just get going?" she said to the others. "Please?"

Gavin placed his hand on one of the porch support beams. "I'm not going back," he said. "You and I both know I don't belong there anymore. It was only a matter of time before I left, anyway. I'll stay in the cabin for as long as I can. When it's not safe anymore, I'll find somewhere else to go."

Gemma didn't know what to say. The idea of returning to the Sanctuary without Gavin didn't feel as good as she would've expected. Only a few hours earlier, during the darkest hours of the night, she'd been debating whether to ask the elders to kick Gavin out of the Sanctuary for what he'd done to Taylor. She hadn't been able to imagine seeing him every day, safe and well-fed, while Taylor was undoubtedly being starved and tortured.

But now that it was Gavin deciding to leave, the idea of losing him so soon after losing Taylor made her feel totally unmoored from every stabilizing force in her life, like a balloon drifting higher and higher into the atmosphere, where it would inevitably burst, sending its fragments plummeting to the earth. She hated Gavin for what he'd done to Taylor—there was no getting around that—but she didn't know who she was without him.

But she would not argue. If he wanted to stay behind, that was his choice. She turned to Brie and Max and steeled herself for more bad news. "I suppose you two are staying with him out of some twisted sense of loyalty?"

Brie dropped Max's hand and approached Gemma cautiously. "Max won't leave him, Gem," she said. "They've been friends since the beginning. And I can't leave Max."

Gemma couldn't hold it together anymore. Tears rolled down her cheeks. She'd barely slept all night, she felt sick, and her nerves were raw. And now she was losing two more friends. "You're making a huge mistake. It's not safe out here. You feel like it's safe since we've been away from the Sanctuary for a few days, but we've been lucky. It wasn't safe for us here before, and it's still not safe."

"You're probably right." Brie pulled Gemma against her chest and delivered the rest of her words in a whisper that only she could hear. "But Max and I prayed about it, and we both feel like God wants us to stay with him." She raked her fingers through Gemma's hair. "If this is what God wants us to do, then He'll protect us, won't He?"

Before yesterday, Gemma would've agreed wholeheartedly. But now? She didn't know what to think anymore. She knew that suffering was part of discipleship. Jesus had told his disciples that they would indeed drink from his cup. They'd taken it to mean Jesus would grant them a place of honor in His kingdom, but that wasn't what He'd meant. He'd known what was coming.

His disciples were going to suffer, just as He'd suffered.

"I hope so, Brie," she finally said through her tears. "I hope you're right."

As she drove away from the cabin, Gemma stared into the rearview mirror at Max, Brie, and Gavin. She couldn't believe that, only three days earlier, they—along with Taylor—had all left the Sanctuary as a team.

And Gemma was the only one returning.

CHAPTER TWENTY-ONE

Seated on Taylor's bunk in the cabin, Gemma dropped her spoon into a bowl of watery tomato soup and stirred the pale-red liquid around, trying to summon an appetite. But she couldn't bring herself to eat anything. Even the faint acidic scent of the soup made her queasy. She'd tried resting in the mostly empty cabin for an hour before dinner, hoping a little sleep would make her feel better, but she hadn't been able to sleep.

It was dinnertime, but she wasn't ready to face everyone in the dining hall. Addie and Sophia would be there, but she wasn't ready to see them yet. She'd successfully avoided them since returning to the Sanctuary because she didn't want to answer their barrage of questions about what had happened in Winter's Dam. She didn't know what to tell them because she didn't know what had really happened in that tunnel.

More than anything, she didn't want to tell Sophia that Taylor wasn't coming home because saying it out loud would make it too real.

Gemma was so thankful for Yost. He and the sympathizers had met with Abram, Oliver, Mia, and the other elders at the trading post earlier in the afternoon and filled them in on the details of the rescue operation. Given what had happened to Taylor, the leadership had been kind enough to give Gemma some space, but they wouldn't let her off the hook for long. They didn't know Yost or the sympathizers, and they would want her side of the story.

She brought the spoon to her lips again and made herself swallow a little of the soup. She had to eat something, or she was going to get sick. Sicker than she already was. When her body didn't reject the soup by sending it back up her throat, she tried another sip. That one stayed down, too.

She put the bowl of soup on the floor.

Good enough.

Gemma grabbed Taylor's pillow and held it against her chest. In her other hand, she held Sophia's flashlight—a cheap, purple plastic-covered one with heart-shaped stickers. Using her thumb, she flicked the light on and off, illuminating a black millipede on the floor like an actor on a stage. The presence or absence of light did not bother the insect as it scuffled across the floor. It continued forward, its many legs moving in unison toward a small gap where the cabin's wall failed to meet the floorboards. Gemma watched its steady advance, marveling at how easily this tiny creature disregarded its tenuous position in the world. It wasn't being cautious. It easily could've hidden until she left the cabin and then proceeded across the floor unnoticed. But it didn't concern itself with Gemma or her flashlight. It had a single-minded focus on progressing toward a goal, and its fear did not motivate its actions—or inactions.

If someone killed it before it reached its destination, it would ultimately have the last laugh. In death, it would give a last gift to its murderer.

Its terrible stench.

Gemma switched off the flashlight and placed it beside her on the bunk. Then, she pulled Taylor's burner phone out of her pocket. Her thumb hesitated over the Photos icon. She hadn't been able to bring herself to look at their engagement photo yet, but she was desperate to see Taylor's face again. She clicked on the icon, and the selfie they'd taken on the beach before returning to the cabin popped up right away.

It was the only photo they'd ever taken together.

The background of the image was almost entirely black, save for a single blot of white—the moon reflected on the lake's surface. In the foreground, Gemma was beaming at the camera. She held the phone in her right hand, her left hand raised to her chin, putting her new ring on full display for the camera, imitating the pose she'd seen from other newly engaged girls on social media over the years.

How stupid she'd been, living in her little fantasy world, posing for this photo as if anyone besides the two of them would ever see it.

Unlike Gemma, Taylor hadn't concerned himself with the camera. He hadn't posed for anyone's benefit. One of his hands lightly cupped her chin while his lips pressed against her cheek.

Gemma's hand shot to her mouth, holding in a cry.

Taylor's eyes were closed. She couldn't see his eyes.

She couldn't see most of his face.

Seeing him again—but not being able to *see him* —shattered her heart. This was all she had—this one picture—and it wasn't enough. Already, she couldn't remember exactly what color his eyes had been. Had they been the color of the morning sky, or had they been more gray than blue? Tears spilled from her eyes, but she didn't bother wiping them away because there was no point. More would only take their place.

She wanted to delete the picture so she wouldn't have to look at it ever again. This image from that beautiful night—a night which had held so much promise—was nothing more than a painful reminder of how quickly everything had been stolen from her. Her index finger hovered, trembling, over the trashcan-shaped icon. She could hardly see the icon through her tears. Finally, out of frustration, she swiped her finger across the screen, desperate to make the picture disappear but not quite ready to destroy it.

A video took its place.

The video of Clyde and Lizzie Fishman's son, Jason, and the grizzled veteran, Marty Glick. The two people who'd died on the football field, both of them murdered by the same Task Force soldier.

Back at the hunting cabin, watching the video had sickened her. She'd barely been able to stomach watching it once. Now, she played the entire thing. When it finished playing, she watched it again. The footage was a little shaky, especially right after the kid got shot, but it showed the whole terrible event from start to finish, leaving absolutely no question as to what had transpired on that field.

Gemma's eyes dropped to the floor, searching for the millipede. She caught only a brief glimpse of the creature before it disappeared inside the wall. Crossing directly in front of her like that had been a bold move—foolhardy, even—considering how many of his relatives she'd squashed with her boot over the past few months.

But he'd done it anyway.

He waited for the right moment—after she'd been dealt a heavy blow—and he went for it. And he made it.

Gemma stared at the cell phone for a long time. The video paused on the image of the dying boy.

And she knew what she had to do.

CHAPTER TWENTY-TWO

The highway unwound before Gemma like black ribbon unspooling, each foot of road carrying her closer to whatever fate awaited her.

Twin beams of light appeared in the distance, a vehicle approaching from the opposite direction. Gemma held her breath, certain that it would be the Task Force and that the driver would somehow know that she was a subversive. The Task Force could make traffic stops. They only needed reasonable suspicion that the vehicle's driver or its passengers were subversives, and they could easily get that from a busted taillight or a past-due inspection sticker.

Gemma squinted through the windshield at the vehicle.

It was a dark-gray sedan with a light bar on the top.

Not the Task Force.

A state trooper.

Her eyes darted to the speedometer. She was only going fifty-three, two miles under the posted speed limit, but she didn't know if the Charger's inspection and registration were up to date. Even if they were, she had no government ID card to give to the trooper.

Police didn't go around hunting subversives—that was the job of the Task Force—but the federal government required local law enforcement to support the Task Force's mission. According to Abram, many of his officer friends had lost their jobs for not immediately notifying the Task Force if they stopped vehicles whose drivers or passengers couldn't produce valid government ID cards. Now, most departments made sure their new hires fully supported the government's mission regarding subversives. Many were former Task Force soldiers themselves.

When the squad car passed by the Charger, traveling in the opposite direction, Gemma briefly locked eyes with the young trooper behind the wheel. He didn't smile or wave, only turned his head to examine her vehicle, looking for violations, probably. Would he find any? She didn't think that

Taylor would've been driving around in a vehicle that had any violations, but she had no way of knowing for sure.

In the rearview mirror, the trooper's brake lights flickered.

No. God, please. Please don't let him pull me over.

But the trooper didn't turn around. The brake lights went out. Maybe he got another call. Or maybe he'd tapped his brakes because he'd spotted an animal near the road. But the vehicle continued on its way, and Gemma breathed a sigh of relief.

Thank You, God.

She pressed the Scan button on the Charger's radio, searching for music to listen to. She needed a distraction, something to take her mind off what she was about to do. But when the numbers finally settled on a station, a single voice came through the speakers, loud and clear.

"...Elevation Ministries. I'm Pastor David Ogden, and I'd like to thank you for joining our Friday evening broadcast. As always, we're coming to you live from Harrisburg, Pennsylvania. I'm eager to share the message our loving creator has placed on my heart tonight. . ."

It was Saturday, not Friday, so the radio station must rebroadcast the live show from the night before. She reached for the Scan button. She'd watched Ogden's television broadcast a few times, and he'd always seemed so fake to her. Fake hair. Fake teeth. Even his skin looked fake, as if too much plastic surgery had stretched it to its limit. He looked like the Madame Tussaud's wax version of himself. The only thing phonier than his appearance were the words that came out of his mouth. She couldn't believe people were still listening to him.

She was about to shut him up by pressing the Scan button, but his words stopped her.

"... spent many years convincing people that Christ was the only way to heaven. I cringe now when I think about all the people I led astray. There are people being held in detention centers because they refuse to let go of the lies I told them. Good men and women who—to their own detriment—refuse to embrace the compassionate reeducation programs. Ladies and gentlemen, hear me clearly, as I speak the truth: Heaven is not off-limits to you. It's not off-limits to anyone! The gates of heaven are wide open, my friends! There is no need to suffer. No need to bear this burden any longer. If you're listening to this broadcast, and you're still in hiding, I'm here to tell you you that don't have to be afraid anymore. You don't have to be a subversive. You don't have to hide. Stop living in a prison of your own making. Renounce...and be free!"

The raucous sound of applause blared through the Charger's speakers. Hundreds of people shouting, *"Yes, Pastor!"* and *"Be free!"* Gemma could almost see Ogden standing on the stage, his arms spread wide, his signature grin widening with every clap. Every cheer.

Gemma couldn't say why she distrusted Ogden so much. Fearing prison, many former ministers had changed with the times, abandoning the Bible and Christianity in favor of new-age religions and the worship of self. They eased the fears of the former believers in their congregations by preaching sermons designed to massage their guilty consciences. But Ogden was different. Like other television evangelists before him, his power came in the form of a monstrous platform and millions of viewers. But he didn't strike Gemma as some charlatan out to shirk people out of their money. There had been plenty of those over the years—both before *and* after the government outlawed Christianity—and Gemma knew their type well.

But Ogden seemed like an entirely different animal.

And—she feared—a more *dangerous* animal.

The preacher's voice thundered over the speaker, silencing the applause before it could die a natural death. *"Listen to me, brothers and sisters. To those of you who have already renounced your old ways and to those who never allowed themselves to be misled in the first place, it is your job to be leaders in this new world. Welcome your friends and family back with open arms when they return to society. Walk with them. Encourage them. Whatever you do, do not hold their past sins against them. Do not! None of this is their fault. Their pastors have tricked them into believing the false premise that Christ is their ticket into heaven. Religious leaders have taught these lies for years. Folks, I'm asking you not to judge them but to embrace them. Forgive them. Help them find their way in this new world."*

On the left side of the road, the trees opened up, giving Gemma the perfect view of Halfway Lake. The white sand. The dark water. It was all so familiar, as if someone had magically transported her back in time to the night Taylor proposed. She searched the beach for him, hoping for a miracle, but he wasn't there.

"I miss you so much," she whispered, running her fingers down the cool glass of the driver's window. The beach dissolved into the trees, as if it had always been an illusion. "You wouldn't give up on me, and I will not give up on you."

Ogden's voice cut into her thoughts. *"Ladies and gentlemen, we're living in a time of significant change, but we are all in this together. We will make it through these trials, and we will emerge stronger as a nation. This isn't about destroying a nation—or a group of people. It's about creating a new nation. A nation of free people. People not saddled down by ancient laws and superstitions. But if we wish to move forward, we must remain unified. We must remain resolute in our mission. This is a revolution against the old ways, and revolutions take time. In extreme circumstances, they may even take violence..."*

Ogden's voice cut off mid-sentence as Gemma snapped off the radio.

A memory flashed in her mind, something she hadn't thought about in more than a decade. One Sunday morning, back when they were still worshipping together in their church, Taylor's father, Pastor Nolan, had warned his congregation that the government would soon come for the churches. They would arrest the ministers and leadership first, but eventually, they would come for the congregations. This would force churches to meet in secret, varying the dates and times of their services to avoid detection.

Of course, everything Pastor Nolan had predicted eventually came to pass—and much faster than he could've ever imagined. However, he hadn't known how quickly people would turn on their own neighbors. Their friends. Their family members. He hadn't realized that meeting in secret wouldn't work for long because people—regular people—would watch the houses in their neighborhoods with eagle eyes, looking for any activity that could be suspicious. Too many cars in the driveway at one time. The same cars showing up at different times each week. The Task Force wouldn't have to hunt people down—at least not at first. They would only need to respond to phone calls from "concerned citizens."

On the ride home from church that Sunday, Gemma had told her parents, with all the false bravado of a nine-year-old, "You know what? If the bad guys come for me, they'll never get me to say I don't believe in Jesus. They'll have to kill me first."

She'd expected her parents to be proud of this declaration, but they stayed silent for a long time. Her mother sat in the front passenger seat, her head tilted toward the window. Gemma had watched her reflection in the glass as she dabbed her eyes with a crumpled tissue.

Finally, Gemma's father had reached into the backseat and patted her knee. "I believe you, sweetheart. You've always been a little spitfire. I bet you'll give those bad guys a run for their money."

Those words ran through Gemma's head as the turnoff appeared on the left side of the road just ahead. The winding road that would take her back to the reservoir.

"I bet you'll give those bad guys a run for their money."

She glanced at Taylor's phone, laying beside her

on the passenger seat. Besides his ring, it was the only thing she had left of him now. And she intended to use it.

"You're right, Dad," she said. "That's exactly what I'm going to do."

Gemma climbed the steps to Letty's front porch, the cell phone clutched in her hand.

From the outside, the bookstore looked vacant. An empty shell, like a corpse. Familiar in appearance but devoid of the spirit that once animated it. Letty's porch swing hung motionless in the calm night air, and next to the swing, a paperback romance novel laid open on a mushroom-colored plastic stacking table.

Nothing had changed since Thursday when Brie and Gemma had searched the store for Letty.

Letty's store just felt like the right place to do what she had to do next. She couldn't go to the elementary school. Not after yesterday. The Task Force would have posted guards there and probably in every other building near the high school. Letty's store was on the other end of town, which seemed safer to Gemma.

Besides, she didn't need to *see* the high school to do what she was about to do.

She was only making a phone call.

The front door to the bookstore was still unlocked, as it had been two days earlier, and Gemma pushed it open, stepping into the familiar scent of paperback books and vanilla-scented soy candles. She locked the door behind her and dropped her backpack on the floor. Then, she proceeded down the aisle. The heat was on, and the interior of the store was warm. Much warmer than the hunting cabin had been. Letty's favorite coffee mug—*It's Not Hoarding if it's Books*—sat on one of the reading tables, a half-inch of congealed coffee in the bottom. A smattering of Lotus Biscoff cookie crumbs littered the table.

Gemma's legs buckled a little at the sight of those crumbs, and she grabbed a chair to steady herself. Only three days earlier, she had visited the store with Taylor to pick up supplies, and—unbeknownst to Gemma at the time—an engagement ring. She had sipped coffee and chatted with Letty while Taylor loaded the supplies into the Charger. So much had changed in the course of a few days.

She peered at the hallway leading to Letty's office and allowed herself a single fantasy. In it, Taylor stepped out of the darkness and walked toward her, a victor's smile on his lips. He would explain how he'd escaped from the Task Force and made his way to the bookstore because he knew it was safe. And he also knew that the bookstore would be the first place Gemma would think to look for him.

All this time, he'd just been waiting. Waiting for her to come back for him.

She closed her eyes, and a low whimper emerged from her lips.

Her eyes burned. Everything burned.

Taylor wasn't hiding in Letty's office. He was gone.

Opening her eyes, Gemma forced herself to keep moving. She made her way back to the office and flicked on the light. Her eyes briefly landed on the rug that covered the entrance to the basement, before she redirected her attention to Letty's desktop computer. The screensaver was on, and a handful of colorful balls bounced from one edge of the screen to the other.

At the reservoir, before hiking back into town, Gemma had checked all of her old social media accounts—Facebook, Instagram, and Twitter. It wasn't vital that they were still active—she could still enact her plan without them—but it would certainly help. One by one, she'd opened websites and typed in usernames and passwords she'd never forgotten. And, one by one, the sites opened up, granting her access to images of friends and extended family who looked healthy and happy, as if they existed in a different universe from the one Gemma inhabited.

It made no sense. Why wouldn't the government have shut her accounts down by now? Carver had produced an entire file on her in Ash Grove. The government knew she was a subversive. Right there, on the side of the road, she'd closed her eyes and praised God.

For the first time in two years, she felt like she still had a voice.

Crossing the office, Gemma lowered herself into Letty's rolling chair. Her hand closed over the mouse, and when the screen came to life, her breath caught in her throat.

Letty's desktop background was a picture of Taylor. He was lugging a box of canned goods down the hallway, and Letty had clearly caught him by surprise. He was looking into the camera, one eyebrow raised, his expression one of good-natured annoyance.

Gemma laughed. And then she cried.

Letty's infatuation with Taylor had caused her to steal a quick picture of him.

And now Gemma knew the exact color of his eyes.

Thank you, Letty. Thank you for this picture.

After allowing herself a good cry, Gemma wiped her face on her sleeve and got to work, clicking on the Internet icon. Taylor's face vanished, and the Google homepage popped up on the screen.

She searched for the office number for Winter's Dam High School.

She couldn't use Letty's office phone to make the call since Captain Haggerty could probably trace the number to figure out her location. Gemma would use Taylor's burner phone to make the call. Afterwards, she would get rid of it.

First, she would delete their engagement photo, and then she would destroy the phone.

She closed her eyes and prayed.

God, please let this work. Make her believe me.

When she dialed the number, her heart was pounding so hard that she thought Captain Haggerty might hear it.

After six rings, a man answered, his voice gruff and impatient. "Yes? Hello?"

Gemma breathed a little easier. Only then did she realize that some part of her had been expecting Private Mullen to answer the phone. But this wasn't Mullen. She knew Mullen's voice. She heard it every night in her nightmares.

She cleared her throat. "I need to speak with Captain Haggerty, please."

"Who is this?" the soldier demanded, wheezing into the phone. He sounded as if his patience was already wearing thin, but Gemma doubted that he had much in the way of patience. "What is this about?"

"I'm calling concerning yesterday's prisoner escape."

A long silence followed. Gemma could no longer hear the soldier breathing. In fact, she couldn't hear anything at all. No closing doors. No one talking. Nothing. The silence was *deafening*. That saying had never made sense to her before, but it did now as she dragged her index finger lightly across the keyboard and strained to listen.

Finally, she said, "Listen to me. You need to put Haggerty on the phone. Now. She's going to want to hear what I have to say."

A loud clunk followed, but the line didn't disconnect. The soldier must've put the phone down. Several minutes passed as Gemma listened to the endless silence on the other end of the line. Finally, there was a heavy thump in Gemma's ear, and a woman said, "This is Captain Haggerty. With whom am I speaking?"

Gemma's right leg bounced, a nervous habit. The heel of her boot rapped against the floor, and she put a hand on her knee to stop it. "Captain Haggerty, I understand you've misplaced a few of your high-value prisoners. Would you like to know where they are?"

"I don't, uh...?" Haggerty sputtered. "Who is this?"

"Who I am doesn't matter. What matters is *what I know*, and what I choose to do with that information."

Silence.

And then, on the other end of the line, there was the distinctive sound of a door clicking shut.

When Haggerty spoke again, her voice was much quieter. Calmer. "What is it you think you know?"

"Well, for starters, I know about the tunnel linking the elementary school to the high school. You know...the one your soldiers left unguarded? I also know about the prisoners in the basement—or the prisoners who *used* to be in the basement. I know that those prisoners have escaped and that they were your only reason for being in Winter's Dam. I know that you're still holding a large group of civilians against their will, even though they have no information that would be useful to you. And—I don't know this part for certain—but I can only assume you haven't let the civilians go yet because you don't want to admit that your mission is a complete failure."

Haggerty's voice grew a little huskier with each word. "I fully intend to notify my superiors of last night's security breach. I'm working on the report as we speak. So, if you think you're going to intimidate me by threatening to—"

"Nothing to hide? What about the boy you murdered? What about the old man? Two civilians. Not subversives. Not sympathizers. Just an old man and a kid." Gemma paused, giving the words time to sink in. "Will you notify your superiors about them?"

"That...never happened."

"The entire town *saw* it happen!" Gemma exclaimed. "One of your grunts shot him down in front of everyone. He was only fourteen. Did you know that? An innocent kid, murdered by the Task Force in broad daylight. His name was Jason, by the way."

"That...boy..." Haggerty sounded as if she was speaking through gritted teeth. "You know nothing about him. He wasn't innocent. He was trying to escape."

Gemma wanted to scream. She'd seen the video. She knew the truth. But she kept her voice steady and even. "An unarmed child. He certainly wasn't trying to escape. He was just a scared kid trying to help his mother. And your soldiers murdered him in cold blood."

"Who are you?" Haggerty demanded. "Tell me your name!"

Gemma closed her hand around the mouse and minimized the Internet so she could see Taylor's face on the computer's background. She wanted to make him proud. To be strong and unafraid. To do what she thought he would've done.

"No one important," Gemma finally said, her eyes locked on the pale-blue computer pixels that composed Taylor's eyes. "Just a subversive with a video in her possession. A video of the Task Force murdering a fourteen-year-old child."

Silence.

Although Gemma couldn't see the captain's face —she wasn't even sure what Haggerty looked like —she could imagine the wheels turning in the woman's mind as she tried to figure out how such a video could exist, trying to convince herself that the mysterious stranger on the other end of the phone line was bluffing.

"I wonder what the public will think," Gemma continued, "if this video ever gets out? What will they think when they see, firsthand, what the Task Force really does to women and children and old men? How many views and shares do you think the video will get? A thousand? A million? Even after the government wipes it off the Internet, you can't wipe away that kind of damage. Do you really trust that your superiors won't throw you to the wolves to save themselves? They'll bury you just like they buried Carver, except you'll still be alive when they do it."

"That isn't possible," Haggerty finally whispered. "There can't be a video."

"Give me your cell number," Gemma said. "I'll text it to you."

Haggerty said nothing, but Gemma could hear her taking slow, deliberate breaths. She could also hear a faint tapping, which she imagined was the captain nervously drumming her fingers on the desk. Then—with no preface—Haggerty rattled off a series of numbers.

Gemma jotted the numbers down on a notepad and then typed them into Taylor's burner phone. There was no way to block the number from showing up on Haggerty's phone, as far as she knew, and they could trace even prepaid numbers. There was probably some kind of app she could use to block it, but even if there was, the government could find a way around it. It would take them a while, though. By the time they figured everything out, she would be long gone, the phone destroyed.

She attached the video of Jason Fishman's murder to the text message and pressed the send button.

"It's coming," Gemma said.

The minutes dragged by, agonizingly slow, as Gemma listened to the sound of the video playing on the other end of the line. She heard the gunshots. The screams. Lizzie Fishman's wails over her dead son.

The sounds fueled her anger.

"What is it you want?" Haggerty asked after the video stopped.

"You've lost your high-value targets. There's no reason for you to stay in Winter's Dam for another minute. I want you to let everyone else go. They aren't a part of this, and you know it. Let them return to their homes, and then you take your soldiers and leave the town."

"I don't have that kind of power."

"Yes, you do, Haggerty. I know how the Task Force operates. This is your operation. If you tell your superiors that the information you received from your informant in Winter's Dam was bad, they'll believe you. They don't have any reason not to. You won't even have to tell them about the escape, if you haven't already, which I bet you haven't. Just order your soldiers to stay quiet. That shouldn't be too difficult. I'm sure you've told them to keep their mouths shut before."

Haggerty gave a mirthless laugh. "And if I refuse to cooperate?"

Gemma sighed. "If you insist on continuing your occupation of Winter's Dam—or if you leave the town briefly to appease me and then return later—I will post this video to every one of my social media accounts. Believe it or not, they're all still active."

She was bluffing, of course. When she destroyed the phone, she would also destroy her only copy of the video. But she had no choice. Holding onto the phone now that the Task Force knew the number was too dangerous. She couldn't stop the Task Force from returning to Winter's Dam, but at least she might get Letty to safety first.

When Haggerty spoke again, her voice was cold and malevolent. "You wouldn't do that. You wouldn't put yourself in that kind of danger. Do you know what we would do to you? To your family?"

"See, that's the thing," Gemma muttered. "You've already taken everything from me. My family. My home. My friends. You've taken it all. That's the beauty of this plan, Haggerty. I have *nothing* to lose."

The captain launched into an obscenity-laced tirade, and Gemma held the phone away from her ear for most of it. At the end of the outburst, Haggerty said, "If you post the video, I'll know who you are. You get that, right? We'll hunt you down, little girl. We haven't taken everything from you. Not yet."

"You're already hunting me!" Gemma spat the words into the phone. "You've been hunting me for years. If releasing this video gets me captured, it will be worth it, *because I'll have taken you down with me.*"

Gemma meant it. She meant every word.

Another long silence on Haggerty's end of the line. Gemma could hear a faint tapping, like the drumbeat of an approaching army. She imagined Haggerty with a pencil in a white-knuckle grip, thumping it against a desk.

"What assurances can you give me you won't release the video, anyway?" No feistiness remained in Haggerty's voice. Now she sounded resigned.

"You'll just have to trust me," Gemma replied. "I'm not dumb enough to put myself at risk for no reason. It's in *both* of our best interests if this video never sees the light of day."

"Okay," Haggerty said. "We'll pull out of the town. We'll need a little time, though."

"You've got twelve hours, Captain Haggerty. If you are still here tomorrow morning, I'll release the video. If you or your soldiers harm anyone else in the town before you leave, I'll release the video. If anything happens to me, I've planned for the video to be released on my behalf." This last part was a lie, of course, but Gemma would say anything to get the Task Force out of Winter's Dam. "It only took you a few hours to occupy the town. It should take you even less to get out."

Another resigned sigh. "Fine. But if that video ever gets out, I will hunt you down and slit your throat."

Gemma didn't hear the threat. She was looking at Taylor's image on the computer screen. The next words slipped through her lips before she could stop them. "There's one more thing."

"What is it?" Haggerty snapped. "What else?"

"The subversive you captured last night..." Gemma's right leg resumed its nervous bouncing. "He is to be released along with the rest of the town."

She waited for Haggerty to respond, a hand pressed to her chest, her heart hammering against her ribcage. Bringing up Taylor had been a mistake. In doing so, she'd given something away. She knew that. Haggerty had something to use against her now.

But she had to do it.

She had to try.

Haggerty's voice became higher in pitch. It was the voice of a woman who'd just realized she had the upper hand in this fight. "Yes, we captured someone last night. Turns out he wasn't a subversive but a Task Force soldier who'd gone AWOL a few months ago. Sergeant Nolan, I believe. I immediately ordered two of my soldiers to transport him to our installation at the Gap for processing and disciplinary procedures. The transfer took place last night, I'm afraid. You're a little too late." The captain almost sounded gleeful. "Was Sergeant Nolan a friend of yours? If so, perhaps he should've chosen his friends more wisely."

Disciplinary procedures.

What did that mean? That could have meant anything.

Gemma bit down hard on the inside of her lip. Hard enough to taste blood. Then, she switched off the computer and glanced at her watch. It was two minutes before nine o'clock. "You've got twelve hours, Haggerty. Twelve hours to get out of town, starting right now."

She ended the call. There was nothing to do but wait.

Actually, there was one more thing, but she *really* didn't want to do it.

However, since putting it off would not make it any easier, Gemma pushed Letty's chair out of the way and dropped to her hands and knees. There, underneath Letty's desk, was a small toolbox. Taylor had used it once when Letty asked him to fix a wobbly bookshelf.

Gemma opened the toolbox and pulled out a hammer.

Taylor's phone was a ticking time bomb. She had to destroy it.

She was taking a chance by destroying the phone now before Haggerty's unit actually left Winter's Dam. But as long as the phone and the SIM card remained operational, they could trace it —especially now that Haggerty knew the number.

Besides, she'd heard the resignation in Haggerty's voice. She was going to pull her unit out of the town.

For a long time, Gemma sat with her legs splayed, the phone and the hammer laying side by side on the floor between her legs. She wanted to look at the engagement photo one last time, but she knew it would be too difficult.

That night would live forever in her mind. No one could ever destroy it.

Finally, she tried to pry open the little door on the side of the phone, but her hands were shaking badly. By the time she'd freed the SIM card from its holder, she could no longer see through her tears.

Was she doing the right thing?

In destroying the phone, she was destroying the only evidence she had of Jason Fishman's murder.

But *not* destroying the phone meant endangering everyone at the Sanctuary.

Gemma prayed through her tears. "Father, please forgive me for doing this," she wept. "But I can't put everyone I love in danger, Lord." Slowly, she picked up the hammer. Part of her expected God Himself to rip it from her hands and hurl it across the room. "I'm so sorry."

She swung the hammer.

The first impact was the worst one. She felt the pain of loss as plainly as if she'd been smashing her own heart into pieces. Segments of the card remained intact, so she kept swinging. She smashed it over and over until nothing remained of the stored memories of love and murder except dozens of tiny shards of black plastic.

She smashed the card until there was nothing left, and then she went to work on the phone.

After it was over—after she was certain there was no way anyone could get any information from the destroyed phone—the hammer slipped through her fingers and landed on the carpet.

Gemma curled into a ball on the floor and sobbed until sleep finally took her.

CHAPTER TWENTY-FOUR

Gemma was back on Dragon's Back.

Not on the fire-scorched mountain of her nightmares, but on the mountain as she remembered it: lush and achingly familiar. She stood on the cracked asphalt between the Station and the entrance to the mine and watched as Sophia's hens—the Golden Girls—circled the base of the playset, absently pecking the ground. Every few seconds, the hens would scrape their claws in the dirt, trying to unearth a stubborn earthworm or grub. But one hen—Blanche—kept scraping until she'd dug herself a small ditch. She settled on top of it and began tossing dirt on herself. The poor thing looked as if she was having a seizure.

I'm dreaming, she realized. *I must be, because the Golden Girls are gone.*

They'd left the hens behind at the Station. They were likely dead by now, snatched up by some predator. A fox. Or maybe a hawk. They had two dozen chickens in a coop at the Sanctuary, but Sophia wanted nothing to do with them. They weren't the Golden Girls. These chickens were White Leghorns, not the Rhode Island Reds to which Sophia had grown accustomed.

Something drew her toward the Station. The building was more decrepit than the last time she'd seen it. The roof had partially collapsed over the section of the Station that had once housed the café, and the forest had made significant progress in its effort to reclaim the building as its own. She could barely make out the porch railing through the thick layers of creeping ivy that had wound itself around it.

How long would she have to sit on the porch before the vines wrapped themselves around her?

Everything felt so real. Almost as if this wasn't a dream but an actual glimpse into what had become of her old home.

She walked around the front of the Station, and her movement caught the attention of Blanche, who glanced up from her dust bath long enough to give Gemma the side-eye. None of the other hens appeared to notice her. A few feet away, Dorothy was tugging a worm free from the dirt, but the poor thing had no time to celebrate as both Sophia and Rose raced over and tried to snatch it out of her mouth. But Dorothy was no fool. She tilted her head back and swallowed the worm whole. Then, she sauntered away from the others, spraying plumes of dust in their faces with her claws.

When the porch came into view, Gemma stopped in her tracks.

Taylor stood at the top of the steps, his back to her.

He was wearing his Task Force uniform, but the blood-red patch was no longer on his left shoulder. Of course, it wasn't. The patch was inside Gemma's jacket pocket. To be sure, she slipped her hand in there, and her fingers glided along the rough underside of the patch.

It's just a dream, she told herself. But she wanted to run to him. To throw herself into his muscular arms. To tell him how much she loved him and how she would do everything in her power to get him back. Her plan with Haggerty had failed, but she would not give up on him.

"Taylor?"

He jerked his head up, and his body went rigid, like an animal sensing danger.

"Taylor? It's okay. It's me."

His shoulders relaxed, but he still did not turn around. "You shouldn't have come back. There are dragons hiding here."

Gemma looked up at the crisp fall sky, a curtain of blue draped over a dense blanket of green. No sky had ever looked so beautiful. "Look at the sky, Taylor. There are no dragons. That was a nightmare. It wasn't real."

But his next words sent a chill down her spine. "They're hiding, Gemma." He brought his left hand up and pointed at the mine. "They're hiding in there."

She glanced behind her at the mine, but there was nothing to see. An idea occurred to her. "Taylor?" she asked him. "Where have they taken you? How can I find you?"

Suddenly, Taylor's body sagged, as if some massive, unseen creature—*a dragon?*—had perched on his shoulders. He lowered his chin as if to look down at something, and although Gemma couldn't see his face, she watched as he shook his head violently from side to side, as if he'd seen something awful lurking in the tangle of vegetation beneath his feet.

"Something's moving," he said. "Something's moving down there."

"What?" She tried to run to him, but her feet wouldn't move. "What is it?"

"The vines...are moving."

Too late, Gemma realized that Taylor's body wasn't sagging. It was sinking. Sinking *into* the vegetation. The vines snaked themselves around his ankles and crawled up his legs, intent on pulling him down. She struggled against the unseen force holding her in place, but it was no use. She couldn't move.

It's a dream, she told herself. *It isn't real. It's only a dream.*

But she didn't believe it.

"Taylor! Tell me what to do!"

"You can't help me!" His voice sounded far away, as if he were already calling out to her from the place where the vines were taking him. "No one can!"

"Stop!" she screamed at the vines. "Please, stop!"

And then Taylor vanished into the porch. Or into the ground. Or into whatever hell lurked beneath the Station. Just before his head slipped out of view, she saw the vines curling around his neck. Choking the life out of him. Claiming him as their own.

When he disappeared, the force holding her in place finally released her. She ran to the porch and sprinted up the stairs, falling to her hands and knees. Her tears dripped onto the porch's decaying floorboards as she tore uselessly at the ivy, searching for Taylor.

"Where?" she cried. "Where have you taken him?"

And then...she knew.

She abandoned the porch and ran to the mine. A quick glance at the playset revealed the chickens were gone. The same thick ivy that had reclaimed the porch—and Taylor—now covered the ground beneath the rusted structure.

She approached the ancient shelter with the canary-yellow coal car and, beyond that, the gaping black mouth of the coal mine. Following the path once frequented by tourists, she descended into the shelter, and the subterranean air enveloped her, cold enough to steal her breath away. Just ahead, the mouth of the mine hung open, the darkness of its throat as black and unyielding as the anthracite coal that diligent miners used to carve out of its belly.

A screech reverberated in the darkness. And then another one. The second one was deeper than the first. More menacing. Hungrier.

The dragons called to her. Taunted her. Beckoned her to join them in the dark.

They thought she wouldn't do it. They thought she was too afraid. And she smiled, because she knew something they didn't.

The game had changed, and *she* had changed with it.

Gemma reached into her pocket, her fingers closing around Taylor's patch.

Then, she stepped into the darkness.

CHAPTER TWENTY-FIVE

A sound ripped Gemma out of her dream.
She raised her head and blinked until the world came into focus, trying to make sense of what she was seeing. Nothing looked familiar at first, but slowly, her mind put things in order. Crowded shelves. Cardboard boxes overflowing with books. Oriental rug.

She was in Letty's office. She must've fallen asleep on the floor, her head resting on her arms. Her throat hurt more than it had the day before, and her entire body felt stiff and achy.

According to her watch, it was just after five-thirty in the morning.

Her head felt fuzzy, like a glass jar stuffed with cotton balls. Keeping her eyes open required an immense amount of effort. She wanted to go back to sleep, to return to the dream, to the mine. She wanted to show the creatures that she wasn't afraid, that the darkness did not frighten her anymore.

Lowering her head to her arms, she allowed her eyes to drift shut.

And then she heard it.

Footsteps.

Coming from just outside the office.

Someone was *inside* the bookstore.

In an instant, Gemma's exhaustion vanished, making way for sheer terror. Haggerty and her soldiers must've tracked her to the bookstore. Had they been able to trace the phone before she destroyed it?

She jumped to her feet and searched for an escape route, but there were no windows, no doors other than the one leading into the hallway—and to whomever was sneaking around outside. She had no weapons. Not even her father's Leatherman. Everything was in her backpack, which she'd stupidly dropped at the entrance of the bookstore.

Gemma's eyes landed on the rug.

She swallowed hard, already dreading what she was about to do. She couldn't fathom the idea of being by herself in the darkness with the spiders and whatever else lived down there. But it was better than being captured and interrogated. Anything was better than that.

She dropped to her knees and began rolling the rug toward the office door. Because the rug was so big, she had to roll one end of the rug a little and then crawl to the opposite end and roll that side. Dust tickled her nostrils, and she buried her face in her arm to suppress a sneeze. It was strenuous work, and she was young and healthy. How did Letty do it at her age?

Gemma had almost uncovered the cellar door when it hit her that she would have no way of rolling the rug back up once she crawled into the basement.

Another thought followed that one. *I'm an idiot.*

Outside the door, shuffling footsteps moved down the hallway, heading for the office.

With one final Herculean effort, Gemma pushed with all her might, shoving as much of the rug as she could in front of the office door. The makeshift barricade would only slow the Task Force down for a few seconds, but at least she'd done something. At least she hadn't just rolled over and given up.

With nothing else to do, she sat back on her heels and watched as the doorknob rotated *excruciatingly* slowly, just like in the movies, as if the soldier on the other side was intent on dragging out

Gemma's distress for as long as possible. Finally, the door swung open, but the bottom corner snagged on the rug.

"What in the world...?"

That voice.

She *knew* that voice.

Letty poked her head through a gap in the door. "Stormy? Good grief...look at this place! I go away for a few days, and here you are, wreaking havoc on my office!"

"Letty!" Gemma grabbed the rug, lifted it above her head, and hurled it toward the center of the room. At least, that was what she felt like doing. In reality, she worked for a few minutes, struggling to pull the rug away from the door while Letty pushed from the other side. As soon as the doorway was clear, the old woman breezed into the room, wearing the same purple sweater, floral blouse, and black slacks she'd been wearing the last time Gemma had seen her.

The clothes were filthy, and she looked utterly exhausted.

Gemma flung herself into Letty's waiting arms and broke down as the old woman held her in a motherly embrace and rubbed her back.

"Enough, Stormy. It's alright. They're leaving."

She lifted her head from Letty's shoulders. "They're...what?"

"The soldiers are leaving," Letty said. "They started loading up this morning, long before the sun came up. We thought they were going to take us with them, right until the moment they opened the gate and told us to go home. They said they had all the information they needed, and they apologized to us for the inconvenience."

Gemma thought of her dream, where dragons no longer soared through the open air but made their homes in the darkness. "Are you sure, though? Are you sure this isn't a trick?"

Letty took Gemma's hand and led her to the front of the store. She motioned for Gemma to look out the window. "See for yourself."

Gemma peered through the glass just as a Task Force Humvee lumbered down the street. Instinctively, she ducked away from the window, trying not to be seen, but the vehicle never slowed. It continued past Letty's store, heading out of town.

"It's okay," Letty assured her. "They're leaving."

But Gemma couldn't relax. Not until the Task Force left Winter's Dam. Even then, she wouldn't be able to relax because she didn't fully trust that Haggerty and her soldiers wouldn't return. She continued to stare out the window and saw people walking in the street. The people of Winter's Dam were indeed returning to their homes.

All except for Jason Fishman and Marty Glick.

They watched as more Task Force vehicles drove by the store. The drivers of the trucks paid no mind to the people walking in the street, not even the ones who stopped long enough to shout profanities, shake their fists, or extend their middle fingers at the convoy. The soldiers ignored it all and kept driving, probably already thinking about the next town.

"Come on, honey." Letty tapped Gemma on the shoulder. "Let's sit down and chat awhile. This old lady is dying for a decent cup of coffee."

While Gemma sat at the table, trailing her finger through the cookie crumbs, Letty got to work brewing a fresh pot of coffee. She returned to the table a few minutes later with identical blue mugs and a small squeeze bottle of honey. Letty took a long sip of her coffee and then exhaled. "Someone ratted us out, Stormy. Someone from the town. I haven't figured out who yet, but I've got my suspicions."

Gemma stared at Letty over the rim of her mug. "Who do you think it was?"

"I believe it was Tim Kertin," Letty replied with a grimace, as if the name left a foul taste on her lips. "*Pastor* Tim Kertin."

"Are you serious? You think a pastor did this?"

"Former pastor. He was one of the first people in town to renounce, and he's gone to visit his daughter's family this week. Plus, he's hunting buddies with Clyde Fishman, and Clyde's got notoriously loose lips." She brought a hand to her forehead. "I figured Clyde wouldn't be able to keep his trap shut when I brought him into this thing, but I did it anyway, against my better judgment. And now look what's gone and happened. The Task Force killed his boy, Stormy."

Gemma nodded. "I know."

The older woman's eyes grew wide. "You know? How do you know?"

Letty sipped her coffee while Gemma told her the entire story, recounting everything from Wednesday's meeting at the Sanctuary to Friday's rescue. She explained that the other prisoners—the high-value targets—were staying at the Sanctuary. All except for Teresa and her father, who had supposedly returned to the town sometime yesterday afternoon.

Finally, she told Letty about Taylor.

About their engagement. And about him being captured by the Task Force.

They were both crying by the time Gemma finished speaking.

"I can't believe you kids did all that for us." Letty pushed herself up from her chair and grabbed a box of tissues from behind the counter. "I've got to call Gerry Tuttle and let him know that

Melinda's safe at the Sanctuary. I'll give him directions so he can drive out there to be with her. He was an absolute wreck last night, worrying about her." She dabbed at her eyes. "Oh, Stormy…I'm so sorry about Taylor. We'll figure something out, won't we? There's got to be something we can do."

Gemma didn't want to talk about Taylor. It hurt too much. So, she changed the subject. "Letty, we expected you to be in the basement with the others. Why didn't the Task Force know about you? Wouldn't Pastor Kertin have given them your name?"

Letty wiped the tears from her damp cheeks. "Clyde talks a lot, but he wouldn't have told anyone about me—not even his buddy, Kertin. Keeping me a secret was the most important part of our arrangement. Clyde knew that. If the Task Force ever found out that I was part of the operation, it wouldn't take them long to dig into my finances and real estate holdings. Those things would lead them straight to the Sanctuary."

Gemma dropped her head into her hands. The coffee had helped a little, but her head was feeling fuzzy again. She wanted to crawl into the nearest bed and sleep for a year. "Letty, I appreciate everything you've done for us, but you've got to stop."

"Stop what?"

She raised her head and gestured to the store.

"This. All of this. You can't do it anymore. You can't keep putting yourself at risk with your signs and your secret cellars. The soldiers could come back. They know there are sympathizers in this town and that those sympathizers are working with a large group of subversives."

Letty narrowed her eyes at Gemma. "And just what do you expect me to do, Stormy?"

"Come live with us at the Sanctuary. We don't need Winter's Dam anymore. We can grow our own food. Raise our own animals. We survived on much less back at the Station. You would love living there. The Sanctuary is perfect. It has everything we need."

"Does it now? And what about the medicine? Are you going to grow insulin for the diabetics in your group? What about penicillin?"

"We'll get it somehow, just like we did before." Gemma leaned across the table and grasped Letty's forearms. "Think of all the people you've saved. You've done more than your share."

"See, that's where you're wrong, Stormy," Letty said, pulling her arms away from Gemma. "All those people I brought to safety...I love them, but I don't have to worry about them anymore. They're already safe. The folks I worry about are the ones who still need saving."

"Letty, the soldiers *will* come back. And what if

next time is worse? Do you think you're invincible? Because you're not. What if they capture you? Or kill you?" The dam burst again, and tears flowed freely down Gemma's sore cheeks. "Taylor wasn't invincible, and neither are you!"

"Oh, Stormy..." Letty came around the table and wrapped her arms around Gemma. "I'm so sorry. I'm so sorry about that handsome boy of yours."

Later, after they'd cried the last of their tears and drank the last of their coffee, Gemma stood inside the door to the bookstore and gave Letty one more hug before she left.

"Are you going back now, honey?"

Gemma nodded. "It's Sunday. Church is at nine, and I want to be there. First, I'll stop by the cabin and let everyone know that the Task Force is leaving and that it looks like everything is over." She ended the hug and raised her eyebrows at Letty. "You're sure you don't want to come with me?"

Letty smiled. "That's one thing I love most about you, Stormy. You don't know when to quit." Then, her eyes grew thoughtful, and she asked, "You've heard of Harriet Tubman? They still teach about her in school, don't they?"

Gemma smiled. "Of course."

"Well, that's good. Lord knows I'm not comparing myself to no Harriet Tubman, but since I started this little mission of mine, I've spent loads of time thinking about her. I've read tons of books about her life and about the underground railroad. She was a hard-nosed woman, that one. And she never let fear impede her mission. One thing she said jabbed me in the gut the first time I read it. Do you know what it was?"

"What?"

Letty kissed Gemma on the cheek and then brought her lips to Gemma's ear.

"I can't die but once."

CHAPTER TWENTY-SIX

Mullen clenched his hands on the steering wheel as he drove through Winter's Dam, still smarting from his brief but infuriating interaction with Captain Haggerty. He kept replaying it in his mind, deliberately stoking the fire that was raging out of control inside of him. He kept his eyes forward, refusing to look at the civilians who were wandering the sidewalks like dumb sheep without a shepherd. If he looked at them, he might just shoot a few of them. Some had brazenly parked themselves in lawn chairs to watch the Task Force leave their town, as if it were a freaking parade.

How many of them were sympathizers?

Mullen briefly locked eyes with one old man in a lawn chair, and the man *grinned* at him.

"Keep smiling, old timer," Mullen grumbled, redirecting his eyes at the road ahead. "If I have anything to say about it, you won't be wearing that grin for long."

Even before he'd arrived at the high school, Mullen had known that Haggerty's unit was pulling out. He hadn't been listening to the radio—he'd spent most of the last two days asleep—but the endless convoy of vehicles he'd passed as he drove into town had given him a big clue. To keep himself calm, he tried to tell himself that Haggerty's unit had gotten the information they'd needed. They'd exposed the network of sympathizers, located the subversives, and all was right in the world. But he knew that couldn't be the case. Not with someone like Haggerty running the show.

To make matters worse, he hadn't heard from Carver since he'd detained that family of subversives at the cabin two nights ago. He'd tried talking to Carver on the drive to Winter's Dam, hoping maybe the colonel could calm him down a little, but he'd received no response.

When Mullen had stepped out of his pickup truck at the high school, the captain had been on her way out the door, a rucksack tossed over her shoulder. The first thing he'd noticed about Haggerty was that her uniform was wrinkled and she had mud on her boots. Next, he'd noticed how big she was. The term *Amazon woman* had flashed through his mind, but that would've implied there was something appealing about her size. There wasn't. She was at least six feet tall, and although she wasn't fat, she was knocking on fat's door. A few more fast food lunches would push her right over the edge. How did she pass her twice-yearly weigh-in? Mullen knew very little about the captain other than what he'd heard through the grapevine about her ineptitude, but her appearance lined up perfectly with the idea he'd had of her.

The ugly cow had no business leading soldiers.

"What's happening?" Mullen had jogged up the concrete stairs to the front entrance of the school. "Where are you going?"

Looking tired and annoyed, Haggerty shifted her rucksack higher on her shoulder. "Who the heck are you?"

Only then had he remembered that he was in civvies. He'd tossed her a quick salute. It was always good to be professional. "Corporal Mullen, ma'am." The ma'am part hadn't come easily. He'd almost choked on it, like a sunflower shell stuck in his throat. "I'm a scout with 2nd Battalion. I'm off this weekend, but I thought your unit could use some help."

"Help?" She looked at him as if he'd lost his mind. "Can't you see we're pulling out?"

What was this cow's problem? Didn't she recognize a good soldier when she saw one? Mullen imagined himself throttling her, landing a punch right square on those piggish lips of hers. Playing the scenario out in his mind was the only way to keep from actually doing it. "Yes, I can see that, ma'am. May I ask why?"

"No, *Corporal* Mullen. You may not ask why, because it's none of your freaking business, and I don't answer to you. Might I suggest you get in your vehicle and roll back the way you came. The highway is right over there." Haggerty jabbed a finger over Mullen's shoulder. "Now, get lost before I notify Lieutenant Colonel Drum of your insubordination."

Then, she'd pushed past him, her rucksack thumping him on the arm.

It had taken every ounce of self-control he possessed not to shove her down the stairs.

As Mullen approached the outskirts of the town, eager to leave the whole rotten experience behind him, a dull throb started up in his head. Originating behind his eyeballs, it was a muted pain that—if left untreated—would eventually progress into a real whopper of a headache. He rubbed at his eyes, trying to massage away the pain. He used to get stress migraines all the time, back when he still shared a roof with his old man.

But he didn't get them as often anymore—not since joining the Task Force.

For most people, their job *caused* them stress.

Mullen's job *relieved* his.

Just ahead, a no-name gas station occupied a small plot of land on the right side of the road. Actually, it had a name: Tom's Quik-E Mart. What a stupid name. But he expected nothing less from this hick town. It was both a gas station and convenience store, a hole-in-the-wall establishment you wouldn't glance at twice unless you were running on fumes or in desperate need of a toilet—or both. Mullen didn't fall into either of those categories, but there weren't many places to stop out here in the sticks, and he needed to get his migraine under control right quick. Plus, it would be nice to take a leak before heading home.

Mullen parked his truck in the blue-outlined handicapped space directly in front of the store. Let someone say something to him about parking there. Just let them. Haggerty might not know how to handle these country folks, but Mullen had a few ideas. He slid out of the truck, strolled up to the glass door, and yanked it open. A bell jingled above his head, and he gritted his teeth at the piercing sound. He wanted to rip the bell down and chuck it through the glass.

The pain in his skull was getting worse by the second.

He glanced around. The convenience store was empty. There were no other customers. Not even a worker behind the counter. Then it hit him. Tom—or whichever local idiot should've been manning the store today—had likely just been released by the Task Force this morning. The guy probably wasn't in a big hurry to return to work.

Perfect. Mullen rubbed his temples. *Just perfect.*

Clerk or no clerk, Mullen needed medicine. The place was unlocked, and the sign in the window said it was open. It wasn't his fault if people refused to do their jobs. He breezed through the aisles, randomly knocking things off the shelves until he found the section with travel-sized tubes of toothpaste and chewable Pepto-Bismol. He ripped a square box of Tylenol from its hook and pocketed it. Then, since no one was looking, he took another one.

The snack aisle beckoned him, and he grabbed three bags of barbecue-flavored sunflower seeds. This little hole-in-the-wall establishment didn't have the Jalapeño Hot Salsa flavor he preferred, but the barbecue would do. Before leaving, he hit the cooler and swiped a Mountain Dew to wash down the pills. He felt no guilt about stealing. If the store owner didn't care enough about thefts to lock his door, then neither did Mullen.

He headed for the exit.

Mullen had one hand on the glass door, ready to push it open, when he spotted the girl.

At first, he thought he was hallucinating. In only ten minutes, the pain in his skull had gone from dull to unbearable. He'd felt nothing like it in his life. Each stabbing pain felt like someone was hammering nails into his cerebral cortex. His mind wasn't working properly, and somehow, it had conjured up the girl from the mountain.

But then he leaned closer to the door, so close that his pockmarked forehead pressed against the glass, and he knew he was wrong.

It was *her*.

The girl from the mountain.

She stood on the porch of the neighboring house. Only, it wasn't a house, it just looked like one. It was actually a bookstore. *Letty's Book Cellar.* Mullen rolled the name around on his tongue. Tasted it. Memorized it.

He couldn't believe it. She was *right there*. The girl from the mountain. The one who had kneed him in the junk and run away from him. The one who had played a role in Colonel Carver's murder. The one whose friends had escaped from the barn fire and made a fool of him.

She was not only alive but standing a few yards away from him. She appeared to be talking to someone on the other side of the bookstore's front screen door. Mullen couldn't see who she was talking to, but it didn't matter.

He would find out soon enough.

As he watched her, the girl turned and jogged down the steps. She headed for the rear of the building, looking a good deal healthier than she had in the spring. Her hair was longer, her skin tanner, her body more fit.

Wherever she was hiding now, it wasn't in some damp coal mine.

Every single one of Mullen's instincts told him to follow her, to attack her from behind and crush the life out of her in the parking area behind the store. But he remained totally still, a hunter observing his prey. Even the slightest movement might alert the girl to his presence. He couldn't just kill her. Not yet. That wouldn't get him everything he wanted. Everything he'd spent months planning for.

He'd been sloppy back at the barn.

He would not make any more mistakes.

After the girl disappeared from view, Mullen backed away from the door. His forehead left an oily smudge behind on the glass. Tucking the sunflower seeds under his armpit, he ran the back of his hand across the damp stretch of his upper lip.

It wasn't hot, but he was sweating.

"Well, now," Carver spoke up in his signature gravelly voice. "Things just got a bit more interesting, wouldn't you agree?"

Mullen felt his mouth widen into a grin. "Good to have you back, sir."

"Good to be back, Corporal. I see we've got some work to do."

"Yes, we do, sir."

When Mullen climbed back inside his truck, he fired up the engine, but he didn't drive away. Instead, he stole a glance at the black duffel bag in the backseat.

"Soon," he whispered. "Very soon."

He switched on the radio, cranked the air conditioning up to full blast, and threw a handful of seeds into his mouth. He tilted the truck's side mirror so he could watch the front entrance of the bookstore, and then he waited, gnawing on sunflower seeds and listening to Lynyrd Skynyrd sing their song about Alabama.

He didn't bother with the Tylenol.

His headache had disappeared.

CHAPTER TWENTY-SEVEN

It was after nine by the time Gemma parked the Charger inside the shed and sprinted for the clearing. She ran for the path that wrapped around the west side of the camp, past the ropes course, all the way to the clearing. She wasn't looking forward to seeing everyone, but she didn't want to miss church.

She needed God today.

Every Sunday, the residents of the Sanctuary—except whomever was manning the security cameras—made their way to a picturesque clearing on the outskirts of the camp. A circle of towering pine trees loomed over the clearing like silent protectors, their branches curving overhead, as if the trees themselves had conspired to conceal the Sanctuary's inhabitants from view as they worshipped. It always made Gemma think of the Ents —those walking tree-creatures from Tolkien's *Lord of the Rings*.

Gemma had just reached the ropes course when someone stepped directly into her path. She skidded to a stop, the tip of her nose inches away from impacting his chest.

"Whoa!" she cried. "Where did you come from?"

Abram Cleary lowered his chin and raised his eyebrows, scowling at her in that paternal way he usually reserved for Taylor. He folded his arms over his chest, his red mustache twitching in what appeared to be barely controlled anger. "I grieved the Holy Spirit with my language three times this morning because of you." He held up three fingers. "Three times, Alcott."

Gemma held up her hands. "Before you flip out, nothing bad happened."

"I'm not flipping out!" Abram bellowed, his voice loud enough to reach the congregants gathered in the clearing. *"When I flip out, believe me, you'll know!"*

She took a step back. She had never seen Abram this way before. Face beet-red. Nearly panting with anger. But there was something else there, too. Something besides the anger.

Pain.

He loved Taylor like a son, and he was hurting, too.

"Abram…"

"Where were you?" he demanded. But before she could answer, he continued to rant. "You think I don't know that you've been gone all night? You think Nolan's capture gives you carte blanche to do whatever you want? To just come and go whenever you please? Because if that's the case, next time, you better stay gone."

"Abram, you don't understand…"

"I understand that you're upset about your boyfriend."

"Fiancé."

Some of the fire left Abram's eyes, and he lowered his gaze to her ring finger. He didn't know yet. None of them did. Not even Addie. He pinched the bridge of his nose. "We're *all* upset," he continued. "But that doesn't give you the right to jeopardize the lives of everyone in this camp."

"The Task Force released them."

Abram blinked at her. His mouth opened and closed again. "Released who?"

Gemma abandoned the pathway and leaned against the nearest tree, exhausted. A variety of feelings swirled inside of her, each one vying for dominance over the others. Pride. Happiness. Fear. Anguish. It amazed her that the human body could host so many emotions at once. "The town. Letty.

Everyone's free. The Task Force left Winter's Dam this morning."

Abram ran both index fingers over his mustache, smoothing it to either side. He squinted at her. "Really? And how did *that* come to pass?"

"Does it matter?"

His eyebrows shot up. "You know what, Alcott? I don't think I want to know what you did—at least not yet. What about the others at the cabin?"

"I stopped in and told them. Brie and Max want us to send someone to pick them up in a few days. Gavin isn't planning on coming back."

"Is that why Brie and Max stayed behind? To change his mind?"

"I think so, but he won't change his mind. He never fit in here."

"He never tried."

But Gemma knew it was more complicated than that. In the distance, she could hear singing— a familiar hymn, "A Mighty Fortress is Our God."

"Should we go to church? I rushed back so I would make it on time."

Abram looked like he wanted to lecture her some more, but he extended his elbow instead, and Gemma linked her arm through his. Putting a hand on top of hers, he escorted her toward the clearing like a father walking his daughter down the aisle.

Gemma's smile reached all the way to her heart.

She had no father in this world—at least not one that she could talk to—but Abram and Oliver were wonderful substitutes. If she and Taylor had gotten married, she would've wanted both men to walk her down the aisle.

"Abram?"

"What?"

"Did you really use the expression *carte blanche?*"

He gave her hand a hard squeeze. "Shut up, Alcott."

✝

In the center of the clearing, two dozen wooden benches formed a horseshoe around a large wooden cross that had been hand-crafted and planted in the ground years earlier by some long-forgotten scout leader. Patches of fluorescent-green moss clung to the age-darkened wood, giving it the appearance of something out of a fairy tale. At first glance, the cross appeared beautiful and sturdy, like the Sanctuary itself. A towering symbol of faith and rebellion. But the moss hinted at the underlying fragility of the wood.

It was a reminder that nothing—no matter how sturdy or well-crafted—lasted forever.

The older members of the group filled the old wooden benches, while the younger people stretched out on blankets or leaned against the trees. Church at the Sanctuary was nothing like the church Gemma remembered. Few people smelled sweet, and no one had manicured—or even clean—fingernails. Most of the men were unshaven. One woman in the group, Belinda, used to be a hairdresser. She kept everyone's hair trimmed as needed, but that was the extent of her services. There was no hair dye at the Sanctuary, and the older women in the group had long ago abandoned the hassle of trying to camouflage the gray in their hair.

Gemma crept between the benches and blankets until she spotted Mia and Oliver. She lowered herself onto the blanket next to Mia, who looked up in surprise and then pulled her into a tight hug. A few feet behind them, Addie sat on another blanket with Sophia sprawled between her legs. Kyle was beside her, a sleeping Weston cradled in his arms.

Running her fingers through Sophia's hair, Addie mouthed *I love you* to Gemma.

Gemma mouthed it back. *I love you, too.* Before she turned around, she noticed Yost leaning against a tree at the back of the clearing, his arms crossed over his chest. He wasn't singing, probably because he didn't know the words. There were no hymnals at the Sanctuary. They sang the hymns from their memories. Yost looked uncomfortable, but at least he was there.

She gave him a brief wave, and he waved back.

The pastor stood at the front of the clearing, directly in front of the cross. The only minister among them, Pastor Jenson, had the honor of conducting the church service every Sunday morning. At nearly eighty-two years old, he had been enjoying his retirement years when the Task Force began detaining Christian ministers. Although he had no desire to spend the last few years of his life in prison, he knew he wouldn't make it long on the run. As the story went, he'd been on the way to turn himself in when he'd asked God to knock him over the head with a sign that he was making a mistake. Five minutes later, he'd pulled into a gas station to get a cup of coffee and found one of Letty's flyers tacked to the bulletin board inside the door.

He drove to the bookstore that same day.

After the congregation finished singing hymns, Pastor Jenson spoke about the persecution suffered by the Apostle Paul and the early Christians as they established the Church. "To say their lives were difficult would've been a monumental understatement," he said. "Death was their constant companion, always following close behind them, breathing down their necks. The people who were against them wanted to prevent the spread of the Gospel at all costs. But what those people meant for evil, God used for good. He used the severe persecution His followers suffered to accomplish His purposes. He wanted them to preach the Gospel to everyone. To share the Truth, no matter the cost, so that everyone heard it. When people threw the disciples out of their towns or tried to stone them to death, it forced them to move on to another town...where more people would hear the Truth. God never gave them the opportunity to get too comfortable."

Gemma shifted on the blanket, listening carefully.

"Consider the possibility," Pastor Jenson said, "that modern-day Christians and the early Christians are two sides of the same coin—bookends, of sorts. Maybe our goal shouldn't be to survive until the world comes to its senses. Maybe God intends for us to *suffer*. And maybe our suffering leads others to Christ. What if, in our suffering, we are being given an opportunity to display true faith to a world that desperately needs it?"

A small hand wrapped around Gemma's, and she looked down to see Sophia on the blanket beside her. The girl gazed up at her with wide, apologetic eyes. Gemma put her arm around her and pulled her close. "I love you," she whispered.

"I love you, too."

"Now, I know what you're thinking," Pastor Jenson continued. "You're thinking, 'Pastor, that all sounds good, but how does God expect me to bring others to the Lord if I'm in prison? Or dead? Isn't it better for me to be free so that I may be of use to the Lord?' And to that I say, 'Yes, dear Christian. Your life is important. Your testimony is important. But your suffering—even to the point of death—will bring more people to the Lord than your life ever could.'"

Silence hung over the clearing at the conclusion of the sermon. The only sounds were the unbroken songs of the insects and the distant squawking of the crows on the ropes course. Finally, Pastor Jenson lifted his hands in the air, signaling for the congregation to rise for the final hymn, "Onward Christian Soldiers." One of Gemma's favorites. When she was a little girl, she used to march in place whenever the pianist played the song in church.

Her eyes fell on the moss-covered cross as she sang.

"Onward Christian soldiers, marching as to war.
With the cross of Jesus going on before."

After church ended, Gemma remained on the

blanket as the clearing emptied and people slowly drifted away. A few of them stopped by to talk to her, but most kept their distance, probably unsure of what to say. Mia stayed longer than everyone else, acting as a sort of emotional buffer between Gemma and everyone else, but she eventually had to leave to help prepare lunch. Their meals were always bigger on Sundays. Turkey was on today's menu, according to Mia. Three wild turkeys, bagged by Abram and Kurt a few days earlier, along with boxed stuffing and creamed corn. A veritable feast by Sanctuary standards.

Alone in the clearing, Gemma stretched her legs in front of her and fixed her eyes on the cross. Pastor Jenson's sermon played on a loop in her mind. That part about suffering for the Truth burrowed itself into her brain like some kind of parasite. Gemma had suffered for her faith. She'd lost both of her parents to the Task Force. She'd lost her home. Now, she'd lost the only boy she'd ever loved. In all of that suffering, what had she done to advance the Truth? What had she done to share God's Word with a sinful and unbelieving world?

Something lurked there, in the back of her mind, a certainty she could've easily grabbed hold of, but she pulled away from it.

Whatever it was, she wasn't prepared to face it.

She jumped as Yost plopped down on the blanket beside her.

She'd thought everyone had left, but it didn't surprise her that Yost was still hanging around the clearing. He knew no one at the Sanctuary, except for her.

He had nowhere else to go.

"I really miss him," Yost said.

Gemma bit her lip and nodded. "I miss him, too."

"I feel like we should do something. I don't know what, exactly. But something, you know? I feel like he wouldn't just be sitting here. He would figure out a way to rescue us."

"I know he would." Gemma scooted on the blanket so she was facing him. "If you can think of anything—any way to get to him—you need to tell me. I'll do anything."

He lowered his head but not before Gemma saw the defeat etched on his face. Despite being ex-Task Force scouts, neither he nor Taylor knew much about the detention centers. Yost picked up a handful of needles and tossed them away, one by one. "Abram asked me to do the pick-ups from now on since I'm the only one with an ID. Kyle Hogue said he would go with me the first few times. I guess that means I'll be sticking around here for a bit."

"You don't have to stay here, Yost. You don't owe us anything. No one knows about your involvement in what happened in Winter's Dam. You could just leave. Go back to your old life."

Yost looked at her. "Could I? After everything that's happened?"

Gemma looked at her hands, her eyes landing on the emerald engagement ring. He didn't need to say anything else. She understood.

"This wasn't what I thought it would be." Yost motioned to the wooden cross at the front of the clearing. "Church, I mean. Not that I had any idea what to expect. I've never set foot in a church in my life, except during raids when I first joined the Task Force. But this... It wasn't anything like what I expected."

"Church wasn't always like this," Gemma said. "It was different when I was a kid. I remember everything being so rigid and structured. We had an amazing minister, but people were constantly finding stupid things to fight about, from the color of the carpet to the kinds of songs we sang. I think some people kept going to church because it was what they'd always done, but they never really *got* what God intended church to be. They were miserable, and they wanted to make the rest of us miserable, too."

Yost wrinkled his nose. "Sounds like a blast."

"Right? But everything changed when the government came after us. We lost our building and everything in it. Then, we lost our minister." She remembered the day Taylor had arrested his own father. The same day he'd shown up at the movie theater to see her. "Those people—the miserable ones—renounced soon after our pastor got arrested. But a few of us stuck together. Instead of gathering in a beautiful building, we met in drafty basements or crowded living rooms. It didn't take long for us to realize that church was so much better when it was pure. Music, prayer, and the Word. That was all we needed. And you know what? There were people in our congregation who'd attended church their whole lives but only really came to know Jesus *after* we lost everything."

Yost nodded as she spoke, his eyes never straying from the cross. He kept tossing dead pine needles to the ground, one at a time, as if he was playing a dark version of 'Loves Me, Loves Me Not.'

"This is going to sound really stupid, Gemma. I almost can't believe I'm going to say it. But...I think *you're* the lucky one. You're on the run. You can't live a normal life. But you've got the life I want." Finally, he looked at her, his eyes overflowing with sadness. "It sucks, you know? I don't belong here, and I definitely don't deserve to be here. But I wish I did."

Her hand found its way to her necklace, the one her father had given to her many birthdays ago. Her fingers traced the chain until she located the clasp, and she unhooked it and pulled it free from her neck. "Here. I want you to take this."

The last of the pine needles fell through Yost's splayed fingers, and he rubbed his palms on his jeans. "Are you serious?"

"You don't have to wear it or anything. Just keep it with you. This necklace means a lot to me, and it's gotten me through some awful times. When you don't need it anymore, you can give it back to me. Okay?" She slipped it into his palm, and his fingers closed around it. "Just take it."

"Gemma, even if I wanted to...you know..." He couldn't even finish the sentence. "I couldn't do it. You don't know all the things I've done. I don't deserve to wear it. I don't even deserve to hold it."

"You're right, Yost. You don't deserve this. And neither do I. None of us deserve God's mercy, but we're so thankful He gives it freely. So, when you're ready, just ask Jesus to come into your heart. Ask Him for forgiveness and ask Him to change your life. It's never too late. Just look at the thief on the cross."

Yost only stared at her. "Who?"

Of course he didn't know about the thief on the cross. How would he?

Gemma's eyes drifted to the cross in the clearing. "When the Romans crucified Jesus, they hung him on a cross between two criminals. One criminal joined the crowd in mocking him, but the other one defended Jesus. Obviously, the criminal wasn't a good guy. They had put him on that cross for a reason. But in the last moments of his life, he realized Jesus was the Messiah. And he asked Jesus to remember him when He came into His kingdom. Basically, he was asking Jesus to allow him into heaven."

"But what did the guy do to deserve heaven?"

She glanced at Yost. "Absolutely nothing. He just believed, and he asked."

The ex-soldier looked flabbergasted. "Seriously? I would've told the guy to go pound sand. But what did Jesus say?"

Gemma smiled. "Jesus said, 'Truly I tell you, today you will be with Me in Paradise.'" She placed her hand on top of his. His palm was sticky with sap. "That's how I know it's not too late for you, Yost," she said. "Because it's never too late."

Swallowing hard, Yost nodded and slipped the silver cross into his jeans. "Thank you." He tore his damp eyes away from hers and cleared his throat. "So, what are you going to do now?"

She tilted her head and gazed up at the crisp, blue sky. According to the radio in the car, it was going to storm later, but right now, it was beautiful. Warm and sunny. The perfect fall day. A day when you could almost convince yourself that life was normal. She thought of her tree stand. Of the solid weight of the bow in her hands. The isolation of the woods.

Time to think. Time to cry. Time to pray.

"I'm going hunting."

CHAPTER TWENTY-EIGHT

Mullen loved hunting.

Parked in front of the convenience store, Mullen spat sunflower seed husks into his empty Mountain Dew bottle and thought back to the days he'd spent hunting with his old man. It was the only father-son thing they'd ever done together. Despite the old man's best efforts at making him hate it—which included repeatedly smacking his son upside the head for "being too loud and scaring away the game"—Mullen had enjoyed the business of hunting. He didn't care for the male bonding part so much as the killing.

He *loved* the killing.

They'd mostly hunted squirrels. The old man had developed a real taste for them, and squirrel pot pie with homemade noodles was his favorite meal. But squirrels were a bugger to clean, especially since the old man's ammo of choice was buckshot. Mullen had spent many meals carefully removing lead pellets from the greasy meat and depositing them on the edge of his plate with the practiced precision of a surgeon. He never saw his father remove any pellets from his meat. The old man probably ground them up with his teeth or swallowed them whole.

To be successful at hunting, you needed good instincts. You needed to be persistent. Above all, you needed to be patient. Patience made good scouts. He had the instincts, and he was persistent, but he had patience in spades.

Mullen used a fingernail to clean the seeds from his teeth. He'd watched the bookstore for hours, trying to get a feel for what was happening on the other side of those walls. To see who came and who went. But the moment the tail end of the convoy rolled out of town, the locals had folded up their lawn chairs and retreated to their houses—probably looking forward to a good meal and a hot shower.

The storm had passed...or so they thought.

With nothing better to do, he worked the puzzle pieces together in his mind. What did he know for sure? He knew that the girl he'd dragged off the mountain six months earlier had, apparently, played a role in the death of a highly decorated Task Force officer. He knew the girl was not only alive, but in contact with whomever was inside that bookstore. And he knew that Haggerty's mission in Winter's Dam was to root out a network of suspected sympathizers, and that the operation had been unsuccessful enough to warrant a hasty retreat.

But what had sent Haggerty running? And why did the girl from the mountain feel safe enough to be walking around in Winter's Dam *before* the Task Force had finished pulling out?

Mullen needed to find out for sure, and there was only one way.

He had to visit the bookstore.

While he was debating whether to go back to the convenience store for another Mountain Dew first, he glimpsed someone in his rearview mirror. An attractive girl with long hair that flowed down her back like oil. She was maybe nineteen or twenty. Skinny, dark, and full of secrets—just the way Mullen liked them.

She went into the bookstore.

Another sympathizer?

Mullen stole a glance at his watch. He'd been watching the bookstore for nearly two hours, and no one else had come or gone. There was an old

Subaru in the parking lot, which he assumed belonged to whomever owned the bookstore, but there were no other vehicles, and the streets were empty.

He could wait until the dark-haired girl left—then he would only deal with one person—but what would be the fun in that?

Mullen hopped out of the truck and walked toward the bookstore.

✝

The inside of the store was even worse than the outside.

There was something pathetic about the place. It brought to mind the dog Mullen's father had given him for his eighth birthday. A hyperactive mutt the old man had nabbed from somebody's yard. Dart had been the name on the mailbox, so they'd named the dog Dart because his father thought it was funny. But it turned out to be the perfect name. The stupid dog was constantly darting into the road, chasing after a squirrel, or a rabbit, or a tennis ball. The road in front of their house wasn't heavily traveled, so he usually got away with it.

But when Dart's luck finally ran out, it *really* ran out.

He'd been chasing a chipmunk when a dump truck ran him down. Of course, Mullen's father had refused to take the dog to the vet. "Ain't no vet going to fix this," he'd insisted. The old man was being cheap, but he was right. The truck had annihilated Dart's hindquarters. What stuck with Mullen, to this day, was how the poor creature had tried to stand when the old man aimed his rifle at its head.

Pathetic.

Mullen wrinkled his nose in revulsion at the bookshelves crowded with wrinkled paperbacks, the scuffed wood floors, the outdated furniture, and the ant traps visible in every corner. The whole place reminded him of a mortally wounded dog trying to stand on legs that no longer existed.

A better person would've put it out of its misery years ago.

"Excuse me? May I help you?"

A chubby old woman materialized like a ghost from the darkness at the rear of the store. She was wearing a purple cardigan that made her look like the dinosaur from those old *Barney* cartoons. The look she gave Mullen when their eyes met was a familiar one. He'd seen the same look in thousands of eyes since joining the Task Force.

Guilt.

"Oh no, ma'am." Mullen gave her a cheerful smile. "I'm just browsing."

The woman wrung her hands in front of her stomach, then she rubbed them on the front of her pants, as if trying to smooth the material down. In reality, her hands were damp with sweat, and she was drying them off. A common nervous tell. She had plenty of them. Mullen could even see her carotid artery pulsing in her neck.

Did she know who he was? *What* he was? Was it that obvious?

Finally, she found her voice. "I'm sorry, but we're closed today."

"Really?" Mullen turned to the door and made a show of looking for the sign, which he'd flipped to OPEN on his way in. "I could've sworn the sign said—"

"It's Sunday," she interrupted. "We're always closed on Sundays."

"Oh, my apologies." Mullen gave her a little bow, his best impression of a gentleman. If he'd been wearing a hat, he would've tipped it to her. "I don't suppose you'd mind if I looked around for a few minutes since I'm already here? I rarely get to this part of the state."

The old hag wasn't stupid. Her expression only grew more suspicious. "Oh, really? Where are you from?"

She wasn't interested in his origin story.

She was testing him, just as he was testing her.

"Perry County, originally." Mullen always seasoned his lies with a little truth. People recognized the truth when they heard it, and it made them more likely to believe the lies. "Grew up outside of Newport. Lots of farmland, lots of churches, and not much else."

He added a chuckle for good measure, but the old woman only stared at him.

"And where do you call home now?"

Mullen had no home, only a cramped apartment he shared with three other soldiers, all of whom hated him. "Actually, that's the real reason I'm here." He took a step closer to the old woman, and she flinched but held her ground. "I don't have a home anymore. Not since my entire family got detained a few years back. They were…" He pretended to struggle with this next part. "Well, the Task Force detained them as subversives, ma'am. I know I'm taking a big risk telling you this, but I'm tired of running. I thought maybe you could help me."

"Help you?" she repeated the words as if she couldn't comprehend their meaning. Then understanding dawned on her face, and her features hardened into a clay mask of anger. "You're a subversive? Why on earth do you think I would help you?"

Mullen felt his upper lip twitch, and he thought of his old man, whose lips used to do the same thing right before he snapped. That lip had been an advanced warning system, like some kind of severe weather alert. Now, Mullen's lip had become his own barometer. He would not stay calm for much longer. Not while the hag lied straight to his face. The girl from the mountain had been at this very bookstore just a few hours earlier, looking a lot better than she'd looked the last time Mullen had seen her. The old woman was playing him for a fool, and he didn't like it. Not one bit.

"Ma'am, believe me, I understand. You've got your own interests to protect. But—"

"Letty? Is everything okay?"

The dark-haired girl came up behind the old woman and put a protective hand on her shoulder. Man, she was even more beautiful up close, the kind of girl Mullen rarely saw outside of the movies. In the dreary darkness of the bookstore, she was the sun. It hurt to look at her, but he couldn't take his eyes off of her.

"I'm fine, Teresa. Just explaining to this nice young man that we're closed. He was about to leave."

The old woman—Letty, apparently, of Letty's

Book Cellar—gave Mullen a pointed look, but he ignored it and turned his attention back to Teresa.

Teresa.

What a beautiful name.

The old woman must've noticed the way Mullen was staring at the girl because she put a hand on Teresa's arm and escorted her toward the exit. "Listen, honey, why don't you head on home? It's been a long couple of days, and these old bones could use some rest. Come back first thing tomorrow morning, and we'll have some coffee and catch up."

Teresa frowned, clearly confused, but she allowed herself to be led to the door. "Okay. No problem. I'll come back first thing tomorrow."

This wasn't going the way Mullen had planned, but that was okay.

It would be more fun this way.

Instead of stepping aside as the old woman probably hoped he would, Mullen moved into the center of the aisle, making himself into a physical barrier between the two women and the door. "Oh, no. Please don't leave on my account."

"She *needs* to go," the old woman insisted, attempting to squeeze her plump body past Mullen. "You and I can talk after she leaves."

"I'm afraid that can't happen."

Mullen seized Teresa's arm and spun her

around so she was facing the old woman. Then, he grabbed his Beretta M9 pistol from underneath his shirt and buried it in the girl's cheek. She didn't scream or cry out in fear but tried to twist out of his arms.

He tightened his grip on her body. She was a feisty one.

The old woman held up her hands. "Please, don't hurt her. She has nothing to do with this."

"I won't hurt anyone," Mullen lied. "I just want to know about the girl who was here earlier this morning. Tell me where she and her friends are. I know you're hiding them."

The old woman groaned as if in pain. There was a table nearby, and she pulled out a chair and collapsed into it. "I don't know where they are. That's the truth. Me not knowing is part of the deal. If I don't know where they're located, I'm not a liability. I just help them get the supplies they need."

The artery in her neck pulsed in time with her lies.

Mullen pressed the barrel deeper into Teresa's cheek. Hard enough to leave a bruise. "Don't test me. You think I won't kill this girl? You think I don't have it in me? Did your little friends tell you about the fire I set? The one at the barn?"

Recognition dawned in the old woman's eyes.

"Oh yes, I heard about that one. They all survived, didn't they?"

Unbelievable. Here he was, with a gun to someone's head, and the pudgy old hag thought it was a good idea to mock him. He didn't want to do it. He didn't want to kill the girl. But the mission always came first. Always.

"I told you not to test me."

Twisting his body, he flung the girl against the wall near the door. She hit the wall hard and crumpled to the floor.

Mullen aimed the barrel at her head.

"I'm sorry," he whispered, tightening his finger on the trigger. "I didn't want to do this."

"I'll call them!"

He kept the barrel trained on the girl, but his eyes flitted to the old woman. "Come again?"

"I said I'll call them. When a subversive shows up at the store, I vet the person first. Then, I make the call, and they send someone here to pick the person up. That's how it works."

Her artery wasn't throbbing anymore. Finally, she was telling him the truth.

"Alright. So, you call someone back at this little hideout of theirs. But you know the location, don't you? Of course you do. You know where they are."

She lowered her head and nodded. "I know where they are."

"How many are there?"

"A lot."

He slammed his free hand on the table. "I asked you how many!"

"Over a hundred."

One hundred subversives, all in one place. Mullen's body trembled with excitement. The gun wobbled in his hand. "Wow. Just...wow."

The old woman pushed herself out of the chair. "I'll write the directions. I'll tell you exactly how to get there. Or I can come with you, if you—"

"Call them," Mullen interrupted.

"What?"

"Do what you would normally do. Call them. Tell them you've got someone waiting. That's what I want you to do."

"But they won't believe me," she rushed to say. "They know the Task Force raided the town. Please. They won't come."

Mullen arched an eyebrow at her. "Something tells me they might get a little nervous if we just show up on their doorstep, unannounced. Something tells me you might even have a plan for that kind of scenario, which is why you're pushing it so hard. So, how about you stop jerking me around? Call them now. Tell them you've got someone waiting to be picked up. I'll be listening the whole time. If you say anything—anything at all—that doesn't sound right

..." He nodded at Teresa. "I'll put a bullet in her perfect little head. How does that sound?"

✝

The old woman made the call from her office.

Mullen stood behind her, his pistol trained on the girl, who he'd ordered to sit on the rolling office chair near the desk. He'd made the old woman put the phone on speaker, and he listened to every word of the conversation. Every inflection. Listening for anything that sounded the slightest bit off. But the old woman was terrified out of her mind.

Not for her own life, but for the girl's.

In the middle of the cramped office, an ugly rug stretched across the floor like a dead snake. Someone had rolled it up, revealing a hidden door in the center of the floor.

The old woman hung up the phone. "It shouldn't be long. A half-hour maybe."

He pointed at the floor. "What's that?"

"The cellar. That's where I hide them until the transport gets here." She squared her shoulders and smirked at him. "Want to go down there? Get the full experience?"

"Nope. But that's where you two are going."

The beautiful girl begged him not to put them down there, but he ignored her and ordered both of them into the cellar. He made the old woman lift the door, grinning as she strained with the effort of lifting it. Then—with his gun pointed at the women—he knelt down to peer inside. A rickety wooden ladder descended about seven or eight feet into an empty cellar with a dirt floor. *Like the name of the store,* he thought. There were no windows. No way to escape. He glanced at Teresa and wagged the pistol toward the hole. "You first, gorgeous."

She fixed him with a frosty stare as she descended the ladder. She was so beautiful it took his breath away. Maybe, when this was all over, he would come back for her. For some fun.

"Your turn, Grandma."

The old woman lowered herself to her knees, wincing at some hidden pain, and then carefully extended one leg over the side.

Mullen could hear the girl down below, trying to guide her.

Somehow, the old hag got both of her feet on the ladder. She descended slowly, one creaky rung at a time. But when only her torso and head were visible and the rest of her body was already in the cellar, she stopped and looked at Mullen. There was fire in those dark eyes of hers.

He didn't much like it.

"This will not end well for you, you know."

He raised his eyebrows. "Really? Why's that?"

"Because you don't have God on your side," she said matter-of-factly. "You don't, but they do."

They. The subversives.

Mullen *tried* not to do it. He didn't want Teresa to think any worse of him than she already did. Not if they were going to have any hope of a future together. He fought himself, trying to resist what his body was telling him to do.

But then Carver spoke up for the first time since he'd entered the bookstore.

"Don't let that woman disrespect you, son."

So, he didn't.

Mullen lifted his leg and kicked the old woman in the chest with his boot. Her fingers lost their grip on the wood, and she tumbled backward, hitting the dirt below with a heavy thud.

"Letty!" Teresa screamed.

The woman did not cry out in pain. Mullen knelt over the open cellar door, and Teresa's heavy sobs drifted up to him, accompanied by a faint wheezing sound.

He knew that sound.

It was the sound of someone fighting for every breath.

"I'm sorry," he said to Teresa. He couldn't see her reaction—it was too dark—but he was still proud of himself for this petty attempt at humanity. "This has nothing to do with you."

Then, he closed the door, shutting them both in the darkness.

The old woman would not be a problem anymore, but he couldn't have the girl following him, so he grabbed the closest standing bookshelf and pushed it over. When the full weight of the bookshelf and its contents crashed on top of the door, the girl screamed.

He left the office, closing the door behind him, and went out to the porch to wait for his ride.

CHAPTER TWENTY-NINE

On the porch swing, Mullen flipped through a tattered romance novel, his mind not on the words but on the beautiful girl with the dark hair. He felt terrible for locking her in the basement with the dying woman, but what choice did he have? He listened carefully, but aside from the creaking of the porch swing, he couldn't hear anything. That was good. If the girl was screaming, no one could hear it from the street. He couldn't have anyone releasing her before he got back. Several times, he thought he could hear her voice faintly, begging him to release her, pleading with him to rescue her from the darkness, confessing that she loved him.

He wanted to go to her—he *would* go to her—but first he had to complete his mission.

When it was over, she would be his reward.

Mullen glanced up at the sound of a vehicle. A Tahoe approaching from the west slowed as it neared the bookstore and then pulled into the parking lot. Mullen closed the romance book and placed it back on the plastic patio table where he'd found it. Then, he stood up, slouching a little and trying to look exhausted, maybe even a little frightened. He thought of the faces of the roaches he'd detained over the years and tried to imitate their expressions.

The Tahoe parked at the base of the porch, and the driver's door opened. A guy poked his head out and gave Mullen a wide smile. Mullen's first impression of the guy was that he wasn't too bright. Friendly enough...but stupid. The human equivalent of a chocolate lab.

"You the one Letty called about?" Dumb Roach asked.

"Sure am." Wiping nonexistent sweat from his forehead, Mullen walked across the porch. "Thanks for coming. I appreciate you guys taking me in."

The passenger door swung open, and another roach stepped out of the SUV, catching Mullen by surprise. He hadn't realized there were two people in the vehicle. This roach was young, blonde, and badly in need of a haircut. He had the look of a surfer, but his eyes were sharp like a hawk's. He squinted at Mullen as if trying to see into his soul.

Joke was on him.

Mullen didn't have a soul.

"Where's Letty?" Surfer Roach asked.

Mullen had expected and prepared for the question. He'd assumed Letty was present for most of these exchanges. "Oh. She went out to get some food. She didn't have time to explain everything to me, but she said something about being away for a few days. I guess most of the stuff in her fridge had spoiled. Sounds like I didn't pick the best day to show up."

Surfer Roach scratched at the pale stubble on his jaw. "Letty left you here alone?"

"Yeah. She didn't want to leave, but it sounded like she was really worried about the food situation. She said the grocery store would be crazy if she waited too long." He offered a shaky laugh. "I told her it was no big deal, but I'd be lying if I said I wasn't hoping you would get here quick."

Surfer Roach didn't look convinced, but Dumb Roach waved Mullen toward the Tahoe. "Hurry, man. Get in. Being back in this town is giving me indigestion."

Mullen wanted to ask what he meant by that, but he knew asking questions wasn't a good idea. Also, why did they want him to get in the Tahoe?

He hadn't expected to have to leave his truck. "Actually, that's my truck over there. I'll just follow you guys, if that's okay."

"The vehicles always stay behind." Surfer Roach gripped the top of the door as if preparing to jump back inside and slam it shut. "Letty takes care of them."

Stupid old hag hadn't warned him about any of this. He should've kicked her harder.

Mullen gave him an indifferent shrug. He stuck his hands into his pockets and pinched the skin of his outer thighs until the pain cleared his mind. "Yeah, she mentioned that she usually deals with the cars, but she said she, because of everything that had happened, she wouldn't have time to do it for a few days. When I suggested following you guys back, she said that was a good idea. She didn't want an abandoned truck drawing any unnecessary attention to the bookstore."

Surfer Roach shot a glance at the truck, which was still parked in front of the convenience store. "Moving it out of the handicapped spot might help," he muttered.

Another stupid mistake.

He could almost hear Carver laughing.

"You serious?" Mullen leaned on the porch railing to look at the truck and then slapped a palm to his forehead. "Oh, man. I didn't even see those blue markings. Besides, the lot was empty when I got here. Do either of you guys have any idea what happened? Letty seemed really worked up."

Dumb Roach shook his head. "It's a long story, man. We'll fill you in when we get back." He pointed at his chest. "I'm Yost, by the way. The grumpy one over there is Kyle."

"My name's Doug." As soon as the words slipped through his lips, Mullen wished he could suck them back in. No one had called him Doug in years. In his old life, Corporal Mullen had been Douglas Mullen, Jr., the old man's namesake. His father had probably thought that, by saddling his only son with his name, he'd be ensuring that Mullen wouldn't go anywhere. Wouldn't make anything of himself. Wouldn't outperform his old man.

But Mullen had proven him wrong. He'd exchanged his name for a rank.

"Good to meet you, Doug." Dumb Roach slapped the roof of the Tahoe. "Let's get out of here. It's about a thirty-minute ride back to the camp, and there's a storm coming."

You have no idea.

"Sounds good."

The roaches got back inside the Tahoe and backed out of the parking space. They waited as Mullen jogged across the parking lot and climbed into his truck. He fired up the engine and put the truck in reverse. A half-empty bag of sunflower seeds slid off the passenger seat and onto the floor, spilling its contents everywhere. The Tahoe pulled out of the parking lot and turned right onto the highway.

Mullen followed them.

It can't be this easy, he thought. *No way will they lead me straight to their hideout.*

When they reached the outskirts of Winter's Dam, Colonel Carver started talking to him again. The dead Task Force commander sat in the extended cab part of the truck, directly behind the passenger seat. In the same spot as the duffel bag. When Mullen realized the colonel had returned, he tilted his rearview mirror toward the roof so he wouldn't be tempted to look back there. But in his mind, he could see Carver, the gym bag perched on his lap, his pale hand sliding back and forth over the smooth nylon, gently caressing it the way a man would caress a favorite pet. Or a loved one.

"This is the day we've been waiting for, son," Carver said. "The girl is so close now. Can you feel her?"

"I can, sir."

"Don't screw around this time. Don't give them a chance to figure you out. Hit your enemy hard and fast, like I taught you. Don't hesitate."

"I won't, sir," Mullen assured his commander. "I'm ready."

Those thirty minutes were the longest of Mullen's life.

Once they exited the main highway, they drove for miles without passing another car or seeing another house. There was nothing on either side of the truck but trees. Mullen searched the woods for hidden driveways or mailboxes but couldn't find any. No wonder this group had avoided detection for so long. It was smart to put their hideout so far from their supply chain.

Dangerous, but smart.

Finally, they came to a bridge that crossed a fast-moving creek. A newish-looking gate blocked access to the bridge and the road beyond it. On the other side of the gate, a sign announced that they were entering Camp Mahantango.

Surfer Roach got out of the Tahoe, unlocked the gate, and pushed it aside. He pointed at one of the nearby trees and gave it a thumbs up. Mullen's immediate thought was that the guy was crazy, but then he noticed a white security camera halfway up the tree, aimed at the gate.

Mullen smiled. The roach was telling whomever watched that camera that everything was copacetic. No worries. Nothing to see here.

After the Tahoe drove through the gate, Surfer Roach waved Mullen through.

"That's it," Carver said. "Make the call."

"Roger that, sir."

Mullen waited until Surfer Roach closed the gate behind them and hopped back into the Tahoe. Then, he pulled out his cell phone, opened the map application, and pulled up the grid coordinates. He put the phone on speaker so the roaches wouldn't see him holding it against his ear.

He called the number.

He didn't want to make the call, not this soon, but he didn't have a choice. Last time, he'd tried to have a little fun, and it had backfired on him. He would not make the same mistake again.

The voice on the other end of the line asked him how many.

Mullen didn't know, but the old woman had said more than a hundred.

"Send buses."

This Camp Mahantango wasn't just any old campground. It was massive, according to the faded map sign he'd just driven past, and most of the buildings he could see appeared to be well-maintained. These roaches were living better than most. Mullen continued driving down the dirt road, passing several painted brown signs with yellow lettering. The signs featured the names of various hiking trails and their lengths.

How did the roaches find this place? Who owned it?

His instincts told him the old hag at the bookstore had something to do with it.

Up ahead, on the left side of the dirt road, was a massive four-door metal shed. Two of the sliding doors were closed, but the other two were hanging wide open. The Tahoe took a hard left into the shed. The open doors reminded him of a gaping mouth, as if the shed itself was surprised to see Mullen pulling up in his pickup truck.

Mullen didn't drive inside the shed.

While the roaches got out of the Tahoe, Mullen screwed a suppressor onto the barrel of his Beretta. The pistol was so long with the suppressor attached that it almost looked like a toy. But he wasn't concerned about appearances.

He needed silence for what he was about to do.

Putting a hand on the driver's door, Mullen glanced into the backseat. No Colonel Carver, but the gym bag was sitting there on the rear seat, exactly where he'd left it.

Mullen hopped out of the pickup truck, holding the gun behind his back.

"Hey, man." Dumb Roach walked toward him. "There's room. Pull your truck inside."

Don't hesitate.

So Mullen didn't.

The bullet slammed into the roach's stomach, hitting the sweet spot just below his sternum, and he fell against the Tahoe, moaning in agony. He coughed, and blood speckled his white teeth.

Mullen swung the gun on the other roach.

Surfer Roach had been reaching for something in the Tahoe, but when the barrel of the gun landed on him, he threw his hands in the air. "No!" he shouted. And then, because he was too stupid to understand what was happening, he asked, "Why are you doing this?"

"Why do you think?" Mullen asked. "You're subversives. You should've died back in the barn fire. It's going to be so much worse for you now."

Surfer Roach squinted at him, confused, trying to piece it all together. When he finally understood, Mullen watched the roach's mouth tighten into a snarl. "That...was...you?"

Mullen beamed at the guy who looked like he wanted to kill him. "People rarely get the chance to right their wrongs. I guess I'm just lucky."

The roach swallowed hard. When he spoke again, it was through gritted teeth. "Please. I've got a wife. We just had a baby."

Mullen couldn't believe it. This disgusting roach with the greasy surfer hair was trying to use his family to connect with him. As if family meant anything to Mullen. As if it was a word he understood. Mullen had no family. No parents. No wife. No kids. Nothing that mattered to him except for the ghost of his dead commander...and the contents of his black duffel bag.

"Thanks for telling me." Mullen raised the gun and pointed it at the roach's chest. "I'll kill them both so you can be together."

He pulled the trigger.

The shot sent the roach stumbling backward, his hands clasped over the wound on his upper chest, blood pooling between his fingers. He fell against the rear wall of the shed and slid to the floor.

Mullen didn't think it was a clean shot, so he raised the gun and pointed it at the roach's head.

That was when he heard the scream.

A *child's* scream.

Mullen pivoted toward the shed's open door, pistol raised, ready to fire at whomever had dared to interfere with his mission. It took a moment for his eyes to adjust to the sunlight, but as soon as they did, he saw her.

The Cindy Lou Who to his Grinch.

He blinked twice, expecting her to disappear. But each time he opened his eyes, she was still there. The girl from the barn. She was a little older and taller but still the same girl. She stood in the middle of the dirt road, pale as a ghost, eyes wide with fear, red hair catching the sunlight in such a way that it appeared to be on fire.

Their eyes locked, just for a moment, and then she sprinted into the woods.

Mullen's eyes darted back to Surfer Roach.

The guy's head was hanging to the side, and his chest wasn't moving.

"Shut those doors in case anyone comes along," Carver growled from behind him, causing Mullen to jump. "Hurry."

"Yes, sir." Mullen quickly pulled the doors closed, sealing the two dead men inside the shed. Then, he spun around, fists clenched at his side, and faced the woods on the opposite side of the road. He caught a fleeting glimpse of red hair just before the girl disappeared into the trees.

"Get after her, son. Whatever you do, don't let that one get away."

Mullen obeyed.

CHAPTER THIRTY

An earsplitting scream cut through the silence of the woods with a knife-like precision.

Gemma's eyes flew open, the terrible sound echoing through her hazy mind like a nightmare she couldn't escape. She sprang to her feet, intending to run, although she didn't know if she was running toward or away from the sound, but something pulled at her waist, flinging her backward. Some kind of strap or belt. She tugged at it, trying to break free even as her half-asleep brain struggled to make sense of the cluster of colors that encircled her.

Leaves. They were leaves.

She wasn't on the ground. She was high above it, in her tree stand.

The void of space beneath her appeared to double as she realized what she'd nearly done. Lightheaded, she collapsed onto the padded seat, the metal shifting ever so slightly beneath her weight. She must've fallen asleep. If not for her safety strap, she would've run straight off the platform and fallen twenty feet to the unforgiving forest floor.

Her back ached from being propped against the tree for too long. The blue sky had disappeared, replaced by ominous-looking storm clouds. It was disorienting, like she'd fallen asleep and woken up in a different world.

But what of the scream? Had she dreamt it?

Gemma leaned as far forward as her safety strap would allow, tilted her head, and listened. She couldn't hear anything at first, but her instincts told her to listen harder. Because something wasn't right. The forest was unnaturally quiet. The normal sounds of the forest, the chatter of birds, the relentless hum of insects, were all gone. Even the trees—which spoke to one another through a series of creaks, snaps, and moans—had ceased their conversations.

Then, she heard it. A deep, unnatural hum, far in the distance. It took her brain a moment to place the sound, but when she did, her body went cold.

The rumbling of engines. *Big* engines.

None of the vehicles they used at the Sanctuary produced that kind of sound. But she'd heard it before. It wasn't a sound she would ever forget, no matter how hard she tried.

Transport buses.

Slinging her bow and quiver over her shoulder, Gemma unhooked from her safety strap and tore down the ladder, jumping off when she was still several rungs above the ground. She raced toward the Sanctuary, already knowing what she would find, but desperate to be wrong. *Praying* to be wrong.

How? The word kept circling in her mind. *How? How? How?*

She avoided the pathways and kept to the woods, skirting the perimeter of the campground, still hoping that she might be wrong. But as she grew closer to the Sanctuary, the grumbling grew louder and deeper until Gemma wondered if it wasn't an engine at all but the guttural groaning of some ancient monster that had climbed up from hell to voice its disapproval with the Sanctuary. She imagined it crawling out of Mire Lake, water cascading down the razor-sharp spikes that covered its back, cloven hooves digging meteor-sized holes in the earth as it made its way down the embankment toward the campground.

The woods ended abruptly at the northern edge

of the lake, and Gemma skidded to a stop, almost losing her footing on the soggy ground. She back-pedaled and flung herself behind the nearest tree, praying that she hadn't been spotted. The compound bow bounced painfully off her left shoulder blade.

Across the expanse of water, four jet-black detainee transport buses were idling near the dining hall. Taylor had told her that the transport buses were basically repurposed prison buses. Like prisoners, subversives' hands and feet were shackled for the ride to the detention center. The dark-tinted windows concealed the wire caging that covered the glass to prevent any subversives from trying to escape, and there would be two armed soldiers stationed on each bus.

Gemma watched as dozens of Task Force soldiers with rifles escorted people she recognized out of the nearby cabins and led them toward the buses. Some people were crying, but most were stoic.

Had they resigned themselves to their fates? Or were they thinking about Pastor Jenson's sermon?

Instead of letting the detainees board the buses, the soldiers sorted them into three groups and made them stand in their newly assigned groups in front of the dining hall.

The groups were men, women, and children.

When the soldiers started to pull children out of their parent's arms, Gemma couldn't stand to watch anymore. She had to do something. She had to find Addie. And Sophia.

She slipped back into the woods and sprinted toward Cabin 4. The cabins assigned to their group from the Station were farther away from the main section of camp. The soldiers might not have reached them yet. Maybe Addie and the others had gotten away. But where would they go? Where *could* they go?

Gemma was almost at the old archery range when she heard a scream, followed by a desperate plea.

"Please, no! Please! Don't take him!"

Dread seized her insides and twisted them like wet laundry. She raced toward Cabin 4. Toward the voice. A voice she recognized by its distinctive Pennsylvania Dutch twang.

"Please!" Addie screamed again. *"Don't take my baby!"*

Moving swiftly through the trees, Gemma kept a thick barrier of trees between herself and the small grouping of cabins. Circling around behind the rear of the cabins, she leaned out from behind a massive pine tree and saw Addie near the firepit. She was clutching Weston to her chest as a Task

Force soldier with black-framed glasses tried to pry the wailing baby out of her arms.

Gemma recognized that soldier. The one with the glasses. He was the soldier from the video on Taylor's phone. The one who had shot and killed Jason Fishman on the football field.

"Stop!" Addie cried. *"You're hurting him!"*

The soldier grabbed the baby's arms, causing Weston to howl even louder. "Then let him go," he growled. "You'll get him back after you're processed at the detention facility."

That was a lie. Gemma knew it, and so did Addie. Minor children never accompanied their subversive parents into detention centers. Children went into the government's care until an appropriate foster family was found. Even if the biological parents eventually renounced and got released, there were no guarantees they would ever get their children back. The adoption process was often fast-tracked, especially where infants were concerned.

If Addie let go of Weston, it was doubtful she would ever see him again.

Addie unleashed a banshee-like scream and twisted out of the soldier's grip. She tried to run in Gemma's direction, but the soldier grabbed a clump of her hair and yanked her backward. She collapsed hard on her backside, her hands reflexively covering Weston's head to shield him from the fall.

The soldier loomed over her. "Hand the kid over now."

Cradling Weston in her arms, Addie whispered, "No."

Somewhere in the distance, black smoke puffed into the sky like dragon's breath. The Task Force must've lit a building on fire. The dining hall, maybe? Or one of the cabins? Gemma silently prayed that there weren't people inside. But the Task Force could burn the entire camp to the ground, and no one would care. The story would never get out, but even if it did, no one would care.

Gemma could feel her life ending. Not her body, not physical death, but the death of her soul, which was so much worse. After losing Taylor, she had nothing left but her friends and the Sanctuary. And now she was losing them all.

Everything that mattered.

Gone.

In the distance, the engines groaned louder. People were screaming now. Crying. Begging. Every few minutes, a lone gunshot rang out. Gemma didn't want to think about those gunshots, but she knew what they meant. She knew. People she knew were dying.

But none of that mattered now. Everything that

was happening on the other side of the camp was nothing but background noise to her, a disturbing soundtrack to the tragedy playing out in front of her.

She couldn't do anything to help the others.

But Addie and Weston...

"Last chance, roach," the soldier said. "Don't waste it."

Addie closed her eyes and began to sing one of her lullabies.

The soldier drew his rifle and aimed the barrel at Addie's head. "Good riddance..."

Gemma's arrow hit him squarely in his chest—a good, clean lung shot.

The soldier looked in Gemma's direction, dumbfounded, and their eyes met for a brief moment. Then, he stumbled into the rocks of the firepit, knocking them over on his way down.

Driven by adrenaline, Gemma raced down the hill to the cabin, her only thought of getting to her best friend before someone else did. When she reached the firepit, Addie was still on the ground with Weston, her eyes wide and unfocused.

Addie appeared to be in shock. "Gemma? What happened?"

It was an impossible question, because Gemma had no idea what had happened. She didn't remember pulling an arrow from her quiver. She didn't remember nocking it. She definitely didn't remember drawing the string or letting it go. Her eyes fell on the soldier, and she was overwhelmed with the feeling that she needed to help him in some way.

But his chest wasn't moving. His pupils were dilated. He was already dead.

And Gemma had killed him.

"We have to go." She slipped an arm around Addie and helped her to her feet. "Right now."

Addie's body felt frail and inconsequential in Gemma's arms, like trying to hold onto a ghost. She'd lost so much weight since giving birth to Weston. Breastfeeding hadn't come easily, and she didn't have a lot of calories to spare to begin with. But when Addie's legs buckled and she crumpled like a tissue, Gemma went down with her.

Somehow, Addie kept a firm hold on Weston, but she sagged against Gemma and wailed, "They've taken Kyle!"

"How do you know? Did you see them take him?"

"No! But he would be here! If they hadn't gotten him, he would be here!"

How could Gemma argue with that? If Kyle was okay, the *first* place he would've come was to the cabin. The fact that he wasn't here didn't bode well. But there was so much loss happening in the woods around them that it was hard to feel anything but numb.

"Where is Sophia?" Gemma asked. "Have you seen her this afternoon?"

"I don't know. Weston and I were napping when the door crashed open."

Another gunshot rang out.

Each gunshot felt like claws ripping through the soft flesh of Gemma's heart. There was nothing worse than not knowing which of her friends had just gotten shot. Which of them might be dying. Which of them might already be dead. She loved so many people at the Sanctuary, but one name stuck out above all the others.

Sophia.

Please, God, let her be okay.

"Gemma...I can't...I can't do this..." Addie extended her arms, trying to pass a still-screaming Weston off to Gemma. "Please take him..." The deep, guttural wail that followed sounded as if it had come from the depths of Addie's soul.

The dead soldier hovered in the corner of Gemma's vision, and although she wouldn't allow herself to look at him, she knew she would never escape him. Not from this day forward, for as long as she lived. She would never forget the soldier or the look he'd given her when their eyes met. The last thing he'd seen before he died was the face of his murderer.

He was a murderer, too, Gemma reminded herself. *And he was going to kill Addie.*

Somehow, those thoughts didn't make her feel any better.

Crouching next to Addie, Gemma grabbed her best friend's shoulders and shook them. Hard. "Listen to me, Addie. If we don't get out of here *right now,* the Task Force is going to find us. They're going to detain us. And they're going to take Weston away from you. If that happens, you're never going to see him again. Do you understand me? Do you think Kyle would want that?"

Addie sucked in a breath, highlighting her hollow cheeks. She was so thin. So terribly thin. "I can't do this without him, Gemma."

"You don't have a choice," Gemma snapped, her voice as hard and cold as marble. "None of us do. Not anymore." Her gaze settled on Weston, and she softened her tone. "You've got to fight for him now." She brushed a finger down Weston's damp cheek, and the baby stopped screaming and stared at her as if he understood. "That's what his daddy would want, anyway. But the choice is yours."

The sound of breaking glass was quickly followed by more smoke. The Task Force had set another fire. This one was much closer. Gemma could see the flames from her spot on the ground. But she didn't move. She stayed next to Addie, waiting to see what her friend decided. Because whatever Addie decided, that was what they would do.

As the flames licked the trees, Gemma thought about how unfair it all was. The Task Force. The detention centers. The raids. How many people—on both sides—had suffered and died for this cause? And for what? Who was it all for?

When Gemma finally tore her eyes away from the flames, Addie wasn't on the ground anymore. She was standing with Weston on her hip. Both of them were staring at Gemma, their dirty faces streaked with tears. They weren't crying anymore.

Standing, Gemma took Addie by the arms and hugged her. Then, she held her at arm's length. "You know where my tree stand is, right?" When Addie nodded, she continued, "Take Weston there. You'll still need to keep him quiet, but it's far enough away that you'll be able to see the soldiers coming long before they reach you. If you see any soldiers, run and don't look back. Otherwise, wait for me at the tree stand. If I don't show up, you'll know what happened. Wait until the Task Force clears the area, see if there are any vehicles left, and drive to Letty's."

Addie winced as Weston playfully snagged a

strand of her hair and pulled on it. He gave his mother a toothless grin, oblivious to the terrible things happening around him. "What about you?" Addie asked. "Where are you going?"

Gemma looked toward the main campground. The fires were getting closer. More soldiers would find Cabin 4 soon, but she had to do something first. It was a long shot, but she wouldn't be able to live with herself if she didn't try. A tiny bud of hope still grew in the rocky soil of her heart.

They'd taken so much from her, but they hadn't taken her hope yet.

"The only place Sophia could be," Gemma said, slipping the bow sling over her shoulder.

"I'm going to Neverland."

CHAPTER THIRTY-ONE

Dark, menacing clouds, swollen with rain, rolled across the sky with the speed of an invading army, easily conquering the thin strip of blue sky over the Neverland tower. The storm clouds and black smoke from the fires combined forces to swallow up the sun, and the unnatural gloominess of the afternoon made the tower look even more intimidating than it usually did.

Gemma jogged across the open field, stealing glances behind her to check for soldiers. The tower rose out of the earth like an enormous grave marker, as if the Sanctuary had known its eventual fate long before its inhabitants. Gemma's eyes could've been playing tricks on her, but the tower looked bigger than the last time she'd seen it. She felt certain that, if she stood on the roof of the fort and reached toward the sky, her fingertips would touch the clouds.

The thought made her shudder.

She didn't allow her mind to drift back to what was happening at the campground, nor could she think about what might be happening with Addie and Weston. Had they made it to the tree stand? Or had they been captured before they got there? She hated herself for sending them off on their own, but she couldn't risk bringing them with her to Neverland.

She reached the base of the tower and whisper-shouted, "Sophia? Are you there?"

There was no response, not the faintest murmur or cry, but that didn't mean Sophia wasn't hiding up there. The wind was picking up, and any hushed response from the girl could've easily been lost to the wind. Besides, if Sophia was hiding, it must terrify her to hear the sounds coming from the camp. She wouldn't reveal herself to anyone, including Gemma.

There was only one thing for Gemma to do, and she *really* didn't want to do it.

The harness was way too small. Abram had adjusted it to fit Sophia perfectly, so it took Gemma several minutes to loosen the straps enough so that she could step into the harness and pull it on like a pair of underwear. Tightening it around her waist, she hooked the carabiner onto the rope that dangled off the side of the tower and tugged hard on the rope. It felt secure. But as she gazed up at the massive wall, she imagined the rope snapping and sending her plummeting to the ground.

Most of the climbing holds were so bleached by years spent baking in the sun that Gemma couldn't tell what color they had once been. Gripping the ones closest to her with shaky hands, she stole another look back at the trail. Still empty. But there was no telling how close the soldiers were to the ropes course. What if they stumbled across Neverland while she was clinging to the side of the tower like a spider on a wall?

They would probably use her for target practice.

"God, help me climb fast," she prayed. "And get me to the top in one piece."

She didn't look at the trail again, nor did she look at the fort on top of the tower. Everything faded away except the wall and her next climbing holds. She didn't even glance down at her feet, afraid that she might have a heart attack and die right there on the tower if she realized how high she was. But she always found the next foothold. When the wind picked up, blowing loose strands of hair into her eyes and mouth, she reminded herself that Sophia—who was only eleven—scaled this wall daily like it was nothing.

The first fat raindrops landed on Gemma's hands. It was strange how quickly the storm had moved in, almost as if God was expressing his anger at what was happening at the Sanctuary. Ignoring the distant flashes of lightning, Gemma kept climbing, doing her best not to think about the vast expanse of open air between her body and the ground. Some of the climbing grips felt a little loose, and now the rain was making them slippery. But those grips weren't what was keeping Gemma on the side of the tower. It was her own body, her own strength holding her up. Strength she didn't even realize she possessed.

What would Taylor think if he could see her now?

"Someday," she whispered to him, wherever he was. "Someday, I'll tell you about this."

The more Gemma thought about it, the more convinced she was that Sophia was in the fort. The girl spent most of her time in the fort anyway, and if she had heard anything bad happening at the Sanctuary, the fort would have been the most obvious place for Sophia to hide. As Gemma approached the top of the tower, she visualized herself crawling into the fort and finding Sophia huddled in the far corner, her tiny arms wrapped around her knees, her expression morphing from terror to jubilation as Gemma pulled herself into the fort, as if by imagining it, Gemma could actually make it happen.

There was another flash of lightning in the distance, followed by a rumble of thunder. The storm was getting closer.

What if the climbing grips got really wet in the storm? Would she and Sophia be able to get back down before the Task Force found them?

She would worry about that later. The fort was so close. Only a few more feet. She kept pulling herself up, faster now, desperate to be reunited with Sophia. They would wait out the storm together—both the thunderstorm *and* the Task Force —in the fort. And then they would climb down and reunite with Addie and Weston.

As for what came afterwards...Gemma didn't know.

She released the last grip and grabbed the edge of the platform, using it to pull herself the rest of the way up. She heaved herself inside the fort and collapsed onto the old floorboards, breathing heavily, her body shaking with relief. Then, remembering why she'd made the climb in the first place, Gemma lifted her head and she searched the corners of the fort for Sophia. There was a pile of paperback books stacked in one corner, and Sophia's pencil sketches were everywhere, tacked to the walls, scattered on the floor. Sophia's life, as she saw it. A beautiful sketch of the moss-covered cross in the clearing. Individual sketches of each of the Golden Girls. Sketches of the interior and exterior of Cabin 4. There was even a sketch of Gemma.

But Sophia wasn't there.

Rain drummed on the metal roof of the fort as Gemma ran her fingers over the sketch of the cross, trying to think. If Sophia wasn't hiding in the tower, then she had to be hiding somewhere else. One of the empty cabins, maybe? Or in the woods?

Gemma searched the inside of the fort again, convinced she had overlooked Sophia.

And that was when she saw it.

A piece of construction paper, laying in the middle of the floor. She hadn't noticed it before because there were papers scattered all over the fort. But someone had tacked this one directly into the center of the floor.

It wasn't a pencil sketch. It was a note.

Gemma pulled the tack out of the wood to free the paper. Then, since it was too dark inside the fort to read the note, she crawled back to the opening, careful to stay low so that no one on the ground would notice her right away.

Another rumble of thunder.

Gemma held the note in shaking hands and read.

The girl says your name is Gemma Alcott. Funny, I never knew your actual name until now, but I expected something better than that. The girl reminds me of you. She ran from me, just like you did back on the mountain. And just like you, she wasn't fast enough. But you won't run from me this time, will you? Because I've got something you want.

Gemma covered her mouth to stifle a scream.

Mullen.

She'd always expected the redheaded soldier to come back for her, hadn't she? The entire time he'd been stalking her in her dreams, he'd been stalking her in real life. And she'd known. All along, she'd felt him closing in on her.

But he hadn't taken her. He'd taken Sophia.

Gemma's world turned to static, so she couldn't see anything clearly. She remembered this feeling —and what came after. First, the static. Then, her vision would constrict until there was nothing but a tiny pinprick of light in the middle of the darkness. She knew the feeling because she'd passed out once before, during an awful high school dance. One moment, she'd been leaning against the wall, dizzy, a red Solo cup of punch in her hand. The next thing she knew, she was on the ground, the punch soaking into her beautiful new dress. When she came to, several of her classmates had been standing over her, laughing.

She closed her eyes. She couldn't pass out now. Sophia needed her.

Gemma concentrated on breathing slowly and deeply. *In through the nose. Out through the mouth.* When the dizziness finally passed, she finished the note.

I don't believe in fairy tales, and I don't believe in God. But I believe in Colonel Carver. He's always with me. He's my god. So, I'm going to ask him to keep you safe. It's important that you don't get detained with the others, because I need to see you one more time. What do you think, Gemma Alcott? Can we meet and finish what we started? —M.

P.S. You have until midnight. If you don't come, the girl dies. If your answer is yes, come alone. If you bring the traitor with you, or if you bring anyone else, the girl dies. If you think I'm bluffing...just remember the barn fire. You didn't really think that fat slob acted alone, did you?

Gemma stared at the note, her heart a block of ice in the center of her chest. Just the thought of Sophia out there somewhere, alone with that monster, made Gemma want to throw up. But Gemma was the object of his anger, not Sophia. Hopefully, he wouldn't hurt her.

But if he hurt her...

Anger welled up inside of her. "Where?" she muttered. "Where am I supposed to go, you piece of garbage?"

How was she supposed to know where to meet him? He had written no location in the note. But when she flipped the paper over, the other side was one of Sophia's sketches.

It was of the entrance to the coal mine, back at the Station.

The mine. Her heart dropped. *Why the mine?*

A noise drew her attention to the fort's opening. She folded the paper up and stuffed it inside her jacket. Then, keeping her body low, she crawled closer to the edge and looked down.

Task Force soldiers. Six of them. All wearing black ponchos over their uniforms. They really were untouchable, weren't they? Even the rain couldn't touch them. The soldiers moved tactically into the field, rifles drawn, each soldier clearing a different area. One of them glanced up at the fort, and Gemma quickly scooted backward, out of view.

"Please don't let them climb up here," she prayed. "Please, God."

Lightning cracked the sky, illuminating the interior of the fort, and Gemma plastered herself tight against the floor, praying that the soldier hadn't spotted her. A strong gust of wind ripped through the fort, sending Sophia's drawings fluttering, but the thumbtacks held them in place.

What would happen if lightning struck the tower? Gemma's traitorous brain produced an image of the fort going up in flames, leaving her with the impossible choice of burning alive or jumping to her death. But the soldiers probably wouldn't be too eager to climb the tower in a lightning storm, would they? The irony of the situation wasn't lost on her. The one thing keeping her safe —the one thing that was keeping the soldiers from climbing up to check the tower—might be the very thing that killed her.

"God, please. Please get me out of here so I can help her."

Gemma remained plastered to the floor of the fort until the storm finally moved away. When the thunder eventually ceased and the pelting rain slowed to a light drizzle, she listened as hard as she could, trying to hear voices. But she couldn't hear anything. No screams. No gunshots. No engines. Nothing. Finally, she crept forward and risked another glimpse over the edge.

The soldiers were gone.

If she was smart, she would wait longer, make sure the Task Force was really gone before she risked exposing herself again, but every minute she wasted was another minute Sophia would have to spend with Mullen.

Gemma looked around for the harness and found it still attached to her waist. She'd never taken the thing off. She slid backward and threw one leg over the edge. The worst part was finding the first foothold. But once she found it, she flew down the tower, barely even noticing how wet the climbing grips were or how some of them felt dangerously loose in her hands.

When she hit the bottom, she tore off the harness.

And she ran.

CHAPTER THIRTY-TWO

Addie and Weston were okay, thank God.

Gemma found them crouched underneath the tree stand, both of them soaked through and miserable but alive. Weston appeared to have cried himself to sleep, but Addie was still sobbing. They looked terrible, but at least they weren't on a bus to some godforsaken detention center. It was a miracle the Task Force hadn't found them. The violent storm had turned out to be a blessing in disguise. Not only had it forced the Task Force to abandon their search, but the rain and thunder had easily covered up the sounds of their cries.

As Gemma approached the tree stand, Addie's head jerked up. She stopped crying, and her eyes searched the woods behind Gemma. "Sophia?"

Gemma said nothing, only shook her head.

Addie's face fell, and the tears started up again. She clutched Weston tighter against her chest, and he let out a single, irritated cry before going back to sleep. "This can't be happening," she sobbed. "I keep telling myself it's a dream. I keep hoping I'll wake up soon."

Crouching next to Addie, Gemma pushed the sweat-soaked hair off her friend's forehead and kissed her just above her brow line. Addie's brown hair was so soaked that it appeared to be black. She was shivering, but Gemma had no way to warm her up. "We have to go, Addie. Okay? We can't stay here any longer."

She'd expected resistance, but Addie nodded and climbed to her feet. She tottered on unstable legs, and Gemma lunged forward, arms out-stretched to catch Weston if Addie passed out or dropped him. Thankfully, Addie steadied herself and nodded at Gemma.

"I'm ready."

"Let me carry him for a bit," Gemma urged, gently prying Weston from Addie's arms. It took little effort. Addie seemed relieved to be handing him over. "You need a break."

"Thank you."

Weston stirred a little but didn't protest the new set of arms holding him, probably because these arms were slightly less damp. They set off at a good pace with Gemma in the lead. She held the baby as tight as she could, hoping that her body heat would warm him. Weston felt heavier than usual because of his soaked clothes, and he definitely needed a diaper change, but they couldn't risk going back to the cabin for dry clothes and diapers. Gemma couldn't hear the engines anymore, so she was pretty sure the Task Force had left the camp. But pretty sure wasn't good enough. They stuck to the perimeter of the camp and used the woods for concealment.

A few minutes into their journey, Addie asked, "Gemma? Where are we going?"

"To find a vehicle. I'll drop you guys off at the hunting cabin with Gavin, Brie, and Max. You'll be safe there."

"Drop us off?" Addie grabbed Gemma's arm from behind, forcing her to stop walking. "What do you mean? Where are you going?"

"To town," Gemma quickly replied, pulling her arm free. She resumed walking so she wouldn't have to meet Addie's eyes. "I have to talk to Letty and let her know what happened. Then, we can figure out where we go from here."

Lying to Addie was a split-second decision. Not that Gemma didn't trust her best friend, but no one from the group could find out about Sophia. No matter what the note said, they would never let Gemma go to the coal mine by herself.

But Gemma knew—with utter certainty—that Mullen would kill Sophia if Gemma broke even one of his rules. In fact, he was probably *hoping* she would break a rule, so he'd have an excuse to kill Sophia.

No. Gemma couldn't risk it.

Mullen was *her* problem.

And she would be the one to take care of him.

✝

The Task Force had not torched the shed. Another miracle.

It was far enough away from the main campground that the Task Force could've easily overlooked it. Since it didn't look like much from the outside, the soldiers had probably driven past it without paying it a second glance.

Gemma crouched on the opposite side of the road for a few minutes, waiting and listening for the sound of any approaching vehicles, but she couldn't hear anything over the rushing creek. Massive tire tracks cut through the mud on both sides of the road, reminding her of a novel she'd once read. *Mortal Engines.* The book was about cities on wheels that moved through the countryside, consuming other cities and their resources. Gemma had never read anything more chilling. What could be more terrifying than a predator city on wheels?

Those black buses, that was what.

When she felt confident the road was clear, she motioned to Addie, and they jogged through the mud to the shed. Gemma didn't have any car keys, and she *really* didn't want to go back to the trading post to get them, but she knew Taylor used to keep a spare key in a magnetic box underneath the Charger's rear wheel well. Hopefully, it would still be there.

"Here. Take him." Gemma handed Weston off to Addie, and then pushed the sliding doors apart, her boots sinking into the mud.

As the doors slid open, she froze.

The first thing she saw was the blood. There was blood everywhere.

And then she saw Yost.

Gemma whispered, "Addie, you and Weston wait outside."

Addie didn't argue.

The door of the Tahoe hung open. Yost leaned against the panel below the driver's seat. He wasn't moving. There was blood all over the driver's seat, and his cell phone was laying on the ground next to him, as if he'd tried to call someone for help. His hands still covered the wound on his stomach, an obviously futile attempt at stopping the blood flow. By the looks of him, most of the blood had already exited his body. Beneath his dark, sweat-soaked hair, his face was the color of fresh snow. Gemma had never seen anyone so pale.

If he hadn't turned his head to look at her, she would've thought he was already dead.

"Yost?"

She couldn't remember his first name. Why couldn't she remember it?

The only color on Yost's face was the dark blood that coated his lips. When he opened his mouth to speak, a trickle of blood oozed down his chin. "Gemma..."

At the sound of her name, Gemma's legs un-froze, and she ran over to him. Dropping to her knees, she put her own hands over his and pressed down hard on the wound. Her eyes darted to his face, searching for signs of pain, but he barely winced.

"I..." Blood dripped from his lips. "I...asked..."

"You asked? You asked what?"

Yost's hands moved beneath hers. He was trying to lift them. To pull them away from the wound. At first, Gemma resisted him, not wanting him to take the pressure away, even for a second. Despite the terrible nature of Yost's injuries, she was still hoping that, maybe, he would live. Maybe God would grant them one more miracle today.

Mike. That was his name. Mike Yost.

But when Gemma met Yost's eyes again, she saw something within them she wasn't expecting. Not pain or fear, but relief. And joy. Seeing those emotions on the face of someone who was obviously dying caught Gemma so off-guard that, when Yost continued to pull his hands away from his stomach, she let him do it.

"What is it?" she asked, pulling her own hands away.

Yost held a blood-covered fist out to her. Opened it. Showed her its contents.

"I...asked..." he repeated.

The object in his hand was her cross necklace, soaked in blood.

With his left index finger, Yost pointed at the roof of the shed. "Never...too...late."

Only then did she remember what she'd told Yost back at the clearing.

"So, when you're ready, just ask Jesus to come into your heart. Ask Him for forgiveness and ask Him to change your life. It's never too late, Yost. Just look at the thief on the cross."

Gemma wrapped her arm around Yost, surprised by the love she felt for him, this man she barely knew. Her fingers closed around his, and he used what remained of his strength to squeeze her hand. "Thank you so much for what you did for us, Mike," she whispered into his ear. "I'll see you again someday."

She'd never held someone as they died before, but she knew the moment the life left Yost's body. She could feel it, the absolute absence of *him.* In an instant, he went from being Mike Yost to an empty shell. Pulling away, she took in his vacant eyes, his blank stare, and she knew that whatever had made him Yost had gone somewhere else. And she prayed—no, *she knew*—it was better than here.

Gemma took the necklace from his limp hand and slipped it inside her pocket.

Outside the shed, Weston unleashed a howl, a sound of pure fury. He must've awoken from his nap and discovered that sleep hadn't improved his situation. He was still cold, wet, and uncomfortable. They had to get him to the cabin. Now.

"Addie, I'm coming," Gemma called out, climbing to her feet. "Just give me a—"

"Help..."

A strained voice came from the darkness in the rear of the shed, the area where the light drifting in from the open doors could not reach. Gemma did not immediately recognize the voice. It could've belonged to anyone. A Task Force soldier. Even Mullen himself. Silently, she removed the Glock from Yost's belt, and then she picked up his cell phone and turned on the flashlight. She headed toward the sound, pistol raised, aware that this might be a trap. Whoever it was...they might kill her, but they would not get past her. She would protect Addie and Weston at all costs.

The weak beam from the phone's flashlight passed over the front of the Charger and continued forward to the area where the voice had come from. And then she saw him: another bloody man crouched on the floor in front of the vehicle. The man had removed his jacket and tied it underneath his armpit and around his shoulder. It took her brain a moment to recognize who it was, but when she did, she cried out, "Addie! It's Kyle!"

"What?" Addie nearly tripped over Yost's outstretched legs as she ran into the shed. When she saw Kyle on the ground, she dropped to her knees and began peppering his face with kisses. Weston stopped crying and stared, wide-eyed, at his father. "Baby? Are you okay?"

"It's just my shoulder." With his good hand, he reached out to touch Weston's cheek. "I might need stitches, but I think the bullet went in and out."

"Oh, thank God!" Addie cried. "I thought..." Her voice trailed off as she wept.

Gemma watched as Kyle embraced his wife and infant son as well as he could with one good arm. She hadn't realized it was possible to miss Taylor more than she already did. Then, she wiped at her eyes. Sophia was out there somewhere—with a monster. They couldn't waste any more time. She only had until midnight. "Kyle? What happened to you?"

He winced, either from the pain in his shoulder or the pain of the memory. "Letty called us for a pick-up. I went along with Yost since he'd never done one before." He glanced up at Addie. "I would've told you, but you were sleeping, and I didn't want to bother you. Anyway, when we got to Letty's, I knew right away that something wasn't right with the guy. I should've listened to my gut."

Gemma knelt beside Kyle and put a hand on his uninjured shoulder. "What guy? Do you remember anything about him? What did he look like?"

"He said his name was Doug," Kyle said, "but that was probably a lie. The guy looked strange when he said it. He was kind of ugly. Red hair and lots of acne scars."

Mullen.

Gemma used her thumb to turn off the flashlight. "We have to go. Right now." She slipped Yost's phone inside her pocket with the cross necklace and then helped Kyle across the shed and into the passenger seat of the Tahoe. Both of them avoided looking at the blood on the driver's seat.

After he was safely inside the vehicle, Gemma checked the Charger for the spare key. It was still there. She turned to Addie. "We have to take both cars. I'll drive the Charger to Letty's, and you drive the Tahoe. You guys should have a vehicle at the cabin, just in case." Gemma didn't add that the reason she wanted them to have a vehicle at the cabin was because she wasn't sure if she was coming back, and she didn't want to leave them stranded. "Are you okay to drive?"

Addie nodded. "But what about Weston?"

"Give him to me." With his good arm, Kyle reached for the baby. "I'm okay to hold him. The cabin isn't far. Yost pointed it out to me when we drove to Letty's."

As they left the Sanctuary, they followed the deep grooves carved into the mud by the Federal Task Force, that ruthless predator city that moved through the country, devouring everything in its path. Gemma took the lead in the Charger, and Addie, Kyle, and Weston trailed her in the Tahoe. Yost's body was in the trunk of the Tahoe, covered with a wool blanket. It hadn't felt right to leave him behind. Not after everything he'd done for them.

They would bury him later, at the cabin.

Gemma drove the Charger through the open

gate, her grip firm on the steering wheel, the emerald stone of her engagement ring shimmering as it caught the sun's waning light. Through it all, she kept her eyes locked on the road ahead.

She never looked back.

CHAPTER THIRTY-THREE

"They're *all* gone?" Max nervously picked at his cuticles, unable to meet Gemma's eyes. Every few seconds, another tiny fleck of skin fell onto the cabin's threadbare carpet. "You're absolutely sure? Because if you guys made it out, there might be other survivors..."

Gemma's legs gave out, and she fell onto the couch—the same couch she'd slept on the night of Taylor's capture. *Survivors.* She hated the term. It implied that anyone who'd gone to a detention center was as good as dead. "We couldn't risk going back to check," she said, a little defensively. She shouldn't have to justify her decision to Max or anyone else at the cabin, especially since they had made the choice not to return to the Sanctuary. "It would've been too dangerous to go back with Weston."

She hadn't mentioned the gunshots to the others, and neither had Addie. It was an unspoken agreement between the two of them. No one else needed to know about the gunshots.

Or about the soldier with the arrow through his chest.

In the kitchen doorway, Gavin rubbed at his bloodshot eyes. He looked as if he hadn't slept in days. "Okay. Max and I will go back to the Sanctuary. We have to check. Make sure no one got left behind."

Max's head shot up, terror etched across his features, and in that moment, Gemma hated the Task Force. There were so many reasons to hate them, too many to count, but the sheer terror in Max's eyes was a big one.

She gave Gavin a sharp look. "You aren't going anywhere tonight. If anyone escaped and they're hiding in the woods, they'll be fine for a day or two. Most of us hid a lot longer than that before we came to the Sanctuary. Right now, your priority is taking care of Kyle and Weston. See what you can do about Kyle's gunshot wound. Keep Weston dry and warm so he doesn't get sick again. I'm going into town to tell Letty what happened. No one goes *anywhere* until I get back."

Leaning against the fireplace, Brie crossed her arms. "I'm sorry, but who died and left you in charge, Gemma? We don't need your permission to check the Sanctuary."

Gemma had expected the most pushback from Gavin, but of course it was coming from Brie. She wasn't used to Gemma asserting herself—none of them were—and she didn't know how to handle it. "You're right. You don't need my permission. But if you go back there tonight, just remember that you're leaving your best friends alone to fend for themselves." She jabbed a finger at the other couch where Addie, Weston, and Kyle clung to each another, their eyelids heavy. "You're leaving Addie here with an infant and an injured husband, all so you can show everyone how tough you are."

"Really?" Brie huffed. "You think that's all I care about?"

"I *know* that's all you care about. You've proven it, time and time again."

Max dropped his hands to his side. There was a spot of blood on one cuticle. "Gemma—"

"Don't bother, Max." The strand of illuminated shotgun shell lights hanging behind Brie briefly flickered as the girl pushed herself away from the fireplace. She blew past Gemma and stomped up the stairs like a teenager having a tantrum. The others watched her go but said nothing.

"I'm going to Letty's," Gemma said. She'd already wasted too much time at the cabin. "Like Brie said, I'm not in charge. Do what you think is best. I'll be back as soon as I can."

The couch springs creaked as she stood. Before anyone could argue, she slipped out the door, eager to leave the musty smell of the cabin behind. It would be dark in less than an hour. So much had happened since that morning when Captain Haggerty had released Letty and the rest of the town. Gemma had counted that as a victory, but her victory had turned into a defeat in a matter of hours.

All of those families ripped apart. The gunshots. The screaming. The fires.

"Gemma?"

She spun around.

Gavin stood on the bottom step of the porch, fidgeting with his hands. He looked different to her, and then she realized what had changed. For the first time in months, the bitterness had abandoned his eyes, and he resembled the old Gavin again, the kindhearted and loyal man she'd grown to love at the Station.

"Can we talk a minute?" he asked.

Gemma glanced at her watch. *6:06 p.m.* Sophia had been with Mullen for at least two hours. Probably more. But she could give Gavin a few minutes. She owed him that much. "Sure."

He led Gemma away from the dimly lit cabin and toward the thunderous sound of the creek. In just a few days, the creek had transformed from a steady but shallow flow of water that one could easily walk across into a wide and fast-moving river. Jagged rocks that were exposed two days earlier were now completely submerged.

Gemma followed Gavin onto the bridge, and they stood in its center, both of them staring into the rushing water below. It struck Gemma that this was the same spot Gavin and Teresa had occupied a few days earlier. Finally, he said, "You're lying, Gemma."

Gemma searched the side of his face, the rigid line of his jaw, trying to figure out what he knew—or what he *thought* he knew. She reached for her neck, searching for the necklace, but it wasn't there. "Lying about what?"

"About going to see Letty." Gavin turned to face her. "I know you. I can tell when you're lying. Where are you really going?"

Unable to withstand the weight of Gavin's stare, she returned her attention to the creek. Her eyes landed on a spot in the water that looked completely smooth. But when she looked closer, she could see the sharp tip of a rock hiding just below the surface, waiting to skewer anyone who jumped or fell into the water. "I'm not lying," she insisted. "I have to get to Letty's. She might not even know about the Sanctuary yet."

"Why can't I come with you?"

"Why would you need to? I mean, have you seen Max? He's a mess, and Brie is unreliable. You can't leave them in charge of the others."

"Gemma, those are all excuses. Distractions. Something else is going on here. Please stop with the lies and just tell me—"

"Lies," she repeated, unable to keep the venom out of her voice. "You know all about lies, don't you?"

Something flashed in his eyes. Something dark. "What are you talking about?"

"You left him." It wasn't a question. Gemma already knew the truth because she knew Gavin as well as he knew her. "You hated Taylor. Not because he ever did anything to you, but because I love him. So, you left him in the basement. You locked the door, and you left him behind. He's gone now, Gavin, and it's your fault."

Gavin shook his head to deny the accusation, but he seemed unable to get the words past his lips. He only stared at her, shaking his head uselessly, the truth written all over his face.

"I'm going to Letty's," she said, pushing past him. "Do *not* follow me."

When Gemma pulled away from the cabin, she

glanced in the Charger's rearview mirror and saw Gavin leaning against the bridge's railing, his head buried in his hands. The sight of her friend, broken and hurting, made something deep within her chest ache.

But then she remembered what he'd taken from her. What he'd taken from Taylor.

A voice whispered in her mind, *One day, you'll have to forgive him.*

"Yes," she whispered in response, "but not today."

CHAPTER THIRTY-FOUR

Gemma's sense of déjà vu as she stepped inside the bookstore was so strong that it almost bowled her over. The bookstore was dark and empty, exactly as it had been the previous night. She felt as if she'd slipped back through time, as if the last twenty-four hours hadn't happened. Her wearied mind grasped onto this possibility, desperate for it to be true. If she got in the car and drove back to the Sanctuary, would everyone still be there? Perhaps God had given her a glimpse into the future so she could change what was about to happen.

She reached into her jacket pocket, hoping to discover Taylor's phone tucked safely away and not crushed into a million pieces. And—yes!—her fingers closed around the cold metal of a phone, but when she pulled it out, she saw it wasn't Taylor's phone but Yost's, the screen smeared with dark blood.

Deflated, she put the phone away and continued down the aisle. The closer she got to Letty's office, the more she realized how different the store felt. There was a heaviness to it, an oppression that hung over the overcrowded shelves like a storm cloud. She'd felt nothing like it ever before.

Gemma froze halfway down the aisle, too frightened to go any farther.

She didn't want to see what was back there.

"Letty?" Gemma called out. "Are you here?"

No response.

An idea occurred to her. Of course Letty wasn't in the bookstore, not this late in the evening, and especially not after spending a few days as a captive of the Task Force. She was probably upstairs in her apartment, already fast asleep in her recliner, a book laying open on her chest. But to get to the apartment, Gemma would have to continue down the hallway, past the office, to the stairway. And she *really* didn't want to do that.

Reaching behind her back, she removed Yost's pistol from her belt and continued down the hallway, gun drawn, her index finger resting not on the trigger but on the metal above it, just as Taylor had shown her. As she inched forward, the wood boards creaked beneath her weight, announcing her presence to anyone hiding in the darkness.

Gemma peered around the corner. There was something on the floor. Something big that hadn't been there earlier.

A body. It's Letty's body.

She reached out with her left hand, her fingers sliding over the wall in search of the light switch. Finally, she found it and snapped it on, bathing the room in the harsh glow of the fluorescent lights that Letty utterly despised.

The office was a complete wreck. The rug was still on the other side of the room, and one of Letty's bookshelves was overturned in the center of the floor, covering the cellar door. Books and papers littered the floor.

And deep within the floor...someone was crying.

Gemma dropped to her knees and began tossing books out of the way. "Letty! It's Gemma!" she cried. "Don't worry! You're going to be okay!"

She cleared the books away fast enough, but the bookshelf was another story. There was no way she could've lifted the thing on her own, even if it wasn't loaded down with books. So, she got on her knees and pushed it. Her boots slid on the floor, and she was dripping sweat by the time she slid it off the cellar door. The bookshelf had barely cleared the door before it impacted the far wall of the office.

Thank You, God.

Shoving the rest of the books aside, she grabbed the handle and yanked the door open. She knelt over the opening and stared into the darkness. "Letty? Where are you?"

"Please," a weak voice drifted up to her. "Help me."

It wasn't Letty's voice.

For several weeks after arriving at the Sanctuary, Gemma had nightmares about being trapped in the cellar. Whenever she awoke from one of those terrible dreams, Taylor would hold her in his arms, his lips pressed to her forehead, until she fell back to sleep. She'd vowed to never again set foot inside that cellar.

Now, she stepped onto the ladder and began to descend.

Nothing could've prepared her for what she saw at the bottom.

Teresa Fallon sat on the dirt floor, her legs twisted underneath her, cradling Letty's upper body in her arms. The girl was almost unrecognizable, save for the waterfall of dark hair flowing down her back. Her face was a mask of dirt and tears, as if she'd been crying for days and repeatedly wiping her tears away with dirty hands.

How long? Gemma wondered. *How long has she been in the dark with Letty?*

The unnatural pallor of Letty's skin. The strange angle of her neck.

"What happened?"

At first, Gemma wasn't sure if she'd spoken the words aloud or just inside of her head. But then Teresa responded in a series of brief sentences, like some strange sort of code.

"A man. With red hair." The girl's hands were shaking, and there was a clicking sound deep within her throat. She clutched Letty's body tighter. "He kicked her. She fell."

A man with red hair.

It couldn't be, could it?

"No," Gemma whispered.

"She didn't die right away." Teresa's entire body was shaking now. "It took a while."

"No."

The world spun like a carousel, slow at first, and then much faster. Teresa twirled away from her like a dancer, and Gemma blindly grasped for the rungs of the ladder to keep herself from falling.

It can't be real. This can't be happening.

But it was.

Letty was dead.

CHAPTER THIRTY-FIVE

"He's going to kill her no matter what I do."

Gemma parked the Charger underneath the small carport behind Teresa's house, but she kept the engine running. The lights were on inside the house, and it looked warm and inviting. She wanted to go inside, crawl into an empty bed, and sleep for a year.

"Who?" Teresa muttered from the passenger seat, her right hand gripping the door handle, ready to get out. She looked a little better now after spending a few minutes in Letty's bathroom washing the dirt and grime from her face, but she was still a nineteen-year-old girl who'd just spent the last six hours trapped in a pitch-black cellar with a dead woman. "Who's going to kill who?"

Gemma's hands slid off the steering wheel and

landed in her lap, palms up. For the first time, she noticed the dried blood on her hands. Probably a combination of Yost's blood and Letty's blood. It was on the steering wheel, too. "There's a little girl at our camp," Gemma heard herself saying. "Sophia. She's like my little sister. A Task Force soldier kidnapped her during the raid today. He left a note for me so I would know where to find her, but it's really me he wants. Not her."

Teresa released the door handle and leaned back against her seat. "Where does this soldier want you to go?"

"The coal mine near Ash Grove. Our old hiding place. That's where he took her."

"Are you going alone?"

"No." Gemma turned the key, killing the Charger's engine. "I'm not going at all."

"What?" Teresa wrapped her arms around her stomach, as if to suppress some hidden pain. "But what about Sophia?"

"He's going to kill her no matter what I do," Gemma repeated. "If he wants me to follow him there, he's already got something planned for me. I would be walking right into a trap, and he would kill us both."

"So, you're just going to leave her?"

"No. I'm going to call the nearest compliance office."

Teresa jerked her head back. "You're *what?* Why?"

"Because I'm going to turn myself in. That's the only way."

"I don't understand. What happens to Sophia if you turn yourself in?"

Gemma pulled Yost's cell phone out of her pocket and stared at the dark screen. "When I call them, I'm going to tell them that one of their soldiers has kidnapped a subversive child from the Sanctuary that was just raided. I'll tell them where he's taken her and that he's planning to hurt her." She raised her eyes to meet Teresa's accusatory gaze. "If I go there alone, I'll get us both killed. If I bring anyone with me, he'll kill her anyway. That's the ironic part. The Task Force is Sophia's only chance to survive."

"But she'll get detained!"

Gemma nodded. "She won't end up in a detention center. She's too young. They'll put her with a family. At least she'll be alive."

Because that was what life had become. Survival at all costs. On that long-ago ride home from church, Gemma had confidently told her parents that she would give the bad guys a run for their money. She'd seen herself as better somehow. Stronger. But instead of giving the bad guys a run for their money, she'd spent the past two-and-a-half years running *from* them while they continued to whittle away at everything she cared about. But she wasn't better or stronger than anyone else. She wasn't some kind of hero for not renouncing her faith. Lots of people had refused to renounce…for a while. She'd held out longer than many, but where had that gotten her?

Alone, with blood all over her hands.

"You're afraid." There was no malice in Teresa's voice. She put a hand on top of Gemma's. "It's okay to be afraid."

"It's not about fear." Gemma gently pulled her hand away. "It's about trust."

Her fear wasn't for her own life, but that she would end up getting Sophia killed. Repeatedly, she'd taken matters into her own hands, barely consulting God, and her rash decisions had directly contributed to Taylor's capture, to the collapse of the Sanctuary, and to Letty's death.

No.

She wouldn't make the same mistake with Sophia.

Gemma dropped her eyes to the phone. It had no passcode, and the signal was strong. There wasn't much battery remaining—only about ten percent—but that was okay.

She only had one call to make, and it shouldn't take long.

Before she dialed the number for information, Gemma closed her eyes and bowed her head. "Father, I'm tired of running. I'm tired of hiding. I went into hiding so I wouldn't have to deny You, but in doing so, I've become a worthless disciple. Everything I've done to survive has done nothing but lead to more pain and suffering for those I love." She pulled in a deep breath. "So, I'm giving this over to You, Father. I'm done denying the truth of who I am. Forgive me for my fear, Lord, and use whatever comes next to increase my faith in You. Make my path clear. And if it's Your will, Father, please rescue Sophia from the lion's jaws. Amen."

Next to her, Teresa whispered, "Amen."

Ignoring her pounding heart, Gemma swiped through Yost's phone in search of the green phone icon. When she located it, she touched it and the message screen popped up. Somehow, she'd confused the text message icon and the phone icon. She was about to touch the home button to exit out of the screen when she noticed that the most recent message was a video message from *Nolan*.

A message from Taylor, sent on Friday, just before the rescue at the school.

Her finger hovered above the screen. She was afraid to click on the message. Afraid of what it might say.

But not clicking it wasn't an option.

Gemma touched the screen, and a video message popped up, a play arrow in the middle of the display. But she didn't press play. She didn't need to watch it again. She could still see every frame of the video clearly in her mind.

It was the video of Jason Fishman's murder.

Below the video was a text message from Taylor.

Sending you a copy of this in case anything happens to my phone, or to me, Taylor wrote. *I think the world needs to see this, man. I've done plenty of things I'm not proud of. We both have. But this kid and the old man are dead. The truth needs to get out, no matter what.*

She stared at Taylor's words on the blood-smeared screen for several minutes, reading and rereading the message until she'd memorized every word. A deep peace settled over her. It almost felt like God was inside the car with her, speaking to her through Taylor's words.

She knew what He wanted her to do.

Teresa put a hand on her shoulder. "Gemma? What is it?"

"It's never going to stop," Gemma whispered, more to herself than to Teresa. As soon as the words left her mouth, she knew they were true. "It's going to keep getting worse until the world hears the Truth."

"What are you saying?" Teresa asked. "Are you going to call the compliance office?"

"No." Instead of elaborating, Gemma reached up and took Teresa's hand off her shoulder. Then, she slipped Yost's phone into the girl's palm and folded her fingers around it. "This phone contains the only evidence of what really happened on that football field. I destroyed Taylor's phone, so this is all that's left. Guard it with your life. Forward a copy to yourself. Do whatever you have to do to protect it until I get back. But promise me that, if I don't come back, you will make sure this video gets out," she said, repeating Taylor's words. "No matter what. Do you promise me?"

Teresa's eyes drifted to the phone, and she stared at it reverently, as if she were holding some ancient and powerful relic instead of a bloody iPhone. Using a fingernail, she scratched at the dried blood on the screen, and dark-red flakes adhered themselves to her fingertip. "I promise."

"Thank you." Gemma didn't know Teresa very well, but she trusted the girl would follow through with her promise. "You should get home now. Your dad is probably worried."

"Yeah." Teresa took the hint and got out of the car. She clutched the phone tightly against her chest, as if she was afraid someone might try to snatch it from her. But instead of closing the door, she leaned inside the vehicle and focused her dark eyes on Gemma. "What are you going to do now?"

Gemma turned the key, and the vehicle's engine roared to life.

"I'm going to end this."

CHAPTER THIRTY-SIX

Gemma pulled into Henry Castern's driveway and parked behind his barn. There were no other cars in the driveway and no lights on inside the house.

Six months after Henry's crucifixion, his farmhouse remained unoccupied.

A sign in the front yard for a local real estate agency featured a rotund man giving a thumbs-up to the camera. The sign had blown over—or someone had knocked it over—and now stood at an awkward angle so that the thumbs-up appeared to be directing any passersby to keep moving. Nothing to see here.

Gemma stepped out of the car into a dark and cloudless night. Why hadn't she thought to grab a flashlight from the cabin? She couldn't even use the flashlight on Yost's phone because she'd left the phone with Teresa.

Maybe Taylor had a spare flashlight in the trunk.

She went to the back of the Charger and popped the trunk open.

And there, laying in the center of the trunk, was Taylor's backpack. The one he'd left in the trunk the evening of the rescue in Winter's Dam.

Gemma's eyes stung, but she did not cry. There wasn't time to cry. She hadn't thought to check the trunk after the raid. She unzipped the backpack and started pulling out the contents and dropping them into the trunk. A spare t-shirt. A half-used roll of duct tape. A small pocketknife. A few black zip-ties. She reached deeper, and her hand closed around something cold and hard. She pulled a flashlight from the depths of the bag.

She smiled gratefully. "Thank you, Taylor."

He was gone now, but he was still protecting her.

Before she closed the trunk, she took one last look at the items from the backpack, her eyes darting between the duct tape and the knife. She tapped a finger on her chin, thinking, and then her hand dropped to her waist, and she touched the firm leather of her belt.

Just in case, she thought.

She grabbed the knife and the tape.

✝

After Gemma locked the car, she crouched by the rear tire and stuck the car keys back inside the magnetic holder. With Yost's pistol hidden beneath her jacket and the flashlight in hand, she set off on a steady jog across the cornfield, heading for Dragon's Back Mountain. There was no way to drive to the Station, at least not in Taylor's car, so she had to make the eleven-mile trek on foot. She intended to jog as much as possible, but even if she walked the entire way, she should still reach the Station well before Mullen's midnight deadline.

Her path through the cornfield took her directly past the spot where Henry had been crucified by the Task Force. Although Henry's body and the cross were long gone, she could still see the square hole where the Task Force had planted the cross in the ground. Seeing it again brought everything back. The flies. The crow. The nails. The blood pooling in Henry's feet.

Gemma picked up the pace, eager to get away from the hole. The land sloped upward, and the field gave way to trees. Before long, the muscles in her thighs burned, and she slowed her pace a little to compensate, hoping to avoid any muscle cramps. She used to hike the mountain regularly, but her body wasn't used to this level of physical exertion anymore. The Sanctuary had made her soft.

That was why God took it away, she realized. *I got too comfortable.*

The last time Gemma had raced up Dragon's Back Mountain, she'd been fleeing from certain death. Now, she was running *toward* it. That seemed fitting, somehow. As if the circle was finally closing. Because she meant what she'd told Teresa. She wasn't afraid of dying anymore. If she died in the mine, at least she would die fighting for something that mattered, instead of cowering under a rock.

No more cowering.

It was well after eleven when the hulking shadow of the bathroom pavilion finally came into view. Gemma had been alternating between walking and jogging for so long that she thought the building was a mirage at first. She kept jogging closer until she could see that the pavilion really was there. So was the old water pump and the rusty play set. There were no signs of the Golden Girls, but she hadn't expected there to be.

Her lungs burned with the exertion of the climb, and a painful stitch settled into her right side. She slowed to a walk and stretched both arms above her head. A short set of stairs built into the hillside led from the bathroom pavilion to the old parking lot, back when the Station had been the Mammoth Coal Mine. She climbed the stairs and stepped onto cracked macadam.

And there it was.

Dilapidated and dense with weeds, but still standing.

The Station.

She hadn't been inside the building since the night she'd stumbled into Taylor on the mountain. It so closely resembled the Station from her dreams that her eyes scanned the porch, desperately hoping to see Taylor. Wishing that, somehow, he might've discovered a way to break through the barrier from her dreams into her real life.

But of course, he wasn't there.

Gemma couldn't understand why the Station wasn't a heap of ash on the forest floor, especially since the Task Force had known of its location since April. One of their favorite cruelties was to destroy subversive hideouts so they could never be used again. Why leave this one standing?

Unless they didn't know about it because Mullen hadn't told them.

The thought made her uneasy. She had assumed Mullen's kidnapping of Sophia had been a crime of opportunity, a spur-of-the-moment decision designed to lure Gemma into a trap. But he'd told her to come *here,* of all places, which meant he'd probably been planning this for a very long time.

To her left, the monstrous mouth of the coal mine beckoned her with a puff of frigid breath against the side of her neck. Turning away from the Station, she continued toward the mine, her eyes focused on its black throat. Everything looked exactly the same, from the wooden benches of the tourist shelter, to the canary-yellow coal car parked on the weed-choked tracks, to the faded sign warning tourists to wear a jacket.

But the mine itself was different. The darkness felt...darker. More sinister. And the entrance looked smaller somehow. The idea was ludicrous. Probably just a trick of the eyes, an optical illusion brought on by her intense fear. But as Gemma descended into the tourist shelter and hesitated next to the coal car, she became even more convinced that the opening was narrower than it had been the last time she'd stepped inside.

Maybe the tunnel really was closing in on her, little by little, slow enough that Gemma wouldn't notice. Perhaps it was biding its time, waiting for her to set off on the tracks. When she did, the walls of the tunnel would slowly tighten around her like a snake's muscles contracting to digest its prey.

A terrible image filled her mind. Maybe she wasn't standing outside of the entrance to the mine. Maybe the dark hole in front of her was actually the mouth of a dragon, and the moment she stepped inside, it would swallow her whole.

Gemma shuddered and pushed the image away. She shined the flashlight into the tunnel. There was nothing to see. Just a dank tunnel with a low ceiling and ancient metal tracks stretching into oblivion. She ran a hand down the rock wall. It felt just as she remembered. Cold. Grainy. Sharp edges. Water endlessly trickling. She wiped the moisture on her pants.

It wasn't the dragon's mouth. It was the coal mine.

But one dragon had found its way inside...and it had Sophia in its jaws.

The thought of Sophia, alone with Mullen, propelled her forward. She pulled the Glock from her waistband and followed the narrow-gauge railway tracks down the West Mammoth Gangway, a trip she'd made hundreds of times before, but usually not alone and never in complete darkness. The batteries in the overhead lanterns had long ago burned out, and the gangway was pitch black. The familiar cold settled on her like a wet blanket draped over her shoulders. She walked at first, hoping to minimize the sound of coarse gravel crunching underneath her feet, but then she picked up the pace into a light jog, her eyes focused on the bouncing beam of her flashlight.

Something's different.

Something wasn't right about the tunnel, but she couldn't put her finger on what it was. It was an eerie feeling, knowing something was off but not knowing what it was. Maybe she just wasn't used to the mine anymore. To the all-encompassing darkness. Above ground, even on the blackest night, there was always *some* ambient light. The moon and stars. The headlights of a passing car. The faint glow of a distant city reflected on the clouds. But in the mine, there was nothing. No light at all. Someone could stand inches away from you, and you wouldn't know they were there until you felt their breath on your face.

But the darkness was an advantage for Gemma, wasn't it? Because she was comfortable with the darkness in a way that Mullen *couldn't* have been. Human beings weren't designed to live beneath the surface of the earth, but Gemma has spent a good portion of the last two years of her life underground. If she could use the darkness against Mullen somehow, *weaponize* it, that might be her only chance of rescuing Sophia.

Something caught her eye.

Light up ahead.

At first, it was just a whisper of light. The trick-of-the-eye kind of light that you couldn't see until you looked away from it. She ran faster, and the light grew brighter, spilling into the gangway. It was a light she knew well. One of the battery-operated lanterns still had a little juice left. It dangled from the overhead timbers just above the first intersection.

Gemma slowed as she approached the intersection, listening, but she couldn't hear anything except the steady dripping of groundwater from the timbers. She switched the flashlight off and slipped it inside the left pocket of her jacket. Then, clutching the Glock in both hands, she spun around the corner, prepared to fire a round into Mullen's chest.

One of the old cots stood in the middle of the tunnel. Sophia was curled up on it, her hands zip-tied behind her back, a long strip of duct tape over her mouth, fiery curls covering her face.

She wasn't moving.

No. God, please, no.

Hurriedly, Gemma tucked the gun in her waistband and rushed over to Sophia. She brushed aside a few of the girl's curls and put a hand on her cheek.

Sophia's skin was ice cold.

Gemma held in a scream as she imagined the

girl's terror as she'd fled from Mullen to the safety of the climbing tower, her own private sanctuary. How must Sophia have felt when she saw the monster climbing up after her? Had she fought him? Of course she had. Sophia was a fighter. Gemma couldn't imagine how Mullen could've gotten the girl down from the tower alive, which meant he'd probably killed her right there in the lookout, surrounded by all of her pencil sketches, and then carried her body back to the mine.

Inside of her, something stretched to its limit, like a rubber band, and then snapped.

She's dead. He killed her to get back at me. Sophia's dead.

Losing Taylor. Losing the Sanctuary. Losing Letty. Those losses—however terrible they had been—paled in comparison to what Gemma felt as she stared at Sophia's motionless body.

She hadn't forgotten Mullen. A vague part of her brain was still aware that he'd drawn her into the mine for a reason. That, even now, she was a tiny mouse in the jaws of a cat.

But Mullen didn't matter to her anymore. Nothing mattered if Sophia was dead. The girl's life meant more to Gemma than her own. If Sophia was dead, she didn't care what Mullen did to her.

Now, all that mattered was what *she did to him.*

Stroking Sophia's cheek, Gemma whispered, "Don't worry, Soph. He can't hurt you..."

Her voice trailed off.

Beneath her almost-translucent eyelids, Sophia's eyes were moving. Her eyelashes fluttered, and then—suddenly—her eyes snapped open in fear, and the girl unleashed a bloodcurdling scream. Thankfully, the tape over her mouth muffled some of the sound. Gemma's body sagged with relief, and she started to cry. "Shh... It's okay, Soph. It's me. I'm going to get you out of here."

Tears spilled down Sophia's cheeks, and she gave Gemma a brave nod.

"Let's get this duct tape off, okay? Then, I'll work on your hands." Using both hands, she carefully peeled the duct tape away from Sophia's mouth. One section of the tape snagged in her hair, and there was no good way to remove it.

"One pull, okay? Just like a Band-Aid."

Sophia winced as several strands of hair tore free from her head.

The tape was off. Now onto the zip-ties.

"Can you sit up for me, honey? Now turn around and I'll—"

"Behind," Sophia rasped, her voice hoarse from disuse—or perhaps from screaming.

Gemma looked up, and she instantly recognized the terror in the girl's eyes.

"Behind you!"

Gemma whirled around in time to see snarled lips, a flash of short-cut reddish hair, and the butt of an assault rifle sailing toward her face.

Crushing pain.

Bright light.

Sophia screaming.

And then...nothing but a vast and horrifying darkness.

Gemma floated in and out of consciousness, aware that something was happening to her but powerless to stop it. Occasionally, her eyelids flickered open, and she saw timbers. Withered ferns. Ancient bolts. A second later, she was back in her bunk bed at the Sanctuary, shivering uncontrollably. Her blanket must've slipped off the bed. She reached over the side of the bunk and stretched her hand toward the floor, groping blindly for the blanket...

And then...someone was carrying her. She felt her dangling limbs, the accompanying sensation of weightlessness. *Taylor,* she thought. *He's carrying me to bed. I must've fallen out of bed reaching for the blanket.* But the hands gripped her roughly and held on much too tight. And the smell wasn't Taylor's. No matter how hard she tried, she couldn't catch even the faintest whiff of cinnamon or smoke or pine trees. All she could smell was body odor and sour breath.

A familiar but repugnant smell that brought one person to mind.

Gemma's heart jolted inside her chest. She forced her eyes open and focused on a single stone on the gravel floor. She was sitting on some kind of bench. Her eyelids felt heavy, as if someone had attached strings to them and kept trying to tug them down. She wanted to go back to sleep.

"Gemma?" Sophia's hushed voice woke Gemma up faster than if she'd swallowed a dozen shots of espresso. "Please wake up! He's gone!"

Gemma snapped her head to the right, in the voice's direction. But the movement was too much, too fast, and the room began to spin. In danger of losing consciousness again, she closed her eyes until the dizziness went away. She counted to ten. When she opened them, Sophia was there, sitting beside her on the bench. Had she been there the entire time? "Soph? What happened?"

"He hit you," Sophia said. "He hit you really hard with his rifle. I thought you were dead, Gemma. There's blood all over your forehead."

"Blood?" Gemma tried to reach for her head, but her arms wouldn't move. "Why can't I—"

"We're both tied up," the girl whispered. "What's he going to do to us?"

The last few days suddenly returned to Gemma in a flood of information, the way a computer screen repopulates itself with icons after a hard re-boot. She could see the file folders popping up on the screen of her mind, each of them containing her memories of recent traumatic events. The loss of Taylor. The raid at the Sanctuary. Sophia's kid-napping. Yost's and Letty's deaths. Returning to the mine.

Mullen attacking her.

Mullen.

Gemma tore her eyes away from Sophia to take in her surroundings. She moved her head slowly so she wouldn't trigger another wave of dizziness. It was dim, but it wasn't completely dark, thank God. Another battery-powered lantern sat on the ground a few feet away, casting its weak light on dozens of people...

People?

Yes. There were *people* in the cave with them. They sat in neat rows with books of various sizes laying open in each of their laps. They were all staring at her.

She uttered a choked scream.

"It's okay!" Sophia whispered. "They're not real, Gemma. They're mannequins."

Mannequins? Of course. The people in front of her obviously weren't real. They were the same denim-clad mannequins that had populated the mine back when the Mammoth Mine Tour was still operational. Gemma's group had removed them all and piled them in the gangway where they wouldn't have to look at them.

That's what was different, she realized. *I knew something was different in the gangway. The mannequins weren't there.*

Overhead, the cave's timbers sloped toward one another, forming a sharp peak, like the apex of a church. An ornate metal structure, almost like an altar rail at the front of a church, separated her and Sophia from the mannequins. Carefully, she turned her head and tried to get a glimpse of what was behind her. Back there, the cave dead-ended in a landslide of frisbee-sized chunks of coal. Directly in front of the pile was an old-fashioned coal cart, the kind that the miners hitched to a donkey's back to transport the coal to the railway tracks in the main gangway.

This wasn't the same place where she had located Sophia on the cot.

He carried me, Gemma realized with horror. *Mullen carried me here.*

She knew exactly where she was in the mine. The old cart behind them had once been part of the tour, designed to show how coal mining worked back in the early twentieth century. Although her group had never used this part of the mine, she knew where it was in relation to the gangway. Very close to the Wishing Well.

The Wishing Well.

The altar rail in front of them was actually the metal grate that had once covered the deep metal shaft of the Wishing Well.

They sat side by side on a bench that had been pushed up against the cart, their wrists behind their backs and zip-tied to the cart's metal side-rails. A silver-skinned mannequin sat on a small ledge jutting out from the wall, his black work boots resting on the pile of coal. His squinting eyes made him appear deep in thought, as if he were trying to figure out why these two girls had suddenly become a part of his workday. Another mannequin—this one sporting an unruly mustache—stood behind the cart, his mouth hanging open as if dumbfounded by the whole situation.

Both mannequins held Bibles in their hands.

Gemma turned back to the mannequins in front of her. Her head throbbed whenever she moved it, but she wasn't as dizzy anymore.

The books laying open on the mannequins' laps. Were those Bibles, too?

She would've bet money they were. There had

to have been at least thirty Bibles inside the cave. She hadn't seen so many in years. They only had two actual Bibles at the Sanctuary, including the one Gemma had found at the old church in Ash Grove. Plus, Sophia had an Action Bible, which she shared with the other children. Those were all gone now. The Task Force always confiscated and destroyed whatever Bibles they found when they detained subversives. Plus, they expected any citizens who found Bibles lurking within the attics or basements of their homes to bring them to their local compliance office for destruction.

But instead of destroying them, Mullen had secretly been hoarding them.

Why?

For whatever cruel fate he'd planned for Gemma and Sophia.

Although she couldn't reach her hip, Mullen would've confiscated her Glock, along with her flashlight. The zip-ties were tight around her wrist, but Mullen had actually done her a favor by tying her to the cart. It gave her a little wiggle room. She could slide her fingers along her belt until she found the black duct tape. Stretching her fingers down the back of her pants, she reached for the pocketknife duct-taped to the underside of her belt. She silently thanked God that Mullen hadn't thought to run his fingers along the inside of her belt.

The knife would've been useless if he'd zip-tied her hands in front of her body, but she'd assumed he would zip-tie her behind her back because that was what he'd done the last time.

Finally, she freed the knife from the tape. She opened it slowly, careful not to drop it. Cutting through the zip-tie would not be easy. The ties were extremely tight around her wrists.

She was going to bleed.

Gemma went to work on the ties. If she could get them off before Mullen came back, that would be something. But the plastic was so tight. It was digging crevices into her skin. Would she cut through the ties before she bled to death? She winced as the sharp blade cut into her wrist, drawing blood that coated her fingers in sticky warmth.

Sophia tried to look behind her back. "What are you doing?"

"Don't look," Gemma ordered. She didn't want Sophia to see the blood or to draw any attention to what she was doing in case Mullen returned. "Are you okay? Did he hurt you?"

The girl's red curls were as black as coal in the dim light of the tunnel. "No. My wrists hurt from the ties, but otherwise I'm okay. But that guy..." She nodded toward the cave's entrance, tears flooding her eyes. "He killed Kyle."

"No, he didn't, honey. Kyle's okay. The bullet went through his shoulder."

"It did?" Sophia wiped her face on the shoulders of her sweater. "Are you sure?"

"I'm sure. He's alive."

Gemma grimaced as the knife dug into her skin again, much deeper this time. She wasn't making any headway with the plastic ties.

Sophia sniffed, clearly trying to compose herself. "The guy with the red hair…"

"Yeah?"

"Well, while you were asleep, he barely looked at me. He kept acting like he was talking to someone else, but there wasn't anyone there. What's wrong with him?"

"I don't know," Gemma answered. "But he doesn't want you, Soph. He wants me. This is all about me."

"Why?"

"He's a Task Force soldier. He and I dealt with each other in the past, right before we moved to the Sanctuary, and I made him angry." She didn't mention that Mullen was the same person who'd tried to murder their group—Sophia included—by setting the barn on fire. "But I'm going to tell him to let you go."

"No!" Sophia cried. "Not without you, Gemma. Please."

Gemma opened her mouth to say that she had no intention of going down without a fight and that the most important thing was that Sophia was no longer a part of the equation, but Mullen came into the cave at that moment, a black duffel bag slung over one shoulder and a roll of something in his hands. Some kind of thin, yellow cord.

Seeing him in the flesh again, as opposed to inside the landscape of her nightmares, was disorienting. He wasn't nearly as frightening as she'd built him up to be. He wasn't as tall as she remembered, only a few inches taller than her, and he looked thinner than the last time she'd seen him, after he'd delivered her into the hands of Colonel Carver. A gross white film coated his lips and the corners of his mouth, and his dirt-caked fingernails picked absently at an assembly of inflamed pimples on his chin.

"Oh, good. You're awake," Mullen said as if they were old friends. "I thought maybe I'd hit you too hard. But you can't blame me for being a little excited. I've been waiting a long time for this."

Gemma fixed him with an icy stare while she continued to work the knife against the plastic. Small, controlled movements so he wouldn't notice. "Waiting for what?"

He dropped the duffel bag and spread his arms wide. "For this! Do you like what we've done with the place? We wanted to make sure you felt right at home."

We?

"I used to come here a lot—after you and your traitor boyfriend got away." Mullen squatted and began unwinding some of the cord from its spool. Then, he opened the duffel bag and pulled out a black box with a long switch on one end. "For a while, I thought you guys might be dumb enough to come back here. Maybe not to live here again, but at least to collect your stuff. The day I realized you weren't coming back was a low point for me. I almost gave up on you. That was when Colonel Carver showed up."

The knife froze over Gemma's skin, slick with blood, and a chill passed through her body. "Colonel Carver is dead."

Mullen continued as if she hadn't spoken. "He said it wouldn't be that easy, that you weren't just going to waltz back into my life—or should I say *hike* back into my life?" He looked up and winked at Gemma. "But he also said that if I served him well, he would lead me back to you. And that's exactly what he did."

"What are you doing?" she asked. "What is that you're holding?"

"Oh, this?" He held up the black box. It vaguely resembled a large staple gun, and the yellow cable dangled from it like an umbilical cord. "This is a firing device. A buddy of mine has a way of getting things. He's kind of like Morgan Freeman's character in that prison movie. What was his name? Anyway, if you tell him what you want, he gets it for you. You've just got to pay for it."

Gemma sawed faster at the zip-tie. She couldn't even feel the pain of the cuts anymore. "What does it do?"

Mullen squinted at her. "Most roaches aren't very smart," he said, "but you're not stupid. You know exactly what this does. When I squeeze the handle, it's going to ignite this yellow cord—it's called detonator cord, in case you're interested—and that's going to ignite the C-4 explosive I planted at the entrance of the mine. I jammed the C-4 into a crevice in the rocks just above the entrance. If all goes according to plan, the explosion should trigger a collapse."

All the breath left Gemma's body. She could hear Sophia crying, but her cries sounded like they were coming from far away. "You can't do that," she whispered. "You'll die in here with us."

Mullen gave her a knowing grin. "What's wrong? You don't want to spend time alone with me in the dark?" He snorted laughter. "You're not the first woman to give me that look. Well, don't flatter yourself. I'll be gone by the time the collapse happens. I won't trigger the explosive charge until the colonel and I are both safely outside. And then..." He clapped his hands together. "Ka-blam!"

The plastic tie snapped. One wrist was free.

Gemma went to work on the other one.

"I don't get it," she said. "You moved us into this cave *after* you knocked me out. We're both tied up. Why bring your little firing device and det cord all the way back here if you've already planted the C-4?" Gemma thought she knew the answer but wanted to keep Mullen distracted and talking for as long as possible.

Long enough for her to cut through the second tie and free herself.

"Mainly to gloat," Mullen admitted with a shrug. He picked at an inflamed zit on the side of his nose. "Colonel Carver and I wanted to see your face when you realized we won. We also wanted to find out what you thought of all this." He pointed the firing device at the mannequins. "We rarely put this much effort into capturing subversives, so we figured you deserved something special. It's nice, isn't it? Knowing that these Bibles will be buried underground with you forever? You Christians love to be buried with your Bibles."

Somewhere deep inside, a fire ignited within

Gemma. The old part of her—the part that knew better—reminded her not to wish death on this man. Mullen wasn't a monster. He was still just a kid himself. An angry, confused kid. What had happened in his life to make him this way?

But as Gemma sliced into her other wrist, another part of her—the part that was expanding like a cancerous tumor—didn't want to understand Mullen. Or to pray for his soul.

She wanted him to *hurt,* like she hurt.

"I don't like that look on your face, roach." Mullen glowered at her. He raised the firing device over his head like a torch. "Don't forget who's in charge here. If you try anything, I'll blow the entrance right now. We're not afraid to die, are we, sir?"

"See?" Sophia whispered. "Who is he talking to?"

"No one." Gemma didn't want to play Mullen's games anymore. With forced restraint, she spoke through clenched teeth. "Carver is dead."

Mullen stared at her. "What did you say?"

"I said Carver is dead," Gemma repeated, raising her voice. "Did you hear me that time? He's dead as a doornail. We killed him in the basement of that church back in Ash Grove. If he's still hanging around, why doesn't he show himself?

Why doesn't he float out of the shadows and rattle his chains at me?"

Mullen didn't respond. Instead, he tilted his head to one side, as if listening to something. He nodded then knelt and gently placed the firing device on the ground near the duffel bag. When he raised his eyes again, they were filled with rage. "The colonel says you're trying to trick me. He says you're trying to escape from me again, just like last time. Well, I won't let that happen."

No. Not yet. Please God, not yet.

Abruptly, Mullen lunged at her, teeth bared, arms extended toward her neck, fingers hooked into claws. He looked like a wild animal. Ravenous. Snarling. Devoid of any humanity.

His hands closed around her neck.

Sophia screamed. "Gemma!"

The other zip-tie snapped. Gemma's hands were free.

Mullen saw the movement behind her back. With one hand still on her throat, he grabbed her left arm, yanked it out from behind her, and took in her blood-soaked wrist, his rage briefly giving way to confusion. "How did you—"

She plunged the knife into his abdomen.

Gemma stabbed him twice, in quick succession, not surrendering the small knife to his body because she still needed it. She didn't think the pocketknife would do any actual damage, but even if it did, she didn't care. She just hoped the pain would slow him down enough so that she and Sophia could get away.

Mullen finally released her wrist and stumbled away from the knife. Clutching his wounded abdomen, he fell against the wall of the cave and emptied his arsenal of profanities, peppering Gemma with them like bullets.

She ignored him and went to work on Sophia's ties, easily cutting through them without nicking the girl's skin because Mullen hadn't made them nearly as tight.

When Sophia jerked her arms free, her small wrists covered in blood that was not her own, Gemma shoved her hard in the back. "Run!" she screamed. "Run to the Station!"

Mullen dove for the girl as she ran past him. The tips of his fingers seized the bottom of her jacket, but she slipped through his grip and ran out of the cave.

"Yes!" Gemma cheered. "Go, Soph!"

Mullen unleashed a furious howl and charged, plowing into Gemma at full speed. The impact knocked the pocketknife from her hand—her only weapon gone—and together they tumbled into the pile of coal.

He threw himself on top of Gemma, pinning her to the ground. She struck at his face, going for his eyes, but he leaned back, easily evading her grasping hands. He clutched her head in both of his hands—she felt his long fingernails digging into her skin—and slammed it against the coal. Once. Twice. The third time, stars filled her vision. Gemma hadn't realized that seeing stars was an actual thing, but apparently it was. They covered the ceiling of the cave, galaxies of stars, swirling around one another, each one brighter than the next.

It hurt to look at them. Everything hurt.

"You shouldn't have done that, roach," Mullen

muttered. Instead of slamming her head against the rocks a fourth time, he bared his teeth at her and squeezed her head between his hands, as if trying to pop it like one of his zits. Spittle dangled from his parted lips.

He's going to crush my skull, she thought.

Suddenly, he released her head and scrambled away from her, one hand clutching his injured side. "That little brat isn't going anywhere," he said, crawling toward the firing device. "None of us are."

The stars faded. Gemma blinked them away. She flipped over on her stomach, and her hands closed around a chunk of coal the size of a dinner plate. It wasn't huge, but it was heavy. She struggled to her feet and staggered toward Mullen, holding the rock over her head like Samson carrying the gates of Gaza.

Just before he reached the firing device, Mullen twisted around and saw Gemma approaching with the chunk of coal in her hands. His eyes grew wide, and his lips twisted into a scream. "Carver!"

The rock landed on his forehead, cutting off his scream.

Gemma sprinted for the cave's exit, praying she could run fast enough to make it out of the mine before Mullen got his hand around the firing device and triggered the explosion.

But then something—or *someone*—stopped her.

She hesitated at the spot where the cave opened into the passageway, her eyes drifting back to the congregation of mannequins. She didn't want to look at them, but it felt as if some powerful force outside of herself was compelling her to look. To *see* Mullen's church scene for what it really was.

Gemma's gaze dropped from the mannequins' blank faces to the confiscated Bibles on their laps, and Addie's words came back to her.

The world needs the Truth, Gemma.

If Mullen blew up the mine, his *true* victory, whether he realized it or not, would come not in burying Gemma alive, but in burying the Truth—which was more precious than any life, including hers—beneath thousands of pounds of rock.

She couldn't let that happen. Not if there was a chance of saving them.

Gemma grabbed his empty duffel bag and ran over to the congregation of mannequins. At the other end of the room, Mullen was sprawled on the gravel floor, moaning and clutching his bleeding head. Between moans, he lobbed curses at her like grenades, but she ignored them and grabbed the first Bible, stuffing it deep inside the bag. Then she grabbed the next one. The illegal Bibles were the small Bibles favored by subversives—easy to transport and hide—but still, the bag wasn't big enough to hold the explosives *and* all of the Bibles. Mullen must've transported the Bibles into the mine on some other occasion. She didn't know if the bag would hold them all, but she would rescue as many as she could carry. She rushed from mannequin to mannequin, stuffing each Bible inside, one after the other, the weight on her shoulder only increasing a little with each book.

When she'd collected them all, there was still room in the bag. Not much, but a little. Then, her eyes fell on the two mannequins on the other end of the room, the one seated with his boots resting on the coal cart, and the one with the mustache.

They both had Bibles...but Gemma would have to get past Mullen to retrieve them.

It would be so easy to just walk away. Mullen was badly injured. The only way he could stop her at this point would be to blow the tunnel before she reached the exit, burying both of them alive. If that happened, the Bibles would be lost anyway. However, if she went back to retrieve the last two Bibles, she would be putting Mullen between herself and the cave's exit. He didn't appear to be much of a threat anymore, but was it worth the risk? Was it worth possibly losing her life—along with all of the other Bibles—to grab two more?

She closed her eyes. *I don't want to do this, Lord,* she prayed. *I really don't. But if this is what You want, please give me the strength to do it.*

When her eyes opened, she was staring into the nearly full duffel bag.

There was just enough room for two more.

Before she could talk herself out of it, she sprinted toward the coal cart. She easily slipped past Mullen, who was still curled up in the fetal position, facing away from her. She grabbed one Bible, then the other, and crammed them both inside the bag. They fit perfectly, leaving no room for anything else. She zipped the bag up and dashed for the exit.

Halfway there, a hand closed around her foot, dragging her to the ground.

Gemma went down hard. The duffel bag slid off her shoulder and smashed into the lantern, plunging the cave into darkness. She couldn't see anything. She dug her fingers into the wet gravel and tried to pull her foot out of Mullen's grip, but he only increased his grip, his sharp fingernails cutting into the sensitive skin of her ankle. "Let go of me!"

But Mullen dug his fingernails in deeper.

"Subversive!" he hissed.

She kicked at him twice with her free foot. On the first kick, her foot sailed through the air, connecting with nothing. The second time, it connected with flesh. Judging by the thick sound of

Mullen's curses, she assumed she'd broken his nose.

He released her.

Pushing herself to her feet, Gemma snatched the duffel bag from the ground and ran in the direction where the cave's exit should be. She knew she'd reached the tunnel because the layer of gravel was much thicker in the tunnels than in the caves. It crunched beneath her boots as she stumbled along in the dark, the sound of eggshells cracking, and Mullen's angry howls faded away.

The darkness welcomed her like an old friend.

CHAPTER THIRTY-NINE

Three-hundred-and-twenty seconds.

That was how long he had to wait.

Mullen leaned against the wall, head tilted back to stop the flow of blood from his nose. He clutched the firing device between his outstretched legs as the countdown continued in his head.

One-hundred-ninety-eight. One-hundred-ninety-nine. Two-hundred.

He knew approximately how many seconds it would take the average female—and this female was *very* average—to run from the cave to the mouth of the mine. His training had taught him to prepare for every contingency, and he had planned what he would do if the roach got away from him. He had jogged it himself frequently, going much slower than his usual pace, and come up with three-hundred-and-twenty seconds to get from Carver's Chapel, as he thought of it, to the mine's entrance.

Of course, the roach was injured and running in total darkness, both of which might slow her down, but she also had the advantage of being very familiar with the mine. She would probably be a little slower, but not much.

The last leg of her journey—that quarter-mile stretch of tunnel that led back to the outside world—was critical. That was the section of the mine that would likely collapse when Mullen triggered the explosion. He was a scout, not an engineer, so he didn't know how far the collapse would extend. Ideally, the roach would end up crushed beneath a mountain of bedrock, but if she went much slower than he'd predicted, she might end up trapped in here.

With him.

That wouldn't be the worst thing. The roach's death, like his own, would be slow and painful. If he could find her in the darkness, he would make her death even more painful as a thank you for his broken nose and for stabbing him in the guts. While he hadn't planned on dying inside the mine, it was an honor to give his life for the cause. Eliminating one more roach in an ultimate act of heroism had a nice poetic quality about it.

Two-hundred-eighty-eight.   Two-hundred-eighty-nine.

Colonel Carver interrupted his count. "She's beaten you again, hasn't she?" The colonel had been quiet since the roach got out of her restraints, and Mullen wished he would've stayed that way. He didn't like the idea of Carver skulking around the dark cave where Mullen could not see him even if he'd wanted to. "I can't believe you let her get away."

"I know what I'm doing, sir." Thanks to his broken nose, the sir came out sounding more like *thir*. He wiped his nose on his sleeve, and a lightning bolt of pain shot straight into his brain. Mullen's old man had busted his nose up plenty of times, but you never got used to the pain. "Trust me. She isn't going anywhere."

"Hogwash. What are you waiting for? Blow the darn thing!"

"Not yet," Mullen replied. "I want her to be crushed. Just a few more seconds."

Three-hundred-and-ten.   Three-hundred-and-eleven.

He closed his eyes and pictured the roach in his mind. She should have been halfway up the railway tracks by now, close enough to see the entrance, even in the dark. That was the primary reason he'd waited so long to blow the entrance. He wanted the roach to see freedom. To feel hope. To believe she was going to live right until the moment the first rock fell on the tracks in front of her.

"You're going to screw this up," Carver muttered. "Worthless little punk."

Three-hundred-nineteen. Three-hundred-twenty.

Mullen's eyes snapped open, and his lip twitched, just a little. But he didn't let himself think about the name Carver had just called him, or how his old man used to call him the same thing.

"It's time, sir."

He tried not to scream as Carver's icy hands, damp with moisture, closed over his own. The colonel's thick, crooked fingers curled around the firing device and, together, they squeezed the handle.

There was a brief delay...

And then the world ended.

CHAPTER FORTY

Gemma stumbled through the tunnel, hands extended in front of her, eyes searching the darkness for any hint of light. The duffel bag hung like a lead weight on her shoulder, slowing her down significantly. But she kept moving, kept putting one foot in front of the other, uncertain if she was running away from danger or toward it.

"Sophia?" Every few paces, she whispered the girl's name in case Sophia was frightened and hiding in one of the many caves. As she ran, Gemma's only prayer was that Sophia had already navigated her way out of the mine and made it to the safety of the Station.

A droplet of freezing groundwater splashed on Gemma's head. She had a vague idea of where she was. She could see it in her mind. After leaving Mullen's cave, she'd traveled through the tunnel until it dead-ended in a T-intersection. She'd turned right into the passageway that connected her group's old sleeping quarters to the main gangway. If she was correct, she would soon reach the main gangway, and from there, it was a left-hand turn and a quarter-mile sprint to the entrance.

"Sophia?"

She only needed five minutes. Just five more minutes, and she would be out.

But did she have that much time before Mullen blew the entrance? Probably not. She likely had only moments left, if that. It surprised her that he hadn't triggered the bomb already. Maybe he *had* tried to blow it, but the explosives hadn't gone off? Or maybe he'd realized that, in blowing the entrance, he would condemn himself to a horrible death. The guy was obviously crazy, but was he *that* crazy?

Up ahead, something caught Gemma's eye, and her feet stopped moving.

Light.

Glowing green light where there shouldn't be any light at all.

This light was *moving*.

Gemma ran toward the light, drawn to it like a bug to a streetlamp. It filled her with hope, that tiny bit of radiance. Hope that she would not die in the dark.

But as she got closer, the light erratically dropped away and disappeared.

"No!" she cried. "Please!"

Gemma ran faster, trying to catch the light, determined to not lose the only hope she had left. If she caught up to the light, it would guide her out of the tunnel, and she would survive. That much she knew with absolute certainty. The heavy duffel bag swung at her side, picking up momentum each time it bounced painfully off her left hip.

The duffel bag swung too far, throwing her off balance, and she went down.

Instinctively, she tried to use her hands to break her fall, and several sharp bits of gravel dug into the cuts on her wrists. When she tried to push herself off the ground, her body wouldn't cooperate. Everything hurt. When she reached down to check her knees, she realized she'd ripped holes in her pants, and the skin beneath felt raw.

She cried out in frustration. "Help me!"

She didn't know who she was talking to. Her own traitorous body, perhaps.

Or God.

But someone answered.

"Gemma?"

The glowing light bloomed in the darkness and

emerged from the opening of a cave on the right side of the tunnel. The light was shaped like a shotgun shell, but longer and thinner. Gemma recognized it immediately. In the outside world, the light cast by the object would be negligible.

Inside the cave, it was the sun.

The green glow stick dangled from a cord around Sophia's neck, illuminating her face. She lunged forward and buried her face in Gemma's neck, and the glow stick dangled between them like a shared heart.

Sophia pulled away and traced a line down the glow stick with her finger. She smiled at Gemma, the glow stick casting her face in a sickly green hue. "Taylor saved me from the dark."

Gemma chewed on her lower lip, fighting the torrent of emotion flooding through her body. "Yeah. He does that sometimes."

Her heart ached at the thought of Taylor, but there was no time for tears, not while the clock was still ticking. "We have to go now, Soph." Gemma brushed hair dampened by groundwater, sweat, and tears away from Sophia's face. They both stood up, and Gemma retrieved the duffel bag. "The railway tracks are right up ahead. We're almost out. We just have to run."

A few paces put them in the main gangway. A quarter-mile away, the entrance was barely visible as a tiny sphere of navy-blue set against the black of the mine. It was like looking down the wrong end of a telescope.

"Look, Soph! It's right—"

A sudden blast of air hit Gemma like a fist to the chest, tossing her to the ground.

The sound followed a fraction of a second later, unlike anything Gemma had ever heard before. A thunderous explosion that shook the whole gangway and caused both of her ears to pop. Clutching her head, she glanced up at the ceiling of the tunnel, her eyes landing on a set of overhead support timbers. She watched, horrified, as the logs directly above her head shifted and settled a few inches lower than before. She imagined the entire mountain collapsing on top of them, squashing them both like bugs.

"No!" she screamed.

Gemma threw herself over Sophia, covering the girl's body with her own, and they both screamed as a storm of rocks—like something out of the Bible—rained down on their heads. She covered her own head with her hands so they bore the trauma from the falling rocks as she waited for the big collapse—the one that would end their lives.

But after a few seconds, the rocks stopped falling.

Slowly, Gemma raised her head and looked toward the entrance. There was nothing but darkness in that direction now. The tiny blue sphere of the entrance had disappeared.

Mullen had trapped them in the mine.

Dust filled Gemma's lungs, and she coughed. Sophia was coughing, too. They couldn't stay in the gangway. It was getting too difficult to breathe. But she didn't want to go back into the mine, either.

Mullen was back there—somewhere.

She turned to Sophia. "Here. Pull your sweater up over your mouth like this." She showed the girl with her own shirt. Then, she picked up the sack of Bibles and flung it over her shoulder. "We can't stay here."

Sophia pulled her sweater over her mouth, and her coughing stopped. With her other hand, she held on tight to her glow stick. Both of her hands were shaking. "What are we going to do?" The sweater muffled her next words, but Gemma understood them anyway. "That was our only way out!"

Oh, but it wasn't. It wasn't the *only* way.

Some part of her had always known it would come to this. That she would eventually have to face the dragon again, one last time. Maybe if she prevailed, her nightmares would finally end.

"Come on," she said to Sophia. "There's another way."

✝

Standing at the base of the ladder, Sophia rubbed the glow stick like a magic lamp, probably hoping a genie would pop out and grant her three wishes. Then, she could wish herself right out of the mine. She gestured to the ladder. "You're joking about this, right?"

"I wish I was."

"I can't climb that."

"Of course you can climb it." Gemma tried to sound more confident than she felt. "You climb the tower at Neverland every day."

"With a safety harness," Sophia muttered. "Besides, this looks way higher. How far is it to the top?"

Four-hundred feet.

Gemma grasped Sophia's shoulders. "It doesn't matter how far it is. We'll pray, okay? We'll pray the entire time, and God will get us through it. Remember, I've done this once before and survived, and you're way more athletic than I am."

That got a tiny smile out of Sophia. "You've got a point."

What Gemma *wasn't* saying was that this climb was going to be much worse than the tower at Neverland. She didn't just have herself to worry about now; she also had to worry about Sophia.

Plus, they had no carabiners. No ropes. Nothing to secure themselves to the ladder in the event one of them slipped on the freezing rungs and fell.

And Gemma would have to make the climb while carrying what felt like a hundred pounds worth of Bibles on her back.

But there was no other way out. They couldn't wait around for a rescue that might never come. Even if someone from Ash Grove hiked up to investigate the loud explosion on the mountain, they would probably just assume that the mine collapsed. They'd have no way of knowing that the entrance had been intentionally blown up or that anyone was trapped inside. Even if they tried to get in, it would take them weeks to break through all that rock.

This ladder was their only hope.

They had to get to the top before the glow stick died.

"You go first," Gemma said. "You've got the light, so you'll be able to see when we get close to the top. Plus, if you slip, I'll be able to catch you."

She purposely left out the part about the hatch, since there was no point in worrying about it now. Sophia could never lift the hatch herself. It was too heavy. When they got to the top, Gemma was going to have to maneuver her own body—plus a duffel bag full of Bibles—around Sophia on the ladder. That would be dangerous on its own, but if the ladder was as slippery as it was last time, it was going to be downright treacherous.

But there was no way Gemma was going to let Sophia climb behind her. If Sophia slipped at any point during the climb, Gemma had to catch her. Sophia's weight might knock them both off the ladder, but that would still be better than listening to the girl scream as she fell and being unable to do anything about it. Also, Mullen was still out there somewhere, and Gemma wanted to stay between him and Sophia.

The soft light of the glow stick illuminated Sophia's bunched eyebrows and flared nostrils. "I will not fall." She gripped the ladder and climbed. "I can do this."

"Yes, you can." Gemma slid the strap of the duffel bag over her head so it was hanging across her back. Then, she noticed something on the ground. Something dark was wedged between the wall of the tunnel and the base of the escape ladder.

The light from Sophia's glow stick wasn't sufficient to see what it was, so Gemma knelt and closed her hand around the object, pulling it out from underneath the ladder. It was rectangular and solid with buttons on one side like a landline telephone. A small antenna protruded from the top.

Taylor's radio.

The one he'd lost when he saved her from falling.

"Oh, Taylor," she whispered as tears flooded her eyes.

The sight of the radio first tore her heart to pieces and then sewed it back together. The radio was a heart-wrenching reminder that Taylor wouldn't be at the top of the ladder to save her this time. She would have to save herself as well as Sophia. But it was also a reminder that God was still with her. He hadn't abandoned her. When Mullen had carted those Bibles into the mine to use against Gemma, God was already there, guiding the soldier to bring the exact number and size of Bibles that would fit perfectly into his duffel bag, so that Gemma could eventually carry them out of the mine.

Similarly, God had protected the radio from being found. It had been down here for months, and no one had ever located it. Not the Task Force. Not even Mullen.

God had wanted *her* to find it, which meant He wanted her to have it.

She tried to turn the radio on, but the battery was long dead. However, it didn't appear to be damaged. Somehow, it had survived a four-hundred-foot drop into the mine. She had no way of charging it, but if God wanted her to have the radio, she was going to take it with her.

But first, she held it against her heart and prayed for Taylor. Wherever he was, she prayed God was guiding his steps the way He was guiding hers.

Sophia paused a dozen rungs up the ladder. "Gemma? What's wrong?"

"Nothing. I'm coming."

She held the radio against her chest for a moment longer. Just a moment.

Then, she tucked it inside her jacket and climbed.

✝

They prayed the entire way, both together and on their own, their whispered voices amplified by the rock walls of the shaft. They sang a few verses of "Jesus Loves Me" at Sophia's request, and then they resumed their separate prayers, each one talking to God in her own way.

Sophia climbed slowly at first, but it wasn't long before her fear seemed to dissipate, and she settled into a steady rhythm. Several times, Gemma had to warn the girl to slow down, partly because it was dangerous to move so quickly on the wet rungs, but mostly because Gemma was struggling to keep up with her.

Whenever their fingers went numb, they would stop long enough to warm their hands in their jackets, just as Gemma had done the last time she'd made this climb. Gemma didn't just welcome the breaks, she *needed* them—probably more than Sophia did. The duffel bag felt like an anchor dangling from her back, and her legs were burning with the effort of the climb. Along with the prayers, that brief bit of rest and warmth fueled her to keep climbing.

Gemma didn't know how long it took them to get to the top. It might've been twenty minutes or two hours. But when the metal door came into view overhead, she almost couldn't believe it. She'd been watching for the door, hoping to prevent Sophia from banging her head against it as Gemma had done the last time she'd made this climb. And then—suddenly—it was there. Directly above them. Only a few rungs away.

Freedom.

Even the weight of the duffel bag seemed to lessen a little. She could already imagine the relief in her back and shoulders when she could finally put it down. "Soph, look!" she cried. "We made it!"

Sophia glanced up at the door, released an excited squeal, and hurried up the remaining rungs.

Wrapping one arm around the ladder, she used her free hand to twist the L-shaped lever, but nothing happened. "I can't get it," she cried. "It feels like it's stuck or something."

"It's okay," Gemma said. "I'm coming up to help."

But it wasn't okay. The duffel bag on Gemma's back was as wide as the ladder. If she tried to maneuver her body around Sophia's, the bag might knock the girl right off the ladder.

If she dropped the duffel bag, though, she could do it.

Above her, Sophia was grunting, the tips of her boots sliding on the rungs closest to Gemma's face as she struggled with the lever. "I still...can't...get it!"

"It's okay," Gemma repeated. She tilted her head and allowed the bag to slide off her back and onto her left shoulder. Her shoulder dipped under the weight, and the strap slid even further. Just a few more inches. She imagined all of those precious Bibles tumbling into the darkness, lost to the mine forever.

The world needs the Truth, Gemma.

"Gemma? What should I do?"

She closed her eyes and put her face against the ladder. The cold metal felt good against her sweat-dampened forehead. "I'm sorry, Father," she whispered. "But I can't lose her, too."

She dropped her shoulder, and the bag started to slide.

And then, from directly above their heads, came the sound of screeching metal. Light and air and voices filled the shaft.

Familiar voices.

Gemma grabbed the ladder, the duffel bag still dangling on the edge of her shoulder.

The hatch was opening.

She could see the night sky, the mantle of stars already growing dim as night pushed toward morning. As she watched, a pair of hands reached down, grabbed Sophia underneath her arms, and lifted her out of the hatch.

Gemma tried to rush up the ladder, but the duffel bag snagged on a rung and flung her backward. Her right boot slipped off the ladder. Her arms couldn't support her weight anymore, not with the added weight of the duffel bag.

Her hands were slipping. She was going to fall.

Someone grabbed her arms.

"I've got you!" he shouted. "Keep climbing!"

The voice was familiar—so familiar—and hope flooded Gemma's broken heart.

"Taylor?"

✝

But it wasn't Taylor who caught her in his arms.

It was Gavin.

Gemma's hope burst like a bubble as Gavin pulled her against his chest. She could hear his heart pounding, and it relieved her that Gavin couldn't see her face, because she didn't want him to see the anguish in her eyes. The memory of reuniting with Taylor in this exact location just six months ago was still too fresh, and the stabbing pain of loss returned with a vengeance.

She was alive, and for that, she felt both gratitude and despair in equal measure.

Max appeared beside her and slid the duffel bag off her shoulder. "Were you planning on staying awhile down there, Gem?"

She gave him a half-smile and turned her head to look for Sophia. The girl stood a few feet away, her arms wrapped around Brie's hips. "You okay, Soph?"

"I'm okay."

When the worst of the pain had passed, Gemma gently extricated herself from Gavin's arms. "Thank you," she whispered. The words weren't big enough to encompass everything he'd done for her, but they would have to suffice for now. "You always show up at the right time."

"Not always," Gavin replied quietly. Before Gemma could ask him what he meant, he cleared his throat and gestured to the duffle bag. "So, what's in there that's worth dying for?"

Part of her expected the Bibles to be gone or to have turned into some other books. The mine had a way of playing tricks on your mind, and it was possible they'd been a figment of her imagination. But when she knelt to unzip the duffel bag, they were still there. Different versions. At least two dozen of them. Maybe more. She ran her fingers over the cover of the one on top. The one the mustached miner had been holding.

Gavin gaped at her. "How?"

"It's a long story. You guys first. How did you find us?"

Extending a hand, Gavin helped Gemma to her feet. "Teresa drove out to the cabin," he explained. "She told us a soldier had kidnapped Sophia, and that you were going after her. She stayed with Addie and Kyle, and we came after you."

"We'd almost made it back to the Station when we heard the explosion," Max interjected." If we had hiked a little faster, we might've been in the gangway when it collapsed..." His voice trailed off.

Gavin picked up the story. "When we saw that

the entrance had collapsed. Brie said we had to get to the escape hatch. She said if you guys were still alive, you would get to the ladder."

Brie met Gemma's eyes and gave her a wink. "This is our special spot, isn't it, Gem?"

"Yes, it is." Something passed between them in that moment, an understanding of sorts. The last time they'd been together in this spot, their situations had been reversed. Gemma had been with Taylor, while Brie was mourning the loss of Max. Now, Brie and Max were together, and Taylor was gone.

There was no reason this realization should've made Gemma feel hopeful, but it did.

If Brie could get Max back, maybe one day, Gemma would find Taylor again.

Leaving Sophia in Max's arms, Brie moved closer to Gemma. "Addie and Kyle are going to renounce," she whispered, low enough so Sophia wouldn't hear. "Kyle doesn't want to do it, but Addie said she can't handle this anymore. She used Teresa's phone to call her parents. They won't be there when we get back."

The news wasn't a shock to Gemma. Addie had been struggling since Weston's birth, and Gemma supposed she'd been waiting for this day to come. But it broke her heart all the same. Not that she was losing her best friend, or that she wouldn't be able to watch Weston grow up, or that she wasn't even going to say goodbye. It was the knowledge that Addie and Kyle were going to stand in front of a camera and renounce their faith in Jesus Christ. It didn't matter if they meant the words they were saying or not. All that mattered was what the world saw.

The world would see two more Christians whose faith meant nothing to them. Two more victories in a very lopsided war.

"Okay," Gemma said. "Thanks for letting me know."

What else could she say?

Gavin stepped closer to her, his eyes clouded with hurt. "Gemma, why didn't you tell me what was going on back at the cabin? I would've..." He shook his head. "I mean, *we* would've come with you. You didn't have to do this on your own."

Actually, I did, Gemma wanted to say. She now understood that Mullen had always been *her* dragon to slay, ever since he'd attacked her on the mountain six months earlier. He would have never stopped hunting her until she faced him and prevailed. But Gavin wouldn't be able to understand that, so she said, "If I didn't come alone, he was going to kill Sophia. He might've been bluffing, but I couldn't take the chance."

Max shifted his feet like he wanted to run away.

He kept shooting nervous glances behind them. "Where is he? Did he just leave you guys in there to die?"

Gemma shook her head. "He never made it out. He blew it with all of us still inside."

"What?" Gavin jogged over to concrete hatch. He gripped the edge as he peered into the darkness. "He trapped himself down there, too? Why would he do that?"

"Because he's crazy." Gemma didn't know who Mullen really was—or what had made him into this type of person—but she knew he was crazy. She leaned close to Gavin and lowered her voice so Sophia couldn't hear the rest. "He's the one who set the fire at Oliver's barn."

Gavin's green eyes darkened. "Are you sure?"

"He admitted it in the note he left in Sophia's fort."

At first, Gavin said nothing, only stared at her. Then, he waved a hand at Max. "Come on, man. Grab some logs, rocks, whatever you can find that's heavy."

"Why?" Gemma asked. "What are you going to do?"

"If he's still down there, we're going to make sure he never gets out," Gavin moved to close the lid of the hatch. "Enjoy the darkness, buddy."

Gemma put a hand on his arm to stop him. "No," she said gently. "Leave it open."

"Leave it *open?*" Gavin gave Gemma a hard look, like he was trying to figure out which side she was on. "I don't get it. Do you want this guy to come after us again?"

Of course she didn't want that to happen. She didn't want to spend the rest of her life having nightmares about Mullen. And she knew that, if he found his way out of the mine, he would continue to hunt her.

But closing the hatch didn't feel like the right thing to do.

"What happens to him is up to God," she finally said. "Not any of us."

They all stared at her like she'd gone mad. All except for Sophia.

Brie moved closer to Gemma, dragging Sophia along with her. "Gem, I understand not piling rocks on the hatch so the guy can't get out. Even *I* don't think that's the right thing to do, and we all know how I feel about the Task Force, but do you really want to leave the hatch hanging open? It's going to be light soon. The light *will* reach the bottom of the shaft. If he wanders around long enough, he'll find the ladder. It will be lit up like a Christmas tree."

Brie was right. Leaving the hatch open wasn't a

good idea. In a few hours, sunlight would penetrate the darkness of the mine, and if Mullen stumbled into that tunnel, the light would appear as bright as a lighthouse beacon.

Gemma pulled her necklace out of her pocket and clutched it in her palm. She wanted to do the right thing. She wanted to do what God wanted her to do. But she also wanted to protect her friends. What if Mullen got out and came after them again? What if—next time—he hurt someone? Or killed someone?

She closed her eyes. *God, help us know what to do.*

When she completed her silent prayer, Sophia's soft voice filled her ears. "That man really scares me," she said. "But isn't locking him in there the same thing as killing him?"

"It absolutely is *not* the same thing." Gavin's frustrated tone suggested he was rapidly approaching the end of his rope. He raked a hand through his unruly hair. "He killed Yost and shot Kyle. I don't want to give him the opportunity to hurt us ever again."

Sophia folded her arms over her chest. "God protected us today, didn't He? Won't He protect us again, if we need Him?"

A feeling of peace settled over Gemma, casting out all of her fears and uncertainties. Sophia was right. Mullen wasn't a threat to them anymore—at least, not right now. If he became a threat in the future, they had to trust that God would take care of them, just as He'd taken care of them in the mine and during the barn fire.

Gemma had prayed for guidance, and God had used the voice of a young girl to tell her what to do. She had an obligation to listen.

"We should at least give him a chance to find his way," Sophia continued. "Even the worst person in the world doesn't deserve to die alone in the darkness."

Gavin had nothing to say to that.

Fighting back tears, Gemma bent to kiss Sophia on the forehead. "You're right, Soph," she said. "Let's give him a chance to find the light."

She took Sophia by the hand, and together they descended the mountain with Gavin, Brie, and Max following behind. In the distance, the sun peeked over the horizon, and the streetlights of Ash Grove blinked off, ushering in a new day.

CHAPTER FORTY-ONE

"Colonel?"

Mullen held his wrist out in front of him and pushed the button to illuminate the screen of his sports watch. The greenish-yellow glow wasn't great—it only lit up the area right in front of him, and it lasted for ten seconds at a time —but it was enough to keep him from walking into walls. He didn't know how long the battery would last. Probably a lot longer than he would, if he didn't find the right tunnel soon.

Of all the days to leave his phone in his truck.

He released the button, and the light went out. Holding the tiny button down for too long hurt his finger. Plus, to push the button, he had to let go of his injured side. The stupid roach had stabbed him a bunch of times. Luckily, she'd only used a pocketknife.

"Sir?" he called out.

Mullen hadn't heard from the colonel since they'd triggered the explosion together, and something about that made Mullen uneasy. He didn't think he'd done anything wrong. The colonel had been right there with him when he'd blown the entrance. Mullen tried not to think about how the colonel's hands had felt when they'd curled around his.

Cold and wet and dead, like a fish.

Shuddering, he pushed the thought away.

At least Mullen had finally killed the roach. In a perfect world, he'd be able to see her body to confirm, but this wasn't a perfect world. At least he had buried this roach underneath a few hundred tons of immovable bedrock. She couldn't have made it out of the mine prior to the collapse. Even if she'd sprinted the entire way, there hadn't been enough time. If she wasn't crushed in the gangway, then she might still be trapped in here somewhere. For her, that would be a death sentence.

Either way, he'd accomplished his mission.

"Hogwash."

Mullen's head jerked up. He fumbled for the light on his watch, and the ghostly, greenish glow filled the tunnel. No one was there. He was alone. But he'd heard the colonel's voice, clear as day.

"Colonel? Where are you?"

No response.

Maybe he'd imagined the voice. After the stupid roach had knocked him upside the head with that chunk of coal, he hadn't been sure of his own name for a few minutes. No wonder he was hearing things.

His anger flared again at the thought of the roach. Who did she think she was, hitting him like that? A big part of him wanted her to still be alive so that he might stumble across her at some point. She would beg him to lead her to safety. Maybe he would pretend that he was going to help her. Maybe he would lead her to his secret exit. Maybe he would even let her see the light of freedom. And then, when she was certain she was going to live, he would smash his boot into her head and send her tumbling to her death.

With a smile on his face, Mullen kept walking, counting on his flawless sense of direction to guide him to safety. He wasn't an idiot. During a previous recon of the mine, he'd found another way out. An emergency exit. A ladder. He'd found it a month ago, when he'd spent his weekend off exploring other sections of the mine. The ladder led straight to the surface. He'd climbed it once to confirm where it went. The climb hadn't been an easy one, and he'd hoped to never have to repeat it, especially in complete darkness. But now that ladder was going to be his salvation.

Mullen pressed the light again, just to see where he was...

And stopped.

He'd come to at a Y-intersection where the tunnel split off in two different directions. But that *couldn't* be right, because he hadn't seen any Y-intersections in all of his explorations of the mine. And there definitely wasn't one between the chapel room and the emergency egress ladder. There were other ways to get to the ladder, other tunnels you could take, if you knew what you were doing, but a left-hand turn out of the chapel room and a quarter-mile of walking should've placed him at the base of the ladder. There weren't *any* Y-intersections along the way; he was sure of it.

The light went out.

Okay, so he'd veered off track into a different tunnel. Big deal. Everything looked different in the dark. The question was, where did he go from here? Backtracking to the chapel room would be the safest choice. If he continued forward from this point, he would risk getting lost in the mine, and he didn't want to do that, especially not without food or water. If things got bad enough, he could lick the water off the walls, but he preferred to avoid that option. He wasn't sure what that disgusting orange fungus on the walls was, but he didn't want any of it on his tongue.

However, backtracking felt so...cowardly. Like something a roach would do. If Carver were there, he would order Mullen to keep going, to press forward, because that was what soldiers did, no matter the circumstances.

But that still didn't answer the million-dollar question.

Mullen pressed the light button, giving himself another ten seconds to examine the intersection. "Which tunnel?" He spoke the question out loud, hoping Carver might hear him and answer.

Nothing.

The light went out.

"Well, I guess it's time to fish or cut bait," he said, repeating one of Carver's favorite sayings.

He entered the tunnel that curved to the right.

Trying to conserve his watch's battery, Mullen went two-dozen steps without using the light. But something wasn't right. He could feel the temperature dropping. Not just dropping, but *plummeting* at least ten or fifteen degrees, which made no sense because the mine maintained a constant temperature. He also felt as though he was traveling downhill, which made little sense. He'd spent months exploring the mine, and there were no downhills.

No downhills. No Y-intersections. No temperature fluctuations.

When he couldn't take it anymore, he pressed the button on his watch.

The ghostly glow returned...and brought a ghost with it.

Mullen froze in place, and the sudden urge to urinate overpowered him.

Douglas Mullen stood a few feet away, the heel of one tar-stained work boot propped on the wall behind him, his leather belt tossed over one shoulder. From his orange safety vest, to his thick boxer's build (which had come in handy for beating wives and sons), to his leathery skin from hours spent in the scorching sun on various highway work crews, the old man looked exactly as Mullen remembered him. Almost as if he'd stepped through a portal directly out of Mullen's childhood.

He certainly didn't look like a man who'd been rotting in the grave for the better part of a decade.

Mullen's eyes lingered on the belt, recalling the many times it had torn into his flesh. "Dad...?" The word caught in his throat. He swallowed hard, forced it down. "What...are you doing here?"

The old man said nothing, only stared at him.

Then, the light went out ... and Carver's voice filled his mind.

"Hit your enemy hard and fast, son," the colonel said. "Don't hesitate."

Mullen pressed the button.

"Yes, sir."

Charging forward, he clenched his fist and buried it into his father's rock-hard stomach. The old man vanished, dissipating into a cloud of orange dust. Then came the pain, spreading like a virus from his hand, to his arm, and finally to his shoulder. Mullen howled in outrage. Outrage at his father. Outrage at the pain. Outrage that there was nothing left for him to hit.

Nothing but that strange dust.

Mullen held his watch up to the wall where his father had been leaning seconds earlier.

Fungus.

The old man had tricked him into plowing his fist into a massive patch of orange fungus on the rock wall, probably breaking every bone in his hand. It wasn't the first time the old man had broken his bones.

Mullen roared, *"WHERE ARE YOU?"*

The light went out.

Still screaming, he charged deeper into the tunnel, intent on catching his father before he escaped. Spittle sprayed from his lips. Some of it landed on his chin. He screamed louder, barreling through the pitch-black tunnel like a runaway freight train. Faster and faster. Picking up speed.

He didn't make a conscious decision to push the button on his watch. It just happened.

The greenish glow illuminated a familiar section of the mine ...

... and the cavernous mouth of the wishing well.

A one-hundred-foot drop. Nothing at the bottom but rock. The metal grate was no longer blocking the shaft because Mullen had removed it and carried it into the chapel. Nothing covered the vertical shaft anymore.

Nothing to stop his fall.

"Colonel!" he cried.

The light blinked out for the last time, and his running feet found open air.

The fall lasted forever.

On a beautiful Saturday afternoon in early November, with temperatures hovering near the mid-fifties, fifty-three-year-old Beatrice Mosely was wrapping up another successful day of renouncements.

Saturdays were always busy at the Region 7 Federal Compliance Office in Snyder County, Pennsylvania. The line had snaked around the squat building with the stone facade and into the parking lot for most of the day. But as the Region 7 Director of Operations, Beatrice knew how to keep things running smoothly. So far that day, the FCO had issued thirty-eight new government identification cards to former Christians.

Only four more to go.

After ushering the previous group out the opposite side of the building, Beatrice picked up her clipboard and headed for the locked entrance. There wasn't much on the notebook attached to the clipboard, except a reminder for herself to pick up ice cream on the way home from work. But because of her size—short and stumpy, as her husband liked to call her—people tended to not take her seriously. The subversives probably saw her as a glorified secretary instead of the Director of Operations.

But when she held up the clipboard, they paid attention.

After disavowing their faith on camera, the government expected subversives to pay—or set up a payment plan, as most of them did—for any associated fines. They based these fines upon the time between the implementation of the National Compliance Order and the individual's official date of renouncement.

Finally, the subversives received their laminated government ID card. All Americans were required to carry those cards in order to purchase food, gas, and any other retail goods. They were also required for all forms of travel. The tiny microchip implanted inside the card—most Americans didn't know about that little chip, and those who did were branded as conspiracy theorists—enabled the government to track the movements of its citizens, particularly those of any former subversives.

In what probably seemed like a last kick in the pants on the way out the door, subversive ID cards included a special designation that identified the person as a former Christian. Just as organ donors had hearts on their cards, and military veterans—like Beatrice's husband—had American flags on theirs, subversives also had a symbol.

Not a cross, as one might expect, but a yoke.

A reminder to never again resist the government's efforts to guide them in the right direction.

Because of the need for quiet during the televised renouncements, Beatrice brought the subversives into the building in small groups. They were filmed, processed, and released all in under an hour. Then the next group came through. By four-thirty that afternoon, the line had dwindled to four people.

Beatrice opened the door and got her first glimpse of the last four subversives of the day. Two females, two males. They were all young—probably in their early to mid-twenties. At the head of the line was a classically handsome young man with sandy-brown hair and gorgeous green eyes. The other young man had curly hair and wore a black leather jacket. He would've been attractive if not for the nasty scar on the left side of his face.

Someone had cut him up badly. Beatrice felt a pang of maternal pity for him but quickly pushed it away.

He'd made his own bed.

Behind the second man was a petite blonde with a pixie haircut. She crossed her arms over her chest, allowing her tattoos to peek out the sleeves of her jacket. She was the only one deliberately staring back at Beatrice. The others kept their eyes down.

Bringing up the rear of the line was a young woman with flowing auburn hair. She wore a gray utility jacket over an untucked flannel shirt, and she stood with her hands tucked neatly inside the front pockets of her jeans. There was nothing remarkable about her, except that her jacket was inside-out. Probably some kind of weird fashion choice.

Kids these days.

Beatrice straightened her back and put on her most official-sounding voice. "Thank you all for waiting. Come on in."

The group moved inside the studio, and Beatrice locked the door behind them. She bent to scratch an itch just above her knee and inadvertently created a run in her pantyhose.

Wonderful.

Oh, well. The show must go on.

"Good afternoon, ladies and gentlemen. My name is Beatrice Mosely, and I'm the Director of Operations here at the Region 7 Compliance Office. I assume you already know how this works, so I'll just give you the highlights. You'll each have five minutes of camera time to use however you wish. But you *don't* have to use the whole five minutes," she rushed to add. "It's closing time, and my staff would like to get home to their families."

Because of budgetary constraints, Beatrice's staff currently consisted of a producer in the control room (Shelby), the cameraman (Nate), and two security guards (Wally and Keegan). The no-frills broadcasting studio aired renouncements live on a dedicated local channel, as well as on their website, six days a week. Judging by their channel's consistently high ratings, people loved watching renouncements. Why, just the other day, Beatrice had read on social media that weekend watch parties were becoming a "thing," complete with themed foods and drinking games. Apparently, one popular game required guests to take a drink whenever a Christian broke down in tears during their renouncement.

Beatrice imagined that people often had to be carried out of those parties.

"We don't care what you say during your five minutes," she continued. "Be as self-promotional as you like. Today, we had two different people pitching their screenplay ideas, and another lady used the opportunity to promote the grand opening of her hair salon. But remember, although some people treat this as their five minutes of fame, this isn't a joke. You *must* state your full name and that you renounce your faith in Jesus Christ. If you choose not to renounce, our security officers will detain you until the Task Force arrives."

Beatrice nodded at the two low-rent security officers on the other side of the room. The older of the two—Wally—was half-asleep with an open Sudoku book on his lap. His partner, Keegan, was only in his late twenties but already balding and startlingly overweight. His stomach hung like a fleshy curtain over the front of his pants, and the armpits of his white uniform shirt were stained yellow from sweat.

"Of course, we'll need to see a valid form of identification before you go on camera. I'll confirm that your name is in our database, and after you renounce, I'll remove you from active status. If you've been on the run, this means you'll finally be able to return to your homes. We will no longer consider you subversives. After you film your segment, I'll have you fill out a bit of paperwork. Then, I'll print your new ID card and send you on your way. Questions?"

The final four shook their heads.

Good. This was going to be an easy group.

"Okay. Would anyone like to go first?"

"I'll go."

Beatrice's head snapped up, expecting to see the blonde pixie.

Instead, the young woman with the auburn hair stepped forward.

"Excellent. May I see some identification, dear? Your driver's license? Passport? Doesn't matter if they're expired, just so that they match."

"Certainly." The young woman took a step closer to her. "Will this do?"

She reached inside her jacket, grabbed something, and pressed it into Beatrice's stomach.

Beatrice looked down and saw a pistol.

Everything happened in a flash of movement. The subversive with the carved-up face produced a gun from inside his leather jacket and made a bee-line for the cameraman, who immediately dropped his Styrofoam cup of coffee on the floor and threw his hands in the air.

Meanwhile, the young woman with the pixie hair raced over to the control booth and kicked the door in—*actually kicked it in!*—as if she'd done it a thousand times before. Inside the booth, Shelby screamed. The classically handsome subversive pulled a revolver on the security guards. He ordered them to stand against the wall and put their hands behind their backs, and they obliged. Neither man attempted to reach for his weapon.

The handsome subversive used the guard's own handcuffs to secure each of them. "Don't do anything stupid," he said, "and nobody will get hurt."

In less than ten seconds, four subversives had seized control of the Region 7 Compliance Office.

"What do you want?" Beatrice stared into the eyes of the young woman who was pointing a gun at her stomach. This girl wasn't the weakling she'd appeared to be at first glance. There wasn't an ounce of fear in those eyes. Just icy determination.

Beatrice had no doubt she would pull the trigger.

"What do you think I want? Just my five minutes of fame."

"You would've gotten that anyway," Beatrice snapped. "You didn't need to bring a gun."

"Something tells me you would've cut me off." The auburn-haired girl wagged the gun toward the camera. "We better get started. After all, your staff wants to get home to their families. It must be so nice to have families."

"Listen, honey. Be careful what you do here. The entire world is watching."

She smiled at Beatrice. "I'm counting on that." She made her way to the mark—a black X taped to the floor a few feet in front of the camera—and nodded to the cameraman. "Go ahead. Start filming."

With the gun aimed at this back, Nate looked at Beatrice for guidance. "Mrs. Mosely?"

"Do it," Beatrice muttered, as if she had any choice in the matter.

With a heavy sigh, Nate pressed the button and pointed a finger at the young woman.

Action, Beatrice thought.

The young woman stared into the dark eye of the camera. "Good afternoon. To whomever is watching this broadcast, I will not tell you my name, because who I am isn't important. Instead, I'm going to show you a video that was filmed a few weeks ago, in a town not far from here. There's a young boy in the video. His name was Jason, and he died defending his mother against the Task Force. An older gentleman also dies in this video. His name was Marty. Neither one of these people were subversives or sympathizers, but the Task Force *still* invaded their homes and illegally detained them—along with the rest of their town—for several days. When Jason tried to protect his mother from being interrogated by a soldier, he was shot and killed. When Marty—an Iraq war veteran—tried to intervene, he was also murdered."

The young woman looked at her friend in the control booth. "Roll the video."

There was a monitor set up a few feet away from Beatrice. It took a few seconds for Shelby to get the video—which had obviously been shot on a cell phone—running. But once it started, Beatrice watched the whole incident play out on the football field, the remains of the beef burrito she'd had for lunch churning in her stomach like laundry in a washing machine.

When the video shut off, the auburn-haired girl's face filled the screen. "Do you think this can't happen in your town? Do you think that you're somehow insulated from all of this madness? This video is proof that the Task Force doesn't care if you're not a subversive or a sympathizer. Jason and Marty were neither of those things. The government trains these soldiers to be killers who make no distinction between guilt and innocence. But they make plenty of *mistakes*," she said, putting air quotes around the word, "and you—or someone you love—might be the next one."

Beatrice wanted that to be the end. She already felt half-sick. But then the young woman pulled a small, leather-bound book from inside her jacket and held it in front of her like a shield. Or a weapon.

It was a Bible.

Beatrice gasped. She hadn't seen a Bible in years. Possessing one was an offense punishable by imprisonment.

The hard look on the young woman's face softened a little. "Now, I want to speak to those who are still in hiding, to those who are thinking of renouncing their faith, and to those who have already renounced. Listen carefully to the Apostle Paul's words from Second Timothy. Write them down. Pray about them. Lock them away in your hearts, where no soldier can ever find them and destroy them. Remember, the government can imprison us. They can hurt our bodies. They might even murder some of us. But they cannot imprison or murder our souls. We have to surrender those willingly."

Flipping to the back of the book, to a page which was bookmarked with a tiny slip of paper, she read: "Keep your attention on Jesus Christ as risen from the dead and descended from David. This is according to my gospel. I suffer for it to the point of being bound like a criminal, but God's message is not bound... For if we have died with Him, we will also live with Him; if we endure, we will also reign with him. If we deny Him, He will also deny us."

She closed the Bible and placed it back inside her jacket. Then, she gazed intently at the camera, as if she could sense the millions of eyes staring back at her, waiting to see what she would do next.

Without speaking, she removed her jacket. Moving slowly and methodically, she put an arm through each of the sleeves and pulled it through until the jacket was no longer inside out. When she put the jacket back on, she rotated so the left side of her body faced the camera.

A blood-red patch sewn onto her left sleeve caught Beatrice's attention. She instantly recognized it as the Task Force's insignia, but someone had sewn the patch on upside-down, so the two intersecting swords now formed a steel cross that appeared to be on fire. The eagle that had once soared across the top of the patch was now underneath the cross, and its outstretched wings resembled a pair of arms bearing the cross on its shoulders.

"This patch once belonged to a Task Force soldier." For the first time, the young woman's face betrayed her emotions. Her forehead wrinkled a little, and her lower lip quivered, but she did not cry. "Despite being taught to hate subversives, he fought to protect us. He sacrificed his own freedom so that others could be free. There was another soldier, too. He surrendered his life for us. And in the last moments before he died, he gave his life to Christ. I'm wearing this patch to honor these men, and to show you that—if you're like these men—it's never too late to change." Running her fingers over the patch almost reverently, she continued, "Sometimes, all it takes to see something from a new perspective is to just flip it over."

Beatrice watched in awe as the young woman brought her hands up and tucked her auburn waves behind her ears, revealing a network of nasty-looking scars on both of her wrists. Aside from the scars, the young woman was ordinary in every way. She could've been anyone's daughter. Or sister. Or friend.

The young woman's left hand inched its way toward her neck, and Beatrice noticed for the first time that she was wearing a beautiful emerald ring on *that* finger.

As Beatrice watched, the young woman pulled something out from underneath her shirt.

A tiny silver cross necklace.

Beatrice squinted at the cross. There was something reddish-brown on it. Rust, maybe?

"Finally, to those Christians who have been wrongly imprisoned in detention centers..." The young woman left her mark and stepped closer to the camera, holding up the cross. "Our group has a message for you. Our message is to hold fast to your faith. Stay strong. Don't give up. Continue to endure these trials. And above all...*never, ever* lose hope."

Along with the rest of the world, Beatrice Mosely held her breath and waited for the mystery woman with the emerald ring and the scars covering her wrists to finish speaking.

"Your salvation is coming."

NOTE FROM THE AUTHOR

Thank you for continuing to follow Gemma, Taylor, and all of their friends (and a few of their enemies) on this epic journey. The final book in The Subversive Trilogy is scheduled to be released in December 2021. I can't wait for you to read it! In the meantime, please consider signing up for my newsletter at http://raenajrood.com to get all the latest updates and special giveaways.

Also, if you enjoyed this book, please drop a quick review (or even just a star rating) at the retailer of your choice. Five stars are appreciated, but any stars will do! Amazon and Goodreads reviews are essential for new authors, and every review and/or rating helps!

Thank you and happy reading!

—Raena

ACKNOWLEDGMENTS

Writing a novel during a global pandemic with three kids at home on virtual learning was a real challenge, and I never could've done it without the help of the following amazing people.

Thank you to Jenn Lockwood for polishing my manuscript and making it shine. It was a joy to work with you. I apologize for my excessive use of commas.

Also, a huge thank you to Lori Thomas for proofreading my manuscript and texting me with every error you found. Some people might find all those text alerts annoying, but I loved them because they meant my book was getting stronger. Plus, I love hearing from you.

To my cover designer, Rachel Rossano: You're a joy to work with and you never yell at me when I ask you to make *just one more tweak* to the cover. Thank you for being such a sweetheart!

To my fellow Christian writer, Jamie Lee Grey: God brought you into my life at *exactly* the right time. I never would've finished this book on time without your advice and guidance. You really were a lifesaver and I hope to be able to repay the favor someday!

Huge hugs to my wonderful beta readers: Kimberly Murphree, Emily York, Lyndie Lei Dison, Pastor Joseph Mott, Joyce Mott, Tandy Oschadleus, and my resident knife expert and unapologetic 14, Jerry Murphree. I didn't know most of you prior to publishing *Subversive,* and one of the best things about being an author has been getting to know you. I'm so thankful to God for bringing you into my life. Your feedback played a huge role in making this story stronger.

My mother, Judy Kissinger, and my mother-in-law, Carol Rood, both read early drafts of this book and gave me the honest feedback and encouragement that only mothers can give. Thank you both so much. I also want to thank my dad, Larry Kissinger, and my father-in-law, Ken Rood, for being wonderful, godly men. I love you both.

The biggest thank you of all goes to my husband, Scott, for giving me the freedom to write, for loving me even when I'm grumpy (which is often), and for being my best friend. To my three amazing boys, Ben, Sam, and George...you crazies are the best gifts I've ever received. You're all way more talented than I am, and I can't wait to see what you do with your lives.

Finally, I want to thank everyone who has taken the time to read my books. You've made my dream of becoming a writer a reality. I pray this series has blessed you and that you will remember to pray for those Christians throughout the world who are already experiencing severe persecution for their faith.

My prayer for this series has always been that God would guide me to make it what He wants it to be. I'm so thankful to my Lord and Savior for everything He's done for me, and I pray for the ability to serve Him through my writing.

To God be the glory, great things He hath done.

ABOUT THE AUTHOR

Raena lives with her husband and three children in rural Pennsylvania, where her hobbies include raising chickens, singing off-key while cleaning, and introducing her kids to cheesy 80's movies. When she's not writing, she spends way too much time thinking about buying more chickens. And possibly a goat.

facebook.com/raenaroodbooks

instagram.com/raenaroodbooks

ALSO BY RAENA ROOD

Subversive: Book 1 of The Subversive Trilogy

Salvation: Book 3 of The Subversive Trilogy - Coming
December 2021 - Available for Preorder Now